RISING TIGER

TARWF 2019-2022

YOUNG WRITERS' MYSTERY STORIES

L.J.M. Owen (ed.)

Clan Destine
PRESS

First published by Clan Destine Press in 2023

Clan Destine Press
PO Box 121, Bittern
Victoria, 3918 Australia

National Library of Australia Cataloguing-In-Publication data:

Editor: Owen, L.J.M.

TITLE: Rising Tiger: Young Writers' Mystery Stories

ISBN: 978-1-922904-57-7 (paperback)
         978-1-922904-46-1 (eBook)

Cover Design by L.J.M. Owen & Willsin Rowe
Design & Typesetting by Clan Destine Press

This book was created jointly by Pilipala Literary, Terror Australis Readers and Writers Festival, and Clan Destine Press. It is not to be used for profit. All rights to the stories remain with the young writers.

Clan Destine
P R E S S

www.clandestinepress.net

CONTENTS

EDITOR'S NOTE

In 2019, when I founded Terror Australis Readers and Writers Festival's Mystery Short Story Competition for young Huon Valley writers, I hoped for 50 entries.

I didn't expect the competition to grow to attract hundreds of national and international entries, nor that the winners would be celebrated at Tasmania's Government House in 2023.

Yet here we are. After four years' worth of brilliant entries from state, national and international young writers, I'm pleased to offer this compilation of winning stories along with a selection of other entries.

2019 – Female Bushrangers

The challenge for young writers in our inaugural competition year was: Ned Kelly, Captain Moonlight, Captain Thunderbolt. Their names are synonymous with desperation, crime and violence.

But at Terror Australis Readers and Writers Festival we asked: Ned who? Because Australia had buckjumping, cattle-duffing, escape artist women bushrangers too.

We asked the young writers to capture the spirit of one of Australia's tenacious, daring female bushrangers.

2020 – Female Detectives

In 2020 we asked: have you heard of Enola Holmes, Juno Jones, or Trixie Belden?

We asked the writers to create their own female detective – real or imagined, human or animal – and tell us how she solves a crime or mystery.

2021 – Scene of the Crime

In 2021 it was all about the science. We set the scene with: dusting for fingerprints, footprints under a window ledge, fibres under fingernails.

Solving crimes isn't just about chasing criminals. It's also about crime scene investigation (CSI) and forensic science: investigating, collecting and analysing clues left behind at a crime scene.

We asked our young writers to create a story set at the scene of a crime. The clues could be as small as a pen or as huge as a murder, as long as the clues left behind helped their investigator solve a crime, mystery or puzzle.

2022 – Agatha Christie in Tasmania

In 2022, the centenary of Agatha Christie' tour of Tasmania, the competition prompt was: Agatha Christie visited Tasmania exactly 100 years ago. She loved it so much she said she hoped to move here one day. If she had, what marvellous mysteries might she have written that were set in her new home of Tasmania?

Let's find out!

We asked the writers to imagine they are Agatha Christie and to write a mystery short story set in Tasmania. They could take any of her stories as inspiration and let their imagination run wild.

Would they write a new version of Murder on the Orient Express, but set on the Ida Bay Railway instead? A Poirot Investigates Hobart, perhaps? Or Miss Marple Enquires on the Apple Isle?

They didn't have to use one of Agatha Christie's characters, in fact were encouraged to make up their own detective to solve a mystery in Tasmania.

Congratulations again to the young writers included in this book. I hope your names grace the shelves of the nation in years to come.

With huge thanks to all the writers, their parents, teachers and supporters, as well as our 2019-2022 judges Bronwyn Chalke, Lindy Cameron, Em Cutting, Julie Hunt, Carol Ann Martin, Tansy Rayner Roberts, Judi Rhodes and Sarah Thornton.

I hope you enjoy this marvellous anthology of 65 mystery stories from young writers living in the Huon Valley and beyond.

Dr L. J. M. Owen
TARWF Director
Convenor of the TARWF Mystery Short Story Competition for Young Writers.

MURDER ON THE OREO EXPRESS

GRACE FU
Hobart, Tasmania

2022 JOINT WINNER
OPEN CATEGORY
AGATHA CHRISTIE IN TASMANIA

A puff of smoke from a blue funnel disappeared into the foggy Tasmanian morning and several boxes were rocked back and forth when the train came to an abrupt stop. A small wooden sign read, the Oreo Express. The train let off one last blow of smoke and the train conductor stepped off the platform, a small tomato in a puffy blue suit, carrying a scanner with a red light flickering. Oranges, apples, cheese and assorted deli meats began piling into compartments. From tiny tottering tomatoes wailing in their prams, to old withering cucumbers that walked with a stick, they all found a place to be amongst the others.

I, Hercule Pineapple, prided myself as a gourmet pineapple, being grown carefully in the sunny days of Queensland. While Queensland was hot and sunny, perfect for growing up fast, Tasmania was the perfect place to keep fruits and vegetables fresh as it was next to the Antarctic-fridge.

I stepped cautiously to the platform, and held my ticket out to the conductor who eyed me, sternly and sent me off on my way. I wrapped my coat tightly around my skin and tottered to compartment four. I twisted the doorknob and steadied myself as the train gave a little jolt. A weary asparagus and heavily-pampered ham holding a parasol, a bowl of stroganoff wearing a crown (I suspected that she was a princess) and a plate of ratatouille with pince-nez glasses perched on its nose, all glanced at me briefly and turned back to their jobs. I made myself comfortable on the leather cushions when a family of onions came in. Before they finished taking out their hats and many layers, everyone looked at each other and burst into tears. I pulled out a silk handkerchief and dabbed it in the corner of my eyes. 'Excuse us,' the embarrassed onion family mumbled as they quickly pulled themselves to another compartment with their belongings.

The others started to talk about if President Pickle was going to retire and other political subjects. Pulling out a small red notebook and a pen, I scanned the room carefully. Attention to detail was crucial. Even on a trip, I needed to keep my eyes open.

A loud horn blew and the train started to pull out of the station. Thick thickets of trees rushed past and I gazed dreamily into the fields of wheat. And slowly, I drifted off to sleep...

The train came to a sudden halt and jostled me awake. Potatoes and onions rolled off the seats and amid the shouts and calls in the cool early morning air, was an asparagus, lying on the floor with its green insides exposed and a sharp fork stabbed in its middle.

The ham next to me gasped and covered her mouth while waving her parasol around in the air. The ratatouille looked up from his book and his mouth hung open. Suddenly, the train conductor barged into our compartment. He too gasped loudly and the leek behind him collapsed, sending the line of vegetables behind her to fall like dominoes.

The line of vegetables stood up and all started to murmur, whispering to each other.

'Murder!'

'Colonel Asparagus is dead.'

'No one to leave the Oreo Express until the murderer is found!' the conductor declared. He tapped on his walkie-talkie twice and signalled to the crew. 'This is Code Black, I repeat, Code Black! Do you read?' The response was a weak 'roger that' and in a flash, the crew were assembled in a row.

Being a detective, I could not resist the temptation to solve the murder. 'Everyone, assure you that I, Hercule Pineapple, will solve this mystery and I promise you will be let get off the train soon.'

A huge sigh of relief escaped the grief and anxiety that circled around the carriage. 'All shall be well wherever Hercule is!'

No time to be wasted. I scanned around the compartment and saw a fruit huddled in the corner trying to make himself unnoticeable and all the vegetables wrinkled their noses in disgust.

'Look at him. Un-brushed hair, smells like sweaty socks long forgotten after a football match and looks a bit foreign.' A nearby eggplant hissed.

'He also carries weapons on his coat.' A corn cob whispered. 'No one can sit next to him. He looks like a criminal.'

The weird fruit raised a hand and began to speak. 'Uh, exqueese me. If I can say somethings, I not really know English. I am foreigner from South-East Asia. Though I have spikes and smell a bit funny, I come here to see if there is any business opportunity.'

He whipped out a business card for a fruit import company and he was the manager. 'Okay,' I nodded. 'You can sit down now, Mr. Dabbah Durian.'

Onto the next one.

'Please, Mrs. Ham, where were you last night?' I questioned.

'Well,' she replied primly, 'I was napping quietly in my seat when I heard someone come into the compartment but I was so tired that I didn't see who it was but I know that he had some glasses on...'

'Thank you,' I cut her off and asked the ratatouille who had put his book down and was nervously fiddling with his glasses.

'Mr. Ratatouille, do you have anything to say?'

'Actually,' he answered, in a heavy British accent. 'I do. I noticed that the princess messing with something in her pocket the whole train ride and when I woke up at night to get a cup of water from the dining train, I saw she was sneaking out of the compartment.'

A gasp rose from the crowd which had formed around us but the princess rebutted his bias. 'I was fiddling with a piece of chewing gum stuck to the inside of the pocket and I woke up last night to go to the bathroom.'

I scratched my head, scanning the room for evidence. A small piece of blue fabric stuck between the doors and I noticed that the artichoke was wearing a blue tie with a chunk missing.

'Artichoke... did you choke the asparagus with your tie?' I asked, half-humorous, half-serious, trying to lighten up the mood.

'No... We artichokes are honest species and we would never choke anybody. In fact, we are signing a petition for the Anti-Choke law.

Also, my stupid husky chewed the chunk off. It has bite-marks and fur around it.'

'Then who killed the Colonel?'

All the vegetables I had asked seemed to have good alibis and I decided to look for more evidence. The crew took the asparagus body out and prepared it to be sent to a forensic department when the Express arrives the next stop. I took out the fork with my gloves and examined every inch of it. I used a wipe to extract the green blood that was left from the body and collected it in a glass bottle. I noticed that there was a small print on the fork, 'If found, return for a reward.'

The fork was tinted gold and the spokes where surprisingly sharper than a normal fork. I stroked my moustache and thought for a moment. I checked the Colonel suitcase and found his money and valuables all gone.

'Aha,' I exclaimed. 'Exactly what I expected!'

I, satisfied with the evidence and made my way to the dining carriage.

'Who was Colonel having supper with last night?' I interrogated once I got there.

'The Colonel talked with some passengers before supper and if I can remember their names correctly, they were: Cairn Corn, Benita Bean, Olly Onion and his family. Supper was served at eight. He ate the meal with three other passengers but I couldn't see who because the light was dim after 7:30.' A nearby pear answered.

'Did you say the light was very dim?' I asked.

'Search the carrot!' I demanded. The heap of foods pinned him down until I called my police officer friend. The carrot was found with colonel's money and valuables all in his top hat.

'How did you know it's the carrot?' asked my police friend, Bill.

'Carrots are full of vitamin A and he is the only one that see clearly in the dark. He must have seen the small prints on the fork and set his minds to steal it.'

'The fork is limited edition,' a fettuccine pasta interrupted. 'They are only 12 of these forks in zee world. It's made partly from 24 Carrot gold.'

'I only know this because I once served a banquet for the Lieutenant and Colonels with those forks.' He added as if to justify himself.

'He must have been fighting over it with the Colonel when he stole the fork and somehow stabbed the Colonel.' I thought to myself.

The carrot was arrested on the spot and confessed that he indeed had stolen the Colonel's fork because he was in lots of debt with the bank and he knew the fork was worth a lot money.

(After he was taken away, he was later sentenced to 12 years of cutting up carrot sticks for a factory that made pre-packaged children's lunchboxes.)

The train tooted three times when it stopped and the carrot was carried and there were cheers all around. One onion was so excited that he bumped into his brother off the train. He hung by the cuff of his skins and hurriedly covered his body with his hands when he realized all his layers were missing.

Another mystery solved. I rubbed my hands together with glee as I stepped off the train and into the country air. Now, all I need is a nice refreshing apple cider from the Huon!

GEMINI

LAUREN BAILEY
Brisbane, Queensland

2021
OPEN CATEGORY
SCENE OF THE CRIME

You won't know what a man is capable of until he shows you. That, you have to learn first-hand. Now, in the field, you learn many things, see many things, but it always continued to surprise me how malevolent and merciless a man's true colours can be. This is a story of the heinous betrayal of Roger Sarmento.

'Detective, Chief wants you on this case.' Began Nicolai.

'What is it?' I asked.

'Car crash. 42-year-old male, not identified, down at the corner of Craven Street and Abbot's Road.'

'Right, let's go...have I interrupted your day,' I followed up with an abnormal degree of sarcasm. 'Let's go!' I left home today without consuming my usual four cups of coffee and clearly it was showing.

'Yep, already on my way, ready when you are.' Nicolai replied crestfallen.

We trudged through the buzzing hubbub of the Saturday morning Police Department with neatly dressed personnel and delinquents alike, to the open doors and past more hysterical mothers and no-good, self-indulged complainers.

'What's Chief got us on a car crash anyways?' I unwittingly asked as I stepped into the branded car.

'Well, even though you are a Detective, chief has the authority to assign any case to your free day that he sees fit.'

'Yes, yes, of course. Nicolai do you know what a rhetorical question is?'

'Yes, it is a question asked that does not expect a direct answer…ah. I see…I'll just…sit here quietly then.'

'You do that.' I replied slyly, glad to have finally won a word bout with Mr Know-it-all.

Arriving at the scene, black skid marks paved the route to the damaged car that lay twisted and warped at the foot of a badly bent lamp post. Smoke cascaded from the popped bonnet, threatening to engulf any person who got too close. Officers stood aground, pushing back nosy reporters from getting their novelty shots as paramedics removed the bloodied body.

'Update.' I ordered.

'Roger Sarmento. Was driving back from the shops when the brakes malfunctioned and he swerved off the road to avoid hitting other vehicles. He crashed into the lamp post and got crushed. Lacerations to the head and torso and a broken arm. He is in an unstable condition, shifting in and out of consciousness so you'd be lucky to get anything out of him, the paramedics don't think he'll make it to the hospital.'

'Brake malfunction, how rare is that?' Asked Nicolai.

'Very. But let's see if we can get anything out of him.'

Walking toward the ambulance, the paramedics gently pulled the white linen over his pale face. A faint murmur pronounced his death as official before they began to pack up their gear to leave.

'Did he say anything before he died?' I asked them.

'Not much. He barely got out a 'dou'.'

'Very well. We'll head back to the precinct and wait for the autopsy.' I said.

Sitting at my desk I flipped a pen through my fingers, pondering at the mysterious death of Mr Sarmento. Suddenly the bouncing child-like figure of Nicolai came charging from his desk, all too ready to reveal his revelation about the case.

'Get this.' Began Nicolai, 'Roger Sarmento put in and received a $6 million policy to life insurance only three weeks ago. It's said to go to his estate in Bowral and housewife, Meghan McClure. Married nine years.'

Nicolai handed me the report and I stared quizzically at the enduring face of Mr Sarmento, eyes mockingly staring into mine.

'Now what's up with you eh?'

'Detective Wilson?'

'What is it?' I asked irritably.

'Autopsy in 10 but they're a bit backed-up so expect some delay.'

'But it's a Sunday.'

Walking into the morgue the brisk smell of chemicals and bodies burned through my sinuses as I changed promptly to breathing through my mouth. Morgues give me the creeps. Dead strangers forced to lie next to each other on a wall in a metal box before being buried or cremated. The morgue attendee waited patiently as we moved through the lines to an immaculate white washed room in the back corner. The pale, bruised body of Roger Sarmento lay still and lifeless on the table. Eyes gently shut looking awfully peaceful and defiant at the same time.

'The body checks out. Death of cardiac arrest and noted other injuries, but none abnormal to the situation. The tox screen is clear showing the body hasn't been tampered with.'

'Are you sure you haven't noticed anything out of the ordinary?' I questioned.

'No. Lacerations and a broken arm, but as I said, nothing weird especially after a crash.'

'What are you thinking Detective? Do you think it's something more than just a crash?' Asked Nicolai.

'I'm wondering why someone would take out a policy to $6 million three weeks before they die in a crash caused by a rare brake malfunction.' I replied. 'Think. If this really was Mr Sarmento, how can we prove it?'

'Umm. Oh yes, looking through his records, I found he has been previously incriminated and jailed for four months for petty theft, if he has any distinguishing marks we can cross reference them with his file.' Said Nicolai.

'Good thinking.' I said as Nicolai handed me the case file and all information on this suspicious character. 'It says he was arrested four years ago, with a...small Gemini symbol on his left ring finger. Does the body have a tattoo on the left ring finger?' I asked the morgue attendee who busied himself with checking.

'No it doesn't. No scarring of removal either.' He replied.

'There appears to be more to you then meets the eye. Let's call down the forensic pathologist to get a better look at who he is because right now, I'm not totally convinced we're dealing with one Roger Sarmento anymore.' I said.

'The body matches the blood works and fingerprints of Roger Sarmento, so I dug a little deeper and brought up his dental records. Charts show that the dental records produced by the body do not appear to have any known previous dental records in any of our databases, and that Roger Sarmento's are quite different. Maybe they were wiped?'

'Or maybe they never existed.' Muttered Nicolai.

'What did you say?' I asked.

'I said maybe they never existed.'

'Why do you say that.'

'Well, now hear me out. Sarmento is originally from East Timor, his mother, who was Australian, moved there once she got pregnant to be with his father. But during the Indonesian Invasion in '75, he fled the country with his grandma after the rest of his family died. They've lived here ever since. So maybe, there was some person related to him that he knew made it out of the country but didn't get documented in Australia.'

'That's very broad.' I replied, flipping through scenarios in my head where this one could be true. 'The funeral is being held in two days at 3pm over at Langley, we'll head over there and see if we can talk to anyone. With any luck, granny's still alive.'

The church sat perched on top of a small hill, a gravel driveway led to the front door. A black shiny hearse sat still at the entry as if mocking the dead. On entering, the polished wooden floor clunked under my heavy boots as I walked to take a spare seat at the back of the hall out of the way. Flowers neatly adorned paved the walkway to the still coffin seated next to the front pew. The faint murmur of weeping friends could be heard as tears were wiped away.

The pastor walked to the altar where he waited patiently for the crying to abate.

'We are here today to show our love and support for Roger's friends and family. Not only have we sensed our own personal feelings of loss over Roger's passing, but our hearts have been drawn toward them, and will continue to be with them…' He began. After a good long while he concluded. 'Now I would like to offer the altar to anyone wishing to give praise to the deceased.'

The pastor stepped down and away from the podium and took a seat next to the organ. Just then an elderly woman of about 90 seated in the front pew next to the casket clasped her oak walking cane and slowly made her way up the carpeted stairs. The solemn thrum of her cane as it hit the floor emanated throughout the hall and echoed in our ears. Her hands shook as she fumbled to get her script out of her cloak pocket, soon laying it on the podium.

She looked around the room at its occupants before looking down and beginning her eulogy.

'I'm sure we all knew Roger as the kindest and most generous person. Opening his arms to support those he loves and otherwise simply to help. It was tragic how he died and I could honestly not see myself coming up here today, but I thought I owed it to him. I am Eden Sarmento, Roger's grandmother, mother of his father. Now that we're on naming terms, let me tell you about a time before this. I had just found out that Amy was pregnant with my first grandchild, or so I thought, and that she was coming over to live in Dili, East Timor, to be with Jose and I was overjoyed, and when I first looked into his shiny eyes as he clasped his tiny hand around my finger I felt pure happiness. Now skip to a toddler. He was a fun, mischievous little fellow, pranks were his specialty. He and his brother, Doug, used to call themselves Gemini Boys. No one could ever control them. Always played the classic switch-a-roo.'

I looked at Nicolai as he wiped a tear from his eye. Rolling my eyes as I turned back to the front. At least one of us was paying attention.

'When he and I moved to Australia it was tough but we pulled through. I tried to give him as normal a life as possible but after his brother died nothing would suffice. He was such an innocent little boy when his childhood was ripped away from him. Nevertheless, he helped me around and we tried to always be there for each other. His life was never meant to end now, but at least he can go back to be with his twin brother. They've been separate far too long.' She concluded.

I looked at Nicolai as realisation dawned, he slowly turned to me and suddenly blew his nose hard, drawing in a long breath.

'That poor lady. Oh…and Doug.' He cried out.

'How did I get partnered with a sentimental baby?' I thought.

'Wait…did she say…' He began.

I nodded harshly and he snapped back to reality as he realised what he missed. We left the church promptly after that.

'I think I have an idea of where we can find Mr Sarmento.'

Getting onto the Hume Motorway we called in for back-up to be sent to the Bowral estate.

'Obscure yet obvious, best place to hide.' I stated.

'Lest bust this psycho.' Encouraged Nicolai.

'Said the guy who cried during his fake funeral.' I commented.

'Hey, it was a good eulogy.'

'Right, well would you mind not crying when you see him 'resurrected'.' Nicolai looked at me obviously hurt. 'I'm kidding.' I amended.

'No you're not.'

'No I'm not.' I conceded with a smile.

We pulled into the long avenue-like driveway paved with trees and greenery that led to an enormous house on top of the small hill. On any other day this house would have been beautiful. A dog ran up to the car and barked excitedly. We heard other cars pull in behind us.

'Cavalry is here. Let's get to it.' Stated Nicolai.

Getting out of the car, the other cops stood behind their doors hand on gun trained for any situation.

'Right…Roger Sarmento open the door.' I shouted knocking on it loudly.

After a second there was a click and the door opened to reveal Mr Sarmento calmly starring back into my eyes. It annoyed me greatly to have this murderer look so calm and content with how this was panning out. The dark eyes made me uneasy but I made sure not to show it.

'Roger Sarmento you are under arrest for insurance fraud and the murder of Douglas Sarmento.'

THE LAST CHANCE

GEMMA BARNES
Woolgoola, NSW

2021
OPEN CATEGORY
 SCENE OF THE CRIME

'This is your last chance, or you're done!' Three short tones sounded. The puddles beneath my shoes splashed cold, mud onto my crisp, white pants. My head hung as I walked slowly towards the building. As I approached, I saw the door was sectioned off by blue and white police tape.

A dishevelled looking woman ran towards me in a blue business suit. 'Boss!' She yelled as she hurtled through the mud, spraying it everywhere. She had almost reached me when suddenly, she tripped and fell straight into the mud, squelching as she landed. Shaking my head, I reached out a hand to help her up. Her entire front was covered in mud as she picked up her dislodged glasses.

'Yes, Miranda?' I asked once she had righted herself.

'Uh, right,' Miranda said, wiping mud off her face. 'So this school was robbed last night.'

'What was stolen?'

'A trophy.'

'A trophy! Seriously?' I replied incredulously. Miranda looked apprehensive as I turned to her. She nodded almost imperceptibly. I shook my head and stalked into the building. Miranda ducked under then police tape and entered the building behind me.

'Nora, wait!' She said grabbing my arm and spinning me to face her. I glared into her warm brown eyes.

Something almost like pity softened her expression as she said, 'Look, I know it's just a silly high school trophy, but this could be your last case.'

I nodded, she was right, she was always right. With a satisfied look she spun and snatched something off a table next to her. 'Here,' she said thrusting a takeaway coffee cup into my hands. The cup was warm in my hands. Taking a sip, I examined then scene before me.

A police officer was dusting for fingerprints on the doors of a glass trophy cabinet. Behind her, another officer was talking to a bald man a suit. I walked over to them, careful not to disturb anything in the 'crime scene'. This was ridiculous.

I cleared my throat and the bald man turned around. Upon seeing me, or possibly Miranda covered in mud, he leaped back.

'Ah, Nora,' The officer said. I didn't recognise him, but then again, I didn't recognise half the people I worked with. 'This is the principal, Mr Edwards,' he said gesturing to the man.

I shook his hand briefly, glad when I could let go of the clammy thing. 'So, Mr Edwards, what exactly happened?' I asked, trying not to laugh at his still horrified expression.

'Well… someone stole our trophy,' he said continuously glancing back at Miranda, who stood slightly behind me dripping mud on the floor.

'When was the last time anyone was here?'

'About four yesterday afternoon.'

'And when did you arrive this morning?' I questioned.

'Nine o'clock, but Ms Watts got here first at about seven,' Mr Edwards said, sweat beading on his shiny head. 'She was the one who reported it missing.'

'Ok. We're done here,' I declared. Mr Edwards' shoulders physically slumped. I marched over to the trophy cabinet to examine its contents. There was nothing to see other than a few trophies and a page from a newspaper article about some competition between two former students.

'What was the trophy for?' I inquired the woman dusting for fingerprints.

'Academic excellence,' she replied. 'It- Miranda!' Miranda squeaked as the woman turned on her. 'You're dripping mud everywhere!' The woman scolded. Miranda backed outside the door muttering about always keeping spare clothes in the car, as I turned back to the principal to find out where Ms Watts would be.

Miranda returned wearing a worn-out pair of jeans and a white t-shirt as I walked down the corridor towards Ms Watts's room.

The corridor was filled with the murmurs of the students inside their classrooms. We turned a corner and reached a green door decorated with brightly coloured handprints. I knocked loudly. It was pulled open by a tall woman with long dark hair. Behind her, a classroom full of students clad in red uniforms had turned to watch the interaction.

'Ms Watts?' I said as she shut the door behind her.

'Yes, that's me,' she replied cheerily.

'I just have a few questions regarding the stolen trophy.'

'Oh, of course,' she said eagerly.

I cleared my throat and began, 'What time did you arrive this morning?'

'About seven,' she said, Miranda scribbling it down in her notepad.

'When did you realise the trophy was missing?'

'Oh straightaway! It's such a big thing, very hard to miss.'

'OK,' I said nodding. 'And what did you do when you noticed it was missing?'

'I called David straight away!' she said clutching a hand to her chest.

'Alright, you can go,' I waved a hand back to her classroom and turned away. I heard the door close behind her with a resounding click. Frowning, I walked back down the corridor to the trophy cabinet.

'I think she was hiding something,' Miranda murmured to me as we walked.

I glanced at her, startled.

'What?' I said incredulously. 'Why would you think that?'

'I don't know, it's just a feeling.'

I frowned at her as we reached the cabinet. The officers had gone, but the area was still surrounded by tape. There was nothing around the cabinet other than Miranda's muddy footprints.

I looked around, my eye catching on something where the wall met the roof. It was small and very hard to see but I could just make out… A security camera! I nudged Miranda and pointed towards the ceiling, a smile blooming on my lips.

'A security camera!' Miranda said echoing my thoughts. We smiled at each other, and then took off down the hall to find Mr Edwards' office.

I banged on the wooden office door, buzzing with anticipation. The door flung open to reveal an angry looking Mr Edwards.

When he recognised us, he stuttered, 'Ah, c-come in.' Mr Edwards opened the door wide and stepped back as we entered.

The room was cluttered with furniture. A large desk sat in the middle of the room, a window behind it. A bookshelf filled one side of the room, the other side taken up by a trophy case. This trophy case was different to the one in the hall however, as it held photos in addition to the awards. I stepped towards the case to examine the photographs inside. They were faded, the sun sucking the colour from them. A photo in the corner caught my eye. It appeared to be a heavily graffitied class photo. A girl with long dark hair stood out to me, she looked almost familiar, but it was too hard to tell with all the graffiti.

Why Mr Edwards would keep such a vandalised photo was a mystery to me. As well as how it became graffitied in a principal's office.

I turned back to face him and saw him sat in the brown leather chair behind the desk. Both he and Miranda were watching me as a sat in a chair across from him.

'I see you have security cameras,' I said crossing my arms. Mr Edwards went pale. 'Care to tell me why you didn't give the footage to any of the officers?'

'I-I-' he sputtered

'If you give the tape to me now, I won't press charges for withholding evidence.'

Mr Edwards was looking slightly green as he nodded and reached into a desk drawer. He removed a small USB. His hand shook slightly as handed the USB to me. I called out a thank you as I raced out.

I had made it out of the school and almost to my car by the time Miranda caught up. We stopped at my car with a spray of mud, and I flung open the boot. Quickly, I turned on my laptop and shoved the USB in. The air smelled like rain, as I opened the file for the trophy cabinet and navigated to last night. A high angle shot of the trophy case appeared onscreen, a timestamp visible in the bottom righthand corner. I skipped forward to four o'clock and set it to fast forward.

We didn't have to wait long. At about four thirty there was movement.

'Look!' I called to Miranda. A boy had walked into the school, straight past the cabinet and down the hallway. We had to find out who that boy was!

I looked towards the school and was startled to see Ms Watts coming towards us carrying a large container.

Hastily, I skipped through the footage, hoping to see the boy's face when he left. There! At five thirty the boy walked back through the corridor and out of the school.

Ms Watts stopped before us, holding the open container out towards Miranda and me.

'I had some left-over brownies and thought you might need some fuel,' she said with a smile. Miranda answering smile was so wide, I thought it might get stuck there forever as she reached in to take a brownie.

When Ms Watts held the container out to me, I spun my laptop towards her and asked, 'Who is this?'

'Oh that's Alistair Walters, he's in my class,' her smile faltered. 'He's not a suspect, is he?'

'Everyone's a suspect,' I said turning away and ignoring the brownies. I pressed play on the footage and began to watch again. Out of the corner of my eye, I saw Miranda give Ms Watts an apologetic look as Ms Watts turned to leave. Just as I heard the first squelch of her gumboots in the mud, another person appeared on the screen. A tall, dark-haired woman ran down the corridor after Alistair.

'Wait!' I called, and Ms Watts turned back around. 'What were you doing here at five thirty yesterday?'

'I was tutoring Alistair, that's why we he was here,' she explained glancing down at my screen. 'He left his laptop charger behind,'

I turned back to the laptop. Another dead end, I was beginning to fear I wouldn't be able to solve this case. Miranda and I watched in silence, the only sound was the quiet squelching of Ms Watts' shoes as she returned to the school. At seven o'clock, a figure dressed in black entered the frame. They walked slowly down the hallway, as though they were trying not to make a sound. When the figure turned to check if they were being followed, their face became visible. I gasped, it was Mr Edwards!

I marched towards the school, Miranda hot on my heels. I didn't bother to knock when I reached Mr Edwards office, and barged straight in. He jumped when the door banged against the wall.

'Why were you here after you said you were?' I demanded, slamming my hands down on the desk. Miranda ran forward and pulled me back from the desk. I stared expectantly at Mr Edwards, waiting for his answer.

When he just stared back at me, I prompted, 'Well?'

'Uh… right,' he said shaking his head. 'I was…'

'Yes?'

'I was using the Wi-Fi to watch the footy,' he said quickly. I blinked at him. That was not what I expected.

'Well do you have any proof of that?' I asked grasping for something, despite knowing he was telling the truth. Mr Edwards pulled up his search history from last night and showed me the time stamp. I felt my shoulders slump as I turned and left the office. Footsteps sounded behind me.

'Nora, wait,' Miranda called after me. I ignored her as I walked back to my car with my head down. The bottoms of my once white pants were now stained brown from so many treks through the mud. The sky looked as though at any second, it would start pouring rain. My feet felt heavy as they carried me back to my sad looking car. Miranda's footsteps had faded, and I was alone. I reached my car and realised that I had left the boot open when I ran to Mr Edwards' office.

Reaching inside, I grabbed my laptop and pressed play in a feeble attempt to find something. Anything. I watched hours upon hours of footage, seeing nothing other than Mr Edwards leaving his office and exiting the building.

This was stupid. It was probably some random person who broke in just because they could and took something as a trophy… literally.

My eyes went out of focus as I stared at the screen. A drop of water fell from the sky and landed on the screen right over the timestamp, making it look as though the time jumped. I wiped the water off with my sleeve and sat inside the boot, out of the incoming rain. I skipped back a few seconds in case I had missed something when I was distracted by the rain. Something grabbed my attention in the corner of the screen. It couldn't be… I went back a few seconds again and there it was! The time jumped straight from 11:38 to 12:03!

There was a whole fifteen minutes missing, but that would mean someone deleted the footage. Someone who had access to security tape. The pieces fit together like a puzzle in my mind. I ejected the USB, placing it in my pocket, then shoved the laptop onto the back seat. I leaped out of the boot, not bothering to close it, and took off into the pouring rain.

I tore through the mud and into the school, pausing only briefly take something from inside. I ran towards Mr Edwards's office, narrowly avoiding slipping on the wet floors. I barrelled into his office, dripping all over the carpet.

Mr Edwards glared at the pooling water as I explained everything to him. When I had finished, he was shaking his head in disbelief.

'One more thing,' I said. 'Does anyone have a key to the trophy case?'

Mr Edwards quickly called the whole school to an impromptu assembling. As the students settled in the hall, I stood in the wings of the stage, buzzing with nervous energy. Miranda approached, her glasses reflecting the fluorescent lights.

'What's going on?' she asked.

'You'll have to wait and see,' I replied, and Miranda rolled her eyes. Mr Edwards approached the podium in the centre of the stage and called for silence. I ignored his speech as he went on and on about who knows what, but soon it was time. I walked onto the stage and stepped up to the podium.

'As you all know, a dreadful crime has been committed in these very walls,' I began, glancing over at Miranda. She mouthed *Too much.* 'Someone stole your trophy and I know who did it!' The audience gasped and started whispering to each other.

'Let's start at the beginning,' I continued, explaining the security camera footage and the three suspects. At the mention of their principal being a suspect, all the heads swivelled towards Mr Edwards in a way they had not when I mentioned Ms Watts. It seemed no one had a doubt in their mind that it could not have been Ms Watts. Finally, I described the missing footage.

'I thought to myself, who would have been able to delete the footage? Then it hit me. It had to be someone with access to the cameras, someone who knew where the footage was stored. Someone who was alone long enough this morning that they would have time to erase part of the footage. Then, I remembered something strange about the crime scene: there was no shattered glass. There is only one person with a key to the trophy cabinet and was here before anyone else this morning…' I paused for dramatic affect. 'Ms Watts!'

Everyone gasped as I pointed towards Ms Watts standing at the back of the hall.

'That's absurd!' she shouted. 'Someone could have stolen the key from my office and deleted the footage last night when they stole the trophy.' All eyes turned back to me.

'You're right, someone *could* have stolen the key,' I agreed. 'But the security footage cannot be accessed until it has been uploaded to Mr Edwards' computer and that only happens at *seven o'clock* each morning. That also happens to be the time you arrived this morning.' The students spun back around to look at Ms Watts again.

Her face had gone red with anger, 'But why would- '

'Because you thought you deserved the trophy. You see,' I said addressing the audience. 'Ms Watts was a student here. She was in the competition to win the trophy but lost at the last second. You can read *all* about the competition in the newspaper article in the trophy cabinet.'

I held the newspaper cutting out to the audience, the students whispered furiously to each other. Ms Watts was now white as a sheet, and several teachers had begun inching closer to the doors as though she would bolt at any second. She looked speechless.

'So, where is the trophy?' I asked. Then, Ms Watts finally made a run for it. She didn't run for the exits though, instead, she ran straight up onto the stage. Ms Watts bolted past me, into the wings, and out the stage doors. A few teachers ran after her, including Mr Edwards who looked as though this was the last thing he wanted to be doing.

Miranda walked up to me. 'Why aren't you going after her?'

'I'm a detective, I don't run,' I said pulling a disgusted face. Miranda laughed as we walked off the stage, and back through the school. Outside, there were three police cars waiting. Leaning against one was my boss. I gulped upon seeing him.

'I guess you aren't losing your job today,' he said, trying to look annoyed but I saw the same warmth and relief behind his eyes that I felt causing through my body.

MURDER ON THE PACIFIC NATIONAL

IZABELLE BORZAK-BELL
Cygnet, Huon Valley

2022
OPEN CATEGORY
AGATHA CHRISTIE IN TASMANIA

Callie ran past as Marion wailed. Daniel tried to block Callie from entering the first aid station compartment, but she pushed past. Jai was dead and she urgently needed to know why and how. Charles looked at her with a bleak expression as she entered and he nodded stiffly to a stretcher on the floor of the first aid station bearing Jai's body. Callie urgently, almost frantically began examining his clothing and body, but there were no immediate signs of puncture wounds or obvious fatal injuries.

'How is he dead if there are no signs or marks?' Callie asked, in shock. Charles shrugged.

'He was maybe crushed, by the looks of it, he was still breathing wasn't he when Charles here found him'

'I gave him a hand to bring him up to first aid and he stopped breathing almost soon as we got here, I reckon.' said Darius quickly from behind Charles. The freight train driver then moved forward quietly and covered Jai's motionless body with his heavy coat.

'I guess we call the police; I expect they'll board once we reach Launceston and want to question everyone.' He then ordered Daniel, Thomas, and Charles to do a safety inspection of all the other wagons. The engineers muttered among themselves.

'I'd better get this train going, get us moving immediately!' He said sharply and impatiently as he strode quickly out of the train car.

Callie looked quizzically at Charles

'Why is Darius so gruff and unemotional?'

'He doesn't seem to be very upset, or even as concerned as everyone else is?' Charles looked down the train car watching as Darius's figure moved out of view and again shrugged. 'Yeah well everyone tends to deal with stress and shock differently, I don't know really'

Callie squeezed Jai's open hand; a tear escaped her eye. *I've seen him manoeuvre inspections between train cars dozens of times and he's always so extremely cautious. How could he let this accident happen?! Or was it not an accident?* Daniel entered the train car; he saw Callie and wrapped his arms around her for comfort. Callie and Daniel moved outside to make room for Marion and Natalie who both wanted to see Jai. Marion collapsing in shock and overwhelmed at seeing her brother's dead body on the stretcher before her.

Callie decided to speak with Marion. As Callie entered the train car, Marion's immediate reaction was to tell her to 'Go away!' But Callie didn't leave the room.

'Marion, its me.' she said quietly. Marion looked up, and she again started sobbing uncontrollably. 'I want to talk to you about Jai.' Callie quietly continued. Marion froze, she looked at Callie, waiting for her to continue.

'When was the last time he spoke to you before he... died?' Marion glared at Callie. As if to say 'How dare you ask me about him?' But still, she answered.

'He kept...t...ell...ii...ng me. That he loved me so much and that I was the best sister in the world.' Callie gave Marion a hug.

'Does he usually say those sorts of things?' Callie asked. Marion shook her head and looked at her blankly.

'So, he only started saying those things. Yesterday?' Marion nodded. 'Do you think he knew.' Callie paused.

'That he was going to die?' Marion stared at Callie with a shocked expression. Callie stood up and began pacing the room. Marion watched her carefully.

'Was he holding anything? When you went to look at him?' Marion nodded. Callie took a step towards Marion. 'What was it?' Marion handed to Callie a silver spoon. 'that's strange'. Callie examined the spoon. Then gave Marion one last hug before setting off to find the other workers to solve the mystery behind the spoon. As a freight conductor, Callie was responsible for the operations and safety of the staff on board. Therefore, it was her job to figure out the if not accidental, death of Jai.

Sadly, no one owned up to bringing a spoon on the trip. But on entering the workers train car, Callie found more unexpected objects scattered all around the inside of the train. She was finding knives, forks and more spoons! But just as she began collecting them, she felt a weird shifting in the floor. The train had stopped...

She got up and went to investigate.

She moved past the other workers and quickly reached the driver's compartment. Darius was kneeling down under the dashboard.

'Why have we stopped?' Callie asked. Darius grunted and pointed to the screen on the dash reading, fuse blown. Callie sighed.

'How long will it take to fix it?' Callie asked. Darius shrugged. Callie walked over to the wall and took a radio off its hook.

'We should get some help.' Callie said. Darius nodded. Callie adjusted the radio until she found the right frequency. A voice at the other end droned.

'Hello, this is freight conductor, Callie Carlton. Reporting a breakdown incident on the Pacific National. We are located somewhere near about half way to Launceston from the East Tamar maintenance depot. The voice told her they were sending out help.

Callie told her companions the bad news. They were stranded there for an hour, and with potentially, a murderer. Luckily, the thrill of attempting to solve the mystery was interesting her. So, Callie went back to her clues; the cutlery was everywhere. The layout was uneven and random. So, when she found three spoons pointing to Charles's day-pack, she was surprised. *Jai might have left these clues*, thought Callie. She checked around to make sure no one was looking then searched Charles's bag. She found a knife with a little bow of ribbon around it. *That's queer.* She thought.

The hour passed by quickly, when the radio buzzed Callie hurried over and whisked it off the wall. The voice crackled and buzzed. 'Help us!' The voice cried out.

'We're being attacked!' The sound of guns firing ended the call. Callie dropped the radio in shock. She couldn't move, just the thought of the scene frightened her. *What is happening!?*

Another call a few minutes later explained that the rescue team had been delayed in the current circumstances. Sadly, these circumstances were that some of the team had been shot. Thomas sobbed, grieving the loss of his brother, of whom had been one of the two rescuers shot.

Callie returned to the radio not long after to check if they were still being rescued. To find the radio smashed.

Callie tried to make some sense of the series of unfolding events. *Was the rescue team killed to stop the murderer from being discovered? So Jai's death wasn't an accident at all! The rescuers must have been killed to buy the murderer some more time?*

She returned to the workers train car and examined the knife she'd found in Charles's bag. Then she remembered something Jai had told her before he died. Jai was from an Indian family; whom were very superstitious. He had even brought a book on superstitions with him. The book would have a superstition on knifes.

Callie searched the train cars for Jai's day-pack. She found it under a bench in the driver's compartment. She delved through it and pulled out a neat little leather-bound book. She flicked through the pages and found a section on knifes.

It said that you should never give a knife to a friend or family as a gift. Or they will become your enemy. Callie nodded slowly. She slipped the little book into the pocket of her jeans and hurried off to find Charles.

'What knife?' Charles asked. Callie held the knife in front of his nose. Charles gave Callie a bewildered look.

'Are you saying that you think that's my, knife?' Charles laughed. Callie nudged him. He stared at her. 'What makes you think that?' Callie frowned.

'The knife was in your day-pack.' Callie said adamantly.

'Why were you looking in my pack? You don't suspect I killed Jai, do you?'

'Well, I'm not sure.' She replied. Charles watched her carefully.

'Is there anything else you wanted to ask me?' Callie shook her head and slunk out of the train car.

Charles is such a kind person. It's stupid I should suspect him of such a thing. But then why did Jai leave the knife in his bag? Or maybe he didn't, maybe the murderer did to make it look like Charles did it! She considered this.

Marion was still a mess. Sobbing and coughing all over the place. She was a delicate little thing. When Callie entered the train car Marion looked up and gestured to the spot on the bench beside her. Callie sat down; Marion held her breath to stop a cough as Callie began asking questions.

'What was Jai like? Was he married? Did he have kids? Where did he live?'

Marion held back a sob, then replied. She explained to Callie about Jai's intentions and family, his trust in other people. His struggle in learning to speak English. The main superstitions he lived his life by. Callie listened patiently absorbing every detail.

By the time Callie left the train car, there wasn't a thing she didn't know about Jai, except why and how he died. Next, she decided to speak with the driver. Darius Walsh was still trying to fix the electrical fault when Callie entered his compartment. When he saw it was only Callie, he resumed his work.

'I need to talk to you about the murder.' Callie pressed.

'What makes you think Jai was murdered?' Darius replied, not looking up.

'I want to know the order of inspections that were ran today.' The driver pointed to the wall where a poster was pinned with a map of the train and the workers names and inspection routines. Callie examined the map.

'Where was Jai found?'

'I think it was train car four.' The driver replied, still not looking up. *Charles was train car one, Thomas three, Daniel five... But Daniel wasn't on his post. He was helping me with my jobs. And Charles was taking over Daniel's post for him.* Callie thought about this for a moment.

'How did you say Jai was killed again?' Callie asked the driver.

'I think he was crushed. The train car he was behind must have been shunted from this end and pinned him.' Callie stared at the drivers boots sticking out from under the dash.

'How do you know that?' She asked slowly, approaching the subject carefully.

'Just a guess.' He huffed.

Callie did not suspect Darius. But it was also hard not to, due to his gruffness and brusque manner. When she returned to the workers train car it was past nine o'clock. The darkness of the night swept over the train car like a blanket.

Daniel was reading, Thomas was snoring, Natalie was staring out the window and Marion was nowhere to be seen. Callie slumped against the wall beside hers and Natalie's packs. As she reached for her bag, she accidently knocked Natalie's over. Callie gasped. Underneath Natalie's pack was a gun. Callie hissed at Daniel to come and look. Daniel scuttled over; his mouth dropped when seeing the gun.

Natalie saw the attention drawn to her pack and went over to investigate. When she saw the gun... she fainted.

'I have a suspicion it's not Natalie's.' Callie frowned.

'She could be faking it.' Replied Daniel.

Callie felt Natalie's forehead. 'No, she's out cold.'

Daniel picked up the gun.

'Maybe it has finger prints of the real owner on it.' He remarked.

Callie took the gun from him and laid it in her lap. She then proceeded to pull a packet of flour from her pocket and sprinkle flour over the handle of the gun.

'Wiped. They knew we'd check.' Callie grunted in a brittle voice. Daniel huffed and went back to his reading.

Callie hopped over Natalie and went to find Charles. Charles was talking to the driver about the blown fuse. When he saw Callie, he smiled. He excused himself from his conversation with Darius and greeted Callie.

'What do you know about the gun under Natalie's pack?' Callie asked.

'There was a gun under Natalie's pack?!' Charles exclaimed.

'Yes, there was.' Callie replied.

'So, you have already found the murderer?' Callie shook her head.

'It's not Natalie's gun.' Charles face went white.

'What's the matter?' Callie waved her hand in front of his face.

'I just, this means the murderer could still be anyone. It could even be you!' Charles ran out of the train car. Callie blinked twice; she wondered why he was suddenly so emotional.

The driver chuckled. Callie looked at him. He nodded to the seat opposite him. She sat down. For a grumpy old man like the driver this was unusual. So, it would be interesting to find out what he wanted.

'What have you found out so far about the murder?' Darius asked.

Callie told him about the cutlery Jai had left as a clue and the knife in

Charles's bag. She told him about the little book of superstitions in Jai's bag. Then the gun under Natalie's pack. The driver looked frazzled when she told him she didn't believe Charles or Natalie to be the murderer. The driver considered this information then told Callie what he knew about Jai.

'Jai was a good fellow. He had some friends very close to him on this train, and he knew of a few incredible secrets. I believe that he told one of them this secret. They told someone else. And what do you know, now he's dead!'

'How did you come up with this theory?' Callie asked.

'Good guess.' He smiled.

'Do you have a theory on the rescue teams murder?' Callie inquired.

He nodded. 'I think the murderer knew he wouldn't be able to go through with his plans if the workers were taken off the train. Especially if one particular worker had figured out who they were. So, to buy themselves more time, they scared off the rescue team and caused the train workers and the train to be stuck here for longer.'

The driver looked proud of himself for coming up with such a theory.

'Another good guess?' Callie smiled.

The driver nodded. Callie looked at her watch, it was a quarter-past ten.

'I'd better get going. Thank you for your insights.' The driver smiled but his face fell when he saw a photograph on the wall beside Callie's hand. He rushed forward to snatch it away, but Callie was too fast. It was a photo of Jai and Darius.

'Are you one of his good friends?' Callie asked. Darius nodded.

Callie gasped. Darius didn't make up those theories, he actually made it happen! Callie began to back away from Darius.

'You. You...' Callie stammered.

'I am Darius Walsh. Driver of the Pacific National. I am friend of Jai Dutta, but he betrayed me and I couldn't let him. I created misleading clues. The gun and other clues you have not yet noticed. I broke the fuse to stop this train. I sent people to hold off the rescue party and buy me more time.' Darius broke off. Callie tripped over, got up and began running. She reached the door at the end of the driver's compartment. It was locked. But she came in this way, how could it be locked?!

Darius was behind her. He pinned her against the door. Then

unlocked it with his keys. His thick beard scratched her face as he moved past her. Suddenly he let go of her. If the train had been moving it would be the end of her, instead she sprained her ankle landing on the train car joint.

Just as Callie began climbing towards the workers train car, she heard a click that made her turn around... Darius was holding a loaded gun pointed at her head. Callie squealed and opened her mouth to call out but as she did Darius placed his finger on the trigger. She froze.

'I caused the train cars to shunt. Crushing Jai and making it almost impossible to figure out who did it.' The driver smirked.

'Tragically because I have told you this, now I will have to kill you.' Callie gulped.

'But it also wasn't me. Wasn't my idea anyway. What can I say? It's not who fired the shot, but who paid for the bullet.'

Callie thought about this. *This meant he hadn't planned for this to happen. It wasn't his fault. He was being paid or forced to do this!*

'You don't have to kill me. I won't tell anyone what you told me.' Callie begged. Darius watched her carefully then began lowering the gun.

But just as he did so... the door of the workers train car opened.

Charles stepped out. Grinning. He stepped on Callie's fingers making her have to balance on the very joint between the train cars.

'Oh, hello Callie Carlton. It is a beautiful night for a stroll, isn't it?' Callie glared at Charles. She had trusted him. She had trusted that he wouldn't have done such a thing. But she was wrong.

'Oh, yes. I did I'm afraid, order Darius to kill Jai. I also locked the door after I left a second ago. But you will understand it was for good reason. Jai had figured out I had plans to steal all the supplies on this train. You see, these electronics and machinery will sell for a very good price, making me very rich!' Charles explained.

'Now, what on earth are you doing Darius. She's not going to bite. Just get rid of her already.' Darius didn't move. Charles rolled his eyes and pulled a gun from his jacket. At that very moment the door of the workers train car opened once more.

Daniel stepped out. He shoved the dazzled Charles out of the way and reached out to Callie. She grabbed his hand and hauled herself into his arms. Darius watched them before disappearing into his train car. Charles shook himself and got up. He glared at Daniel and made for the driver's compartment. Daniel laughed. Not letting go of Callie, Daniel tripped Charles, causing him to hit his head on the train car joint. Knocking him out cold.

The next day, the rescue team successfully reached the train. Tying up the dizzy Charles and grouchy Darius. Callie was in the papers for solving the mystery of Jai Dutta's death. Marion was forever grateful to Callie. Callie returned home with Daniel, vowing to herself to never again work on a train.

AN UN-FUR-GETTABLE CASE

ELENI CHAPMAN
Perth, Western Australia

2021
OPEN CATEGORY
 SCENE OF THE CRIME

December 1st

It's official – I am now a fully fledged detective, ready to take on my first ever case. It's a horrible sight, too. It started this morning when I woke up to Mum's cry of despair.

'Look!' she yelled. 'Look!' I rolled out and rubbed my eyes. Dad was already thumping down the stairs.

'What is it?' he asked. 'Are you alright?' Mum wailed again.

'I'm fine …' By that time, I had joined them downstairs, gaping. Mum was fine, but the living room was definitely not. Just a day ago it had been all set up ready for the Christmas month, but now it was utterly trashed. The Christmas tree was turned on its side, the top hanging at an odd angle, its trunk half snapped off. The stockings were strewn all over the floor and several photographs on the mantelpiece were chipped or broken. Tinsel was scattered all over the carpet. My brother Arthur tottered in on his chubby little legs and promptly burst into tears. His twin brother Timothy, in Mum's arms, followed suit. Jennifer,

upstairs, had no idea what was going on but started crying all the same. Mum and Dad busied themselves trying to calm Jennifer and the twins down, but I stayed in the lounge room to survey the damage. This could only be the work of...a criminal.

December 2nd

Whoever it was certainly didn't have a heart: messing up an innocent family's special Christmas decorations! There were kids at my school who didn't celebrate Christmas, but even they wouldn't do something like this. I decided to make a list of my suspects.

Mum
Dad
Arthur
Timothy
Grandma
Grandad
Uncle Max
Uncle Sam

These were the obvious ones, because they all lived in or had keys to the house. But I went back through and crossed them all off again. Mum wouldn't have done it, because she was the one so upset about it. Neither would Dad, because he complained all day yesterday about how much his back hurt from putting up 'that blasted Christmas tree!' and he wouldn't have put all his effort to waste. I reckoned Arthur and Timothy could make that much mess if they tried, but they both love Christmas so much I didn't think it could be either of them.

Grandma, Grandad and the uncles hadn't been round since two weeks ago, and none of them could have done this either. So it must have been someone from outside the house. Were we the victims of … a burglary?

December 3rd
Mum has no respect for my detective pursuits. She took down all the portable security cameras from around the house that I had so painstakingly put up.

'Elizabeth, I don't want you following our every move on your phone. I think you're taking this a little over the top, sweetheart.' I just scowled at her. Just because I haven't been to university, or even high school yet, doesn't mean I'm not a qualified detective at age nine.

Then she said I had to go to school, even though all I wanted to do was stay home and look for evidence. I stormed out the door in a huff. Then I had to storm back in because I had forgotten my backpack. It kind of ruined the dramatic effect. When I was finally at school, I realized I was excited to tell my friends about what had happened.

Maybe we'd even get in the news! I sat down next to my friend Oliver and told him what happened.

'So … your Christmas tree fell over?' he blinked at me. Sometimes even Oliver can be a bit thick.

'Yeah. And a lot of stuff was cracked and broken and there was stuff scattered everywhere. And I think we got burgled 'cos there was no-one else home who could have done it and we might get to be in the news!' I gabbled excitedly. Oliver shrugged.

'Cool.' Then he went back to disassembling his pen. I shook my head in disgust.

December 4th

I decided to make a list of further suspects. I had ruled out anyone in my immediate family, so who else could it be? I chewed my pen for a while, before writing:

Mrs Fields (the crazy old lady next door)

The postman

The Uber Eats delivery person

Oliver

Still none of these seemed likely. I slowly crossed them all off my list. I sighed and lay back on my bed. Who could it possibly be?

December 5th

I lay awake all night last night trying to think of a way to get some more evidence. Suddenly, I knew just how I could do it! I ate and dressed quicker than I ever had before, and was out the door before Mum or Dad could stop me. I couldn't wait to get to work. I got to school half an hour before it started, which was just what I wanted. I walked into the library and logged onto one of the computers. I opened up my email account. I opened the leather address book in my lap. It was from Dad's office, and had the names and email addresses of most of the people in our street. I carefully typed them all in. Then I started drafting a message.

Dear Neighbour

I live on 24 Crabapple Avenue and recently have experienced some upsetting events on my property. Would you perhaps have seen any suspicious activity around the area in these past few days? I

would much appreciate any insight you could give on this matter.
Thank you,
Elizabeth Myles

I pressed send, satisfied with my work. I spent the rest of the time googling 'mysterious trashing of house' but found nothing. Sigh.

December 6th

Today I could get cracking on the detective work, at least. I grabbed a roll of clear tape and some powder. I had to make do with a jar of baby powder because Mum told me off for using up her good makeup products. Speaking of Mum, she walked in just then, as I had finished sprinkling powder on the surfaces around the scene of the crime.

'Elizabeth, what on earth do you think you're doing! Stop it, you're getting powder all over everything!' Well, yeah. How else did she think I was going to get some decent fingerprints of the thief? Everybody knows that cops use powder and a brush to catch the culprits. She should watch more crime shows.

'Oh goodness, it's in the carpet ... and the couch ...' she rushed off to get a broom and a sponge. While she was gone, I managed to lift a few sets of fingerprints from the shelves and sofa armrests. She shooed me away, armed with a mop and a duster, as I lifted the final print.

I took them back up to my room and opened my craft drawer. I frowned and opened more drawers.

'Daaaaaaaaaaa-aaaaaaaaaaaaaaaad, have you seen my black cardstock anywhere? I thought I bought a new pack last week!'

'Um ... no, honey. Sorry.' I sighed. I stuck the pieces of tape with the fingerprints onto pink card instead. I had to squint to see them, but it was something. However, what I saw there was extremely disappointing. Instead of clear evidence, as I'd hoped for, there were only blurry, distorted ... pawprints?

'MILLY!' I yelled. My cat walked in and rubbed her head against my legs.

'How dare you contaminate my evidence!' I scolded her. She just tilted her head at me, then walked out, swishing her tail. She's a rather sassy cat.

December 7th
With the disappointing results of yesterday's attempt, I was delighted
to find a reply to my earlier message when I sat down at the school
computer today.

> Dear Elizabeth
> I am troubled to hear that you have been experiencing upsetting
> events. No, I have not seen any suspicious actions around the area.
> However, I would like to make a complaint about that cat of
> yours. Minty? Marnie? Melanie? Whatever its name is, please stop
> it from entering my garden and shredding my rosebushes or I will
> have to inform the council.
> Sincerely,
> Cheryl MacDonald

I swallowed. Was that a threat to my cat? I'd better make sure Milly
didn't get over the fence. again.

December 8th
There were no further breakthroughs today, just another email from a
neighbour.

> Elizabeth
> The only 'suspicious' activity around here is your cat banging
> around in the garbage bins in the middle of the night!
> I think I still have a couple of horse tranquilisers in my shed...
> Mr Brian Murphy

Oh no! Surely Mr Murphy couldn't tranquilise Milly! I would have to
make sure she didn't get up to any more mischief in the night. Poor cat!
What did all the neighbours have against her?

December 9th
Thankfully, there were no more Milly threats today, but no further
breakthroughs. It seems this criminal may have left no traces ...

December 10th

My goodness, today was an interesting day. Mum and Dad attempted to recreate the pretty Christmas scene in the living room, but it wasn't the same with a half-mangled tree. Timothy walked in, took one look, and started screaming. Arthur and Jennifer joined him. To be honest, I didn't blame them. The felt Santa hanging above the mantelpiece now more closely resembled a disembowelled zombie than a round, chuckling man. Christmas in our house would be a melancholy affair.

December 11th

There was another email message today. I gulped when I saw it sitting in my inbox. Not another threat to put my cat to sleep!

> Good afternoon, Elizabeth
> In regards to your email, I have indeed seen some suspicious activity in Crabapple Avenue. There have some been some mysterious noises at night, and I have seen a silver Toyota car with three people in it parked in front of your property lately.
> Take care and proceed with caution in your investigation.

There was no closing signature and the email was just a bunch of letters and numbers. My heart beat faster. What was that car and those people doing at our house? Could they have been responsible for the burglary? But how did they get in? And why would they destroy a Christmas set-up?

December 12th

Today I decided to interrogate Mum and Dad about the information I had received from the anonymous sender.

> Me: Hey Mum?
> Mum: (suspiciously) Yes, Elizabeth? You haven't used up all my makeup powder again, have you?
> Me: No, I was just wondering. Have you noticed anything out of order around the place lately?

Mum: Other than your disaster site of a room, no.
INTERROGATION CLOSED. AND NO, MUM, I AM NOT
TIDYING MY ROOM.

Me: Hey Dad?
Dad: Are you about to ask for extra pocket money or something?
Me: No! Why does everyone automatically suspect I've done
something wrong?!
Dad: I don't know … (looks meaningfully at me)
Me: Okay, we agreed we would not speak of the incident with the
missing eyebrow.
Dad: Hey, I didn't bring it up.
Me: Let's just get on with it. Where were you at the time of the
crime?
Dad: What crime … you mean the wrecked Christmas display?
Me: Yes.
Dad: Uhhhh … at work.
Me: Mmm – hmmm. Any valuables missing?
Dad: My salmon! My beautiful, gourmet salmon I had been
saving for my favourite dish has disappeared! (sobs dramatically)
Me: I meant valuables.
Dad: Salmon is valuable! No, no, my beautiful salmon (breaks
down).
INVESTIGATION CLOSED. DAD, YOU NEED TO GET
SOME HELP.

December 13th

Aaargh! It's been almost two weeks since the crime and I still don't have
a suspect. The trail will have gone cold by now. If only Milly hadn't
ruined my fingerprints with her clumsy paws, I might have actually
caught a criminal! And my family is no help. Dad going on about his
stupid missing salmon … who cares? Other than Milly, she loves salmon.
I glance over to the window and jump. There's a silver Toyota parked
on our drive! With three people in it! I can barely breathe. What's going
on?

December 14th

I tossed and turned all night. Every time I drifted off, that car popped back into my mind. I couldn't shake the feeling. It was early next morning when I woke with a start. I peered out the window and my heart skipped a beat. The car was still there, and the people, dressed in dark suits and sunglasses, were leaning casually against the hood. I lunged for my phone and dialled 000. Now that I actually had a suspect for the burglary, I felt more nervous than I had ever imagined. What if these people would go further than wreck our Christmas tree? But before I could press Call, I stopped. My dad was hurrying down the steps, down the drive, tidying his hair, and approached them. They talked for a while, then my dad came back inside. The car drove away. I ran downstairs, my heart racing.

'Dad, who were those people?' He gave me a weird look.

'You know who they are! You don't recognise Janet, Shane and Paul?' I felt silly now. They were Dad's work associates. They had been around for countless meetings and dinners and were always dropping in some paperwork for Dad. They were like family to us. I guess I had been overreacting. But that left an important question: who had committed the crime?

December 15th

Today, I went back to my email inbox. If the mysterious people were just Dad's fellow accountants, who had sent that email that put me on a false trail? I read the message again. Maybe it was even sent by the culprit, to throw me off the trail!

> Good afternoon, Elizabeth
> In regards to your email, I have indeed seen some suspicious activity in Crabapple Avenue. There have some been some mysterious noises at night, and I have seen a silver Toyota car with three people in it parked in front of your property lately.
> Take care and proceed with caution in your investigation.

I took a closer look at the email address that had sent it.
L2oe00vi9r@mail.net

Hang on one minute! The unscrambled letters and numbers of the address spelt ... Oliver and his year of birth, 2009! I glared over to the other side of the computer lab. Oliver was looking sheepish.

'I just wanted to give you a real detective case to solve!' he said. I stormed away.

December 16th

I was working at my desk today, trying to piece together the evidence. But nothing made sense. I was just ready to give up the case when Milly ran in and jumped onto my lap.

'Hey, Milly,' I sighed. 'Now, you be a good girl, okay? I've been having some complaints from the neighbours about your mischief.' She just purred and licked me, then leaped onto the desk.

'Eeeewwww, Milly! You smell like old salmon!' I yelled. 'And you're getting your dirty pawprints all over my clean desk!' She leapt off the desk and I chased her through the house.

She ran down the stairs into the garage and into an old basket. I stopped. Inside the basket were six tiny, wet kittens. Milly purred and licked them all. They were lying in a sort of nest made from ... shredded Christmas tree, fabric and tinsel! Suddenly it all made sense. Milly had taken bits and pieces from the living room and the neighbours' gardens to make a nest for her kittens! She had stolen Dad's salmon to eat, and of course I found pawprints at the scene of the crime! It wasn't that Milly had contaminated the evidence: she was the evidence!

'Oh, Milly!' I cried. One of the kittens squeaked and snuffled. I grinned. This was better than any Christmas display.

FORCE OF NATURE

RUBY KELLY
Garden Island Creek, Huon Valley

2019 WINNER
OPEN CATEGORY
  FEMALE BUSHRANGERS

There are some things people talk about that they want no one else to hear. They will go into a locked room or far out into the bush, but wherever they go I have a habit of finding out. I slip under the door or slide through the bushes, and though they feel my presence I am ignored, for I am as old as Time itself.

I have been everywhere, seen everything, and oh the stories I could tell you! But today I shall tell you a story I have been waiting a long time to tell, about a girl named Caroline.

I have known many people like her across the ages, people with something a little wild about them, people constrained by their society who loved me for the fact that I am free, able to come and go as I please. But there was something about her that kept drawing me back, compelling me to blow through her hair and rustle her skirts.

Many a glorious hour I have spent blowing along the creek flats, racing her as she rode on her horse, Fury. Tearing through the tree tops or whistling through the garden, there has scarce been a moment in her life when I have not been present in some small way, from the day she was first wheeled outside in her bassinet to the time I took my last mournful farewell, blowing through the crowd as she swung from the gallows.

I remember her as a child, crossing her eyes at her teacher while I slipped through the cracks in the wooden walls, enticing her to come out and play. I kept company with her as she grew, skipping rocks down at the creek or howling triumphantly as she stood on top of the cliff after a long climb. I would blow softly to dry her tears after her numerous fights with her mother and on warm winter nights I would swirl air laden with wattle blossom through her open window to help her sleep. In those days I was her only friend.

I remember swirling distrustful around Mr. Alden when he came to her house, and following them on their walks. I moaned sadly at their wedding and in the months that followed, as his true nature showed through, I would sing through the treetops bringing memories of a happier time to remind her that there was a life out there worth living.

As it became clearer than ever that Herbert Alden's company was one better avoided than sought, Caroline would spend hours out in the bush behind the small house, hiking along the cliffs and following the creek, trying to forget about the mistake that had tied her life to that of a scoundrel. It was on one of these rambles that she first met Elizabeth.

A young girl, scarcely sixteen, she was crouched behind a rotten log by the creek and running a high fever when Caroline found her. Later, Caroline found out that she had taken to the bush in hopes of avoiding jail time for stealing from her employer. For now though, Caroline's only thought was to get her home and into a bed. She took the girl to the hay loft above the stable, not wanting to risk Herbert's wrath by bringing her to the house.

It was three days after this, during which Elizabeth remained in the loft, slowly regaining her strength, that Herbert decided he would bring home an aboriginal servant girl. He stumbled in late one night, swearing and cussing as he crashed around in the dark, a silent shadow following on his heels. He'd got her cheap, he explained drunkenly. A bargain. No, he didn't know her name, and he didn't care either. Call her whatever darn name you like.

She didn't speak much those days. When Caroline asked her name, she simply replied with Maddy. She was observant though, and it didn't take her long to work out that there was a third member to this small family, and she nearly scared Elizabeth senseless one afternoon by appearing by her bedside in the loft. She handed Elizabeth a cup containing a dark brew, and instructed her to drink it.

That was the start of the bond between these three women that would last right to the end of their short lives.

Exactly a week later the inevitable happened. Herbert had been growing more and more reckless, and one night he awoke Caroline to grab her valuables and saddle up. The police had cottoned on to him and they had to flee he had a brother in Melbourne who would hide them until it all blew over. But Caroline didn't want to go.

'No,' she screeched, 'I'm sick and tired of watching you make a mess of our lives, and I'm sick and tired of the fact that I can't do anything about it! I hate my life! Do you hear me? I hate it!'

Herbert stared at her a long moment and then laughed. 'Do what you will, woman. Go back to your family if you like, but if you think they'll harbour the wife of a criminal you've got another think coming. It's me or nothing girl.'

He made for the door, and when he saw she wasn't going to follow, took the money out of the bread bin and rode away.

Caroline wrapped her arms around her legs, crying and shivering. She couldn't stay here, not with the troopers coming, yet where could she go? This life wasn't fair. She would give anything, *anything* for a chance to make her own rules, and get her own back on all the people who told her that she would never make do if she didn't learn to curb her reckless nature. Suddenly she stood up. They thought she had a reckless nature? Ha! She'd show them reckless. After all, what did she have to lose? Her reputation had vanished with Herbert, now the only thing left to her was her life, which she would spend in one final fling of glorious rebellion.

Shoving on her clothes, she grabbed her pistol and went to the kitchen for food. She was met at the door by Maddy, holding a bulging hessian sack. 'I've got food,' she said, 'matches too. Should last us a while, but I know how to get more when we run out.'

Caroline paused, and said, 'Maddy, I'm running away. Looking for revenge, so to speak.' She cringed, realising how silly it sounded, 'You – I'm not – you don't have to come with me.'

Maddy only smiled. 'It seems I could do with a little revenge of my own, sometimes. Besides, you wouldn't last a week out there by yourself. I'm coming with you. You'll bring the girl too, of course.'

'Of course,' Caroline agreed weakly. Elizabeth climbed onto the back of Fury, Maddy took the packhorse, and as they followed the track down into the gully, I went ahead of them, freeing the moon from the clouds.

I have seen this before many, many times, and I knew where it would end. Too many times I have witnessed as some bright, young person, lit by an uncontrollable fire within, has thrown away their life trying to get revenge on a world that just didn't understand. It is sad, but it is a fact. And now it was happening to my Caroline.

Their first act was to steal two horses from a nearby farm, one for Elizabeth and one for Maddy. After that first theft their raids grew more and more daring. Holding up the mail coach, robbing the Governor on his way home from a meeting, they kept on. After each raid they would retreat back to the ranges, Maddy's skill combined with Caroline and Elizabeth's knowledge of the area making them almost impossible to track.

And not for lack of trying, either. Dozens of troopers were out scouring the bush, and the price on their heads was up to eight-hundred pounds, yet they still remained uncaught.

I shouldn't have helped them. It was going against the ancient laws of nature, and was only delaying the inevitable anyway. Perhaps by helping them I was doing more harm than good, but this didn't stop me from blowing away their tracks, or dropping a limb in the path of a searcher who got too close. Something in me kept going back to the small girl dancing in the sunshine, and I couldn't bear to see that flame extinguished. Silly, I know. I am a force of nature. What does it matter to me what the humans do to themselves? I have seen thousands, millions, of humans come and go and one more shouldn't make any difference. It did, though.

The last night was warm and friendly, and as they rode down out of the ranges. It felt as though nothing bad could ever happen, even the guns in their hands looked more like some sort of toy than an instrument of murder. They were out to rob a special coach. Word had come to Caroline that it would be passing through that evening. What her informant had failed to mention, however, was the strong armed police escort.

As soon as the first shot was fired, they knew they had been tricked and tried to flee but the shot had alerted troopers in the surrounding area that the girls had been sighted, and hoof beats sounded behind them. The second shot killed Maddy on impact. Elizabeth screamed, and her horse reared back on its hind legs. She slipped, and her body slammed the ground, gun spinning from her hand before she had time to let off a shot. At the sound of Elizabeth's scream, the fight seemed to go out of Caroline, she dropped her gun and slowly raised her hands, as the circle of troopers closed in around them.

They were captured and tried later that same week. Elizabeth was pardoned on account of her considerable youth, but Caroline was charged with robbery and the murder of one policeman, and sentenced to hang.

It had to happen, of course it did. One cannot defy the law without reaping the consequences. I know this, and yet this knowledge didn't stop me from mourning the little girl I once played with. And as watched Herbert rise to become a successful business man, I couldn't help thinking that perhaps this world isn't as fair as it's meant to be.

Years passed, and people forgot the beautiful young girl. Caroline lived on only in the history books and in local legend as a ruthless bushranger, head of a small gang that once roamed the ranges.

I tell this story to remind people that there was more. There always is. Every criminal, no matter their crimes, was once a little baby, and no person is wholly evil, just as no one is wholly perfect. More than that though, I tell it to myself, to keep my young friend alive, forever dancing in the warm sun beneath the wattles down by the creek.

THE DETECTIVE OF THE MORN

MAILEA LEARY
Dover, Huon Valley

2020
OPEN CATEGORY
  FEMALE DETECTIVES

In a world where both humans and animal shifters
known as 'morns' exist…

JULY EIGHTH, 'THE MEETING'

The room was quiet with tension, those in it seemed to only be using looks of mistrust for an odd sort of communication.

Time felt as if it was ticking away by an hour a second.

Something had went wrong while discussing certain matters, not helping the already wary impressions of each other.

It was silent until the door was swung open, a girl with black, shoulder length hair and a patched up pinafore dress stood in the doorway.

'A child?' One of the guests questioned confusedly. His face held a look of displeasure.

Noticing his scowl, she held it with her own.

'If it isn't Lia!' Shouts a man sitting at the end of the table 'Is there something you want?' He asked innocently.

'Yes…' she said hesitantly 'could you take a look at the preparations for tonight's party?'

'How could I say no?' He stands up and holds out his hand to his daughter before he waves goodbye to the guests.

Close behind, followed Scrat, the tiger quoll, Henry, the Masked owl, Leon, the Brush-Tailed Possum and Alik, whose shifted form was unknown, although she assumed it was some foreign animal, because of his accent.

Along the way, she noticed Scrat in the corner of her eye looked a tad nervous, he was just in a meeting with some dangerous yet important figures after all, so she hadn't thought much of it. She knows the people who helped raise her, Leon, Scrat Henry and Alik, were not the friendliest outside of the village.

She'd heard stories whispered by morns passing through. It wasn't by any means a hidden truth that their heroes were often the villains in the lives of outsiders.

But it was all worth it in the end, because the village was happy. Villagers greeted her father, to them, he was known as the 'Hero of Morn'. He entered the main hall, while she waited, thinking about different topics, like 'humans'.

Her nose wrinkled slightly. She was always told to despise them.

As her thoughts continued her father and Alik had quietly exited the building 'That was splendid!'

'I'm glad you think so, everything seem safe?' She asked.

'Yep, all good!' He said, grinning 'I should get back to work though, what're you planning to do this afternoon Lia?'

She hummed in thought before answering. It was a wonderful day with the sun out.

'I think I'm going to hang out in the shrubs...' she said, looking to the trees overhead.

He bows before walking off somewhere with Scrat and Leon at his sides, while Alik and Henry followed suit at his back.

As her feet crunched over sticks and bark, Lia hummed softly, sometimes imitating a birds song, other times trying tunes off the top of her head. But it wasn't too far into her adventure when her gut twisted, as if trying to warn her, so she heeded it.

A small animal, covered in bristly, black fur, stood on all fours, replacing Lia. Ears twitching, voices could be heard not too far ahead. The southeast guard towers appeared to be struggling. After prancing over fallen man ferns and Tea tree plants the destination was reached.

Lia, the small animal, stood in a bush, whatever it was had the guardsmen's full attention, as they didn't notice her at all. Her ears listened into the rushed conversations,

'A HUMAN!!'

She froze and all went quiet.

Lia's eyes slowly looked around, her heart pounding, a young boy stepped into view.

As he took another step, the animalistic instincts of the guards must have snapped. Quolls, snakes and even dogs pounced out from their hiding spots, semi-circling the boy.

He backed away with his hands out in front of him.

He quickly turns around sprinting with a face of terror.

The news spread around the den like a bushfire on a windy day.

Lia's father had a face of stone, his expression stern, letting Alik, Henry and Leon discuss the situation, but Lia had noticed Scrat was missing, he was probably somewhere among the chaos.

Presents and a speech replaced the party.

That night the village went to sleep disappointed and scared.

JULY NINTH, 'THE INVESTIGATION'

The next morning, Lia woke to loud screams and doors being slammed. She didn't question anything for a second, she was up from the bed and out through the door. She followed a big clump of voices as she ran, the streets were near empty. Stopping at the edge of the crowd, she tried to push into it, but gave up as no one budged and shifted to crawl through.

The strong scent of blood hit her nose.

Claw marks scraped up and down different surfaces, clumps of feathers and mattered fur decorated the floor, blood splatter painted the walls. It reeked of death.

Lia stood in silence.

Leon and Henry had a lot of enemies, she knew that, she also knew she had to leave this matter to the adults. But she was furious and sad.

Two dead and one missing, Scrat.

She breathes in trying to think rationally before stomping off to her father's quarters. She slams the door open with a stern face. Her father, who had just been doing some sort of paperwork looks up at her.

'Lia! darling you have a bad habit of doing that, slamming open doors and barging in, don't you?' He said.

She notices Alik in the corner of the room, for a second she thought she saw bruising around his neck.

She turned her gaze back to her father.

'Did you find 'em yet?'

He cocked his head.

'Y'know! Those villains who murdered Leon and Henry!'

His eyes hardened.

'No Lia, I haven't done much regarding that. I'm too busy.'

'I'm going to find them then!!' Their eyes met once again, challenging each other. It only ended when her father, in a very certain tone simply said 'No.'

She looked away, frustrated, trying to reign in her anger.

She found herself alone her room.

"Hero of morn' my foot!'

She paced around in anger, she couldn't do anything, but she just wasn't able to sit still. She needed to do something. She grabs a long strapped bag hanging on a hook, next is a small first aid kit and then a torch from under the bed.

She heads to the door, breathing a little heavily.

'Sorry dad.'

She turned a few odd corners instead of directly heading to her destination as an attempt to not cause suspicion. Around the back, an underground tunnel opens up to a few loose floorboards inside, only a couple of people knew about it.

The room was quiet and nothing like a place full of fond memories anymore.

The first clue she looked at were the claw marks, too big to be from either of the victims.

Using her devil's nose, she finds Scrat's and a foreign scent. After a small search, she followed Scrat's scent back from where she entered, her nose picked up something else she hadn't notice before, there was the faint smell of blood.

She's lead through the gate of the village and into the bush, she kept going until she couldn't move.

Red hand prints decorated trees, as if Scrat had began staggering and using the trunks for support. She grouched in frustration when she reached her shifted forms limit, she needed to rest, she couldn't follow the scent as a human.

Not far from the spot she found a nice place to nap, a giant boulder. Lying back, she decided to give her mind a break also.

But it wasn't long before she caught a soft crunching noise against the leaves and twigs. The footsteps clearly weren't that of an animal's. She crouched behind a tree, waiting for the person, although to her surprise, it wasn't someone from the village, but the human from the day before.

Her heart raced 'what should I do?.'

He was only two metres away when she leaped out at him, knocking the boy to the ground, he cried out. Working fast, she used the straps of her bag to tightly bind his wrists.

'Well it's nice to meet you too, miss.' He mutters, spitting out the mud from his mouth.

After a short silence, she clears her throat 'I'm Lia' her voice deepens 'and I'm here as a detective!'

'Sure.' He says flatly, not convinced.

'And you're a suspect!'

'What!?' Now he reacts.

'Well 'maybe', on July 8th at around 3:15, you intruded a morn village's territory and between seven and five on the eighth and ninth, two morns were murdered in the main hall.' She states.

'But I ran away after a bunch of shifted morns started growling at me way before any of that!' He protested.

She pursed her lips, sceptical, before noticing something sticking out of his pocket 'Hold still for a sec–'

'What're–'

Ignoring his questioning, she grabbed the object, her hand pulled back with a piece of checkered fabric, she uses the very last of her shifted forms energy to smell it.

'Scrat!' He'd often worn checkered flannels and this one was covered in his scent 'where'd you get this!?' She glared.

'Geez, I picked it up about fifteen minutes ago, down that way.' He points to the bushes.

'It was just lying around?' She asked.

'Not exactly, it was in a bush, I wasn't able to get a good look around, something in the shrubs... scared me off' his face flushed, embarrassed.

'Lead me there.' She commanded, he looked at her, wide eyed.

'Um, okay... name's Nathaniel Cheung by the way, but you can just call me Nate.'

'Nice to meet you, Nate, now then, can you please take me to the location?'

'S-sure, but can you untie-'

'Nope.'

After a walk of silence they reached the desired destination.

She cursed herself for not resting enough to replenish her shifting abilities, as she was, meant she couldn't sense anything out of place. Eventually she slumped against a tree, frustrated.

From above, a croaky old voice greeted them, making them both jump.

They looked up, sitting in a branch sat a very short middle-aged women, cackling.

'What the-?' There were two of them, they shifted between currawong and human forms.

'Hey I'm Bonnie! And this's mama!' The chick cheered.

Lia stared with the fabric gripped tightly in her hand.

'Mama! Mama! Look that's the fabric that fell out of our nest!' The youngest shouted and pointed at Nate a second later 'and isn't that the boy who picked it up and left even after we called out to him?'

'So that's what spooked you earlier? Currawong morns?' Lia tried to hold in a giggle.

'Well it's not exactly ours either, last night an injured man staggered through here, but his shirt got caught on a branch and left that piece behind.' Said the mother.

'Scrat?' 'What did he look like?' She asked.

'We didn't see him...' Bonnie answered 'Nel did.'

'Huh?' There was a rustling sound and something swooped down from the branches, a large eagle showed itself before shifting into a girl around Lia's age.

The old currawong squawked 'This's Nel, my eldest daughter, as you can see, she looks a little different.'

'Nice to meet you Nel. I'm Lia, that's Nathaniel, we're told by your... mother, that you witnessed an injured man come through here. Did you see what he looked like?' She questioned.

Nel scoffs 'I did see an injured man come through here, he went that way' she points east 'his hair was brown.'

'Uh, thanks Nel, so he went east?' Lia asked

'Yep, I started following him, but stopped when he entered the city.' She said casually.

'Wait! You followed him?' She was flabbergasted.

'Yep, he didn't seem to notice me.'

'Can you take us there?' Lia asked and hears Nate gasp beside her, not liking the idea.

'Hm, Nope, all I remember is the direction he went, but I'll still come along.' She jumped down from the tree.

'What? Lia asked, confused.

'WHAT!?' Yelled the mother currawong 'You're not going anywhere! You're only fourteen!'

Lia apologetically smiled up at the currawong, with no intention of telling her that her daughter was entering a murder investigation.

She felt Nate tug at her arm before speaking 'You do realise that I can lead you to the city, since this's the way I came, right?' He said.

She mentally face palms 'oh yeah... well, will you?' She asked hesitantly.

'Only if you untie me.' His said.

She looked at the human with uncertainty. She always thought humans were down right evil, but he hadn't tried anything.

She sighed in defeat 'Fine...' she loosened the bindings and he rubbed his sore wrists and they jog after Nel.

'We'll stop in about ten minutes.' She decided.

'I have a few matches for a fire.' Nate said.

They settled under a tree, with Nel perching above them in a branch.

They chatted quietly until Nel shushed them, she had shifted into her human form and was climbing down from the tree.

'There's something approaching and fast.' The eagle whispered, she turned to Lia, but froze when bushes began rustling as something ran their way.

Lia quickly pulled out her torch and stamped out the fire, they all started running instinctively with their pursuer close behind.

They followed the dim light of the torch while the chaser didn't seem to have a problem with the darkness, swiftly dodging everything.

In the corner of her eye, Lia caught a glimpse of what she assumed to be a shifted morn, 'A lynx!?' She'd read about them in books, they were definitely not from around there.

She tried not to think about it and focused on running.

They only stopped when they reached the hard pavement of the city. Nate welcomed them to Hobart and they decided it was best to stay at his house.

Nel and Lia slept in the garden shed and she felt her anxiety wash away, she'd made her first friends.

JULY NINTH, ' SOLVED'

The next morning, they found themselves at an old warehouse. 'The trail goes right through those doors.' Lia said, referring to Scrat's scent. They both stared, gulping.

'Hey Lia, I think I need to do something before we go in, but I'll need to quickly run back home.' Nate said, already turning to walk away.

'What?' She asked, tugging at his arm.

'This's really important, I promise I'll be right back! Don't enter without me.'

She nodded, giving up.

But she couldn't sit still...

Going against what Nate ordered, she pushed the doors open and entered. Something leaps out at her, she runs, but is soon cornered.

'S-Scrat?'

He shifted, showing himself to be who she suspected. 'You found me.'

She stood up to face him 'Why did you run away!?.'

He winced 'He would've killed me, just like Leon and Henry.'

She had a suspect.

'Alik, d-did he-'

'Nope.' He cut her off.

'W-what? Then who... a stranger? a guest from the day before?- No it couldn't be!'

'But you're not entirely wrong, Alik dumped the bodies, that's what I saw, but he didn't attack me.'

'How d'you he didn't do it then?' She asked.

'He wasn't the one who had murder in his eyes.'

'Dad...'

'That was fast, don't you trust him?' He smirked, but grimaced from pain a second later.

A loud squawking echoed outside 'Nel! That was a warning, we gotta go!'

A second later the doors were roughly pushed open and the lynx from the night before springs out at the quoll.

'Alik, drop him' a voice said, Scrat who was raised up into the air a second ago fell to the ground with a thump.

'Dad..'

He didn't look back, instead he started kicking the lynx.

'You useless waste of space!' He hit him again and again 'You can't even transport a couple of dead bodies!'

'DAD!' She screamed out, but he didn't even flinch, when he was done, he moved onto Scrat, smiling with each hit.

'Did you say something?' He asked as if nothing was happening.

'Why are you doing this?' She mumbled.

'It's punishment!' He said cheerfully.

Her gut wrenched with fear.

When he gives one last punch he turns around, heading her way.

'You killed Leon and Henry.' She whispered.

'Mhm.' He confirmed with no guilt.

He approached with a deadly grin but there wasn't any time to react when a flash of orange and black zoomed past her eyes.

A second later, her father was pinned to the floor.

Her jaw drops. A tiger sits on her father, making it impossible for him to move with the weight.

'What did you drag me into Nathaniel! This better go on my record as self defence!'

Grumbled a man behind her, who she figured out was the tiger.

'Don't worry dad-'

'WHAT!?' She yelled at Nate.

'This is my dad, Mr. Cheung.' He said proudly.

'Yo.' Greeted the morn.

'Wait you're a morn?' She asked Nate.

'Nope, I've got the blood in me, but I'm a human, just like my mum.' He answered.

'A human and a morn...?'

Everything gets sorted out when the officers arrive and the clues are all connected. Her father had murdered Leon and Henry when they protested against his plans to take over human towns, he sent Alik to create a murder scene to cover it up.

Alik's bruises around his neck were also caused by her father, as punishment for Scrat getting away.

When it was reported that Lia was missing, her father sent out Alik again, hence the reason why they got chased by the Eurasian lynx. The next morning she was escorted back to the village and cleared up the misconception and lies about humans.

From that day onward, she was known as the 'Detective of Morn.'

THE CASE OF A LIFETIME

BRILEE LOVELL
Huonville, Huon Valley

2020
OPEN CATEGORY
 FEMALE DETECTIVES

My name is Chelsea Anderson. I am 20 years old and I live in a busy city by the sea in South Australia. It's not very bright and welcoming, but it always has that fresh sea smell.

In my family is my Mum, my Dad, my older Sister Victoria and my younger Sister Phoebe.

I am a tall young woman with mid length blonde hair. My friends always say that they would change anything about themselves for my beautiful freckles. I had always wanted to be a detective but my parents wanted me to be a veterinarian like my older sister Victoria, but I was determined to follow my own dreams.

When I finished school, I applied for a junior detective course at a university out of town. My sister Victoria always had my back, she told my parents that I worked with her at the Veterinarian clinic.

3 years later
I now have a great job as a detective. My parents still don't know about my real job, but Victoria keeps reassuring me that they would be okay with it. I'm not too sure about telling them just yet.

Mum rang me just before my shift at work finished on Tuesday night. She was crying and asked me to come home immediately. I quickly got my stuff and raced toward the door as my boss Chief Williams called me into his office, his tone sounded serious. I walked in and sat on the chair closest to me. The way he stared at me, I knew it was important.

'Don't freak out' he said, 'But your little sister Phoebe has gone missing'.

'What!', I shouted at him.

'She was last seen by your mother this morning when she dropped her off at the school gate', he explained.

I looked at my watch, it was now 5:30pm.

'That was more than 8 hours ago!', I yelled.

He told me that this case could be mine.

I knew that it would be a big risk, knowing that my parents would have to find out about my real job. But now I didn't care, my sister was in danger and I knew I was the one person who could find her. I told him that I would like this case more than anything.

I raced home to see my family. It seemed like forever but I finally drove into the driveway. As I grabbed my handbag and keys I could see Mum, Dad and Victoria through the window all sitting on the couch crying. I opened the door and entered the living room. I sat on the ottoman in the centre of the room and joined their conversation. I had to pretend that I had no idea what was going on, I didn't want to blow my cover. I heard the story again for the second time. I stealthily pulled Victoria aside. I explained how I was in charge of Phoebe's case and Mum and Dad would soon be finding out about me being a detective.

'It's about time!', she told me.

'I'm so nervous', I said. 'When will be the right time to tell them?'

She didn't have an answer, but advised me not to wait too long.

We walked back into the living room together, as if nothing had happened.

Mum went into the kitchen to make dinner, but the rest of us sat awkwardly in silence. When dinner was ready, we sat at the table, but none of us could bear to eat. Phoebe was always the one to start conversations and make jokes. Now it was like our family was being torn apart. I began thinking over and over in my head how I would tell my parents about my job and the case.

'Mum, Dad', I said just loud enough for them to hear me. They looked up from their plates.

'There is something I need to tell you', I said nervously.

'What's wrong?' Dad asked.

'You know how Victoria says I work at the clinic'? 'Well it's a lie', I explained, 'She covers for me'.

They looked concerned.

'So where are you getting your money from then?' Dad asked.

'I work as a detective in an office just out of town' I told them, 'And I have been given the opportunity to solve Phoebe's case'.

I was finding it hard to swallow as I waited for a response.

'So you knew about this Victoria?' Mum asked.

'Yes, I'm sorry I didn't tell you', Victoria replied with a scared look on her face.

Mum and Dad looked at each other, got up from the table and left the room.

I could feel myself going red and tears started falling from my eyes.

'You did the right thing', Victoria said as she put her hand on mine.

When I woke up the next morning I was so nervous about the day ahead. I didn't get much sleep that night, I was so worried. I got dressed and walked to the kitchen for breakfast. No one was to be seen, but I could hear Victoria in her bedroom talking on the phone. I cooked myself waffles, but I only managed a couple of bites. I grabbed my bag from the bench, but before I could walk out the door Victoria came out of her room calling for me. 'What's wrong?' I asked her.

'Good luck today', she replied.

As I reached for my car door, I saw mum in the front yard. I walked over to her, becoming extremely nervous at this point.

'Morning Mum' I said, not knowing what her response would be.

'Morning, how did you sleep?' she asked.

'Not that good', I replied.

'What about you?'

'The same, she said.

'I will find her mum' I said as I walked to my car.

I arrived at work feeling really anxious, I was about to start the search for my missing sister. As I entered my office I saw some folders and papers sitting on my desk with the name Phoebe Anderson, along with a photo of her, my sister. I began to feel emotional but I knew I had to hold it together. I already knew Phoebe's personal information like when she was born, where she lived, who her family were and what school she went to, so that gave me a start. Once I had filled in all the usual information, I knew, it was time to officially interview my parents.

I hopped in the car and travelled to see my Dad at 'Australian Builders'. I parked my car outside of the construction site and walked in. I had to put on safety glasses and a hard hat for my own protection. I found my Dad climbing on some scaffolding as high as the third story and when he saw me he came straight down.

'Hi Chelsea', he said as he came closer to me.

'Hey Dad' I replied.

'Have you found her?' he asked

'No not yet Dad, I am still gathering evidence and I need to ask you some questions about Phoebe's case'.

Dad said he knew Phoebe's class was going on an excursion that day. That was really going to give me a starting point and help me with the case.

I kissed him goodbye and went on my way.

The next stop was home to interview Mum. I knew this was going to be awkward, but I knew I had to do it. I drove in the driveway to see Mum sitting on our balcony with a cold drink in her hand. As I got out of the car she quickly walked up to the car hoping I had some good news.

I asked her the same questions as Dad but with a little bit more depth. She told me that she had signed a form to say that Phoebe's teachers were completely responsible for her during the excursion.

I said goodbye to Mum and headed to Phoebe's school to speak with her teachers. It was lunchtime and all the students were outside playing when I arrived. One of Phoebe's friends Georgia recognised me and ran up to me.

'Hi Chelsea', she said.

'Hello Georgia', I replied.

'Is Phoebe okay, she is not at school', she asked.

I didn't want to scare her so I just told her she was sick and would be back in a couple of days.

'Hope she feels better soon', she said as she ran away with her other friends.

I walked into the office and asked where I would find the grade 2 classrooms. The lady from the office gave me directions along with a visitor badge. Once I found her classroom, I knocked on the door and a young woman with the name Miss Zane on her badge greeted me.

'Hello, Miss Zane', I said looking up from her name badge.

'Hello, please call me Allie', she insisted.

'I am here to talk to you about Phoebe Anderson', I said.

'She was last seen by her family entering these school grounds early Tuesday morning', I explained to her.

'Is that why she is not here today?', she asked.

'Yes, sadly it is', I told her.

'As I have been told, she went on an excursion with you that day'.

'That is correct, We went to the museum', Allie replied.

'Is that the history museum in Adelaide? an hour's drive from here', I asked her.

'Yes it is', she said.

I asked her a few more questions and discovered that they hadn't done a headcount before they left the museum because they were running late. I told her that it is compulsory for her to do a headcount before you leave, especially on a school excursion and that it was her responsibility as the class teacher. She apologised greatly before I let myself out of the classroom.

On my way back to the station I thought through all of the information I already had. How mum signed a form so Phoebe could go on an excursion. How she was seen going to school, and how her teacher didn't do a headcount before they left the museum.

When I got back to the station I didn't want to face anyone, I was emotional enough as it was.

Thankfully I didn't see anyone and headed straight to my office. I wrote down all of the information I had gathered and put it in order of events and it led me to believe that Phoebe never arrived back at school. What if she was still at the museum all by herself? or worse someone had taken her before she could get on the bus to come home? Just thinking about it made me feel sick, and what was worse I had to find my own sister. I sat in my office for a while, just thinking about what I would do next. I gathered all my files and went to see chief Williams. I sat with him and went over the evidence I had.

'I plan to go to the area where the museum is located, to see if Phoebe was still around there', I told him.

'This is a great start to the case', he began. 'But the only way I can let you go is if you have backup', he continued. 'We don't know what to expect, and it is better to be safe than sorry', he explained.

'Who will I take?', I asked him.

'I don't have any free time, sorry but I'm sure one of the junior detectives would enjoy the adventure', chief Williams said.

I thanked him and went to find someone. I knew that the junior detectives were in class today, but this was an emergency. I came to room 309 and knocked on the door. A tall young girl with long brown hair and blue eyes opened it and welcomed me in. I explained the situation to their teacher and asked for permission to talk to the students. She gratefully agreed for me to do so.

'Hello everyone', I announced. 'If you don't already know me I am Chelsea Anderson, I am in my first year as a professional detective,' I told them.

They all looked excited.

'I am about to go on a case out of town, but I need someone to accompany me', I said.

'This is important and I need someone responsible and ready for an adventure', I explained.

Everyone was so excited and eager to do it.

'ME, PLEASE', everyone was asking.

'Who do you think has worked the hardest and deserves to go?', I asked the teacher.

She pointed to the same girl that had opened the door for me, and said 'I'm sure Zoe is up to the challenge'.

Zoe looked proud with a huge smile on her face. She stood up and we walked out of the classroom.

'Nice to meet you Zoe', I said to her.

'Where are we going?', she asked.

'We need to go now, but I'll tell you on the way', I said urgently.

As we walked out to the carpark, she was telling me almost EVERYTHING about herself. I was glad to get to know her, but she wouldn't stop talking! I told her a few things about me and the case, and that we were looking for my sister. An hour later we finally arrived at the museum. It was a very long trip. As Well as being sick of talking to Zoe I just wanted to find Phoebe and bring her home safe and sound. As I got out of the car Zoe was already doing laps of the park in front of the museum with a huge smile on her face. I don't know if she was looking for my sister or what, but I was happy she was enjoying this trip.

'I will go to the toilets over here and have a look', I told her.

She gave me a thumbs up, as she attempted to look through the windows of the museum building. Sadly there was no sign of Phoebe.

I went back to check on Zoe when I saw her talking to a security guard.

'We are detectives trying to solve a case', I heard her say. 'You have to let us in!', she was demanding.

I rushed in and pulled her aside.

'Sorry', I said to the guard as we slowly walked away.

I gave her a dirty look. We had to stay the night, so we needed to find somewhere to sleep. I took out my phone and managed to find a local airBnB. We stayed there but I didn't get much sleep. All night I could hear Zoe snoring from the bedroom next door.

At 6:00am I got out of bed and went into the living room, Zoe was already there eating breakfast and watching t.v.

We decided to go door knocking around the neighbourhood and ask them if they had seen Phoebe. We grabbed a photo of Phoebe from my files and began our mission. It was around 8:00 by now and we hadn't come across any new information.

Our first stop was a street called Tupad Lane where 5 little kids under the age of 9 were playing together. We thought this was a good place to start. We knocked on a house with the address, 4 Tupac Lane. A very polite lady in her late 40s answered the door. We explained who we were, what we were doing and showed her the photo of Phoebe. She told us, 'My friend down the street had taken in a young girl off the streets, but I don't know what she looks like'.

'Thank you so much', I replied gratefully with a grin on my face.

'This helps a lot', Zoe pitched in.

We basically sprinted down to number 10. I had butterflies in my stomach, I was so nervous.

As I knocked on the door Zoe looked at me with a hopeful expression on her face.

When the door opened my heart was beating faster than ever. Before I saw who had opened the door, I held up the photo of Phoebe and asked if they had seen her. When I noticed who was standing opposite me, my eyes widened and tears started falling down my face.

'PHOEBE!', I yelled.

She had the biggest smile on her face as I went in for a hug. We held each other tightly and cried.

After we had calmed down, the family invited us in to have morning tea. There was their Dad, their Mum and two young girls about 6 years old. We sat in their living room with snacks on their coffee table. The Dad told us the story.

They were playing at the park in front of the museum when they saw Phoebe sitting on a bench all by herself. She had tears rolling down her eyes, so they approached her. She told them that her school bus had left without her, while she was in the toilet. They took her to their house and welcomed her in. They were going to start looking for her family today, just before we got there. We thanked them gratefully for taking care of my sister.

We said our goodbyes and headed home.

We dropped Zoe off on our way home.

I had phoned Mum, Dad and Victoria as soon as we had found Phoebe, so when we drove in the driveway they were all there anxiously waiting and were running up to the car before I had even stopped. I was so glad to have Phoebe back with our family.

Later that night when Phoebe was in bed, Mum told me how proud she was and how glad she was that I was following my dreams.

I went to sleep that night knowing I had made my family proud, and I could now openly follow my dreams.

WHEN YOU PIECE THINGS TOGETHER

LULU LOVELL
Bundoora, Victoria

2021
OPEN CATEGORY
  SCENE OF THE CRIME

Prologue

Tears stream down my face, each droplet like acid, burning my face. My Mum shouts at him to leave. She tells him to go away and never come back. My Mum despises his irresponsible behaviour and his incapability to look after me. She hates that he spends valuable money on drugs. She hates everything about the person he is. But she is still finding it hard to tell him to go. Mum decides to pack our stuff and leave. Too many bad memories here. New house, new family, new start. I will never forget this night. ~

Soaring down the main road, I notice the clouds are mainly stratocumulus ones. It is funny how I spot things like this. Most people that look out car windows notice things like shop sales and advertisements, not usually the shapes and heights of clouds. I consider telling my Mum the technical names of the clouds out the window, but I know she would not appreciate this fact.

'Really, Luna. When will you have thoughts that aren't so abnormal?' That is what my Mum said yesterday when I told her that I saw twice the amount of blue cars that I saw red, and three times more white cars than I saw grey. I have to keep my cloud discovery to myself, even though it is agony. I give my Mum a haughty look even though she has no idea why. It is the sort of look, that if an adult spotted it, they would say 'don't give me attitude'. We turn off the main road and near my street. When we turn into it, I am not the only one who notices the multiple police cars and metres of crime scene do not enter tape.

'Murder!' says Damian. Of course he would assume that. I am surprised he is already at the scene.

His school finishes fifteen minutes later than mine, and most of the time he stays late with detention. He probably wagged.

'I highly doubt there has been a murder.' I say logically. But I guess in our colossal city there is bound to be some homicidal people. I run through what could've happened. There could've been a burglary, but Ms Delhi would be talking with the police if that happened and I can't see her anywhere. If there was an assault, Ms Delhi would be in an ambulance being taken to hospital. I drag Damian over to a policemen that doesn't look relatively busy, but when we approach him he sighs deeply like he has no time for us. I am about to ask him what has happened but he gets in first.

'Ms Delhi. Murdered' says the policeman. I digest the statement. My heart pounds harder and faster, my breath becomes dry and raspy.

'You found a body?' I utter, blinking back tears.

'Yes. Well not me, personally, but some others did. I can't stand anything gory and gruesome!' Admits the policeman. I want to ask why is he is a policeman when he can't stand the sight of blood! But I figure if we want some answers, we'd better not ask him any questions that might irritate him.

'Y'know who did it?' Ventures Damian. This is a reckless question. The policeman starts yelling at us, but mainly Damian.

'How the hell would we know already?! We only got the call at twelve thirty! We were gonna call an ambulance, but she was already dead. We guessed she was murdered at night as the blood was dry and from the state of her body, we could see she'd been dead for a while.' I look past the caution tape, but the only odd things I can see are the front door off its hinges, and a slight crack in the front window. Who is behind this?

It has been a week since Ms Delhi's funeral. I hated wearing black, and it was ironic as Ms Delhi thought black clothes should be illegal and that they are utterly depressing. I am looking at a picture of Ms Delhi that her brother said I could keep. I compare Ms Delhi's face to a picture of my Mum on the wall. They look freakishly similar. The Mum I am looking at is a great deal younger than the one sleeping in her bedroom at this minute. Ms Delhi was younger than my Mum, but the Mum and Ms Delhi I am looking at are both around the age of thirty. Mum has kept to herself more since Ms Delhi's death. I make Mum a cup of her favourite minty tea, and let it steep in her most treasured mug. It displays the words 'love is never-ending, and neither is the kettle'. When I bring her the tea she doesn't stir. I place it next to her, but it will probably be cold before she wakes, and cold tea is seriously depressing.

Three weeks after Ms Delhi's funeral, I am lying in bed, restless and awake. I squirm, toss and turn, as many thoughts whizz through my mind like lighting. Who did it? Is the thought that pops up the most. Why did they do it? Is also wallowing in my head. Who and why. Who and why. The well of clues has ran dry and the police have almost given up. I haven't yet. I have to do this for Ms Delhi. I remember how Ms Delhi used to cook meals for us some nights when Mum had a fatiguing day at work. And how the night we moved into the house next to her, she came over, cooked us dinner and let Mum cry on her shoulder. Mum wasn't sad that she told Dad to go, she was upset that it didn't work out and downcast that she picked him up in the first place. At least that is what I told myself.

If the police find out who did it, then it won't be hard to determine why. A few threats and the criminal reveals their motive. The police might not try to find out why. If they've caught the culprit their work is done. But wouldn't it be so distressing not ever knowing the criminals reasoning? The case would be empty and meaningless.

The next morning I wake after only achieving one or two hours of sleep. I look in my mirror and see two dark, baggy rings under my eyes. I have a serious case of bed hair, and apart from my rosy hot cheeks, my face is pale and washed out. I slog to the bathroom to shower, and afterwards I begin working on digging deeper into Ms Delhi's killing.

By noon, I haven't established anything new. I feel defeated, so I call it a day and get into bed. The next morning I see a postman ride past and leave mail. The postman leaves something in Ms Delhi's mailbox. It must be a letter from a friend that don't know she is dead. Ms Delhi had loads of friends. She got along with everybody. I go collect it, feeling that

I should read it on behalf of Ms Delhi. It isn't addressed to any specific person, it just has her address on the front. I tear it open. It reads:

Luna,
I know something you haven't found yet. I know something crucial about the death of her. Want to know what it is? Meet me at the house she was murdered at, on the 5 of June at 11 at night. I'll tell you everything I know. You can win your family back.

An innominate letter. Another lead that pulls me back into the dark hole of crimes. Why was it delivered to Ms Delhi's mailbox, and not ours? Who is this anonymous person and how do they know my name? When they say, you can win your family back, are they assuming because Ms Delhi and I were close that we were family? And do they mean winning her back by finding out the truth? I search my mind, going right back to the dark depths of my brain, but I can't think of who this can be. They say they know something, which means they must have done a personal investigation on the crime. This could be the key to me unlocking the secrets of Ms Delhi's murder.

If I choose to meet this unspecified person, I will be diving into a sea of danger. I haven't the faintest idea who it is. Curiosity is fatal.

The next night, I slip on my white sneakers that aren't so white anymore. I realise that white will stand out too much in complete darkness, so I pull on my black Nikes. I creep to the front door and gradually inch it open. Once I am outside, I walk casually to the next house's front yard. Ms Delhi's front yard. Maybe I shouldn't call it her house. She doesn't live here anymore. But I guess her spirit might. The caution tape still surrounds the house, but it won't stop anyone from ducking under. The door has been boarded up with wooden planks, but I know where her key for the back door is hidden. I am shaking as I step into the house. My legs wobble, my fingers quiver and I don't blink for almost a minute. I forget what I am here to do. Listen to what they have to say. I hear a car pull up and then, I hear a gunshot. I know why they are here.

Thud, thud, thud. Footsteps. Human footsteps. Is must be the murderer. Someone capable of killing Ms Delhi. If they killed Ms Delhi, they can certainly kill me. Thud, thud, thud.

My first thought is to run. Ignoring that thought, I go and hide. I look around the room I am in. Ms Delhi's bedroom. The very room where she took her last breath in. I dart to the wardrobe, open the door and jump in. I am surrounded by some flowy skirts, and long dresses. I breathe in the reassuring scent of Ms Delhi. And then I wait. Whatever they are looking for is taking them a long time to find. It feels like hours go by as I hunch in that wardrobe.

I hold my breath, as a torch beam floods the room. I look through the crack in the door and see the figure of a man. He is wearing a grey shirt, a black coat, black jeans and black leather loafers that look too expensive to wear going around killing people. What if he steps in some blood? Maybe he is not planning on pulling the trigger or drawing his dagger tonight. I can't see his face from this position. He turns away to face the mirror that Ms Delhi used to use it apply her makeup. She would powder the lids of her chocolate brown eyes, then outline her pale pink lips, and lastly she would lightly brush her plump cheeks with rouge. He raises his torch higher to look at it. He looks into the mirror like he fancies diving right in. This angle enables me to get a glimpse of his face. He looks a little like me. Same nose, similar eyes and face shape. I know exactly who this is. At that moment, I start to put the puzzle pieces together.

I get the corners. This is my Dad. I find the edge pieces. He wanted to kill my Mum. I fill in the middle. He wants revenge. He wants me to himself. Or maybe he wants to kill me too. He knew I was onto him and he knew I would come here. He is smart. Smart enough to trick me at least. I can't believe I didn't see this coming.

He takes a step towards the wardrobe, and my heart stops beating for a second.

'Luna.' He whispers, and I almost faint. 'I know you are there,' he continues and my heart drops to my stomach. He pulls out a knife coated in dry blood. My breath speeds up and I bite my lip so hard it bleeds. 'This is the same knife I used on your Mum.' He smells the blood and he smiles dreamily. For a second I think he is going to lick it. I remember that he doesn't know who he really killed.

'You didn't kill Mum. You got the wrong house. I don't live here.' His smile fades away.

'I killed the wrong person?' I don't answer him. He knows I am not lying. His fists are clenched like he wants to punch something. 'Well, bye, Luna. I have unfinished business'. No. I grab at his legs but it does nothing. He leaves the room. I can't stop him. I am not strong enough. I crumple into a heap. When I finally rise I race out of the bedroom. I see him lying on the floor. I got it wrong. His unfinished business wasn't to get my Mum. His remorse caused him to kill himself.

Blood surrounds his chest, his knife lays solitary on the floor next to him. He has no pulse, and his chest is motionless. This isn't what I want, so what do I want?

Mum rushes in. She sees the body, and figures it out as quick as me. We weep for each other, we weep for ourselves and we weep for Ms Delhi. We haven't cried together for a while. She holds me in her arms. It feels warm. So I don't let go.

ALICE AND THE MYSTERY OF THE CRYING BABY

CLAIRE MACDONALD
Hamilton, Queensland

2022
OPEN CATEGORY
  AGATHA CHRISTIE IN TASMANIA

Silence crept over the town. The moon hid behind the misty clouds, scared of what the night had to bring. Only a little cottage, in the midst of Penguin stirred. A tiny baby with bright blue eyes rocked in her cradle not knowing that danger lurked in the shadows. Quiet footsteps scurried through the small house leaving not a footprint at all behind. Eyes of fury darted back and forward as they continued to creep inside a dark room. A large smile reached across their face as they headed towards their target. Arms grasping for its prize, a loud pitched scream was let out and could be heard from a mile away. Slowly the voice deafened, and the unknown person charged out the door, leaving nothing but a crying baby behind.

'It's been two days since the incident and there had been no lead' exclaimed Elizabeth, dancing her way towards her little sister.

A young girl with light brown hair watched the tall, elegant girl intently as she jotted down some notes. 'I just don't think the police are doing enough, that poor baby is left alone without her dear mother' said Alice Parker, as she continued to study the plots of the big crinkly newspaper.

It was a cool Saturday morning with many flowers and blossoms reaching up to greet the suns warm light which sprinkled over the town of Penguin. Many people surrounded the small building, the police assuring everything would be ok. Gloomy faces hid in their houses, sorrowful for the disappearance of Esther Brown. Esther was well known to many of the citizens of Penguin, as she had a great sense of humour and an infectious personality. The mysterious disappearance hit Alice like a bullet. Alice and Esther were great friends since the day they were born. 'Sister, I need to do something about this, I can't lose Esther' she spoke. 'Alice, you know very well that we can't stick our noses into other people's business, there is a reason that we leave work for the men of our world' the older sister said as she took a seat next to her younger sibling. Silence crept into the small living room as the two sisters stared outside through the small window, while slowly drifting off to sleep.

A warm glow of light shone through the tiny room, sending a message towards the girl sleeping in a comfy bed piled with blankets. The little area was filled with antique objects such as vases made a hundred years ago and riches more valuable than diamonds. Outside of the small room, the church bells sung a sweet and calming song that ringed calling the people to join the happy day of Christ. Alice quickly changed clothes to her Sunday best which a beautiful white dress with big puffy sleeves. She swiftly raced down the spiral of stairs where her father was waiting for her to arrive. Her mother died giving birth to dear Alice and her father usually was out working. He was a doctor which meant he was often away, but when it came to the church it was their time to have fun together. Grasping each other's hands, they walked out the door wondering what this event had to bring.

After a long 20-minute walk, they reached the tall, ancient building, which towered over the rest of the town welcoming everyone inside. Inside the church, was long pews embellished with the finest fabric in the city. The walls had stained glass everywhere and one with Jesus holding the cross above his head. Already the room was filled with many people ready to start the usual Sunday mass. Sitting near the front of the chapel, her sister Elizabeth sat at the front, next to her husband Edward. A priest walked up the stage, wearing a long, colourful robe that hung to his knees. 'Help, he's going to kill me!' screamed a lady outside. The people of the church ran out to find that there was nothing, but mists left behind.

Another morning rose at Penguin. Creating a cup of tea, Alice sat on the balcony watching the sunrise joyfully dance in the sky. Unlike other girls her age, she didn't need to worry about kids or husbands or jobs as she didn't have any. Her father always told her she needed to find true love like Elizabeth did but no one came to mind. To Alice's delight, many birds gathered on the porch, performing their sweet carol to her. Ideas swirled around her head as she watched the concert. Suddenly the image of Ester screaming flew in her brain which made Alice wonder even more. 'Is what happened to Ester and the mystery of the church connected?' she spoke to the birds. The question spined around unanswered. From the balcony, you could see the whole of Penguin even from the distance of the house. In the distance was the uniting church which watched over the rest of penguin.

Then something caught her eye. Down the corner was a house of brick. 'Ester's house' she exclaimed. Rising from the comfortable chair, Alice walked down the flight of stairs and ran out the door to figure out hidden mysteries that stormed her head. Racing to the old paddock, she grabbed one of the golden horses that grazed in the field. Hopping on the horses back, Alice adventured through the mist wondering what she would find if she went to the scene of the crime. After a while she reached a small cottage made from brick. Vines spread over the house; the garden filled with flowers. A large oak door was wide open, welcoming the young teenager inside. Lying there in the distance was a small baby rocking in her small cradle. 'Oh hello dear Margaret' said Alice bending down to see the bright blue eyes that stared at her. Will find her I promise'. Soon after, darkness fell over the small-town sending Alice home. She jumped on her bed and closed her eyes wondering what the night had to bring.

The moons bright light waltzed in the night sky, as the people of Penguin slept below. The small detective lay in her bed, eyes wide open, the world agitating her sleep. Inventive ideas swirled her head wondering if they would be answered. Her long brown hair covered her face as she twisted and turned under the covers. A feeling of darkness crept up her spine, as she thought about the mysterious scenario. Slowly getting up from the uncomfortable bed, she quickly put on a jacket and went out for a midnight stroll through the dark neighbourhood. As she opened the door, she noticed a soft motor sound that ringed in her ears. The big gushes of wind warned her to be cautious. Her feet darting towards the sound of the ocean, Alice could see the cold blue sea dance across the golden sand.

As she got closer, she noticed a dark figure as black as the night sky looking down at a pile of rocks and stones. Interested of what this suspicious person was doing, she hid behind one of the tall trees, hoping the unknown person couldn't see her. Deciding to creep closer to the figure, the sound of the waves became louder until a cacophony rushed through her ears. After she got close enough to see what was happening, Alice noticed that the mysterious person was gone. Below her she could see the same piles of rocks that the shadow had examined but they were scattered around. Suddenly, she noticed a small handle popping out of the smooth sand.

Her heart pumping rapidly, she reached out to pull the handle wondering what it had instore. To Alice's surprise, it opened to a ladder that went down and down and down. She slowly creeped down, her hair standing on end as she continued to go down the wooden ladder. Finally, she got to the bottom of the cave like area which was lit up by a million glow worms that shone in the dark archway. Continuing to explore the dangers of the cave, she noticed a cold shiver run down her spine. A cold hand grasped her by the shoulder and before she could scream, they disappeared without a trace.

Her eyes slowly waking up to a cold breeze hitting her face, Alice could se water surrounding her as a person with black fabric covered over her face pushed her towards a small tree. The moon beamed down at her, as she noticed where she was. The land below her was small and bumpy against her feet and faintly she could see small penguins scavenging up the slope of sand. Two other islands were close by to the land she was standing on and she could see the mainland of Tasmania look down at her. 'The three sisters' she muttered under breath so her captor couldn't see.

Suddenly the mysterious person pushed the victims head and Alice felt a freezing feeling come over as she sank deeper and deeper into the soil. Tears started streaming down her face as someone's warm hands grabbed her by the legs and pulled her towards the centre of the earth. Alice couldn't believe her eyes. Under the earth of hope on of the three sister islands was a secret base like no other. It was piled with riches and jewels and had real gold and silver inside the walls of the unknown cave. Her eyes darted down at her ripped night gown and the long hair that was filled with sticks and twigs. A man wearing old rags came out of the darkness and assisted the mystery person with placing Alice in a small wooden chair. Suddenly the worried mistress found herself tied to a chair by rope that twisted and turned around her. Slowly the black creature started taking off the fabric that sealed her identity which caught the teen by surprise.

'Elizabeth!' cried Alice shocked that her older most trusted sister was staring at her. Standing in front of her was the woman she once known as her favourite sister but with envy shining through her brown eyes. 'We have done it Fredrick; it will be done tonight' exclaimed Elizabeth. The man next to her grinned as he the chains that bound his legs rustled as he came closer to the prisoner.

'Hello Alice, little girls like you should mind your own business, I am Fredrick Howard one of the convicts that work in and out of this passageway that we built years ago' said the gentlemen cunningly. 'I have had enough of being waiting for father to give me my allowance, this plot of Fredrick's gives me a chance for the future I wanted, and I won't let a puny sister ruin it' The older sister stated.

Alice's eyes turned red as tears streamed down her face, as she noticed a woman also tied to a chair next to her, begging for food and her baby. 'You only were the distraction, tonight we will set a bomb at this island which will attract the police and we will get to steal the money from the bank which is rightfully ours and by then the two of you will be dead so bye bye sister' Elizabeth said as she chuckled her way out of the secret base, Fredrick following after. As Alice turned to her dear friend Alice softly asked 'how should we get out of here?'

Once the evil captors left the dark cave that Alice was stuck in, she started plotting a plan to get out. Only a tiny beam of light shone into the secret base. Her eyes darted back and forth waiting for a brilliant idea to pop in her tired head. Noticing the riches below her feet, she grabbed a glass goblet which had the someone's name engraved into it. Finally having an idea dance in her head, Alice quickly placed the goblet at the beam of sunlight pointing it at the rope that contained her, which quickly burned the rope into smithereens. She quickly jumped out of the chair and helped her best friend Ester get to her feet. Together, they raced up the millions of stairs to the top of the island, hoping they could be on time.

Taking a quick glimpse at the view, they quickly found the old convict passageway that led back to their hometown. Ester raced to the police station while Alice went back to the island to deal with the bomb that may destroy not only the island but the whole of Tasmania. Fixed to one of the trees, was a large bomb which was tightly wrapping itself to the tree by a code. The timing of the bomb was in twenty minutes. Her heart told her that Elizabeth still wasn't bad and that she still cared about her even though she chose the dark side. Panicking, she quickly wrote her name, but an error sign appeared. Then she tried the word that she feared her sister had chosen. Money. The bomb suddenly clicked and she threw it on the floor and smashed it with her foot. Knowing that her sister's plans had now been crumpled like paper, she ran back to Penguin. Her heart felt with sadness of the betrayal. When she got back, she could see a tall policeman tightly holding Fredrick Howard's hand and Ester, hugging the baby that she left a few days ago. Suddenly a voice filled her ears as she heard her sister yelling at the top of her lungs as she ran away. 'You haven't seen the last of me' she shrieked as she disappeared into the darkness.

THE MYSTERIOUS AFFAIR AT SHIRLEY'S

AVA MCMAHON JONES
Kingston, Tasmania

2022 JOINT WINNER
OPEN CATEGORY
  AGATHA CHRISTIE IN TASMANIA

PROTESTS INCREASE AS WORKING CLASS CITIZENS
DEMAND AFFORDABLE GROCERIES

PRESSURE MOUNTING ON STATE GOVERNMENT
TO LOWER PRICES OF EVERYDAY ITEMS

GUEST LIST FOR FUNCTION TONIGHT: WHO'S
GOING AND WHAT DIFFERENCE WILL THIS MAKE
TO THE COST OF LIVING CRISIS

The bell rang and the tram slowed to a stop. Cicely Lowell stepped off onto the busy Sandy Bay Road and almost immediately collided with another person. The stranger grabbed onto her shoulders and helped her to her get her balance. She straightened and thanked the stranger, not looking up. She was about to walk off when they said

'Always one for the dramatic entrance. One may have even thought you didn't recognise me.' Cicely looked up and sighed in relief.

'Oh, Jerald.' She said, smacking his arm lightly. 'I thought I had collided with someone, well, you know…' She trailed off. Jerald smiled.

'Easily offended?'

'I was going to say important, but yours works too.' Jerald feigned offence and they laughed, drawing a few glances from around the street. Jerald seemed to feel the people looking at them because he immediately tensed up and suggested that they start walking. They walked in silence for a few blocks before turning off the main road and down a quieter street. The buildings were incredibly grand. Cicely looked around in stunned awe for a moment, before collecting herself and turning to Jerald.

'Jerald, you mustn't let them bother you. We are here as guests of one of the most important people in the city. Are they?'

'No, because they too are some of the most important and absurdly rich people in the city. Because they too are some of the most pompous-'

'Jerald!' Cicely reprimanded. 'Don't insult people like that. Even if they are ridiculously dressed and live in wildly overdecorated mansions with too much food to eat in a lifetime while we are trying to afford everyday groceries. Even if they are pompous, sometimes painfully stupid, superficial idiots who are too far disconnected from the real issues of our society to even notice real problems when they're right under their powdered noses.' Jerald tried to restrain himself but couldn't. His roaring laugh broke the peaceful air of the street and Cicely couldn't help but join.

'Honestly, though. Please try not to insult them. For whatever reason it may be, they are trying to help us. All we need to do is stick out this ridiculous function and then things might be better'

It was at this moment that a door opened just ahead of them. The house that the door led to was tremendously grand. It was one of the finer houses on the street and out stepped a man who was dressed from head to toe in the finest dinner party suit, hat, and shoes that the pair walking down the street had ever seen. Cicely could feel Jerald shifting uncomfortably next to her, obviously feeling underdressed already, despite wearing his finest clothes. The man looked around and saw them. Cicely could have sworn she saw a flicker of what could have been disgust in his eyes, but it was gone almost immediately and replaced with a large smile.

'Hello! Are you here for the function?' His tone was friendly, but Jerald did not respond.

'Yes, sir.' Cicely said, trying to enunciate her words. She had been told before that she tended to slur her words, and she did not wish to appear dull in front of a man who wanted to help them. Or a man who was already disgusted by them. He nodded.

'Shall we walk? Shirley's house is only a block or two. I thought a bit of a stretch would be good for me, so I decided not to take the car, although the night is proving to be a little chilly, isn't it?' He kept talking, and Cicely and Jerald shared a look. Driving? People with their sort of income could afford only to either walk or take a tram when they needed to go somewhere. And now this man was complaining about not taking a car two blocks because it was just a little bit cold? He was the one in the three piece suit, Cicely only had a thin cardigan to protect her bare arms from the chill.

Nevertheless, they reached the venue of the function and found it ridiculously decorated. A banner across the entrance, a decorative pile of champagne glasses stacked higher than Jerald was tall. Flowers decorating every wall, and to top it all off, a massive crystal chandelier hanging from the ceiling of the drawing room, which is where they all gathered to 'mingle' before dinner.

They were greeted by an enthusiastic woman named Shirley Martin, who Cicely and Jerald had seen in the papers. She was quite a controversial character. Supporting the working class, while encouraging the federal governments tax increases. She was loved and hated on all sides of the political and economic spectrums. She was a socialite and highly political, never failing to express her opinions in The Mercury. Jerald hated her.

Two long hours later, it was time for dinner. Before starting what looked like a delicious first course, they made a toast. To the suffering middle class and to the hard work done by Miss Shirley to put together this function and support those that are suffering. They drank, and all began eating the food.

By the second course everyone was asleep.

When they woke up, Miss Shirley Martin wasn't there.

Ivy Lawrence was just packing up in the office when she got the phone call. It was the police department. Ringing about a disappearance at the high profile function that was running that night and they needed a detective on scene stat. Ivy sighed.

'Sir, I'm not sure if you realise but it is half past nine, most of the detectives have left.'

'Most?' The chief of police said over the phone. Ivy rolled her eyes.

'Well, sure, most. I mean there's only one detective here at the moment, but they may not be who you are expecting.'

'I don't care. Get them down here and get them down here now. This is a high profile case.' The call ended there. Ivy sighed. She picked up her bag and started out towards the tram. She'd pick up some food along the way.

Ivy got off on Sandy Bay Road, eating a pie bought from a pie seller on Macquarie Street who was packing up. It was somewhat room temperature, but better than nothing. She turned down St Georges Terrace before turning right onto Colville Street. She saw police gathered around the entrance to the front garden. All attendees were gathered outside. Ivy walked up to the chief.

'Hello, sir. You requested a detective?' The chief of police turned to her.

'Yes, where is he?'

'She, sir. I think you'll find I'm a woman.' The chief sighed and turned away before turning back.

'Was there no one else?' Ivy could feel the exasperation rising in her.

'No, sir. I told you over the telephone that there was only one detective still at the agency, that detective being me.' Ivy could feel that the chief was about to continue patronizing her, so she cut him off. 'I assure you detective; I am fully qualified to be in the field. I am experienced and learnt from no other than Hercule Poirot himself.' That left the chief of police silent. Ivy nodded and walked into the house, the chief following her.

'Sir, I'm Ivy Lawrence, detective with the Australian Detectives Agency. I have 12 years' experience in the field.' She said, not turning around.

'Thomas Aldritch, chief of police at Police Tasmania. 23 years' experience in the field.' Ivy turned and held out her hand.

'Pleased to meet you, Mr Aldritch.' They shook and Ivy turned back to the scene of the crime. 'Nothing has been touched, has it Mr Aldritch?' He shook his head.

'Police have received strict orders that by no circumstances are they to touch anything. Everything is how it was when they woke up.'

'Woke up?'

'That's how the disappearance occurred. The guests all fell asleep.

They woke up and she was gone.' Ivy looked around the room and walked over to the chairs.

'Where was Miss Martin seated?' Mr Aldritch nodded in the direction of the head seat.

'Her function. She was seated at the head.' Ivy walked over and her eyes were immediately drawn to the dried blood. Then she tilted her head and looked at the tablecloth. The white was sharply contrasted to the deep red of the blood that had splattered onto it. Ivy examined the area more closely. Numerous drops on the plate, the glass, the cutlery, and the napkin. This was no disappearance. This was murder.

'Mr Aldritch.' Ivy said. 'Please collect the suspects and bring them into the living room.' Mr Aldritch nodded and left the room, leaving Ivy.

She walked down the hall and turned into what she believed was the living room. Within a few minutes, all guests were seated in the living room. Ivy turned to address them.

'Good evening. I am Miss Ivy Lawrence of the Australian Detective's Agency. I am here investigating the disappearance of Miss Shirley Martin. However, I have reason to believe that Miss Martin has been murdered.' The suspects gasped.

'Now, in order to set things right, I will be interviewing you one at a time upstairs, with Chief Aldritch as a witness. We will start with…' Ivy trailed off while looking at the guest list. 'Miss Cicely Lowell.'

The two women walked upstairs and into an informal living room, Mr Aldritch trailing close behind. They closed the door and sat. Introductions were exchanged and then Ivy started asking questions, notebook out, pen poised.

'Could you please recount what happened tonight? After you arrived at the function?'

'I arrived with Jerald at around 6 o'clock. Dinner was to be served at 8, but we were all to arrive two hours in advance so that we could discuss what needed to be progressed. And we did, for a while.

'I was with Miss Shirley, discussing accessibility to different areas of the city for the working class, and how much impact transportation costs have on our incomes. A real discussion, and she seemed very interested, but I couldn't help but be a little suspicious of her, what with her supporting the government's tax increases. Nevertheless, I spoke with her. Jerald was standing off to the side. He hates the upper class. Including Miss Shirley. Gradually more people got involved in the conversation Miss Shirley and I were having. They were all interested and seemed like they were interested in helping us. But Jerald refused to participate. There was music playing, and Peggy Lee's *Ain't We Got Fun* started playing. Anyway, Miss Shirley exclaimed something like

"*Oh, what a great song! Perfect for an occasion such as this!*' I could see Jerald tense. I could tell he was going to pick a fight. She could see it too. So she said

"*Oh, Jerald! This song is almost an exact description of your situation, of what we're trying to change. That's what tonight's about, isn't it? It's for the working class- for your- benefit.'* That's when Jerald snapped. He said:

'*Shirley, did you ever think, that by throwing this, you are spending hundreds of taxpayers'- working class dollars? We paid for your cooks, for the food, everything. Not directly, but we did. Because all money that goes in and out of your pocket is taxpayer money and you rich don't pay taxes. The ones who need the money the most are the ones who give it away. Yes, that song describes our situation exactly, but we don't have fun. We work and we work to give up our money so you can get richer. The song is right about another thing, the rich get richer, and the poor get poorer. But we don't have fun.'* Then he went outside for a smoke.' Ivy was writing all of this down very hurriedly. Cicely continued.

'So just before dinner, I went to the restroom. On my way back, I heard Shirley and another guest talking. Tall fellow. He wanted to know why she even bothered with us. We just need to be put in check. The tax increases would keep us in line and then Shirley could be generous with *her* money. 'But cutting taxes, it would prevent most of the upper class from getting half their income. The upper class are starting to turn their backs on her. She'd be doing something she that she would regret. She explained that she was determined to try cut taxes for the poor but put more in for the rich. He wasn't happy about that. He said that it'd be her funeral. And she said, knowing some of the people here, she wouldn't be surprised if it was.' Ivy looked up.

'Thank you Cicely. You can go.' Cicely left the room, and the other guests came through one at a time. It was the same story from all of them.

Ivy went downstairs and back into the dining room. She approached the door into the servants' entrance and found it locked. She went outside and around to the entrance to the kitchens. She went inside. On the wall was a table layout. Next to it was a roster. She took both.

Heading back into the dining room, she examined the table. She went and took one of the glasses, shaking it lightly and sniffing it. She could smell something. Traces of a sleep drug. *Blackmores sells stuff like that.* Ivy examined each of the glasses, hoping for a sign. She found it.

All suspects were gathered in the living room once again. It had been 30 minutes since Ivy's discovery concerning the water glasses, 28 minutes since she sent out police officers all throughout Battery Point to search every car in the vicinity. 2 minutes since the body of Miss Shirley Martin was found in the back of a car 5 blocks away, with a slit throat. Ivy began talking.

'This evening I was brought here to investigate the disappearance of Miss Shirley Martin. Quickly, I realised that all of you had a grudge against her. She was very controversial. Hated and loved on both sides of the spectrum. At 9.20 all of you woke up after falling asleep right there at the dinner table. You were all drugged. A pharmaceutical drug probably sold by Blackmores that caused you all to fall into a heavy sleep for a short period of time was put in your drinks. This could only have happened in the kitchens. One of the staff.' Ivy looked around, looking for signs of smugness or relief, anything, no matter how faint. 'However, they worked under orders. All of you were biased against Miss Martin, but who was it that would take it one step too far and murder her. About 5 minutes ago we found the body of Miss Martin, in the back of a car, with a slit throat.

'Jerald. You were the one that I first suspected. Of course. You were very open about your opinion of her, and you are outwardly very cold. It would make anyone think that you would do it. But it soon became clear that you didn't. Cicely told me that she overheard a conversation between Miss Martin and a very tall man. Cicely is above the average height for a woman, so for a man to be *very* tall, he would have to be very tall. There are a few men that fit that description.' Ivy started pointing. 'Mr Farn, Mr Pence, Mr Pall, and Mr Tristan. The man that Cicely overheard was warning her against supporting the middle class, or she'd regret it. Or, in his words, it'd be 'her funeral'. Miss Martin presently replied, 'knowing some of the people here, I wouldn't be surprised if it was.'

'I also inspected the dining room, and that's when I discovered our culprit. In order to complete the crime, they could not have been drugged. I tested all the glasses, and all of them were drugged. Then I realised, they mustn't have drunk from the glass. Mr Pall, no lips have touched your glass. You did not fall asleep. You slit the throat of Miss Martin while she was asleep and you convinced your nephew, who is part of the staff here,' Ivy held up the roster, 'to drug the champagne. You then locked the entrance to the dining room from the kitchens, and carried Miss Martin's body out to your nephew's car which you then drove and parked 5 blocks away, in order to get back in time for everyone to wake and so no one would notice your absence, isn't that right? You did not support Miss Martin and you knew the only way to stop the tax increases for the upper class coming into play and then cutting off just over half your income, because you work at the taxes office, and most of your income comes from taxes paid by the poor, was to kill the most influential person in favour of these changes.' Mr Pall paled. Then he ran towards the nearest window and leapt out. Mr Aldritch barked an order and officers from all around the block circled Mr Pall before he could escape.

One day later, Ivy hopped off the tram to find the agency building surrounded by reporters. She approached and suddenly she was being bombarded for a statement. She went up onto the steps of the agency and turned to face the growing crowd.

'There is only one person I would like to thank at present,' she said. 'My mentor, Mr Hercule Poirot, who taught me everything I know.' She looked to the back of the crowd and saw the man with the funny moustache smile.

GIRL DETECTIVE

AMELIA PATERSON
Huonville, Huon Valley

2020
OPEN CATEGORY
  FEMALE DETECTIVES

My name is Faye, I was brought up in a small town called Bunbrook. My life is about me and no one else. All I want to do is be a detective and I won't let anyone stop me from doing so and one day I'll have my first mystery.

'There is a new student in our class, his name is Ben' called out the teacher. 'Great a new person' I thought sarcastically. I was probably the only one thinking that cause every girl I saw that day stared at him like he was a god. Thankfully, everyone stopped because the bell went and ran out of class. As I was walking home, Ben was weirdly walking behind me looking stressed. 'That's strange'.

Morning arose and I turned on the tv to wake myself up. 'Breaking news' it said, 'there's been a murder in Bunbrook'. That sentence was music to my ears. 'Damn I have to go after school'. I was bummed, I didn't really listen to whatever the teacher was saying the entire day. Everything was normal even though there was a murder. Luckily, the bell rang so I could finally leave.

I was running home and Ben wasn't behind me. I packed my things and was on my way to the crime scene. 'How am I going to get in' I thought. I passed a donut shop and luckily there were cops inside and I could get a treat. 'Wow that murder was pretty rough' a policeman said, 'you know we got to go back' 'yeah' 'it was kind of weird that he was missing a ring though' 'yeah'. I snuck in their van and sat there quietly waiting for them to start driving. I had to wait for a bit of a while but then I heard a huge sigh. I was confused 'who's there' I whispered. 'Is that you Faye? It's me Ben from class'. I was gob smacked what was he doing in the van? 'Ben why are you in this van?' I said as the van started.

'I…I am here t…to find out who murdered the guy' he replied with a stutter. 'Cool, same actually'. The entire drive was awkward, he looked very stressed. The car ended with a halt and we started going out the back door. 'We're right in the middle of the crime scene' I whispered happily. We were at a farm and it looked like it was only him who lived there, as I looked over the body writing down my thoughts. 'Dead bodies are a bit grosser than the movies' I joked to Ben. This poor man got shot straight through the head. The house didn't look that interesting until I went into the bedroom. 'What are you doing' whispered Ben as I was going in. 'I'm going in the bedroom, now leave me alone I want to solve this mystery myself!' Ben didn't leave but he didn't follow me in either. As I slowly walked around him. It looked like a normal room but had creaky boards especially in one spot. I started kicking it as hard as I could with my foot.

'I can hear something' 'Quick it might be the murderer' called a cop. I wasn't thinking, the police were coming and quick. I looked around frantically luckily to see a cupboard in the corner of the room. 'Where coming in!' they yelled. The door swung open just as I shut the cupboard door. Then they finally left not checking the cupboard, how dumb. I slowly opened the cupboard and ripped up the board. 'What the hell!' it was a picture. There was a mother, father and a boy. 'Maybe there connected to the man's death' I left and saw Ben just waiting frantically outside the door 'Hi, let's go'. We went into the van and waited as the police went in later and drove back. 'We've got to find out who these people are' 'do you know'? Asking Ben didn't really help since he wasn't paying attention.

I went to the library to look for newspaper articles to see if that family had any history. Ben and I grabbed a year's worth of newspaper each and looked. 'This is kind of boring' said Ben. I flipped through a couple more pages until I found the perfect article. It said, husband murders wife. I was shocked. 'Ben, I found it the father stabbed his wife and now is in jail. We've got to go there.' 'I'm not sure that's a good idea and how would we even get in there.' 'I've got a plan.' 'This was kind of recent, so we've got to pretend we're reporters and get in contact with him, then we ask him about the photo.' 'naah, I don't think he'll cooperate' Ben said as if he knew the man. 'Why do you think so.' 'No reason' he answered shrugging.

We went along with my plan since Ben didn't have a plan and tried finding a disguise. We went to a shop and Ben got a mustache I got a scarf and sunnies and we both strutted out and planned on stealing a car. 'We have no choice Ben we've got to otherwise how are we going to get there' 'NO it's a felony!' Ben never agreed with what I said. 'Do you want to find this guy or not!' I was so angry he isn't any help. Next minute the perfect car passed the shop. I urged Ben towards it, and he rolled his eyes and followed.

There was a scary man who stepped out the car 'go distract him from shutting the door quick Faye' said Ben. I was walking towards the man looking distressed. 'Help me' I lied 'someone stole my purse, please help.' I started leading the man away and Ben started entering the car. A while later I said, 'Um thanks for helping but I'm going to be late' 'well I'm sorry we couldn't find your purse.' The man was so nice I almost felt bad, but I didn't. I ran back to his car and just saw Ben sitting in the drivers' seat. 'What are you doing! Start the car' 'I don't know how! Quick you start it he's coming.' I turned around and the man saw us sitting in his car and was running towards us. I reached over Ben and hotwired the car. 'How do you know how to do that.' 'What do you think, movies of course.' I started the car and Ben pushed the pedal as hard as he could, and we rushed off straight to prison.

It was a pretty long drive, and we were hoping that we weren't going to get pulled over, then we finally made it to the gate. 'Hello dear sir' Ben said in a cheery accent. 'I am Mr. Even, I am from the newspaper agency...' Ben didn't know what to say, he looked back at me, until I filled in with 'Tempo.' 'Yes assistant, Tempo I would like to question this man.' Ben showed the picture and the officer let us in. He took us into a room where no one was listening just as we wanted and let the father in.

'Hello' I said starting the conversation. 'I have a couple questions to ask.' I looked over at Ben trying to hide his face. 'Cut it out' I said nudging him. Ben continued. 'My name is Faye.' 'Hello Faye, my names Jack' he answered. 'I was wondering if this is you in this photo.' The man looked like he was going to cry. 'Yes, that's my wife and I with our son.' Tear's started pouring down his face. 'It wasn't me; I've been framed!'

'Do you know who from?' 'No, but you got to help me get out.' He had a grin that looked like he was crazy and said those same word over and over, like he was possessed. 'Jack, do you know this person too?' I was curious while passing him the picture. He was shocked 'Yes, that was my butler, but what is he doing dead, he was meant to be looking after my son.' 'Help, dear son come on Ben where are you, help me' Jack was going crazy. I pulled Ben aside 'Ben do you know this man?'

Ben didn't answer for a while as he was watching Jack rocking back and forth in his chair. 'YES!' he called out. I had so many questions. Well first thing, why did Ben fake he didn't know who the victim was. Second thing was, why'd he kept it a secret, and third thing is, is he the murderer. 'Ben tell him that you're his son, I think he should know before he loses his marbles not knowing where you are.' Ben went over to his dad and took off his disguise. 'Dad, I've missed you so much' Jack was surprised it was him. 'Son.' As they were reuniting, I was very suspicious of Ben. Why didn't he tell me he knew the butler? 'We got to go Ben.' Jack was a bit calmer now. 'Well goodbye son, visit me again soon.' 'I will, goodbye.'

The car drive was pretty silent I didn't know if I should ask anything. 'Um Ben can I crash at your house, if that's ok?' 'Well it is closer' he replied, 'so ok.' Ben did look a little stressed. When we arrived, Ben ran as quick as he could inside. He's definitely hiding something. 'Hey Ben, wait up.' It was pretty dark inside, and he was running around trying to find something. I turned on the lights to see Ben looking under a coffee table. 'Ben what's going on?' 'N...n... nothing.' Ok' I said slowly. 'Um, I'm going to go to sleep now, you probably should too.' Ben showed me where I was going to sleep, and I waited till he left. I heard a door slam and I started looking around. It was a pretty normal house. I opened the door to Bens room and there was a door to the attic.

I tip toed over to the attic door and tried jumping for it. 'Damn, I can't reach.' I went back out and got a chair from the living room. I opened the door for a second time and there was a creak. 'Faye, what are you doing?' Ben was rubbing his eyes. 'Why are you trying to go into the attic?' I ignored him and placed the chair down continuing to open it. I climbed in and Ben followed silently behind me. It was a dark space with cobwebs everywhere. I turned on the light and there were pictures of the butler everywhere. The pictures had knives and darts through them. 'It's you, isn't it.' Ben came out from the darkness of the corner with a gun pointing at me.

'Ben you don't have to do this just put the gun down.' 'Why did you have to find out, we were friends.' Ben started crying. 'Now I have to kill you too.' 'Ben just put down the gun.' I started to panic. 'How should I kill you Faye? Hmmm.' He shot the floor in front of me to scare me. How am I going to get out? Th…the window? 'Well your done for, get ready to die.' I jumped and the bullet went straight into my leg. I screamed in pain as I landed on the floor of the front yard. I limped to our car across the street and hid.

Everything became really dizzy. I couldn't hear anything all I could feel was my blood oozing from my wound. I couldn't speak and I was all alone. 'I'm going to die' I thought. I passed out and was confused as I awoke in a hospital. 'Why am I doing this if I'm going to be this close to dying.' I will never forget the story behind me forever wanting to be a detective. Occasionally I remember the day when I decided that I wanted to be a detective.

It was a normal morning, and I was about six. A person broke into my mum, dad and I's house. I woke up to a window getting smashed open and my dad and mum ran into my room making sure I was all right. Then a man burst in. 'Oh, what do we have here.' The man raised his gun, and two bullets were fired. My parents fell to the floor and I was left there. There was no reason for him there. Then the man jumped out the window and ran. The detectives never found him and now I strive to be the one that will find murderers for other people and maybe just maybe find the one that killed my parents.

I got up from my hospital bed and tried walking but fell. 'Anybody! Can I get a hand?' A nurse came into the room and helped me up. 'How long have I been asleep.' 'Only a couple days, you really shouldn't be getting out of bed.' She helped me get back into bed and left. 'How am I going to leave this place?' 'I have got to find Ben.' The only big question I have is why, why did Ben killed his butler? What did the butler do to get Ben to kill him?

I had a couple day's in the hospital thinking of many reasons why and the only reason that makes sense would need me to visit Jack. My wound hadn't completely healed so I was worried that something bad was going to happen. I slowly creeped out my hospital room and went down the stairs. A nurse yelled that I was missing, and I started walking faster. 'Excuse me Mrs., what are you doing?' a nurse asked. I had to think of something quick. 'I was going to get my clothes, there just in a car outside.' That was a horrible excuse, but it worked. I highjacked a car and was off to Jack.

'Hello again.' I hoped that the policeman would remember me. 'Hello, you're the assistant of Mr. Even aren't you?' 'Yes, I am, now I am here to request another meeting with Jack.' 'Well of course! Right this way.' The policeman took me in the room that we were last time and brought Jack in. 'Take as much time as you need.'

'Hey, Jack you remember me?' 'Yep.' 'So, I would like to ask you a few questions about the relationship between your butler and your wife?' 'My butler and my wife?' 'You believe me don't you, he killed her you know.' 'It was one night, and I was in the living room. Ben was asleep and my wife, Belle was downstairs. My butler got up and went downstairs with Belle. A blood curdling scream came from there and the butler left with blood on his hands.' 'But how did he frame you.' 'We had an argument that was very loud which the neighborhood heard just before which is why she was downstairs to have a break. 'Do you know why he killed her.' 'No.' The picture must've been a trophy then. I was very confused, but I had to go back to Ben to find out more.

I arrived at his house scared as ever jumping back through the attic window. 'Ben! Where are you, I need to talk!' I was terrified he might have his gun. The house was dark, and the lights didn't work. 'Ben do you know why your butler killed your mum. Answer!' 'It's because he loved her!' Ben came out right in front of me and turned on a torch. Holding the gun at my head.

'So that night I went to bed and mum was downstairs having a fight with dad so I went to go check on mum but our butler was with her saying 'Jack doesn't deserve you so if I can't have you than no one can!' over and over. Then mum screamed really loudly, and I remember watching her drop to the floor as I ran into the room.' So now you know everything, prepare to die. I was scared that I would feel the pain I felt before. Pain came from my leg. Damn my bullet wound opened, I have to think fast. I ducked, he shot, I twisted the gun from his hand and pointed it at his head. 'Don't you dare try shooting me again!' 'Now tell me where your phone is before I shoot you' Ben pointed in the direction of the phone. I dialed 000. 'Hello there is a guy that has tried to kill me twice.' The lady on the phone was surprised and sent over some policeman. The policeman burst through the door and jumped on Ben to hold him down and I dropped the gun.

They questioned me for a bit, and I told them everything. Then stripped Ben of his belongings. One thing that surprised me is that he had the ring 'so that's what he was looking for' and they saw it ring from the butler that was missing, so Ben was sent to jail for murder. As they were taking him out of his house, he looked at me as if sending him was a mistake, but he got what he deserved, JAIL FOR LIFE. I rolled up my pants to check my wound because it was hurting, and blood was everywhere. I fell to the ground as pain struck me like a brick to the face.

I was in the hospital for a long time to heal and I became famous as the detective girl of Bunbrook. Also, Jack got out of jail since he didn't kill anyone. Knowing Ben's, the murderer makes everything add up. Like how he was in the van already hiding and how he was stressed all the time.

Now I wait for my new mystery to begin.

WILLOW GRACE BLACK

LILY PETERS
Ranelagh, Huon Valley

2019
OPEN CATEGORY
  FEMALE BUSHRANGERS

Chapter 1   FAREWELL

One day in 1840 a child was born in Hobart. She had blue eyes like her mother and silky black hair like her father, she was given the name Willow Grace Black.

The Black family lived on a very small farm and were very poor. Willow was small for her age and had a special gift, she could sneak anywhere and no one would hear her coming. She had quick, light fingers and could take anything without anyone knowing.

Willow's father, James Black, was a bushranger when he was young but stopped when he had a family.

On Willow's 14th birthday her family only had a loaf of bread and butter. James said that he would go and steal two pigs from the neighbour's farm.

Willow watched her father from her bedroom window and to her horror a police officer saw James jump the fence and went to see what was going on. Willow tried to warn her father but he could not see her. As James jumped over the fence with two pigs under his arms, he bumped into the police officer.

'What are you doing with my mum's pigs?' he asked.

'My family are hungry and poor,' said James.

'That is no excuse,' shouted the officer as he pulled out his gun. 'Drop the pigs and put your arms in the air.'

The officer grabbed James and took him to the carriage and put cuffs on his hands. Willow and her mum Emma ran outside.

'Please,' begged Willow. 'Please let him go.'

The officer ignored Willow.

'What is his sentence?' asked Emma.

'He will go to Port Arthur to work for us, he will stay there for 7 years,' said the officer as he climbed into the carriage next to James and flicked the reins.

Willow watched her father until he was out of sight.

Chapter 2   THE CAPTURE

A few days later Willow was starving and Emma had given her the last bit of bread and butter. At 1:00 at night Willow heard something outside. She got out of bed and walked to the window and looked out, it took a minute for her to realise what she could see.

Three figures were rummaging around outside. One of them had their hands in a bin and another was climbing the fence to the police officer's mums farm and came back a minute later holding what looked like a pig and then all three of them left.

Willow climbed back into bed and fell asleep.

Willow got up early in the morning and went outside to the place where the figures were rummaging in bins, the sun was very bright and hot and there was not a cloud in the sky. Willow tried to remember what had happened last night and she couldn't shake the feeling someone was watching her.

A few days later Willow went outside to the vegetable patch and picked the last lettuce and carrots and went inside. Emma was sitting in a chair by the fire looking very thin and ill. Willow walked to her mother and gave her a carrot she ate it with in a second and thanked Willow.

Willow walked into the kitchen and chopped the lettuce and carrots and put them in two bowls and took one to Emma. Willow ate her serving of vegetables very fast.

Later in the afternoon, Willow went back outside to the vegetable patch that was just a pile of dirt and weeds she pulled most of them out. Half an hour later Willow had all the weeds out and in a big pile, she started to walk back to the house and she saw three pairs of eyes watching her through a nearby bush, two blue and one green, and, without thinking Willow found her legs taking her behind the bush. She stopped half way, afraid of what she would see, and she felt two hands grab her arm.

Afraid to look down she tried to pull her arm free and felt another pair of hands grab her and pull her into the bush. The next second she was asleep.

Chapter 3   THE JOB

Willow woke up in a carriage with a bag on her head. It was raining. She did not remember it raining at home?

Willow tried to stand up but fell back down for her legs were tied together. Willow tried to take off the bag on her head but it was no good her hands and arms were bound tightly to her body. Willow gave up after a minute or two because voices could be heard a few inches away. Willow stopped moving.

'Are you sure she is up to it?' said a squeaky voice, that of a girl who sounded the same age as Willow.

'I'm sure, I've been watching her for over a month with a bit of training, she will be the world's best Bushranger. The way she can sneak around most of the time, even while I was watching her, I could not find her and then she would be right in front of me,' said a different voice. It was a boy called Ben and he sounded no older than 17.

Willow sat frozen, she could not believe what she was hearing how did these people know she was good at sneaking around.

The rain was pouring now and Willow was soaked sitting in the back of the carriage, after what seemed three whole hours the carriage came to a stop and Willow felt two hands grab and lift the bag off her head, the rain felt lovely on Willow's face.

'We need someone who can sneak around without being seen, we need you Willow,' said Ben.

Willow saw the three pairs of eyes, two blue and one green. The boy named Ben who had spoken had green eyes and short blond hair and was very tall.

'You need me?' asked Willow.

'Yes we need you,' said the squeaky girl called Meg, who was the same age as her but was a lot taller with long curly black hair and magnificent blue eyes.

'Why do you need me?'

'Because you can sneak around without being seen, can't you?' said the third kid.

This boy, Noah, had blue eyes and messy black hair down to his shoulders.

'Yes,' said Willow.

'We are very poor and hungry and you are too,' said Noah, the blue-eyed boy.

'So what do you need me to do?'

'You see Willow, we are some of the most wanted Bushrangers but none of us can sneak in the dead of night like you. If you helped us we could all be rich. Anyway, let me introduce us, I'm Ben, this is Noah,' he gestured to the boy with blue eyes. 'And this is his little sister Meg.'

'Hello,' said Willow.

Willow thought about their request, well I guess I have nothing to lose. 'Ok I'll do it, what's the job?'

Ben smiled.

Chapter 4   THE PLAN

A few weeks had past and Willow had made three new friends and Ben wanted to do the plan that night.

'I think we should go over the plan one more time,' said Willow in a shaky voice for she was very nervous.

'Ok,' Ben said.

'But we have gone over the plan 5 times already,' said Meg.

'It can't hurt to do it 50 more times little sis,' said Noah sarcastically and in a very good impression of a Mother.

Ben ignored him. 'Ok, the bank sits along the river, it's not heavily guarded so it shouldn't be too hard for Willow to get past the guard on duty if we do it at night. Willow needs to pour the sleeping potion that Meg has already made into the guard's drink. Once the guard is asleep Willow needs to steal the key and quickly pack up as much gold and coins as she can. We will all be waiting in the dark at the back window by the store room of the bank, ready to catch the bags of gold. We have maybe 5 minutes from start to finish before the guard wakes up.'

They waited until night fell before setting of. Willow crept across the road and walked in the shadows she was going over the plan in her head, what if I get caught? I won't be able to run very fast with the gold. She tried not to think about this. It took 5 minutes until they got to the bank, no one was talking. Ben, Meg and Noah said bye to Willow and then they were swallowed by the darkness.

Willow got out the potion Meg had made from gill root and lavender and crept along the wall of the bank. When Willow got to the entrance, she saw two guards one was drinking a coffee while spinning keys on his finger, she seized her moment and walked towards the guards being careful to stay in the shadows. Willow opened the lid of the potion and waited, then Willow heard a shout behind her and shaking from head to toe slowly turned around to see a man running across the road.

'I just found a deserted camp, the embers in the fire are still hot. I bet it's Meg Robin, Noah Robin and Ben Kay.'

'Honestly Thomas, not this again, do you really think Meg and Noah Robin and Ben Kay would just come and camp under the stars when they know we are right here?'

'No,' said Thomas. 'You're right Oliver, but we still should check it out.'

Willow was scared, so they had found their camp! Willow looked away from the men and saw that Oliver had put his mug down and the other man had gone with Thomas to look at the camp. Willow walked forward and tipped the bottle of gill root and lavender into the mug. Willow watched Oliver gulp down the potion and coffee, he swayed on the spot and then fell to the ground and his mug smashed next to him.

Willow snatched up the key and bolted inside the bank, she ran as fast and as quiet as she could until she stopped at the door of the gold room, she unlocked and opened the door as quiet as she could and ran inside. She picked up as many bags as she could and ran out and down the corridor, she went into the store room and climbed on to some boxes and slowly lowered the bags.

'Well done Willow,' whispered Ben and she ran back down the corridor back into the room with all the gold, snatched up the rest of the gold and ran into the store room, she tossed the rest of the gold out of the window before jumping out into the night, where Ben, Meg and Noah stood holding the gold.

'Let's go!' Said Ben and they ran back to the camp. When they were opposite the camp Willow remembered that their camp had been discovered.

'Wait! Two police might be in our camp, hide in the bushes with the gold and I will go and see if they are still there.'

So Willow bravely crept across the road and hid behind a tree, she could not hear anything, she looked out from behind the tree to see a deserted camp but all their stuff was scattered everywhere. She ran back to the others and they all went back to camp.

'It's not safe to stay here any longer, we will have to leave.' Ben said.

So they packed up their stuff and went back to Willows home On the way, Willow stopped and bought as much food as she could. When she got home, she found the house a mess, she cleaned up and realised just how hungry she was.

So, she made some food, gave some to the others and went upstairs to Emma's bedroom with a tray of food. Emma was asleep and very skinny.

'Mum wake up. I have got you some food.'

'Willow?' said Emma. She sat up. 'Where have you been?'

'Long story, eat this and I'll tell you.'

Later, Emma and Willow went down stairs and Willow introduced the others and Emma let them stay in their house for as long as they needed.

'Thank you Missus Black,' said Meg.

From then on they lived happily with new gardens and they sold vegetables for money and helped the poor when they could. The Blacks, Robins and Kay were no longer poor.

7 YEARS LATER

One day Willow was out in the garden when a police carriage arrived. Willow ran inside and told Meg, Noah and Ben to hide upstairs, Emma and Willow went outside to find an officer and James climbing out of the carriage. James smiled at Willow.

'Father!' She cried. Willow ran to James and hugged him, Emma did the same.

The officer got back into the carriage and rode off. The family went inside and Willow introduced James to Meg. Noah and Ben and he listened to Willow's adventure with delight.

'I have heard of this tale in prison, it's all anyone could talk about, even to this day, the bank robbery is one of the greatest crimes ever committed. Tales were told of a brave Bushranger who changed Hobart town for the better. Who would've thought it was my brave daughter! I'm very proud of you Willow.'

Willow smiled. Maybe there was more she could do to change this great town for the better. She looked over at Ben and they both smiled, they had had the same thought.

THE END

WHAT HAPPENED BEFORE DINNER

ROSE PULLINGER
Hobart, Tasmania

2022
OPEN CATEGORY
  AGATHA CHRISTIE IN TASMANIA

I shoved open the gate with my hip, and flakes of green paint came off on my uniform. As always, the gate creaked in that way that reminds me of steel wool being scraped along a pot. It clunked shut behind me. And then there was quiet, before the sound of running footsteps shattered the silence. I spun around.

Pelting towards me, her two wonky pigtails skimming behind her, was Charlie. I slipped my bag off my back and stretched out my arms toward her.

She rammed into my stomach, and reached her small, sticky hands as far as they'd go around me. I kissed the top of her head, and breathed in her smell of gingerbread and pencil lead and oranges and grass.

'Did you have a good day?' I asked her, and she tipped her head back and gazed up at me.

'Yes!' she said. 'I did a drawing of a cat, but it's not as good as Mummy's . . .'

I lost track of what she was saying as we traipsed up the path. I couldn't think of anything except doing homework and helping Granny make dinner and looking after Charlie, because Mum's a cleaner and was working at the hospital later, and Dad was still away - it was his brother's wedding. Airfares were too expensive for all of us to go. My thoughts buzzed and sparked and I felt almost frantic. My French essay was due tomorrow, and I'd barely written half of it.

Our kitchen is cramped and cluttered and tiny. Charlie's pencils were strewn over the floor, and pieces of paper littered the table and the bench.

'Here's my cat!' Charlie beamed up at me, and I smiled at how very proud she was of the wobbly, scribbly picture that looked something like a possum crossed with a bush.

'Oh, wow! You like drawing cats, don't you?'

'Cats are my very favourite animal. I wish we had a cat. If we did, I'd take it on walks.'

'Take a cat on walks?' I said, making my eyes big and astonished. 'No. Way. Imagine a cat on a lead! Maybe you should draw a picture of that.'

'Yesss!' cheered Charlie, and she plonked on the floor to draw a bright blue cat.

I'd sat down at the table with my laptop and workbook, when Mum came dashing down the stairs.

'Oh, Anna, sweetheart.' She pressed cool lips to my forehead. 'How was school? Sorry, I've got to go, my boss called and I need to fill in for Nadia.'

'Oh,' I said. 'But–'

'I'll see you tomorrow morning, if I'm home before you leave for school, okay?'

She wrapped me in a hug.

'Bye, Mummy,' Charlie said from the floor. Her tongue was poking out the side of her mouth.

'Hang on - Mum, wait – what about dinner?' I asked.

Mum said a word that made Charlie look up from her drawing and gape at me. 'I'm telling Granny you said that!' she told Mum triumphantly.

'Sorry, Anna, I forgot - your Granny's at knitting club, she'll be here about seven, when I was supposed to leave. Can you start dinner?'

No, I couldn't. I had a French essay to write, and Charlie would be running around, and asking me questions, and I'd just remembered that I'd left my French textbook at school and we weren't supposed to use Google Translate. (Whoever made up that rule has never studied French.)

But when I looked up at Mum, I noticed how tired she looked and how many lines there were around her eyes.

'Yeah, that'd be easy,' I said.

I wished ordering fish and chips counted as starting dinner.

The kitchen clock ticked on, each dry click reminding me that it was nearly 6:30 and Charlie would be getting hungry.

I hit the red cross to close Google Translate with a decisiveness I didn't feel. Outside, night had fallen, and the dark was deep and velvety. Stars were spattered across the sky, white specks of paint on black paper, and Hobart twinkled and glittered below, a city made purely from pinpricks of light.

I pulled a pan from a cupboard, filled it with water, and set it on the stove. I pulled a packet of spiral pasta from the pantry and was about to open it, when I realised Charlie wasn't in the kitchen.

I rubbed my forehead, almost certain I could actually feel a headache starting. 'Charlie?' I called out, but no chirpy, giggly response came floating down the stairs. In fact, the house was so quiet that silence itself seemed to be echoing off the walls.

'Charlie?' I called again. 'Charlie?'

There was no response. Charlie was probably just . . . in our room? Looking for her favourite toy, Cat the cat? I remembered her asking me about dinner. 'Potato tray?' she'd said curiously. 'No, Charlie,' I'd told her as patiently as I could. 'We're not having potatoes for dinner, and we're not eating off a tray either.' I remembered her delightedly showing me her completed picture. I remembered her announcing something to do with spying and 'good potatoes.' She was probably climbing on our bunk beds.

I ran up the stairs. The seventh from the top step creaked, as always, but it made me jump so hard that I nearly toppled over.

I walked down the corridor. Our carpet is faded, but also soft and squishy, like moss soaked with dew.

'Charlie!' I yelled again, and my voice sounded more panicked and more frenzied than I'd intended it to at all.

The door to our room was shut, and on it, Charlie had stuck up a yellow cat in pride of place, only slightly askew. Seeing the messy, spiky lines, which were just so utterly Charlie, made my heart beat harder than ever.

What if I couldn't find her?

What if something had happened to her?

Reality seemed to be teetering and trembling, about to tip over and spill into nothingness. I closed my eyes, willing Charlie to appear, to squeeze me in her pudgy arms, but when I opened my eyes, it was only the yellow cat that stared back.

I rested my hand on the picture, just for a second. And then I twisted the handle and pushed the door.

It didn't open. I shoved it again, with my hip, and this time it opened with a loud bang. I peered nervously into the room: our desk chair had fallen on the floor. It had been jammed in front of the bedroom door.

My eyes skittered around the room. Over the bunks, the desk, the wardrobe.

No Charlie. I couldn't see her anywhere.

She wasn't anywhere.

I stepped into the room. Cat the toy cat was perched on Charlie's bunk, the bottom one, and I grabbed her for something to hold. I could feel terror lodged in my throat, as if it was an actual, literal stone. I tried to think through the fear, but my breath was coming fast and sharp, and tears were pooling in the corners of my eyes so fast I couldn't blink them away.

A cool breeze from the open window brushed my cheeks, light as a whisper. The night outside seemed even blacker in contrast with the bright light in the room.

I crossed to the window and gazed out. Where was Charlie?

Tear dripped down my cheeks, falling properly now, and I forced out her name again, calling into the night. 'Charlie! Stop hiding, it isn't - it isn't funny anymore!'

The dark absorbed my words. They were gone.

Just like Charlie.

It hit me quite suddenly. I couldn't believe I hadn't thought of it before.

Why was the window open?

The window was never open.

I turned and sprinted back across the room. Back down the stairs. I had that feeling that I was in a dream. You know? When things feel unreal and impossible, as if you're floating above yourself, or cocooned in cotton wool so nothing can hurt you?

It's real. The words thudded into my head. Their truth sent me spinning, reeling, from the unthinkable-ness of what was happening.

Charlie. Charlie. Charlie, who stuck out the wrong finger when drinking tea/apple juice and pretending to be a princess. Charlie, who commando crawled up the stairs to practice her spying. Charlie, who ate 'melonwater' while singing songs of her own creation, dribbling sticky pink juice down her chin.

I snatched a torch off the bench and stepped towards the door.

It opened before I got there.

Granny was home early.

'Hello, my dear. Knitting club was wonderful today. Janice brought in some passionfruit and banana muffins, isn't that fancy? And I dropped several stitches, I was so amused by Enid's story, but I think my scarf will come good in the end. Haven't you put the pasta on yet, dear?'

'Hello, Granny,' I said. My grandma is slight and dainty, with papery folds of wrinkled skin that just about droop off her face. She was wearing an uncomfortable looking black dress, and her masses of wispy white hair were piled up on her head. 'Granny, I've just got to – do something outside.'

Charlie. The word thrummed in my head in time with my heart. Charlie.

'Where's the little one?' Granny asked expectantly. She'd somehow already managed to pour the pasta into the pot.

'Oh – she's – upstairs. I think.'

You mustn't ever worry your granny, Mum always said to me. She's getting older.

And an unconscious grandma was the last thing I needed.

'Of course she is. Of course she's upstairs.' Granny looked at me. Her eyes are clear blue, and I got the funniest feeling, in that moment, that she could see right into my head.

'I've got to go outside.'

Charlie.

Charlie.

'Isn't she a funny thing then?' muttered Granny. 'Isn't she a funny thing?'

'See – see you soon.' My voice trembled. My stomach wasn't filled with butterflies: it was filled with snakes.

Because my sister.

My sister.

'Don't cry, Anna,' Granny said. 'We'll find her, you silly thing.'

'I – what?'

I pressed my palms to my face; my cheeks were damp. I breathed in sharply, trying to stop the tears.

They kept falling. Faster, faster, faster.

Granny's arms were suddenly tight around me. I remembered Charlie hugging me, only a few hours before, and yet a lifetime ago.

Charlie.

Charlie.

My tears blobbed onto the coarse fabric of Granny's dress, creating a wet patch on her shoulder.

'There, there. It's alright. Anna, my dear, it's alright.'

Granny was rocking me slightly, swaying side to side. 'It's alright,' she whispered again. 'It's alright.'

I straightened. My nose was running, but I didn't wipe it.

'Anna.' Granny guided me to a kitchen chair, forced me to sit. She sat herself, and took my smooth hand in her wrinkled one. 'Anna. Where's Charlie?'

'I don't–' I gasped, choked. 'I don't know, I was doing – my homework and – I was distracted – I can't find her, she's not in her room, the window's open – and she's gone, what if–' I shut my eyes, just for a second; the tears didn't stop falling '–what if someone's taken her away? And we can't get her back?'

'You dear thing. She'll be right as rain, Anna, I promise. Tell me everything. What did you do tonight?'

I breathed out through pursed lips. Breathed in. Out.

'I was doing my French essay. I was worried I wasn't going to - finish it in time, and so I was distracted. And – and Charlie, she was drawing a cat, she was talking about potatoes and eating potatoes off trays, and showing me her pictures, and then she went upstairs to – I think to do spying, you know, and that was ages ago, but now–'

'And the window in her room was open, you say?' said Granny thoughtfully. 'Hmm. Come with me.'

'I thought maybe she was in the cubby–' I started, but Granny shook her head.

'Anna,' she said firmly, 'I know where she is.'

Granny stood up and clip-clopped over to the torch I'd left lying on the bench. She grasped it tightly, and marched up the stairs, straight-backed and rigid as ever. She didn't pause at our bedroom door for any sentimental stroking of the yellow cat picture; she opened the door briskly and strode right in.

The window was still open, the curtains blowing in the breeze. Granny peered outside.

'Hmm,' she said. 'I see.'

I thought of Charlie jumping on our bunk beds. I thought of Charlie booing out on me from behind the wardrobe door. I thought of Charlie tucking her five dolls (Rainbow-wonder, Wonder-magic, Rainbow-magic, Rosetta, and Migglenorablina) into bed each night. I thought of Charlie hugging me, gripping me, as if she'd never let me go.

'Granny,' I said. 'I think we should call the police.'

'Nonsense,' said Granny sharply. She flung one leg elegantly over the window-sill, then the other. Then she jumped, and was gone.

I think by this point I was crying again. I remember biting my tongue and the salty taste of blood flooding my mouth. I remember climbing out of the window after Granny and banging my knee painfully on the metal edge. I remember rolling my ankle when I landed on the grass outside.

The moon was a thin crescent in the sky, a creamy gold against the inky black of night. It was so beautiful, but I barely noticed it. The air was freezing, cold enough that the skin on my arms puckered. I barely noticed that either.

I stumbled after Granny. She was strutting along ahead of me, her shoes making floomp noises whenever they hit the grass. She walked out onto our street, and glanced one way, then the other. She started striding down the hill towards the bushes on the side of the road.

I ran after her. It was, again, as if I was dreaming. Or hallucinating. I felt delirious and dazed and as if I had to concentrate to keep a grip on reality.

'Anna,' Granny hissed from ahead of me, and the sound of her voice startled me. It sounded eerie, disembodied. 'Anna, come here.'

I hurried to catch up with her.

'Look,' she said. And she clicked on the torch.

After nearly pitch-blackness, its light was almost blinding. Granny pointed it over the clump of bushes, illuminating first the odd-shaped leaves and pointed twigs, then a raggy orange cushion.

And finally, Granny played the beam of light across a little girl. There was mud in her hair and a cut on her cheek. I noticed a tear in her leggings. Spiky twigs and sticks were digging into her back.

She was fast asleep, and a delighted, mischievous grin twitched on her lips.

The girl was Charlie.

I didn't know whether to burst into tears, or yell at her, or hug her harder than I ever have before.

So I settled for all three.

I took a gulp of hot chocolate, and it burnt my tongue. My face was puffy and red and still sticky with tears.

'Anna, dear,' said Granny softly, 'I told you we'd find her. Because I knew we would.'

Granny was sitting on the couch, and Charlie's head was in her lap. When Granny breathed, Charlie's eyelids fluttered.

I took another swallow of hot chocolate so I didn't have to say anything. Everything was still shaky and blurry, as if reality was smudged at the edges.

I felt like I had to keep staring at Charlie, just so she wouldn't vanish into thin air.

'Anna, dear. We've found her. Everything will be right as rain.'

I nodded, once.

And then I spoke, my words too fast and jumbled together so it was hard to tell one from the other. 'Granny - Granny - it was just luck we found her, really, and if - we hadn't -Granny, if we hadn't, it would have been my fault and I keep thinking, what if we hadn't?'

'Anna, dear,' Granny said gently, 'we found her. And we found her because all the clues were there. NOT because we were lucky.'

I couldn't help smiling at that. My eyes drifted to the orange cushion on the floor by the heater. The cushion had just gulped down a saucer of milk.

The 'cushion' was a cat, a stray cat, called Potato, according to Charlie.

And Charlie had desperately wanted to meet Potato the stray. Potato tray.

So, she'd finished her drawing and ran up the stairs. She'd jammed a chair in front of the door – 'Like a real spy!' – and clambered out of the window. She'd soon found Potato behind the bushes, and Potato had curled up next to her, at which point she'd promptly fallen asleep.

I couldn't help thinking about my little sister, alone, at night, on the road, with an ugly, stinky, flea-ridden and possibly aggressive cat.

I couldn't help thinking about what would have happened if Granny hadn't solved the mystery.

'Granny?' Charlie said groggily, from where she was laying. 'Can we keep Potato? Please?'

Granny sighed, and as her eyes met mine over Charlie's head, I knew that, in that moment, we were both thinking the same thing: Charlie will never change.

In case you're wondering, we did keep Potato. There's some things four-year-olds can do that no one else can, and convincing my parents that keeping a filthy and vicious cat is a good idea is one of them. Charlie will never realise how lucky she is to possess such powers of persuasion.

And if I hadn't been distracted by my French essay that day? I would never have realised how lucky I am to have my clever, funny, gentle, determined, incredible sister.

She's Charlie. And despite everything, I couldn't live without her. Even if I tried.

THE SECRETS SHE LEFT

QUEENIE SHI
Sydney, NSW

2020
OPEN CATEGORY
  FEMALE DETECTIVES

CHAPTER 1

Holliday stepped out of her car parked in front of Dolphin Square, scanned around for the crime scene. It was not far from here, only a couple of rods away at the wharf of the Westminster Boating House, with her colleagues walking in and out of the cordoned zone in urgency. She looked at the grey and lifeless sky, a feeling that it's going to rain soon rose in her heart. The birds shrieked than flew away from the river bank.

'Ma'am,' Edward reported 'Gabby just called that they've ID'd the victim. Elisabeth Jennifer Harmon. She turned thirty-seven in June. Was a criminal prosecutor.'

Holliday picked her eyebrows, queried, feeling like she already predicted everything, 'Is that the prosecutor that was said to never lose a case?'

Edward nodded and swallowed, 'Yes. Gabby also said they've just contacted the victim's husband, Mr Harmon, and was told that he will come back from the first plane from Birmingham.'

For a few seconds, it felt like choking something for Holliday. Scott Harmon's constant mysterious and poised smile popped in her mind. After a century, she squeezed a sentence out of her teeth, 'Tell him to come to the Westminster Police Station to confirm the victim's identity then.'

Walking into the cordoned zone, the atmosphere was even icier inside. Holliday approached the body lying on the shore and knelt to see the details. Elisabeth Harmon had a delicate face with curly silky hair. A wound cut through the front part of her slender, swan-neck, nearly chopping off her whole head.

'Doc!' Holliday exclaimed to Marco Bailey who was off talking to another officer, 'When are you taking this to examination?' She pointed to the body of Elisabeth.

'As soon as you finish finding what you need.' Marco Baily yelled back.

Holliday stood up, gesturing to people from the forensic department to take the body away.

Walking out of the autopsy room, Holliday couldn't help trembling. At the end of the corridor, she saw Edward talking to a man in a black suit, with pale blond hair and a pair of deep, blue eyes, like the ocean. There was evident melancholy in his eyes, softening the blue depth of his eyes.

'Mr Harmon, DI Griffin is here.' Edward reminded.

Scott Harmon turned to Holliday, nodding to show that he acknowledged that she was here.

Holliday felt some bitterness in her heart. Seeing the family of the victim was the worst part of an investigation.

'My condolences, Mr Harmon–'

Scott Harmon interjected, there was determination but also weariness in his tone, 'Inspector, let's just get down to business instead of wasting time on formalities, you ask whatever you need to ask.'

Holliday and Edward exchanged a look.

Holliday led Scott Harmon to the autopsy room. It was only silence between them. The sounds of the footsteps echoed in the empty corridor.

'Where were you last night from ten to eleven?' Holliday summoned up her courage.

Scott Harmon glanced at Holliday, answered like his authority had been questioned: 'I was with my assistant Margot Knowland, in Birmingham.'

That was quick...just like it was being prepared. Holliday thought.

She pushed to open the autopsy room, the motionless atmosphere paralysed every single nerve of Holliday's body.

Scott Harmon moved toward the table where his love lied. He closed his eyes in agony. When he walked away and opened his eyes, he pushed his golden glasses and said: 'Our wedding ring is gone.'

CHAPTER 2

The Harmons' house at Chelsea was a residence of warm colour tones of coral, champagne and coconut. *She must have put a lot of effort for a happy and comfortable life for her family.* Holliday thought. The fragrances of fresh flowers adorned the rooms swirled in the air. It was hard to believe that the mistress of this residence already lied cold.

Sergeant Lincoln who just walked out of the Harmons' bedroom, suggested 'She's young, beautiful, and full of energy'. He smirked, 'She must have had a tangled love history.'

Holliday glared at Lincoln with annoyance - these older generation officers always put an equal sign between beautiful and flirty.

'Griffin' Lincoln didn't notice Holliday's irritation, 'Look at this.'

'Remember, I'm your boss. So next time, you will address me as ma'am.' Holliday warned him and took over the small box.

It was a box covered with velvet of burgundy colour. Holliday carefully opened it to see what is inside. She felt her nerves tightening and her breaths speeding. 'Could the missing ring be in this box?' She assumed.

There was nothing inside.

She asked Lincoln, 'Where was this found?'

'The victim wrapped it with a pale yellow linen fabric and put it inside her jewellery box.' Lincoln pointed at the dresser behind the unlocked door to Elisabeth Harmon's bedroom.

Led by the front desk lady of Crown Prosecution Service, Holliday held the ring box tight in her hands.

The front desk lady knocked a door lightly and they heard a sleepy sound 'Come in.' Holliday opened the door and saw Scott Harmon flipping through a folder. He looked more energetic now than he did before. He just kept yawning when they spoke last.

'Good morning, Inspector Griffin.' He put the folder aside and stood up.

Holliday skimmed through this office. It was so organised that you could not even see a piece of random paper nor a book put on the table. Just like his wife, this Prosecutor Harmon is known for a clear system of doing things.

'First of all, I want to thank you for moving out so quickly, that helped.' Holliday bowed, 'I hope that you and your family are all coping with this.'

'It was just hard to speak to the children about it, my mother will be taking care of them for a few months.'

'Have you seen this box before?' Holliday asked, showing the burgundy ring box to Scott. He sighed, looked aside and removed something on his left hand. Holliday sat down. It was a diamond ring, glowing under the light. She couldn't help gasping its beauty in admiration, but meanwhile also feel sorry for its tragedy.

Holliday shook her head to keep herself far away from sorrow, 'How would you describe your wife?'

For a second, Scott Harmon smiled gently 'Lizzie was a good mother. She always knew the best way to educate the children. She's a little bit of a workaholic... which you probably know because of her reputation. Now, she's, I could only hope that- Excuse me.'

He rubbed his eyes and began to sob.

Biting her lips, Holliday asked 'Were you each other's first spouse? Did you notice anything different about her recently?'

Nodding, Scott Harmon began his memory 'Anything different about her....'

He thought for a moment 'Her last case which happened two weeks ago, it was a splendid victory for her. But since then, she always talked about that she felt like she was being followed. She began to isolate herself from the family, which as I say it probably had something to do with what happened.'

'Thank you for your time, Mr Harmon.' Holliday stood up, she skimmed this office once again before she left.

CHAPTER 3

Taking off her shoes, Holliday rushed to the meeting room.

'Ma'am, you are finally here.' Gabby, a fresher constable, chuckled, 'We've all been waiting for you.'

Putting her feet in her high heels again, Holliday demanded loudly 'I need every single detail about Elisabeth Harmon's last case.'

She braced her hands against the table and continued 'Mr Harmon told me that our victim felt like she was being followed since she won the case.'

Sergeant Lincoln rolled his eyes and asked 'Didn't we agree on that this is a crime of passion? Why aren't we looking over her past love interests?'

Holliday felt her anger and rage grew in her mind, she didn't like being opposed nor questioned, especially by somebody that always doubt about her abilities. But he was right, their man could just be one of Elisabeth's past suitors.

'Thank you, Sergeant Lincoln.' Holiday took a deep breath 'I'll certainly take that in.

Harmon claimed that his wife had no time for socialising even though there were quite a lot of people going after her. But we don't know if he knows everything. Edward, you and Gabby, remember to go to talk to the neighbours, asking them if they saw anyone suspicious recently. I'll go to CPS's office again, inquiring if anything happened after our victim won the case. Lincoln, you can go to tech to check the cameras near Thames river bank.'

But before they all went off, Edward proposed 'I think taking off the ring is also a symbolic thing to look at in this case. She appeared to love her husband, and it was her wedding ring, I'm pretty sure she wouldn't throw it away and it wasn't in her house either. I talked to Doc earlier in the day, and he said there were some minor scratches on her ring finger, post mortem, could it be caused due to the criminal taking off her ring? If so, why does this ring matter to the murderer?'

'If they think Elisabeth has somehow insulted this ring, or she doesn't deserve to be loved.'

Holliday shivers in the cold air in the Ministry of Justice, a young lady walked to her and smiled charmingly 'Good afternoon, Inspector Griffin, I believe you have come to see Specialist Prosecutor Juliette Young.'

'Yes.'

Juliette Young was an old lady that still kept her elegance. She wore a grey dress with a black shawl and pearl necklace and earrings.

'Please do take a seat, Inspector.' Offered Ms Young.

Holliday managed her coat and sat down on the armchair 'Good afternoon, Ms Young. I'll go straight into my questions if you don't mind.'

Seeing Juliette Young nodding to give consent, Holliday asked: 'How do you feel about Elisabeth Harmon?'

'Oh, young Elisabeth. I feel so sorry for her sudden,' she paused and looked at Holliday, her hands holding the arms of the chair unnaturally, 'You know. She was a stylish woman who brought joy to the office, and justice in the court.'

Holliday thought for a moment and continued 'Did anything happened after she won the case?'

'Well, it was a murder case where a swimming coach was charged with killing his student. His wife was very angry at Elisabeth. She came to the Ministry, asked to see her. And she was very aggressive. Wait, Inspector, I know what you are going to ask, she had dark brown hair, about 5.4 feet tall.'

It felt like discovering a brand new land for Holliday, her eyes shined like stars in the night sky.

Excitedly, she stood up and shook Juliette's Young hands. Holliday gave her a deep bow of ninety degrees and said gratefully 'Thank you, Ms Young. You gave us a lot of useful information.'

CHAPTER 4

Walking out of the Ministry of Justice, Holliday received a call.

'We have something here.' It was Gabby's cheerful voice, 'Two days ago, at about half-past nine, a few people in Elisabeth Harmon witnessed her argument with a woman with brown hair.'

Holliday held her breath tightly.

'She had a knife in her hand and it looked like to one of the witnesses that she was threatening Mrs Harmon.'

'How did Elisabeth Harmon reacted to her holding a knife in her hand?'

'According to Mrs Lawrence who lived a few doors from Mrs Harmon, she was quite freaked out about somebody coming to her house at nine o'clock with a kitchen knife in her hand.'

It seemed that all questions are clear now, this lady probably committed the crime, and what they need to do is to find the evidence they need, but another question appeared in Holliday's mind.

She asked, 'If the problem between this woman and Mrs Harmon had already been promoted to such a serious stage where weapons are involved, why did she not report it to the police force straight away?'

Numerous theories zoomed through Holliday's brain.

'Ma'am? Are you there?' Gabby and Edward asked with concern on the other side of the call, 'Are you okay?'

Holliday didn't answer until this one notion in millions flashed through, she screamed out certainly 'What if she felt guilty about something she has done to her? And also, I have been thinking about one question, if it was a woman, why has she chosen this certain style of killing the victim? It the criminal is a woman, she's more likely to poison her victim instead of trying to chop off her head.'

'Alright, ma'am, Gabby's just searching it up.' Edward's prim voice came through the other side of the call, 'She got it!' He screamed with eagerness.

'Execution is widely known as a punishment, in a form of taking lives due to the process of law. Maybe the criminal thinks that Elisabeth Harmon deserved to be punished?'

'Wait a minute, these all fit together, she wanted to punish Mrs Harmon for some reason, and so she chose to execute her instead of doing it more efficiently. She took off the ring after she tried to execute her.'

Discussed Edward and Gabrielle, completely ignoring their superior who was trying to figure things out.

Holliday waited patiently until they finished chattering 'Just make sure that we have the evidence to prove her guilty.' She bit her lips, pressing down the worries that they may not be able to find the evidence.

The garden of the Millers' house was all different from the well-managed front garden of the Harmon couple. The grass seemed to have not been trimmed for about two weeks or maybe more. Wildflowers grow, scattered on the lawn.

Edward knocked on the door, Holliday glanced at him, hinting him that she will speak to this Ms Olivia Miller.

A woman opened the door, she had a walnut brown hair and hazel eyes with a touch of baby blue in it. But she looked tired, just as that she hadn't been sleeping for days, her voice was also husky 'Good afternoon, how can I help?'

Holliday took her police licence out of the pocket of her jacket 'DI

Griffin and this is Constable Riemann, we wish to speak to Ms Olivia Miller.'

The lady in front of Holliday twisted the handle of the door uneasily and finally answered, 'That's me. Come in, officers.'

Olivia Miller escorted them to sit down on the couch in the living room and sat down on the armchair next to the couch.

Holliday threw her eye on Edward, telling him to begin. Receiving the order, Edward put a photo of Elisabeth Harmon on the coffee table.

'Do you know her, Ms Miller?' Looking into her eyes, Holliday probed.

'Well,' Olivia Miller shrugged her shoulders, 'I know that she was the prosecutor that took my husband's case.'

'She was murdered yesterday night between ten and to eleven. Where were you yesterday night?' Edward interrupted, Holliday, glared at him with rage.

'I was,' Olivia Miller looked across the living room.

Seeing that Olivia Miller have nothing to say, Holliday gave Edward a look at asked 'Can we take a lot at the house?'

Olivia nodded, her eyes leaked out some despair. Edward stood up and walked directly to the dresser that Olivia Miller was staring at. Holliday waited for the news with her left hand holding her other hand tight, her hearts jumping like a deer and her stomach full of butterflies.

'Ma'am, we found Elisabeth Harmon's missing ring.'

EPILOGUE – TEN YEARS LATER

Feeling the soft sunshine touching her face, Holliday jogged along the River Thames. The morning sky is filled with a faint fragrance, the night rain washes away all the dust, and even. the fragrance of the jasmine is exaggerated in the damp air, moving with the wind and reaching every breath. She stopped, looking at the figure in front of her, in black suit, with pale blond hair, still tall and straight. The tall and slim girl next to him in black uniform had a delicate face with the exact pale blond hair as her father.

'Mr Harmon, good morning.' Holliday jogged passed, 'And to you, Miss Harmon.'

Scott Harmon grinned, he looked at his daughter proudly, 'Hi, Inspector Griffin. Meet Anneliese, my youngest one.'

Indeed, he should be proud, Anneliese was an exact copy and paste of her mother. The young girl greeted Holliday, 'It's a pleasure to meet you, Inspector Griffin.'

Holliday grinned back, Scott Harmon said, 'Now, Anne,' he handed his daughter her school bag, 'School's only a hundred metres away, would you like to go there yourself?'

Anneliese Harmon smiled like the may sun and left.

After a long time, he spoke again. Showing her a photo, 'Elisabeth left this in her folder for the Miller case. I knew you would be interested in it.'

It was an old photo of two girls standing in front of an orphanage, one with blonde hair and the other one with beautiful hair of walnut brown. They were all smiling so happily, above the girls, there were scribbles in pink of 'Elisabeth & Olivia'.

Holliday frowned and asked, 'Is this?'

Scott smiled to the sky, just like how he would smile to his beloved 'Smart as Elisabeth, she already thought of the pathway her murderer will go. She did value friends more than family.'

THE GREAT JUPITER!?

SAILA PERERA
Huonville, Huon Valley

2020 WINNER
OPEN CATEGORY
FEMALE DETECTIVES

WAITING
PLACE: RED HOUSE
TIME: 10:00

'By any chance do you know why the President wants to see me?' asked Sanaya.

'I don't know anything ma'am, so please take a seat and I will inform you when you are allowed to go in,' said the Secretary.

As Sanaya sat down, more concerning thoughts filled her head. What happens if she embarrassed herself in front of the President? What happens if she failed the job she was entrusted with?

AWKWARD SILENCE
PLACE: HEXAGON OFFICE
TIME: 10:25

It was too late to turn back, the Secretary asked her to come into the President's office. As the doors opened Sanaya noticed how amazing the office was. It had a beautifully patterned floor and paintings on each side behind the President's desk. Sanaya loved art, it was something that always stood out to her. Sanaya couldn't look for any more artistic details in the room because she was distracted looking around the room for the President himself.

A smartly dressed man entered the room and asked Sanaya to take a seat. This wasn't the President, it was his advisor, Mr Longford.

Once Sanaya took a seat next to Mr Longford there was an awkward silence. No one said a word for a minute or two. Mr Longford was busy fiddling with a file. Suddenly the door on the left side of the President's desk opened. Mr Longford immediately stood up and Sanaya joined him.

MEETING THE PRESIDENT
PLACE: HEXAGON OFFICE
TIME: 10:30

The President was wearing a smart suit. It was perfectly tailored. It was navy blue and had a slight spiral pattern.

'Sorry for being late,' said the President.

'What should I say?' Thought Sanaya.

President Krummph broke the silence saying, 'Thank you for coming Detective Sanaya, I have heard that you are one of the best detectives'.

Sanaya's heart skipped a beat when the President said this.

'Thank you for inviting me Mr President' replied Sanaya.

Mr Longford then explained that everything they discussed at the meeting had to be highly confidential.

THE CASE
LOCATION: RED OFFICE
TIME: 10:40

Your case is to find a HACKER! said President Krummph.

'A hacker? You chose ME to find a hacker?' said Sanaya.

'Sanaya our country is in danger. This hacker, you are assigned to find, has hacked into one of my most important files to…uh….launch deadly missiles to start a nuclear war, and we want to arrest him before he does any more damage' explained President Krummph while staring at Mr Longford.

'You are putting a lot of trust in me!' said Sanaya excited.

'Yes, now move on, you will need to choose an undercover name. Normally we choose the name, but you can choose yours, Sanaya' said the President.

Sanaya thought for a while and remembered that when she read a book about The Planets organisation (her favourite group of detectives) the only planet that didn't have a detective yet was Jupiter so with that she made her decision.

'Can I be, Detective Jupiter?' Asked Sanaya

'Of course, Detective Jupiter. This hacker may be very dangerous so you will have access to our weapons room. My secretary will show you everything. I would like you to start immediately,' said the President.

'Yes, Mr President. Sir, may I ask one more question?' asked Sanaya.

'Yes you may,' said Mr President anxiously.

'Why are you putting only me on this important case?' asked Sanaya curiously.

'Well...' Said the President pausing to look at Mr Longford 'Because the more people that get involved, the more chaos there will be. Anyway, here is the file they hacked. The only thing I ask is that you don't go into the chapter named 'LET GO', this is where the codes are. Don't worry, this is in the last part of the file. We couldn't take it out, so we put in a sensor. If you go into it, you will alert my agents' continued the President while handing over a hard drive.

'Thank you, Mr President,' said Sanaya.

'My secretary will show you to your room/office and everything else,' said the President.

Before she could say another word, Mr Longford hurried her out of the office and shut the door. When the doors closed, she couldn't hear a thing because it was a soundproof room.

Sanaya had mixed feelings, excited, nervous but mostly scared, this was only on the inside.

The first rule of being a good detective, 'Never show fear'.

After settling into her room/office and getting to know the building and the staff, she studied her case but found nothing important and so she called her foster mother, Lisa

CALL WITH LISA
LOCATION: HER ROOM
TIME: 15:45

Sanaya knew that the case was confidential, but she called Lisa on a secure phone line. Sanaya trusted Lisa with her life.

'It has been three hours and I still haven't found anything Lisa!' said Sanaya 'I have read everything that I'm allowed to read, and all the hacker left me was a little picture of a red planet. Why can't I just read THAT chapter? I'm hopeless!' Continued Sanaya gloomily

'You are not hopeless Sanaya! I feel like all you need is a little break. Since you were 9 years old, you wanted to go to the Red House and visit the bowling alley, sleep in one of the bedrooms and eat at the restaurant! But now that you are there, I don't see you doing anything but stress!' said Lisa.

'So, are you telling me to relax while there is a dangerous hacker on the loose?' asked Sanaya.

'Only for an hour, it will give you a clean start and it might be an eye-opener for the case!' explained Lisa.

'Ok, you are right. I will go for a swim in the pool. It looked huge from the glimpse I got!' said Sanaya smiling 'Thanks Lisa'.

'No problemo Miss Detective, you should go now and swim. Love you!' shouted Lisa.

'Love you too Lisa' laughed Sanaya as she cut the line.

THE HACK
LOCATION: RED HOUSE POOL
TIME: 17:00

Sanaya swam for an hour and she loved it. Her mind was free of the case. She got out of the pool and went to her room. After she had a shower, she felt refreshed and couldn't wait to get back on the case. After a few minutes, there were loud knocks at the door. Sanaya rushed to open the door as it seemed urgent.

Five agents came crashing through and grabbed Sanaya by her wrists. Mr Longford walked in.

'I knew I couldn't trust you,' Mr Longford said with a frown on his face.

'What are you talking about?' asked Sanaya scared and confused.

'We got an alert that you opened that forbidden chapter half an hour ago. We were busy and only saw the notification now,' said Mr Longford angrily.

'I HAVEN'T GONE INTO THAT CHAPTER AND I WASN'T

PLANNING TO! HALF AN HOUR AGO I WAS SWIMMING,' screamed Sanaya in pain.

'DON'T LIE TO ME!' shouted Mr Longford.

'I AM NOT! I WAS IN THE POOL,' said Sanaya.

'We have security cameras there. You two go check them,' ordered Mr Longford to two of the agents.

Mr Longford kept on staring at Sanaya with his angry green eyes.

Five minutes later the agents came back and confirmed that she was at the pool.

'Oh. I'm very sorry. I take things too dramatically sometimes. I'll just leave you to work' said Mr Longford with an awkward laugh.

Someone had hacked Sanaya's laptop!

When she turned it on there was a message displayed…

It said:

Come count and the Find words Me for passage time: UNDER SECOND
If you understand, you will find the two passage of life and M.M of it!

It had a red planet! This meant that it was a message from the same person that hacked the President's file!

CRACKING THE CODE
LOCATION: SANAYA'S ROOM
TIME: 18.45

It was a hard code which meant it was going to take time to decode. Luckily her dad (Ethan) had taught Sanaya methods of decoding as he was an expert in the decoding field. As Sanaya started decoding the mysterious message, memories of Ethan and her practising decoding came flooding back. Tears started building up, but she had to control her emotions as Ethan would have expected her to, now that he was gone.

She worked on decoding through the night.

Sanaya looked at the clock and it read 23:30. She decided to pour herself a cup of coffee and while sipping it she started studying the message again and suddenly everything made sense.

The decoded message was 'Come and find me in passage M.M. Count the words for time' Since there were 12 words in the important message it meant that Sanaya had to meet someone in M.M passage at midnight, but what did M.M mean?

Sanaya searched up what M.M could stand for and the first thing that showed up was the name of a famous singer called Marlin Macroe. Sanaya thought that it was a funny coincidence until she read an article about how Marlin Macroe was found escaping through a passage under the Red house. This passage was found under President Krummph's bedroom which meant only one thing.

GETTING INTO THE PRESIDENT'S ROOM
LOCATION: DIFFERENT LOCATIONS IN THE RED HOUSE
TIME: 23.32

Sanaya didn't have to sneak around the Red House because the Red House was always awake. Sanaya used her weapon advantages to borrow a dart gun, smoke shooter and an alarm muter. Sanaya planned to use the dart gun on the guards outside the President's room, the smoke shooter was just in case someone walked in on Sanaya breaking in and the alarm muter was for the alarm that alerts agents when there is unauthorised movement inside the President's room.

PERFECTLY, UNPERFECT PLAN
LOCATION: OUTSIDE THE PRESIDENT'S SUITE
TIME: 23.45

Sanaya's 'perfect plan' didn't go as perfectly as Sanaya would have liked it too, but that didn't hold her back.

The second rule of being a good detective, 'adapt quickly to change'.

The guards spotted Sanaya and approached her before she could shoot them with her dart gun, so she had to improvise. Sanaya used her smoke gun to distract them. She then shot them with her darts. The darts had a formula which would make them unconscious for half an hour and forget everything that had happened 10 minutes before they got shot. Sanaya was nervous about what would happen if someone walked in on her since she had used the smoke gun, but it was too late to turn back.

FINDING THE HATCH
LOCATION: IN THE PRESIDENT'S SUITE
TIME: 23.50

When Sanaya got into the apartment she covered the alarm. This part was easy. Now it was time for the hard part, finding the hatch to get into the secret passage.

When Sanaya got into the President's room, she checked under his desk, near his bed and on the roof and everywhere else but there was nothing. The last spot Sanaya had to check was the walk-in closet. The closet was HUGE! It even had a painting. A painting? Sanaya found that suspicious.

When she went up to it, she noticed that Marlin Macroe's signature was on it! Sanaya used all her strength to lift it but it was too heavy. There was only three minutes left until she had to meet the mystery person. Sanaya felt hopeless.

'Finally, I get a huge case and they are going to find me in the President's closet! Not only did I trespass into his room, but I shot two agents' thought Sanaya.

She leaned on the wall in exhaustion – and it moved! That's impossible, right? No, it wasn't. When Sanaya turned around the painting made a cracking noise. Sanaya pulled the painting aside and there it was, the secret passage!

Sanaya ran down the steps and hit flat ground.

THE MYSTERY MAN
LOCATION: IN THE SECRET PASSAGE
TIME: 23.59

Sanaya checked her phone for the time and saw that it was 11:59 pm. She started walking but she was still on guard. Sanaya suddenly noticed a strange figure behind her. The stranger grabbed her but since she was on guard, she was able to pin him down to the ground.

The third rule of being a good detective, 'always be on guard'.

'Who are you?' exclaimed Sanaya. There was no reply.

'I asked, who are you?' repeated Sanaya.

'I see you worked on your moves since the last time we met' laughed the mysterious man.

Sanaya was confused at how calm the stranger was. It was also strange at how familiar the voice sounded.

'Sanaya, help me up,' said the voice.

Sanaya was amazed at how the stranger knew her name. Her body had a mind of its own and started standing up. Once they were both standing up again, she asked....

'I demand you to tell me, WHO ARE YOU?'

The stranger took off his hood and mask. Sanaya recognised this face immediately.

'I thought you were dead?' said Sanaya weakly 'You had a funeral!'

'Was the coffin open?' asked the man.

'No. I just assumed that, that was how a funeral was done' replied Sanaya.

'Well, it was staged. Anyway, why haven't I got a hug yet?' asked the man.

Sanaya hugged him tight and said, 'Why have you been hiding dad? I've missed you so much'.

I had no choice. I have been under the radar because the organisation I work with, suspected that the President was leaking private information about the country' said Ethan tearing up.

'What private information?' asked Sanaya

'I can't discuss it. All you need to know is, if he sells anymore, this country will be in a lot of danger!' explained Ethan.

'The President gave me a job to find a hacker. Do you know what that is about?' asked Sanaya.

'What did he tell you?' Asked Ethan.

'That there was a hacker who hacked a file that had nuclear launch codes and I had to find the hacker before it got too dangerous so the President could arrest them. I was also given a hard drive, but I couldn't go into a file called 'LET GO' because that was where the actual codes were' replied Sanaya.

'I knew from the day you were hired that you would be put on this case and that's why I sent the coded message' said Ethan, ' I knew you would decode it!', ' I was the one who opened 'LET GO' but it doesn't include nuclear launch codes. That chapter has information and agreements the President has with the groups, but we need more evidence to arrest him' said Ethan while looking at his watch. 'It's 00:15 Sanaya, you should go because the President normally settles in his room at 00:30. I love you' said Ethan while tearing up again.

'No don't leave- but before Sayana could finish her sentence a cloud of thick smoke covered him and by the time the cloud was gone, Ethan was gone too. Sanaya found a note on the ground. It had a phone number on it. Sanaya put it in her pocket and looked at the time to see that it was 00:19 which meant she didn't have much time. Sanaya ran back the way she came.

THE EVIDENCE
LOCATION:PRESIDENT'S CLOSET
TIME: 00.21

When Sanaya got back to the closet, President Krummph was already in the room but he wasn't alone, he was with Mr Longford! Sanaya felt sweaty and didn't know what to do. She then heard them talking and decided to listen. While listening in she realised that they were talking about what her dad had just told her, selling information! At that point, Sanaya felt that recording the conversation would be great evidence for her Dads organisation.

Mr Longford left the room after the conversation and the President went for a shower.

Sanaya then ran down to the secret passage and called the number her Dad had left her. Her Dad answered and told her to send the recording to that number immediately and to wait where she was until he showed up.

After a while, she heard a lot of footsteps coming towards her. It was her Dad and his team.

'You have been a great service to us and I'm so proud to be able to call you my daughter. We finally have enough evidence to arrest Ronald Krummph and Nathan Longford and it's all thanks to you' said Ethan.

'Who do you work for Ethan?' asked Sanaya as she heard helicopters and other vehicles.

'Have you heard of The Planets?' asked Ethan.

'Of course I have! They are my favourite detectives!' replied Sanaya.

'Well let me introduce you to them,' said Ethan.

One by one Ethan introduced the detectives who were there and explained that he was apart of it. Sanaya looked at her dads' jacket and spotted the logo of the organisation and saw it was the same logo from the hacked files, a red planet. This confirmed that it was her Dad who had hacked everything.

While all of this was happening The Planet's security team rushed into the Presidents Suite and arrested Ronald Krummph while a second-team arrested Nathan Longford.

Sanaya finally sat down and noticed a female figure walking towards her. The lady then said,

'How come I haven't been introduced to the hero?'

Ethan said, 'Sorry Marlisa. Sanaya, let me introduce you to Detective Mars. I know she is your favourite detective'.

Marlisa hugged Sanaya and cheerfully said, 'Thank you so much for helping us! You know what, why don't you join the organisation? We have an opening for one person or, as we say, one more planet'.

Sanaya froze. Her dream was finally coming true.

'So?' asked Marlisa

'I would love to! Thank you, Marlisa!!!' replied Sanaya excitedly.

'I am extremely happy! What will your name be?' asked Marlisa

Sanaya replied, 'Can I be, Detective Jupiter?'

THE IMPOSTER

VERONIKA TSVETKOVA
Georgia, Europe

2020
OPEN CATEGORY
  FEMALE DETECTIVES

I walked in the dark room. There were scarlet roses lying on the table and 6 plates arranged in a circle. There were bits of food left on the plates and crumbs all over the table. I imagined how this room was filled with light and people who were talking, laughing, eating and not even imagining what could happen next. Now the room is dark and dusty. It was my job to investigate the situation and find out what actually happened but it seemed like I would need more time then I thought.

My boss announced that I am going to be working by myself, and all I have is one week. I've always loved my job until this day. Today seemed like a nightmare; I was supposed to ask people who lived next to the house where the accident happened if they heard or saw anything strange. Surely enough, I left that for the evening and then completely forgot about it! Well never mind, I thought, tomorrow will be better.

'Hello, and who are you supposed to be?' asked a lady with a warm smile while opening the door.

'Oh I'm just a person who works in the agency.' I smiled back. Telling her that I'm a detective would sound a little weird and creepy since she might not even know what happened a week ago.

'I assume that you came here for the information about that house.' she replied calmly pointing at a posh cottage standing on the other side of the road.

'Yes,' I answered 'so you do know about the accident.'

'Of course I do! I knew all of the people personally.' she said. 'Let me lead you through my house and give you all the information that I have. Come with me.' she slowly walked in her house and turned on the lights as I followed her, looking at all the paintings and china dolls that she had, all sat on a cupboard. Everything in her house seemed ancient.

'Oh I haven't introduced myself have I? I'm Lily.' explained the lady as we sat on her sofa.

'So,' I started. 'You said that you knew all the people there personally, who was there?'

'oh , there were 6 of them. All of them were my old friends.

'And all of them got poisoned?'

'yes , unfortunately.'

'So you say that there were only 6 of them.' I asked as she slowly stood up and walked away.

'Sorry just making myself some tea, would you like some?' asked Lily.

'Sure.' I replied, patiently waiting for her to come back. When she finally came back with 2 cups of tea I asked her once again if there were only 6 people.

'Yes, there were. Oh and I came there before the guests came.'

'So you were there during the accident?' I asked.

'No, but I was there before the accident.' she answered, slowly sipping her tea.

'Did you notice anything strange?' I asked.

'Oh no, everything was completely fine.' she said very calmly as I took a sip of tea. The tea tasted strange, I've never drank anything like that before. Suddenly I started coughing really hard, the lady didn't even budge to call the ambulance. She was just peacefully sitting there, sipping her tea, although I never finished my job, I still knew who poisoned the family and the guests on the night of the accident.

SUSPECT COFFEE SHOP

GEORGIA WIESE
South Guilford, Western Australia

2020
OPEN CATEGORY
 FEMALE DETECTIVES

There's been a murder. After spending 10 years in detective work for this town and spending the whole of my 30 years of life watching it grow to become the safest, most comfortable place one could only dream of, I wouldn't have even thought to imagine such a thing. Such a despicable action causing the whole of Winding Willows such terrible pain and grief. Such monstrous activity. Such… such… disgust!

'AGENT EVERLY SKANIK AND AGENT THOMAS PHELLOP, MY OFFICE. NOW.' Sergeant Barnes screams as my partner and I dash down corridors and upstairs to end the infinite, ear-piercing cries.

'Yes, Sergeant?' I half whisper as we scurry through the office door and into the perfectly decorated room. It's filled with small, ancient statues that are known to provide health, success and guaranteed love for the rest of ones' life. Though Barnes always informs us that such beliefs in marbled creatures are ridiculous.

I can't help but think though, as these dragons and lizards and bugs are so sacred to our culture, festivities and ancestry shouldn't we be allowing the public to worship them freely?

Generally, if it were on of my colleagues I would speak up and say something considering I am one of the most valued associates due to my long work life here, but, I don't wish to be fired on the spot and have to become a doctors daughter, following in both of my parents footsteps.

'I need BOTH of you on this case at once before the townsmen never leave their houses again' he deliberately exaggerates both. This is because Thomas and I generally work on the same cases, but at different times and for different parts.

'Already on it.' Thomas speaks with a sort of precision that's never escaped his mouth before.

We start to make our way in towards the town centre. As we step into the towns' square and arrive in front of the coffee shop, I feel a hollowness erupt inside of me. There is no one here. Not a single soul aside from Thomas and I. I detect a sudden urge of desperation inside of me. I've never felt so lonely, so isolated, so scared, so worthless, so... small. The town looks isolated, with no one here. For some unknown reason the town just looks dustier, older, sadder. None of this is helping with the state of my mental health right now.

There are a billion and one things thrashing against the inside my head is if they could just destroy my skull and run away. Where will we get the keys for the coffee shop? When will everything go back to normal? Will anything go back to normal? Will everyone eventually just forget about what happened? Will this happen again? Who is the killer? Why would they kill? Where are they now?

'C... can...can I help you?' a frail young lady steps out of the alleyway in a uniform crinkled with an old rustic scent. The uniform is one of the café.

'Yes, actually you can.'

'We are going to need the keys to the coffee shop Candles and Coffee, and seeing as you are wearing an employee outfit, I would assume you know someone who has the keys?' Thomas backs up my first statement with the perfect question.

'I don't have them, but the owner John Meadow does, he lives on Third avenue house 27.' She says with deep uncertainty.

'Wait I shouldn't be telling you this, um...umm... he...' The woman whispers as she cuts herself off mid-sentence.

'Nice try but you can't fool private agents that easily' Thomas gives away with almost a laugh at her attempt at deception. Before we can say anything else, she hurries back down the alleyway and out of sight. As we trudge towards the third avenue, I silently ponder about why Thomas would just blow our cover like that. Anyone could have been listening, watching, recording, plotting. Maybe asking him why he blew our cover will give me answers. I find myself wondering what to say but then deciding it best just to leave normal problems for easier times.

Walking up to the front steps of the owners' lot I feel a surge of drive. How dare this murderous villain disrupt this sanctuary of love. The world seems to acquire a tinge of darkness, almost as if someone has draped a blanket over it.

Before I can even knock at the door a man who looks to be in his 50's opens the door with a furious swing, wielding a gun in one hand and a butcher's knife in the other.

'If either of you are the killer, I suggest you back away and leave this town before I shoot the both of you!' the man says with a ting of frustration.

'I'm not the killer!' I say as a rushed response, completely forgetting to add Thomas in my plead for innocence.

'And how can you prove that exactly?' the man speaks with more nervousness than assurance.

'Listen John, I understand that you must be scared out of your skin right now but so is everyone else, so I advise you to drop the weapons and let us speak with you in peace.' Agent Phellop speaks with such calmness that he makes it look like dealing with murders is a part of his everyday schedule.

After chatting privately with the founder and owner of Candles and Coffee and securing the keys we unlatch the lock and step quietly into the café, and oh what a mess it is. I silently swear hoping it will keep my mouth shut and my feet grounded so I don't scream and run out wishing I'd never chosen this job in the first place.

There, lying on the floor was a young boy who looked to be 6 or 7. Surrounded by a pool of blood, covered with dirty tear drops and whispering secrets. He knows, and we don't. There is a massive gash in the side of his head so big it has cut through the bone showing bits of now useless brain and a knife where his heart lies silent and dead. As if Thomas read my thoughts, he says aloud what I couldn't seem to link together.

'Isn't it obvious? He was clearly stabbed in the head with something sharp and quite strong which lead to the shortage of brain function and then stabbed in the heart and left to drown in his own blood.'

'How did you get that from this?' I speak as a cold, cruel shiver tiptoes down my back.

'It's quite straight forward really, I thought you were a good detective?' Thomas tries to lighten up the mood with a joke that is not necessary at all, let alone appropriate as to what we have walked into. Though I let it go because humour is how Thomas deals with loss.

It's day two of the murder of whom we researched and figured out to be young Riley Smathin. The young boy was aged six at the time of his death.

He lived in a full house with his parents, one older sister, two older brothers, younger twins, a dog, a cat, and 3 fish.

On a Saturday morning, Riley was out to breakfast with only three of his siblings, Juanita, Jack and Ben, all of which happen to be older. We managed to get in contact with the Smathin family quite quickly due to the small population of the town.

Speaking to all three of the siblings they had told us basically the same story. They went with Riley to get him breakfast as he had won an award at school the previous day they also needed to pick up some items for their mother, seeing as the grocery store was on the way to the café. They all chipped in and bought him a croissant, a hot chocolate and a cookie. The reason they did this for him and none of their other 5 siblings is because this was the first award he'd received ever in his short education.

After coming home from the shops, they all said Riley went out to play on his bike with 5 of his siblings until it was lunch time. We were then informed that he went out to draw on the driveway with some chalk until he got bored, when he decided to play inside with his toy cars and dinosaurs.

He was called for afternoon tea which consisted of scones with jam and cream. The rest of his afternoon was filled with playing cards and running around on the back lawn until it was time for dinner. After dinner had ended, he then went to bed.

We also spoke with his mother, Kayley Smathin who said she went in at 10:00pm to check that he was asleep. He was snoring quietly and peacefully all tucked in and warm.

The next morning when they'd searched the house and couldn't find him anywhere, they called the police station asking for a search party to look for him because they'd rung all of his friends parents to see if he went to their houses.

Approximately 2 minutes later the police were phoned about the sighting of a dead body belonging to a young boy and so they sent a unit of officers to go check the crime scene, because never in the history of Winding Willows has anything like this happened. That is when we were contacted.

As if the murder of small Riley wasn't enough, we were contacted again this morning about a similar case.

Thomas and I trudge down a path that feels it has been paved with tragedy, loss, tears and a pain so scary it felt as if I were tiptoeing across a ledge 5mm in width. As we arrive at the Bakers' I spot John Meadow peaking his nosey head around the sharp, red, bricked corner of a dirtied alleyway.

The first thing that screams panic, warning, fear and suspicion throughout my body is the question; what is he doing back there? Thomas yanks me out of my wondering mind with a look so dirty the trash cans would be jealous. We continue with our next case but as I look back behind me for reassurance, I see that old John Meadow is not there anymore.

'Skanik? Everly? Hello? Earth to Everly?' I snap back into reality wondering why Thomas is so focused on me right now.

Keys. Of course. I have the keys! We needn't take any trip to the owner of Bread by the Dozen because she dropped them right off at the station to traumatized to do anything with them.

As I fumble the key into the side of the lock, I realize I'm not focusing. What will I see? Will it be gorier than Riley? Will it be the same as Riley?

I twist the key with a sharp flick of my wrist and turn the doorknob to find something truly horrendous.

A girl. I recognize her as 11-year-old Amelia Parge. I'm friends with her parents. This one is going to hurt more than before.

There is no knife, no brain, no heart, no blood. A girl strapped to a chair with her neck snapped. Quick. Painful, but quick. Whoever this murderous killer is truly has no soul. No soul and no heart.

But I need to focus. The pain of trying to clear my head almost hurts more than looking at the sight in front of me. Almost.

'So, Mister I'm So Good, what happened here?' I try to tease Thomas, but it comes out as a strained, hurtful insult.

'Well, Miss I Need To Step Up My Game, again, it really is obvious, she was told to tilt her head to the side or she'd be killed and then they must have dropped something rather heavy on her head otherwise her neck wouldn't have snapped' Thomas says as if he were recounting an event instead of making an educated guess.

I secretly kick myself for being a fool and not adding everything together. How could I let someone who is five years younger than me just walk into a massive job like this with no hesitation and so far, guesses that seem to be quite accurate?

After marking the crime scene and scanning the area for any clues we turn to leave so we can get to interviews and computer screens. But out of the corner of my eye I see the most secreted yellow sticky note in a place I didn't even know existed. Snuck on the side of the counter is a little flap, and in that flap is a yellow sticky note

'You start interviewing Thomas, I'm going to do another quick scan of the area' I call.

I pick up the sticky note. I find the most shocking thing that could be a massive link to the puzzle. My little yellow sticky note read: make sure you keep a close eye on that coffee boy, you can't trust everyone.

John Meadow is a coffee boy, John Meadow could be the killer. But nothing adds up. Why would the owner to Coffee and Candles be holding a gun and a knife when we knocked on his door? But why is he creeping in and out of alleyways? Who is he watching? Why is he watching them? Why was his employee so scared when we asked about his house? Why would he be leaving notes trying to blow his cover?

Now I would contact the sergeant, but I don't have enough evidence. One measly note and the recount of him peeping around the corner. Useless. For now.

I gasp for thin air that seems non-existent in the moment as I thrust my body up to a sitting position. 2:37 in the morning. My brain is surrounded by ambushing weakness. My throat has suddenly shrunk with a dryness so indescribable. My legs frail as I try to stand up to reach the light switch. I'm drowning in my own sweat. Water. I need water.

I crawl to my bathroom and flick the tap on with as much force as I can gather from my weakening shell. I push against the top of the counter and lift my upper body forward. My head is now drenched in ice cold water.

I let myself fall to the ground and lay there in a crumpled heap. After what feels like hours, I find the will to move and slam the light switch on. There is water all over the countertop and the tap is still running. I gently turn it off and head towards my bed to get more rest.

As I move towards my resting place, I feel a stabbing pain in the side of my stomach. I look down to find a gigantic, bloody wound in the side of my torso. As I rush past my bed to get to my first-aid kit I see a knife. Covered in warm blood. Blood that hasn't dried yet. All over my bed and all over the floor. The realisation hits me like a punch to the guts. someone just tried to kill me.

I wrap my stomach up in a bandage that quickly turns from white to crimson red. Now that my mind is clear enough to think I rush myself to the hospital. I'm losing blood. Fast.

I wake up to the sharp clang of metal as the blinding sun forces my eyes open. I look around with what little concentration I have and conclude that I'm somewhere unknown, in a white room, with a drip connected to me. As if timed perfectly, my Dad walks in.

I just found out I suffer from serious stab wounds causing my stomach not to digest food properly and my boss wants me up and ready by the end of the week. Does this man not understand the that I can hardly open my eyelids let alone chase down a killer? Clearly not.

I've got to stay in this uncomfortable, plain bed for three months, there is no way I am getting up in a week. There is one thing I am desperate to do though. Study the crime scene that took place in my home.

Breathing is a struggle. Opening my eyes is a struggle. Even thinking is a struggle. I can't live like this. I must get up. I gather all the strength I have left and turn my body over. BANG. The world starts to dissipate in front of me. But blacking out isn't an option. I pick my withered body up and yank the drip out of my arm. My blood drips on the floor and on my hospital gown. More stains. I really need to get used to the fluid keeping the thought of death in everyone's mind.

THE MURDER AT BELLENHOFF MANOR

GRACE WINSPEAR
Hobart, Tasmania

2020
OPEN CATEGORY
FEMALE DETECTIVES

Let me get straight to the point.

My name is Jane Porterly and I was a female detective for most of my life. While I was in the business, I had to remain discreet. Being a young female in the 1900s was an incredible advantage in the detective business. A female is ignored, overlooked. A man can never believe a woman is more intelligent than he. And that is what one must use to one's advantage.

So I worked with the police in utter discretion, but when I finally retired, they refused to give me the credit I deserved. I pride myself on being quite a headstrong woman, so I wasn't about to throw a hissy fit and then accept it and go back to my embroidery. I simply told them I would get my reward, one way or another. So this is what this is. A recount of my first mystery, the beginning of a wonderful journey into the world of danger, murder, and intrigue.

I was an incredibly inquisitive child. I had a sharp wit and insatiable curiosity. I was constantly amazed by the world around me, and nothing pleased me more than climbing trees or diving in the duck pond. When I was 10 however, father called me into his office and told me what was expected of me.

My brother Philip had died of polio only three weeks beforehand. He was five years old. His absence was a terrible, terrible thing. When I heard he was dead, I cried for days, and afterwards felt hollow and hardened. I didn't think anything could ever upset me again.

'You are now the only child bearing my name,' said father on that fateful day. 'So you have to ensure a good reputation. As you are a girl, this means you must marry someone rich and respectable and give birth to many sons. I want no more of this silly adventuring nonsense. You are a girl, not a boy, understand?'

I wanted to say that marrying someone and giving birth was my nightmare. I wanted to say that adventuring wasn't only for boys. I wanted to yell, and shake father, and ask him why he was so ashamed of me. But I swallowed my pride and nodded demurely. If I upset him he would have tossed me out of the house, and I would've ended up in a factory or god knows where else.

So a governess was hired, and I stopped climbing trees and started needlework and pianoforte. It killed me. All the clothing in which I could barely breathe, the dull afternoons correcting my posture, and learning which spoon is for which kind of dessert.

I could feel myself becoming more and more respectable. My unique spark began to fade away. It seemed there was no way out for me, and I began to lose hope that I would ever escape from my dreary life.

But then, when I was thirteen, I discovered detective novels.

Delving into the world of murder and mystery, I realised that it was exactly what I wanted to do. I spent many sleepless nights at my windowsill with my favourite thrillers, squinting in the faint light of the moon and turning the pages as quietly as I could.

Sherlock Holmes was my favourite, but it irritated me that all the characters were men. I searched for any detective novels featuring a female lead but there were none to be found. All that the women seemed good for was fainting or wooing or screaming over dead bodies. It seemed perfectly ridiculous, and I promised myself I would never scream over a dead body, no matter the circumstance.

Unfortunately, I didn't keep that promise for very long.

It was a week until my seventeenth birthday, and mother, father, and I had been invited to a party at the Bellenhoff manor. This was no surprise since mother and Diana Bellenhoff were best friends, and the Bellenhoffs were well known for their wild nights.

We were dressed in our most fashionable attire. Mother, ever the traditionalist, wore the largest dress she owned and slipped on her most expensive white kid gloves. I took a more modest approach, with a pale blue gown and a string of pearls cold against my neck. We did our makeup giggling, although it took quite a lot of foundation to cover the fresh bruise staining mother's cheek.

We arrived just after seven o'clock, and it had begun to drizzle. We hurried up the front steps and I cast a worried look at the foreboding clouds encroaching on the dusky sky. Father pulled on the enormous bell-rope hanging by the front door and an angry clanging could be heard from inside. A few moments of silence followed, and then the large doors creaked open, and noise and light spilled into the cold night air.

'Olivia! Richard! Jane!' Diana Bellenhoff stood in the doorway, resplendent in black sequined dress and white mix stole. 'So pleased you could come!'

'We're so grateful to have been invited.' Said mother with a gracious smile.

'Of course.' Diana leaned in close. 'To be honest, the rest of the guests are rather dry company. I need some dear friends to entertain me.'

'Of course Diana,' my father smiled. 'I hear that Colonel Sanders is attending. His war stories are known to have people falling asleep even before the coffee is served.'

A bubbly laugh escaped Diana's lips.

'This is why I need you all here.' She said with a grin, opening the door wide. 'Come in! You must be freezing to death out there.'

Our trio stepped through the doorway into the grand hall, and as my parents shook the rain from their coats, I marvelled at the splendour of the room we stood in. I had never been inside the Bellenhoff's house before.

It was twice the size of our living room and a dazzling marble white. A large, colourful mosaic occupied one wall, and an enormous glittering chandelier was suspended from the ceiling.

'Pretty, isn't it?' Came a voice from beside me.

I jumped and turned to see a young girl in a pale pink dress sporting an impressive hairdo staring up at me.

'Yes. It is rather magnificent.' I replied.

'That chandelier is 300 years old.' The girl stared up at it. 'The house has been in my family for years.'

'You must be Lord Bellenhoff's daughter,' I concluded.

'Elizabeth Bellenhoff in the flesh.' Elizabeth took my hand and shook it heartily. Thus sealing a lifelong friendship, although neither of us knew it at the time.

We followed Diana into the parlour and were introduced to the other guests. There were four in total. Lord Bellenhoff, Colonel Sanders, Letitia McCarson and Mr Hildendorf. They all seemed pleasant enough, although father was right about Colonel Sanders' war stories, and I spent a pleasant hour mingling and chatting, and I learnt a great many interesting things.

Leticia McCarson was a widow. Her husband had perished in a carriage crash only a few weeks beforehand. She had briefly courted father before he met mother, and apparently, it broke her heart when he left her.

Colonel Sanders had fought in the Great War and subsequently had no hearing in his left ear. He and father had been best friends until a falling out during the war since father refused to sign up. Colonel Sanders had gone without him, and when he came back, father had married mother, who had been courting Colonel Sanders when he went away to war.

Mr Hildendorf owned an extremely successful law firm, he was excellent at keeping guilty people out of jail. And by the looks of his leather shoes and golden cufflinks, he was making quite a lot of money from it. Father had hired him for a legal matter some time ago for some matter concerning a friend of his. Mr Hildendorf had won the case, and it was only afterwards that he realised his client had robbed him of half his savings.

There was a strange frostiness in the room all night. And once I had gathered information on everybody it wasn't hard to see why. Everyone hated father.

Elizabeth and I got along splendidly, however. I learned she was thirteen and the youngest of three. Her older brothers had left home already, and she loved detective novels almost as much as I. She always carried around a notebook and pencil on her person for that very reason.

We were in the middle of a heated debate over the usefulness of Watson, and Diana had just left to get more appetizers when the lights buzzed, flickered, and shut off entirely. There was the sound of general panic, a struggle, and… a gunshot. The acrid smell of gunpowder filled the air and then pandemonium ensued.

'Stop!' came a voice.

Everyone obeyed, and an eerie silence filled the parlour. There was the sound of a match striking, and Lord Bellenhoff's face was dimly illuminated by low candlelight.

'This happens all the time.' He said. 'These new electric lights are a terrible bother. In a few moments, everything will be fine.'

We waited, and eventually, the lights blinked on and everyone could see again.

'There. It's all alright.' Said Lord Bellenhoff, blowing out the candle.

'Did you hear a gunshot?' Murmured Elizabeth.

I was about to respond but was interrupted by hellish screaming. I looked to see mother bent over father, tears streaming down her cheeks. I was confused, but when I saw the cherry blood staining his chest, and the dull stare of his eyes, I knew.

He was dead.

I allowed myself one tiny scream, only one, and then I folded up all my emotions and put them in a drawer. There was a mystery to be solved.

And I would be the one to solve it.

Elizabeth and I retired to the nursery. The police had been called, but because of the storm, they couldn't access the house. The parlour had been shut off, but even so, I was avoiding downstairs entirely. One of us was the murderer and I didn't intend to be the next victim.

'First of all,' I said to Elizabeth who was lounging on the rug, taking notes. 'I believe we can rule out both your mother and mine since yours was not in the room at the time and I know my mother. She would never do anything like this to her husband.'

'Agreed.' Said Elizabeth. 'So everyone else is a suspect then yes?'

'Yes. Colonel Sanders and father had a terrible falling out, whereupon father married his lover. Leticia was courting father when he married mother, so she may be harbouring some resentment towards him due to that. And Mr Hildendorf blames father for someone stealing half his money.'

'What about my father?' Asked Elizabeth.

'We can rule him out too. He and father were thick as thieves.'

'So we have three suspects with perfect motives and perfect opportunities.' Said Elizabeth sighing. 'It always seemed so easy in the books.'

I gave my assent, and we began brainstorming ideas as to who could be the killer. An hour of this turned up nothing, so we agreed to split up and look for clues.

I was hurrying down the hallway when I bumped into Leticia, her face quite red and blotchy from crying.

'Oh sorry, dear.' She said mournfully. 'I didn't see you there.'

'It's quite alright Leticia,' I said graciously. 'We're all a bit shocked, and not quite ourselves presently.'

'Oh!' Leticia burst out crying again. 'It's horrible, isn't it? A murder. Right here in this house!'

'You didn't happen to see anything did you?' I wondered as I consoled her.

'I only wish I had!' Leticia blew her nose loudly on her handkerchief. 'I was far too panicked about the dark to notice anything. Dear Richard! I probably shouldn't say this to you dear, but I have loved your father for a long time. And I was going to tell him tonight that I was finally done with him. I was ready to close that chapter of my life forever and now look at what's happened!'

I hugged her tightly.

'Don't worry Leticia,' I said. 'We will bring the killer to justice.'

And with that, I ran off to find Elizabeth, Letitia McCarson had just ruled herself out.

I found Elizabeth in the kitchen. Once I explained breathlessly about Leticia, she revealed that Mr Hildendorf was also innocent. He had indeed been robbed, but it had been insured. And the sympathy he received had helped him win several extra cases and his beautiful wife, Maria. Diana had told her this a few moments ago, but Elizabeth had disappeared before Diana could ask why she was so curious about motives for murder.

'So I suppose that leaves Colonel Sanders.' Said Elizabeth. 'But we can't just accuse him because he's the only suspect left.'

Right on cue, Colonel Sanders strode into the kitchen. When he saw us, he tipped his hat sorrowfully.

'Hello, girls.' He said. 'What a terrible time it is.'

I said hello back, but Elizabeth was frozen to the spot. When the Colonel turned away I leaned towards her.

'What's wrong?' I whispered.

'Look,' Elizabeth said shakily, pointing to the gun poking out of the Colonel's pocket.

My blood ran cold and I turned completely white. We were in the room with the murderer! Suddenly my fear turned to anger, this man in front of me had killed my father. I wasn't going to let him get away with it. Despite Elizabeth's frantic protestations, I strode up to him and tapped him on the shoulder.

'Why do you have a gun?' I demanded.

Elizabeth let out a little squeak of terror.

'I see what you're getting at, young lady,' said the Colonel. And to my horror, he pulled out the gun and pointed it at me. I held my breath, waiting for the sound of a gunshot and the pain of a bullet entering my chest- 'But this old thing hasn't worked in years.'

He gestured for me to take it and I realised this was true. The gun was caked in rust and obviously hadn't been fired for a long time.

'I keep it on me for sentimental reasons.' Said Colonel Sanders wistfully. 'It was the first gun I ever fired and I consider it my lucky charm. But rest assured I would never lay a finger on your father, the war taught me to respect honour above all else, even petty revenge.'

'Sorry Colonel,' I said, ashamed.

'It's quite alright.' The Colonel took back the gun and re-holstered it. 'This is quite a shocking time for everyone. It's only natural that you're upset.'

He strode out of the room and I turned to Elizabeth.

'Well, that was a bust.' She said disappointedly. 'Don't get me wrong, I'm glad we weren't stuck in the same room as a murderer, but now we have no clue as to who it might be.'

'Let's just go back to the nursery,' I said, disheartened. 'The police are coming soon, we can let them figure it out.'

We tramped dejectedly up to the nursery to find mother bent over, rummaging through a toybox.

'Mother?' I asked.

'Jane!' She said, straightening up. 'I was just looking for a handkerchief. I seem to have made mine quite sodden.'

'I'm so sorry mother,' I said, leaning in to hug her. She squeezed me back tightly, and as I leant sadly on her shoulder, I saw something peeking out of the toybox that she had just been poking around in.

When she pulled away, I leant down to investigate. I grabbed the thing, and as I pulled it out I realised that it was a gun. A working one, sleek and shiny. I turned in horror to her, not quite believing it.

'Mother?' I could barely speak. 'What is this?'

I saw then in the recognition in her eyes that it was hers. She had done it. Millions of emotions coursed through my body. Panic. Grief. Fear. I noted the tension in her stance and pointed the gun at her before she could run.

'Don't move,' I said.

'Jane,' said mother. 'Don't be silly. Put the gun down.'

'Why did you do it?' I asked in a strangled voice. 'Why?'

'Do what?' She asked innocently.

'Don't play the innocent here mother.' I said. 'I know this is yours. I KNOW WHAT YOU DID!'

'I had reason.' Mother hissed. 'Don't pretend you didn't see the way that monster treated me. Treated you. He only ever cared if I produced a son, and when little Philip died, he blamed me. You think that bruise on my cheek was from running into a doorframe? You think he hasn't been hurting me for years? He was becoming unhinged, dangerous. So I did what I had to do.'

My hand wavered, I could see from her face that she wasn't lying. I was so unsure. Father had never been a kind man, but did he really deserve to die for it?

'I chose to liberate myself from his tyranny,' mother continued. 'And if you just put the gun down and join me, we can blame it on someone else. Everyone here hates him, and it's no mystery as to why.'

I looked at mother's pleading face, and down at the gun in my hands. I could do it. I could pretend like nothing had ever happened, and mother and I could go home to safety and love. It would have been so easy.

But I didn't.

I told the police everything when they arrived, and as mother was taken away, I finally let myself cry. For in that evening I had both learned about my parents' terrible actions, and lost them in one fell swoop.

It hurt too much for words to express.

THE NIGHTINGALE'S LAST SONG

RUBY STEPHENSON
Kenmore, Queensland

2021 WINNER
OPEN CATEGORY
SCENE OF THE CRIME

A path of yellow lights illuminated the lavish opera stadium. Walls lined in the softest red velvet, ornately designed pillars stretching to the ceiling, hundreds of esteemed guests flitting around in fanciful clothing. Bernice Bennett oozed with excitement as her parents slowly weaved their way through the crowd.

From the time she could walk, the Royal Opera House had become a second home to Bernice. The warm glow of lights, the dome shaped ceiling and England's very own Nightingale, Madam Sherrie, comforted her like nothing else. Her voice soared through the cavernous stadium and pierced into even the coldest hearts. Bernice's stomach was aflutter. The lights were dimming and the colossal curtains encasing the stage finally parted.

A bright white spotlight followed Madam Sherrie as she walked gracefully forwards with a bowed head. Her deep pink bodice decorated with white ruffles and bell sleeves blurred into an extravagant explosion of pink satin that trailed behind her. She was the picture of health and beauty; rosy cheeks, pink lips and eyes that shone as though reflecting moonlight. A beautiful melody drifted from the orchestra pit. The opera performer raised her eyes to the audience.

Bernice did not realise that she had been holding her breath until the first sweet note danced through the air. Madam Sherrie began. The entire audience – once raucous and distracted – were deathly silent. Not a murmur would dare to interrupt such captivation that entranced a crowd of four thousand. Bernice felt like a snake being charmed. The music washed away all her previous nerves and sailed her away. It was nearing the climax of the first act. Madam Sherrie exploded with the highest note yet when she was cut short. Nobody saw a person, few saw the hand as it lashed out from the back curtains but everybody saw the crimson blood trickling from the Nightingales slit throat. She stumbled forwards gasping for air. Reaching into space with milky eyes before dropping to the floor.

Dead.

The audience stared at her still body on the stage in shock. Somebody screamed and chaos broke loose. People were stampeding out of the building like a herd of wildebeest. One man rushed forwards onto the stage, muttering 'no' over and over again. Bernice and her parents were still sitting down facing straight ahead. Her heart was hammering in her ears. How could this be happening? It was then and there that Bernice decided this would be her breakthrough.

Since she was a young girl, she had always wanted to become the first female detective. So far, the most progress she'd made was setting up an office. Nobody would entrust real problems to her; nobody believed that she would be able to solve them. However, there was no question in her mind now as dark blood gurgled from the singer's throat. *She* would solve this case.

'Darling, we must get going.'

'No. I am staying here. You leave, I'll be fine.'

The Duke and Duchess had emerged from their horrified stupor and were attempting to drag Bernice out of the opera house away from the crime scene. This was a crucial time in an investigation and she would most likely never get another chance to observe evidence and interview witnesses. Bernice lifted her head high and removed her emotions from this already overly complex equation. To discover the murderer, she needed to act fast.

Bernice made her way onto the stage as her parents departed arm in arm. The only local police officer – Constable George George – had arrived at the scene. Anybody with half a brain could see that he would be of no help to this investigation. His rotund shape was awkwardly standing off to the side offering comfort to the grief-stricken man sobbing. This in itself was a mystery. Up until now, the prince was only known to be involved romantically with one woman: his fiancée.

Walking swiftly onto the stage, Bernice began an amateur investigation. She collected a sample of blood in a small vial as well as a saliva swab and some of Madam Sherrie's hair. Blood had pooled around her form and soaked into her magnificent costume.

Kneeling in the centre of this mess was the prince. He did not notice Bernice's approach and only startled slightly at her touch. His tear-stained face and bloodshot eyes said it all.

'Hello. I am Bernice Bennett, daughter of the Duke and Duchess of Kensington. I will solve this treacherous crime but I need your help. Meet me in the royal box in fifteen minutes.'

The puffy eyes of a broken heart followed Bernice as she walked away to wait. Her heart was beating out of her chest. She never could have dreamed that an opportunity like this would've fallen into her hands – gruesome as it was.

The door to the royal box was encrusted in a gold design strewn with tiny shimmering leaves and flowers. It had plush seats and the best view in the entire building. Bernice could only get in due to her parents rather convenient friendship with the security guard. Staring at the second hand rotating on her watch, she waited patiently for the prince to come. The tinkle of a bell announced his arrival.

'I appreciate you joining me in these sensitive times. From what I have already been able to deduce, yourself and Madam Sherrie were secretly lovers. Am I correct?' A glance upon his face was like reading an open book.

'We were so much more. We were soulmates.' His voice cracked with a flood of emotion.

'Are you not engaged to Lady Purcell?'

'Yes, but I do not love her. I was to escape with my love this very night'

'Ah, I see. We must get to the bottom of this. Would you be so obliged as to come to Kensington Manor early tomorrow? There is plenty to discuss and no time to waste but exhaustion is yet to overwhelm you.'

'I shall be there. Goodnight.'

The weary man trudged from the royal box with a weak sense of hope.

Perhaps this strange girl could find justice for my love, he wondered as he left to return home to a dark house and cold supper.

Bernice rushed into Kensington Manor at an hour to midnight. The biting maliciousness of London winter had kept her wide-awake and rosy-cheeked. Waiting for her was her mother, incredibly worried for nothing good ever became of young ladies wandering around the streets at night.

'What kept you so long at the opera? I've worried myself half to death.'

'Constable George wished to interview any witnesses and you must understand his unorganised fashion. It took far longer than expected. I'm sorry mother, I should have called.'

'See that you do next time. I'm just glad you have returned safely however, you must go upstairs to bed at once.'

'Goodnight mother.'

Bernice hurried to the attic with a candle lit and fleece blanket in hand. There was not a chance of her sleeping tonight; the cogs in her brain were spinning out of control. Once atop the winding staircase, she opened the attic door and slipped inside soundlessly. Books were scattered all throughout the room, sometimes in neat piles but mostly strewn randomly across the panelled wood. It was a quaint room and could only fit a desk, two chairs and a bookcase but Bernice had filled in every nook and cranny. Tiptoeing between pillars of precariously balanced true crime tales and detective files, she sat down at the desk, brought out a fresh sheet of paper and began what was to be a long night of gruelling investigation.

The weak sunlight did not awaken Bernice however, the wintry rain pouring into the open attic window did. During the early hours of the morning she had finally given in to sleep still sitting at the desk. It had been a long night but Bernice did not feel she was any closer to solving her first mystery. Groggy and soaking wet she stumbled down the stairs to dress and wait anxiously for the prince to come by. She did not need to wait long as he arrived shortly after her waking.

'Hello Prince Wilton. Follow me to the attic and no need to worry about chaperones. My parents know this is strictly official business.'

He only gave a slight nod and walked behind the girl like a shadow. It seemed that a nights rest had done the prince no good; the bags beneath his eyes were like caverns and his skin was a sickly colour. Already his face seemed tightly drawn across his bones.

They arrived in the attic and slumped into two mismatched armchairs.

'Firstly, I shall need to ask you some questions. What were you doing at the opera last night?'

'I was watching my love sing her last song before we were to escape out the back to be smuggled to China on a merchant ship.'

'Were you with anybody?'

'Yes, my fiancée would not let me go alone for she loves the opera.'

'Was your fiancée aware of your relationship with Madam Sherrie?'

'No.'

'You are cert–'

'I am certain.'

'How did she react to the performer's death and your reaction?'

'She did not see my reaction. She went to the lavatory before the murder and only returned after I had finished speaking to you.'

'How did you and Madam Sherrie fall in love?'

'I still remember the first time I saw her so vividly. My parents took me to the opera last Christmas – what to watch I cannot remember. She flittered on stage like an angel. I met her afterwards and we walked around town all night undeniably infatuated with one another. It was difficult to hide my strong affections in front of my family and there was many a time where they suspected I was engaging in secret affairs. Then, after two glorious months, my parents decided to arrange with the Purcell family for their daughter and I to wed. I had no choice in the matter. While on the surface it appeared that the two of us were meant to be, I was still deeply falling for the sweet singer. During those times, I could sneak away at all hours of the night to spend time with Madam Sherrie. After my engagement with Lady Purcell, I could not seem to escape her. I could not even leave her behind me the night we planned the escape. I felt terrible imagining how she would feel when I left her at the carriage and never returned. Nevertheless, fate has repaid me for my wrongdoings and I shall never be happy again.'

He began to heave uncontrollably with guttural bellows of grief. Bernice sat back awkwardly and waited for him to finish before they could continue. All she could focus on was progressing the case and finding justice for Madam Sherrie. It took five minutes and a glass of water before he was functioning properly again.

'Please describe is your relationship with Lady Purcell.'

'In all honesty it is highly confusing. She mainly wants to marry me for wealth and I do not wish to marry her at all yet here we are; forced together by our parents. The conversation is awkward but we have managed to fool everybody into believing we were the finest couple of the season.'

An idea blossomed inside Bernice's mind. Could it be possible that the murderer was a woman? One nobody would ever suspect. One that was trusted. One that could get away with murder.

'Has she ever had suspicious of your secret relations?'

'Not to my knowledge. Although she has been rather gracious of the whole situation, which leads to believe she had already some suspicion of what was occurring.'

'Does she know you are here?'

'Yes, she is picking me up in a quarter of an hour to prepare for our wedding.'

As if they had summoned her, a shrill noise echoed throughout the house to the attic.

'It seems she is early. I truly am sorry to cut this short.'

'Don't be concerned, we had plenty of time. I shall escort you out.'

Bernice's mind was working at a mile a minute. There must be some way to get evidence from Lady Purcell without arousing her suspicions, she thought.

A crime of passion and a crime of love do not always need evidence; whether she knew facts or only her own instincts Lady Purcell must be the murderer and Bernice would find a way to prove it.

Lady Purcell was undeniably a beautiful woman. The sharpness in her eyes and the forced-nature of her smile were the only visible indicators of the malice behind that vanilla-scented skin.

'Hello Lady Bennett, it's so…wonderful to see you.'

She looked the younger girl up and down, sneering at her simple frock and shoes.

'Yes, you as well Lady Purcell. The prince and I were just discussing how you should come in for some tea. I have a cup prepared already.'

Bernice pulled a steaming cup of tea from behind her. Jerking her hand forward, she spilt it all over Lady Purcell's outstretched satin glove.

'Oh how dare you insolent girl. You are lucky I have another pair of gloves for my wedding ceremony. We must be departing at once!'

'Wait. I am terribly sorry. Please let me redeem myself by washing and returning your glove. We have the finest lavender oils here imported from Sweden and Genevieve is a truly splendid launderer.'

'If you insist.'

She placed the soaked glove in Bernice's hand and huffed like a bull before marching the poor prince away.

Unbeknownst to Lady Purcell, Bernice had just gotten hold of the key to her investigation. She skipped up to the attic to set up a forensic investigation. The chemist downtown supplied luminol by the litre; it would be no concern to test the glove, but first other DNA needed to be extracted. Fingerprints. Many were found on the opera house curtain and backstage that didn't match to any of the crew members. If she could just have something to test them against, they might get closer to uncovering the mystery behind Madam Sherrie's murder. Bernice couldn't be certain this was the right track but it was better than nothing.

She carefully collected the fingertip samples from the glove, storing them away to compare to crime scene evidence.

Bernice tipped a litre of luminol into a bucket. If her suspicions were correct, the chemical compound would react with iron in the haemoglobin and detect trace amounts of blood in the fabric. She slowly lowered the glove; allowing it to soak in the liquid. Splotches of glowing blue light were splattered over it. This was enough evidence to confirm what Bernice had suspected all along. There was only one thing left to do and one place left to be.

'Do you, Lady Purcell, take thee, Prince Henry Wilton, to be your wedded husband, to have and to hold from this day forward, for better, for worse, for richer, for poorer, in sickness and in health, to love and to cherish, till death do you part'

'I do.'

'And do you, Prince Wilton, take thee, Vera Purcell, to be your wedded wife, to have and to hold from this day forward, for better, for worse, for richer, for poorer, in sickness and in health, to love and to cherish, till death do you part.'

'I, I–'

'STOP!'

Bernice burst into the wedding ceremony, waving Lady Purcell's glove in the air like a madman.

'You must stop the wedding at ONCE. Vera Purcell is none other than the cold-blooded killer of Madam Sherrie.'

The crowd gasped in shock. Who was this strange girl, intruding on weddings and making absurd accusations?

'Please, don't be ridiculous girl. You are interrupting the ceremony.'

'Must I spell it out to you in front of everybody?' The bride was silent.

'Fine. Lady Purcell, your family is in great debt. Your engagement to the prince secured you financial stability and welcomed you into the world of parties and pretty dresses. However, once you discovered the prince loved another your future in this world became...blurry. You turned to the only other solution you could think of. Murder. This was clearly a woman's crime; a man could never think to subject their victim to such humiliation as you did to dear Madam Sherrie. Simply slipping backstage during the performance and slitting the singer's throat then escaping by hiding underneath the stage while everybody panicked. As you didn't wear gloves to commit the crime you left a number of fingerprints at the crime scene. When you were beneath the stage, wearing your gloves once more, blood dripped through the cracks and seeped into the fabric. I commend you on your excellent hand washing skills but luminol quite beats laundry powder.'

Bernice had to stop and breathe. The audience was completely silent. A shadow of understanding fell across Lady Purcell's eyes as she realised there was no way out of this.

'What do you have to say for yourself?'

The bride smiled but it didn't touch her lifeless eyes.

'Well done.'

She bolted down the aisle, proving to the crowd that she was guilty. Bernice stepped to the side and let her run straight past through the large oak doors and straight into the beefy body of Constable George.

'Miss, ye're unnar arrest. Put yer 'ans behind yer back.'

'Ugh. Get your grimy hands off of me!'

The prince ran from the altar to Bernice to congratulate her.

'I never would have known it was her. I can't begin to thank you enough. Have you ever considered becoming a proper detective? I'm sure I could figure something out to repay you.'

'That would be wonderful.'

Bernice left the church feeling elated. The first of many successful cases closed. All she needed now was a warm bath and a cup of tea.

THE CLUE OF THE ASCENDING LETTER

SEBASTIAN HARVEY
Auckland, New Zealand

2022 WINNER
YEARS 5-6 CATEGORY
  AGATHA CHRISTIE IN TASMANIA

It was New Year's Eve in Coles Bay. All the townspeople were gathering for the annual celebratory picnic. Every year the venue changed. Last year it was in the town centre and the year before that it was near the Swan River. This year the picnic was in a paddock behind Mayor Emmanuel Lomax's newly acquired property, an old church converted into a house he had called Lomax Hall. Before, it had been painted white, but had recently changed to black by Jack O'Brien, the original owner. It was a small nineteenth century colonial building. There was an enclosed porch and triangular gables and the steeple with a bronze and gold cross on top. There were stained glass windows depicting forgotten saints and biblical prophets from the past. Along the left-hand side of the house was a gravel path with multi-coloured flower beds with rose bushes behind and there was a polished marble statue centred in the middle of a ring of buxus.

We walked or rode our bikes along the old dusty stretch called Flacks Road. Once people got there, they walked along the path for about two minutes before they came to the paddock. There was not a cloud in the sky and it was incredibly hot. There was a light zephyr tickling at peoples' legs. On the grass, ten trestle tables covered with yellow and green gingham cloths were set up. Each table had two vases of banksia on them and there were containers of cutlery next to them and individual beer glasses engraved with the guests' names to indicate where they should sit. The tables were scattered around the paddock with a barbeque next to each one. There were bowls of nibbles laid out and also people were carrying extra provisions. The townspeople circled around their tables making friendly conversations forgetting the quarrels of the previous year.

At our table sat Mayor Emmanuel Lomax, a tall skinny man of fifty-three years old, salt and pepper hair, a sallow complexion, a silly button nose and thin lipped. He wore a casual suit which was grubby and creased. Emmanuel's new girlfriend Rae Brown was with him. As well as being his girlfriend she happens to be my mother. She had long, naturally dark blonde hair, soft skin tanned by the sun, with little make-up. She was wearing a straw Panama hat, dark sunglasses, a sleeveless top and varied coloured and patterned silk trousers. The previous owner of the church, Jack O'Brien, was forty-six years old, still handsome but weary looking. He was an outdoor type with a ruddy complexion, wearing a white singlet and beach shorts. The brother of Emmanuel Lomax was called Vic and was three years younger than him and was tall with light brown hair, a pleasant face and wearing a blue polo shirt and white beach shorts. Emmanuel's ex-wife Suzy Gage was a similar age to the Mayor. Her hair was an unnatural black produced by a bottle. She wore too much make-up and a loud lime green and orange floral patterned dress. The Mayor was sitting at the top end of the table. On his left was his brother, and on his right, his girlfriend. At the other end sat his ex-wife and beside her, to the left, Jack O'Brien, and I was sitting on her right.

On the barbeques sizzled a mixture of pork, beef and vegetarian sausages and patties. The tables had baskets of buns, white bread and sourdough, butter and relishes lined up along the centre in military precision. Surrounding the picnic area were Tasmanian blue gums with glossy dark green leaves and white flowers. People mixed, talking to each other as they found where to sit. Beer was poured and people started on the nibbles.

Suddenly, an eerie sound came from above the treetops, and then emerged like a comet came a large flock of yellow tailed black cockatoo calling out in their dreadful wail. They descended into the blue gums to feed on their seeds. Everyone left the tables gathered in groups surrounding the tree line to watch this amazing spectacle. Dumbfounded that such a breath-taking event had occurred on such a stunning day. When everyone returned to their tables they sat down and started eating again. First up were the sausages and patties which everyone happily devoured. The Mayor made a toast 'We are all gathered today to celebrate the promise of a good year ahead, good farming, good economy, and a year that delivers better sausages than today's'.

Emmanuel took a gulp of his beer and started to choke. He clutched his heart before falling down, face first, into his meal. Everyone began making noises of panic. It wasn't only the wailing screams of the yellow tailed black cockatoo but also that of everyone gathered there. People ran screaming for someone to phone the ambulance. Soon you could hear the sirens screaming, slowly approaching. The noise was unbearable. Children shrieked and ran off into the blue gum bush, while others stood still shocked by what had just happened. I stood up and went to find my mother. Searching through the sea of people...

I was shocked by what had just happened and the effects still hadn't kicked in. I felt like a boat in the middle of a raging storm, until I found land, my mother. I found her around the back of Lomax Hall, slumped in a flower bush crying inconsolably. Her dress was stained with dirt and her make-up had become rivers of muddy water running down her face. The mascara around her eyes had also run giving her the appearance of a Tasmanian devil. I said to her 'Let's go home'. She silently nodded her head and I helped her up and we slowly walked back to our bikes and slowly, mournfully pedalled home.

After the autopsy it had been discovered that it was not heart failure. It was poison, one that must mimic a heart attack. Someone had poisoned the Mayor Emmanuel Lomax. I overheard this information at night when my mum had thought I was asleep and had received a phone call from the coroner telling her the news. They were still trying to figure out which type of poison it was. They couldn't identify it. So, as my mind drifted off to sleep, I made a plan the next day to visit the picnic site to find out who had poisoned Emmanuel.

My favourite writer was Agatha Christie and her detective, Hercule Poirot. His cleverness using psychology and extensive knowledge of human nature weeded out the criminals. Of course, he does take physical evidence into account but more often than not it is his combination of order, method and his 'little grey cells', that does the trick. I was going to follow the master.

I pedalled through town and saw a notice on the community notice board saying that Emmanuel's funeral had been planned for the following Sunday. This meant I might not have long to solve the mystery. I continued pedalling and turned onto Flacks Road and rode for two hundred metres before turning onto the gravel driveway of Lomax Hall. I parked my bike outside the door and walked along the gravel path. All of the roses had mysteriously wilted, perhaps in sadness at the sudden and unexplained death of their new owner. I continued until I arrived at the picnic field. Emmanuel's body had been removed but nothing else had been touched. I went over to the table I had been sitting at and began to search for a few clues. I first checked the food but by now it was riddled with maggots and flies and starting to decay. Those maggots must have arrived overnight so that meant that it was impossible to find out if the food had been poisoned but anyway, everybody had eaten the same. Then I remembered that the glass Emmanuel had been drinking from after he returned to the table had a short name on it. So, that gave me 4 four suspects…

First, Emmanuel's ex-wife Suzy

she hated him because he was physically and emotionally abusive.

The second, his brother, because when Emmanuel and Vic were young they both had a crush on the same girl and Vic felt that Emmanuel stole her from him.

Third, the girlfriend, my mother, who did not really love him and was just there for the money.

The fourth, the previous landowner, Jack O'Brien. Emmanuel had bought his property from him cheaply when Jack got into financial difficulties and taken unfair advantage so he had reason to be angry.

I sat at the table, nearly overcome with the stench of rotten food, bewildered. I had to recreate a picture of the table before Emmanuel collapsed. I made a mental picture trying to see if there was anything that did not seem right. Everyone was sharing the same food and drinking beer. Surely, if there had been poison in the food or beer, others would have collapsed as well. Could something have been switched? By whom? So many at that table had a motive to do Emmanuel harm. I needed to look at my mental picture closer. Something worried me. But nothing was clear. What had happened?

Then it became blindingly clear. When the Mayor stood up to make his toast, the glass he raised had a short set of letters, much shorter than his own name. I peered closer to the picture in my mind. Was it three or four letters? Four. That means it could not have been the people sitting on either side of him. Their names had only three. It could only be Suzy or Jack. Which one? Both had very good reasons to do away with the Mayor. Which one? I made mental eyes into microscopes. The glasses must have been switched when people left the table to see the amazing flock of cockatoos. Then I knew. The last letter of the glass containing the poison went above the line not below like y. It was the k of the name Jack.

THE DISAPPEARANCE OF CAMERON SANDERSON

MYA ANDERSON
Cairns, Queensland

2021
YEARS 5-6 CATEGORY
  SCENE OF THE CRIME

Cameron briskly walked through the deserted alleyway, often looking back to see if anyone was following. Any small movement or sound made him jump hastily then continue his way through the backstreet. The only sound was the constant dripping of water from rusted, leaking drainpipes and the occasional noise of rats running in the dying leaves. Cameron was shaking head to toe with nerves, even for someone who hid their emotions well, he was clearly disturbed about something....

Cameron was a well-structured, handsome man with a mop of black hair, bright blue eyes like the ocean and a pale, flushed face. His eyebrows were bushy like a forest (that's what his mum said) and there were dark shadows of tiredness under his sparkling eyes. Cameron looked a lot older than he was, most people think he is 17 but he's only 15.

The pitch-black alleyway continued as Cameron sped up his pace, overwhelmed by its earie presence. He had been walking around for ages...he could not remember why he was there or how he got there. The last thing he could remember was setting off for a walk as the sun was setting but that was all. How could he be so foolish to end up in this place!? Deep in thought he barely noticed a shadowy figure emerge from the never-ending darkness. Cameron stumbled in shock then instinct kicked in and he ran for his life. The mysterious figure was close behind, nimbly dodging rubbish bins and any other obstacles stopping him from reaching his target. Fear engulfed Cameron as he saw the obscure figure take something out of his jacket...

And that was the last anyone saw of Cameron Sanderson...

2 weeks later

THE WEEKLY POST created by Bailey Brown.

MYSTERIOUS MURDER basketball player quits?

Cameron Sanderson remains unfound. Police have confirmed the fact that there was a murder and continue to search the area. They still have no leads on who the killer was but advise people to stay in groups. Now the question is, *Is there a killer among us?* Nobody knows.

Hugo Taylor quits basketball after a huge argument with basketball player for the Australian giants (also Hugo Taylors team). its said that they smashed their NBA winners trophy. Maybe their breakup will cause the whole team to part!? Keep reading for more info on this interesting topic!

Mila's (Cameron's younger sister) chocolate brown eyes sparkled with tears while reading the weekly post. 'He can't have been murdered,' she squeaked, 'he just can't have been.'

Mila could not get over his death. She just did not believe it; she would not believe it. He could not have died. Any moment he would come through the door explaining his disappearance. With her face still wet with tears she pushed back her light brown hair and ran her trembling fingers through her blonde highlights. Mila put her head in her skinny arms whilst biting her lip painfully.

'Of course, he was murdered, you're 13 so I guess your small brain doesn't get it' barked Hazel, Mila's older sister, although she was being rude her bright blue eyes also had tears gently falling from them. 'You're just way to self-absorbed to even have the smallest amount of hope. Cameron would be disgusted!' moodily hissed Mila. She instantly regretted saying this at the devastated look Hazel gave her before storming out of the room and vigorously slamming the door. After a while of staring at the wall daydreaming, Mila decided to pass the time looking at her photo album. She always loved pouring over the photos and happily reliving the time they were taken. As she turned the page she saw a family photo of her, Hazel, Cameron and their parents. She smiled as she remembered how it had been taken at Hazels 16th birthday party a year ago. It was Cameron's favourite photo and he always kept a copy in his pocket wherever he went. Mila looked again at Cameron's smiling face, how she wished to see him again. Despite what the paper had said, the police had done nothing. They seemed to be afraid to do anything about it, their duty was to protect and serve, to be brave, but they still appeared to be scared. If they were not going to investigate then someone would have to…maybe they could hire a detective but no…that still would not work. Suddenly an idea came to her like the need to sneeze, she could find who killed Cameron! With an unexpected rise in energy, she ran to the phone to talk to the police.

'Yes, hello umm can I please talk to a police officer involved in the investigation of the disappearance of Cameron Sanderson'.

'Yes, young lady I will hand him over.'

After a long minute she heard, 'This is officer August speaking'

'Hello, can you please tell me everything you know about Cameron Sanderson's murder, clues or leads would be great.'

'What? A-are you a spy or some-something, wait Chase i-is that y-you I have n-not told anyone p-please don't hurt m-me…I've got to go s-sorry…'

Mila was not expecting that sudden conclusion. Who was this Chase person? Why was the officer so afraid? Mila desperately thought, her mind was thinking so rapidly she could not understand any of her thoughts. After a while she decided it was best not to come to a conclusion until she checked the crime scene.

The following day she woke up, roused by her alarm clock. She got up yawning and clumsily fumbling around trying to turn off the alarm clock. She got ready to go as quick as she could then got her old, rusted bike and rode to the crime scene.

It was deserted and barren concealed by the mist. Bright yellow police tape was strung around the area reading 'keep out'. Carelessly, Mila ducked under it and scanned the area there was nothing but blood and dirt. The police had put a sign next to the blood reading 'proof A, blood on floor'. Mila got closer and the blood did NOT look like blood, it was too red and had the wrong consistency. Mila got down to her hands and knees and sniffed. It distinctively smelt like tomato sauce but there was only one real way to find out if it really was. She scrunched up her nose, dipped her shaking finger in the 'blood' and put it in her mouth. The moment she tasted the unmistakable flavour, she knew it was tomato sauce. With a surge of energy Mila got up scanned the area and followed some red footprints, there she found an empty tomato sauce bottle! And they say this only happens in fairy tales light-heartedly thought Mila. But that was not the most important thing, now she knew in her heart that Cameron was alive! She got up, carelessly throwing the sauce bottle aside, ready to find her brother wherever he was...

After a while of snooping around the crime scene she managed to find marks in the dirt that looked suspicious. Mila's uncle was a keen hunter and had taught her how to track wild animals and survive in the wilderness. Looking closely at the patterns on the ground she realised that something or someone heavy had been dragged from this spot. Out of the corner of her eye, Mila spotted a familiar photo half buried in the dirt, it was of Hazels 16th birthday, Mila now knew that if she ever wanted to see her beloved brother again, she would have to follow the track. She used her hunting skills to follow the trail until it finally came to a stop outside a house. The house was painted black and had barely any windows, the ones that were there were suspiciously boarded up. Wildly shaking with the unpleasant knowledge of what could be beyond the creepy exterior of the house, Mila slowly walked up the faded stone steps leading toward the door and knocked. She stood there for a moment realizing the terrible danger she may have put herself in. Remembering how most families keep a spare key under a door mat she thought, what are the chances? There was no door mat but there was a dusty statue of a cat, she kneeled down and lifted it up to reveal an old key. Mila picked the key up still not believing that happened because of the incredibly small odds. She placed in the keyhole then turned it gently. There stood Cameron looking miserably down at his feet across the hall of the entrance. 'Cameron!' she cried hugging him, she really did not expect this to go so easily. But Cameron pushed her away and whispered, 'Go away Mila, Chase will kill you. Go now! Please, he will kill our entire family if you don't go.'

'NO, I won't go, and I already called the cops so you will be fine!'

'Mila, the cops are dead scared of him, they know where he is already so if they have not come yet then they are not going to come now, go please!' pleaded Cameron desperately.

But Mila was not taking no for an answer she grabbed him and pulled him with a great deal of strength and ran off with him. She ran with him all the way back to her bike.

'Mila please, Chase will kill us all let me go please…'

She grabbed her tie dye scarf and tied it around his neck to prevent him from talking. Then they got on the bike and rode back home. Mila could still not believe how lucky that all was, first the tomato sauce then bringing Cameron home. It had all happened so fast she thought she was dreaming the entire thing!

But at last, she was bringing Cameron home.

A CRIME FROM RIGHT UNDER THEIR NOSES

ALEXIA CHATFIELD
Toorak, Victoria

2021
YEARS 5-6 CATEGORY
  SCENE OF THE CRIME

I feel my heart beating fast and adrenaline running wild through my body as we head closer to the house. There we see a lady crying with devastation, her eyes as red as chilli and filled with tears. We walk slowly, closer and…

Hi, I'm Prue and I work for a secret spy and detective agency. I have been working here for five years and have become quite the expert. Find a clue, catch the criminal, and you solve the case. No, you really thought it was that easy, haha! No way! Every step we take in a crime scene is filled with investigation and science but this case was like no other, just wait and see. It was a cold autumn day at the Clue-2-Clue Spy and Detective agency and it was almost time to go home and relax. However, the special agency red phone started to ring loudly. It was as loud as an evacuation alarm during an earthquake and permeated through the entire building. My good friend and colleague Dawn, who I have known since kindergarten, ran quickly from her desk to the special red phone. She was naturally concerned but was also intrigued to see what the case may be.

'Hi, this is Dawn from Clue-2-Clue Spy and Detective agency. How can I help you?' said Dawn.

'Please, please now, come now,' the lady said in a distressed tone. 'She is my life, my happiness, my joy. Please find her.'

'We will find her for you,' Dawn stated with her usual calming and direct manner.

'Don't worry, we're coming there now, it will be ok,' Dawn said.

'But who is lost?' she asked.

'My doggie Kaaju,' the lady replied through her tears and wailing.

'Oh no,' said Dawn, 'that's horrible, we're coming there now and we will find her'.

We ran to the lady's house, it was an emergency and we needed to get there as soon as possible! There stood a small, but loving and homely dwelling filled with colour and surrounded by hundreds of beautiful flowers, but this hid the emergency swelling inside.

'Please help, please, my little Kajuu is missing and she is probably sad and hungry, and needs to come home,' the lady cried in devastation.

'When did you last see her?' enquired Marge the other detective that joined myself and Dawn.

Marge was relatively new but a very hard worker and had good experience when she did a stint working in another detective and spy agency in Europe.

'This afternoon,' the lady said, 'I was giving her cuddles and hugging her sweet face, and I went upstairs to make her food and she was gone!' she screamed in despair.

'Hmmm,' mumbled Dawn. 'That is very strange indeed'.

We were all so confused, but we knew somehow, we would solve this case. 'Mam do you know if you have any holes in your fence?' I said.

'There are no holes, but there is connecting door to our neighbours' house but it is always locked,' she stated.

We all rushed towards the fence to investigate the connecting door.

'Whaaattttttt it's oppeeeennn,' she exclaimed.

We all crowded around the connecting door and Marge then noticed what looked to be foot prints on the ground. Together we laid our special magnifying glass closely to the ground. This revealed large footprints that could not be children's and certainly was not animal prints.

'Prue, Kaaju was left outside with the door closed, but could the thief be my neighbours,' pondered the lady. 'My neighbours were always jealous of Kaaju and they have keys to the door,' the lady exclaimed.

'I'm not sure,' said Prue, 'but we will get to the bottom of this.'

They all proceeded through the connecting door towards Mr and Mrs Lucaza's house. There sat Mr Lucaza sleeping on his front porch and snoring as loud as a bear.

'Mr Lucaza, Mr Lucaza wake up now,' said the lady shaking him to wake.

'Ah ah, oi oi, what are you doing? Can't you see that I'm sleeping?' Mr Lucaza said with a big yawn.

'You stole my beautiful puppy Kaaju, where is she?' the lady screamed.

'What nonsense are you talking?' he said.

'You know what I mean, you stole Kaaju from my backyard through our connecting door. Now give her back!'

'My sweet Sunshine, I didn't steal your beloved Kaaju. Today was my bowling day. I have only been back for 10 minutes and was having a quick nap,' Mr Lucaza said with conviction, waving his ticket that displayed his bowling score for the day.

'Oh, we're so sorry!' everyone, including Sunshine, said in unison.

'We thought it was you because of the door,' Marge added.

'That's ok,' Mr Lucaza said as he fell back to sleep.

'Wait' I said walking to the door. 'I have an idea. When I was on my first day of the agency, John Rusty, a veteran of the agency, gave me a tour of the building. He took me into the agency's science lab and showed me a special invention he made a few years ago. It's a gooey potion that can be used to identify the footprints of anyone. He made it for a case he was working on at the time.'

I quickly told Dawn and Marge about this and together we told Lady Sunshine. Dawn rushed back to the agency headquarters to source a tub of the potion. In what seemed like lightning quick time, Dawn was back with the special potion in hand.

Three, two, one, we carefully poured the gooey galaxy coloured potion onto the footprints near the door in the fence. It started to bubble and glimmer and letters started to appear. J, O, H and soon enough it was all revealed, it was John Rusty!

'It was him?' I asked with disbelief, 'maybe that's why he was missing from our morning meeting this morning?'

Both Dawn and Marge could not believe it either. Surely it could not have been one of the Clue-2-Clue gang. We are here to solve mysteries and help others, and not to cause trouble.

We have to investigate though. Together we ran to John's house to find out more. When we arrived, there was no answer when we knocked repeatedly on the door.

Marge said, 'We have to go around the back and investigate.'

Together we climbed John's fence and began to head to the backyard.

On the ground near the fence sat small strings of what seemed to be fur. I quickly pulled out a small tweezers from my detective bag and held the fur in the palm of my hand.

'Sunshine, does this look like Kaaju's fur?' I asked.

'Hmmm' said Sunshine staring at the fur, 'yes I think it does,' she said.

We kept walking through the backyard and soon came across John sitting quietly on his back porch. John was whispering quietly to a small cute puppy on his lap. 'Oh no, I think that is Kaaju,' exclaimed Dawn.

Straightaway John knew he was caught. 'I'm sorry, I'm so sorry' John cried. 'I just miss my little Rowdy so much.' John had previously had a beautiful puppy called Rowdy, who one day had run away at the park and could not be found.

'I know you miss Rowdy but you can't just steal other people's dogs,' said Marge sternly.

'Yes, Kaaju is everything to me,' exclaimed Sunshine. 'How dare you steal her!'

John felt truly terrible. 'I'm so sorry, I really am. I just needed her, my whole family needed her, I thought she was going to make us happy again,' John said. 'I'm so sorry, I will give her back immediately'.

'I understand,' said Sunshine compassionately. 'I did not realise you had lost your beautiful Rowdy and how much pain you and your family were in.'

Recognising the despair of the situation, Sunshine had an idea. She had received a gift certificate many months ago for the Rainbow Crest Street Pet Shop, the most luxurious pet shop in town. The certificate was given to her by her good friend Pearl, who she had helped move house.

'Oh, thank you so much,' John said with great excitement, 'and again I am so sorry for taking Kaaju and causing you all this worry'.

Sunshine had accepted John's apology and knew all to well the pain of losing a loved pet. Now Sunshine had her lovely Kaaju back and John was all set to find a new, loving dog.

That's all thanks to the Clue-2-Clue Spy and Detective agency.

THE ROBBERY

FINN CONNOLLY
Lauderdale, Tasmania

2021
YEARS 5-6 CATEGORY
 SCENE OF THE CRIME

Mr. Scones Stepped onto the stage with a heartwarming grin 'Good Evening Fleur, yes it is true we have caught the culprit for this recent crime. But for all of you out there watching this, to understand this case we need to start from the very beginning.'

Silent as a mouse, sneaky as a fox, as dangerous as a bear! A single pin was dropped on the cold stone floor. A man and a bird with a mission, crept into one of the most famous well known Museums in the world unnoticed, The Louvre! A Security Guard who was tired, cold and fed up, sat watching his security camera, slowly he started to doze off but not because he was tired because something special was slipped into his office that night, something that made people very sleepy!

As the Man and the bird crept further into the museum a guard woke up to a strange clicking noise on the floor in front of him. At first he thought it was just his imagination, but before he knew it he was thrust to the ground, and everything went black. 'A pity these guards are so useless, I was hoping for a better fight!' said the man.

'Squawk, Iago agrees, Iago agrees!'

'Hush Iago you'll start an alarm or something, at least you're sticking to your code name for once though.'

'Anything for the Boss, anything for the Boss, squawk!'

The man and the bird fell silent as they arrived in the great gallery where thousands of treasures were stored, each one worth billions. Every treasure was tempting to take but both of them knew very well they only needed two. If they stole any more, people would notice and thousands of soldiers and police would be sent after them like a pack of wolves chasing a delicious chubby sheep.

The man pulled out two pieces of thin metal and shoved them into the locked power box next to him. He spun them around a couple of times until a loud click was heard, the hinges of the box door gave in and snapped off, the metal clattered to the ground but all the guards were either out cold or sleeping so they had nothing to worry about. The man flicked the switch inside the power box and all the lights in the hallway dimmed and then went black.

In front of the man and the bird thousands of tiny red security lasers beamed. The man had been watching and learning everything he could about this museum, so much that even the thousands of tiny killer security lasers didn't worry him in the slightest. In a simple movement he flicked on a torch he had been carrying in his bag. He pointed it at the top of the ceiling from where the lasers shone. When the man did this the lasers started to dim and fade and started turning a pale white colour. When this happened the man and the bird strode on through walking through the now useless lasers without a care in the world.

They stopped when they reached a statue made out of beautiful stone carved perfectly, it was worth billions of euros in France and probably even more in other countries! They smashed the glass case it was sitting in with a powerful hammer. Glass shattered to the floor and a soft crunch echoed through the hall as the man walked through to snatch the statue and take it for the keeping.

The next place they stopped was very obvious and probably the most valuable thing in the whole gallery, The Mona Lisa! Without hesitation, the bird hooked his beak around the screws holding it in place and twisted until they all came undone. The statue and the Mona Lisa were probably the smallest things in the gallery. But they were very valuable.

Once the painting and the statue were in the bag the man was carrying, the bird and the man ran towards their exit out of the newly created crime scene, the sewers! When they arrived at the ladder that descended into the sewers, they checked they had everything and had left nothing incriminating that could identify them. Satisfied, the man opened the manhole lid and took a deep breath in, the smell of rats and dirty rain water flooded into his nostrils, but he didn't mind as he had succeeded in his mission. So with another deep breath he put his left foot on the first rung of the sewer ladder, and descended into darkness.

The morning after the robbery (that nobody really knew about yet) a news station was one of the first to report due to connections at the Louvre. They were in the process of interviewing some crime reporters and guards who were there at the time. 'Good Morning and Welcome to Bonjour News, this is Fleur Dupont live from the Sunnyside Paris News Station.'

Bonjour News was one of the most popular news stations at the time of the robbery and lots of people liked to tune in whenever they could, especially if it was about a robbery that happened in the people of France's most beloved museum.

'As some of you may already know, there was a robbery at the famous Louvre museum in Paris last night. Bonjour News is here with all the latest developments to inform the people of Paris!'

Despite the fact that Bonjour News interviewed people on the case and those that were there the night it happened not much information had actually come to light as most of them were either off duty, or out cold.

'Today it is my great pleasure to introduce Mr. Harry Scones, the well-known crime reporter, to our station on this fine morning. Say Mr. Scones what have you and your fellow policemen found out about this shocking robbery?'

'Well Fleur,' replied Scones, 'we haven't found out much yet since we've only been on the case for a couple of hours now, but we assure you everything is perfectly safe. We have found an interesting colourful feather that we ruled out as a kids craft feather, but just to be sure we have taken it to the lab to double check. Even something as insignificant and small as a feather could be a major clue into finding whoever did this.'

'Well thank you so much for joining us Mr. Scones, it has been a great pleasure. Moving on now we are joined by a security guard from the robbery last night. His name is Jean Bonaparte and joined the Louvre security guard association five years ago. Say Jean, what do you remember from last night?'

'Well Fleur to be honest not much, all I remember really is waking up from my sleep to a strange clicking noise. I thought it was just my imagination but before I knew it I was thrust to the ground, and then everything went black!'

'Well thank you Jean for joining us this morning, I hope being thrust to the ground hasn't hurt you that much. Well folks thanks for listening, that's all on that subject for the moment, but tune in later on today for more info,' Fleur signed off.

Deep, deep, deep, underground in an abandoned bunker from World War Two, a man and a bird sat, stashing their treasures and listening to the radio to make sure nobody suspected them.

'We have found a colourful feather that we ruled out as a kids craft feather, but we've taken it to the lab just to double check,' said the man on the radio.

'How many times did I tell you to be careful, you waste of feathers!!!'

'I'm sorry, Squawk, boss, I didn't know I had lost one.'

'Well sorry is not going to cut it, thanks to you my whole operation could be blown! Get out of here before they use your stupid feathers to track me here, go on leave! Or I'll shoot you!!!!'

'Squawk, yes boss, yes boss.'

'Go leave now!!!!' were the words the bird heard echoing through the bunker as he flew away, and then there was a gunshot.

As Bonjour News promised, they were back with groundbreaking robbery news! 'Hello and welcome back to Bonjour News this is Fleur Dupont, and I am now live from the Louvre in Paris which is where the robbery two nights ago occurred. Joining me again is the wonderful. Mr. Harry Scones, the man of the moment! Take it away Mr. Scones.'

Harry stepped onto the stage with a confident smile and took a deep breath, then opened his mouth, and went back to the start. 'Hello Fleur, yes it is true we have groundbreaking news about this heist. As I said last night we took the feather to the lab and the results are in! It turns out this feather belonged to a Rainbow Lorikeet, I know it doesn't sound that exciting, but Rainbow Lorikeets are not native to France so we believe that this rainbow lorikeet was part of the robbery. This lead us to searching registry files of Rainbow Lorikeets being brought into Paris. Nothing came up, we also checked Parisian zoos none of which contain any Rainbow Lorikeets. This brought us to the conclusion that this

Rainbow Lorikeet was brought into Paris illegally! Which proves that this Criminal hasn't only committed a crime by robbing the Louvre, they have also committed a crime by bringing an unregistered animal into this country! We needed to find this bird, to lead us to the criminal. We broadcast yesterday to the whole nation that we were looking for a rainbow lorikeet to match the feather we had found. We got lucky! A local man rang our number to tell us he had found a dead Rainbow Lorikeet who fitted the description perfectly. He had found him in an abandoned alleyway near the Louvre. All we had to do then was go to the alleyway where the lorikeet was found and look for clues. We knew the criminal would freak out when he found out we had found a colourful bird feather that we could use to track the bird with. So he had to dispose of the bird so his cover wouldn't be blown, it seemed to us he shot the bird! We used this information and found a trapdoor not far from the alleyway that lead to an abandoned bunker from World War Two, we called reinforcements and charged into the bunker, but unfortunately found nothing, we were obviously too late. Just as we were about to give up our search we heard a faint humming noise coming from above, muffled due to the bunker. As we climbed out of the bunker we looked up and saw a helicopter flying up above. The helicopter door swung open and there the criminal was holding a gun, with an awful grin on his face. He knew he was going to get away for sure, and so did we. He would have gotten away if it wasn't thanks to one special Rainbow Lorikeet. As we looked up at the sky we saw the crafty Rainbow Lorikeet speeding towards the rotors on the Helicopter. It seems that in a show of avian genius the lorikeet had a final act of revenge on the criminal, earlier he had staged his death by using the statue that he had covered in kids craft feathers, faking his corpse. The genius bird then sacrificed himself in that final moment before he was sucked into the rotors, just so he could help us bring his ex-master to Justice!'

Harry Scones beamed. 'And that's how we caught that despicable villain! Well that's my news Fleur what about you?!'

ELEMENTS

DILA GOKCE
Ironside, Queensland

2020
YEARS 5-6 CATEGORY
 FEMALE DETECTIVES

'No! Please don't do this to me Catherin! Don't do this to me!'

Alana and Lucy had lost their mum a long time ago, when a big rock rolled over her, at least that's what they were told. Since that time, they were looked after by Catherin, the head of their tribe. They weren't allowed to speak or even think about their mum. They always felt like they were different to the other people, like if they had something special in them…

The sun brightly shone into the Alana and Lucy's room as they woke up, ready to start a new day. They got up and walked to the exit of their small tent and found themselves with their tribe, like they did every day. It was a beautiful place to live, the forest was covered with lush-green trees and a clear river with colourful fish in it.

As they walked towards the river Lucy was holding a torch, just in case they had a bear attack. Suddenly she tripped over a rock and dropped it. The fire flew towards her hand instead of spreading out. She didn't know what to do, this was extraordinary. Alana looked at her sister, like if she was a monster. Lucy did some movements and the fire did it as well. She was controlling it. Alana was shocked to see that her sister had powers. Lucy looked at her big sister, smiling as she played around with her new powers, careful not to burn down the trees around them. She was a Flame-bender. But this was only in stories!

'Stop there you!' yelled a deep voice. It was the strong men from their tribe.

'You know that you shouldn't be playing with new things. Now come here, we have to put you in prison, this is a command by Catherin!' he continued.

Alana couldn't believe that Catherin commanded these men to capture her innocent sister. She had to stop them.

As they were getting closer and closer to Lucy, ready to put their filthy hands on her shoulder, Alana put one hand out and yelled out 'Stop!' The men stopped. She couldn't believe what she had done. And she held her hand up in the air longer, so the men wouldn't get closer to her sister. Her sister looked at her, amazed.

'I think you can control people because there is water in our blood and you can bend it! This means you are an Agua-bander!' Lucy cried.

They couldn't stay here for long because their tribe didn't welcome new things. They had to run away. They both looked at each other and nodded. Wait, what? Could they speak to each other without actually saying a word aloud?

They ran as fast as their tiny legs could take them. The other people couldn't hear them, so they didn't know where the two girls were going.

They ran until they could no more, they finally stopped to have a breath. Their hearts were pumping harder than ever, and sweat was sliding down their red, puffed cheeks. That's when they noticed what was standing in front of them. The girls' legs began to shake with fear as they had never seen a creature like that before. A centaur was standing right in front of them. The centaur didn't seem to be scared of them at all, actually, he was smiling.

'You must be Lucy and Alana, oh how nice to meet you! We were waiting for you for years!' the centaur exclaimed.

The girls looked at each other, astonished. They didn't know what to be confused of, the centaur itself or the centaur knowing them?

'How do you know us?' Lucy asked with surprise.

'Everyone knows you! You are the two daughters of Sheila!' the centaur replied.

The two sisters looked at each other, not knowing what to say. How did the centaur know them and their dead mother?

'My name is Jake and I am one of the centaurs in the wizarding world. You seem like you don't know that you mother can bend the four elements, FLAME, AGUA, DIRT AND WIND.' continued the centaur.

'You two seem confused, I, I mean us, all the creatures and wizards in this world thought she was dead, but we overheard Catherin from your tribe saying that it was beginning to be too hard to keep her in a metal case. This means that she is still alive, needing to be saved. We needed you, the two daughters of the strongest wizard to help us rescue her.' Said Jake.

Now the girls were putting two and two together. Catherin knew that their mother had powers, so she locked her up and told them that a humongous rock killed her. They didn't know if they should be happy or mad. There was a chance that they could see their mother again, but they were angry at Catherin, lying to them.

'If you want to save your mother, then hop on my back!' continued Jake.

The girls did what he said, and as soon as they were on, the centaur turned into an eagle and flew off. They didn't know that centaurs could turn into other things.

'I know what you are thinking. Some centaurs can turn into other things.' Said Jake.

'That's cool!' replied Alana.

After some time, the eagle started to descend and finally they were on the ground. In front of them stood a big hut.

'Okay, you two wait here, and I will transform into a rat and go in to see where they are keeping your mother.' Said the centaur and transformed into a rat and went in the hut.

'I guess we will have to wait here.' Said Lucy using her powers.

'Ugh! I hate waiting!' replied Alana loudly, bending down to sit next to her sister.

After what seemed like hours, Alana finally said 'I can't wait anymore! I am going inside!' and stood up.

'No! Wait! We have to wait for Jake!' said Lucy, but it was no use. Alana headed towards the hut.

As soon as she opened the door, she saw forty-seven soldiers standing in front of her. In a blink of an eye, she was captured and covered in steal so she couldn't bend water and put in a tiny room. But she wasn't the only one there. Someone else was there.

'Who are you?' said a strong voice, from next to her. Even though Alana couldn't see, she knew that this was her mother's voice.

'Mum! Is that you?' she yelled out.

'Alana? How did you come here?' replied her mother.

Alana couldn't be any happier. Even though she was covered in a steel armour from head to toe and hanged up on the wall, she was next to her mother.

'Mum! I, I mean we, Jake the centaur, Lucy and I came to save you from here!' said Alana.

'Where are they?' said Sheila.

'Well, Jake went in and right now he is looking for you. And for Lucy, I left her outside.' Replied Alana.

'Wait what did you say? You left Lucy outside?' yelled Sheila.

But Alana didn't have time to answer because a rat ran into the room.

'Jake?' asked Sheila.

'It is me! It has been a long time since seeing you, old friend Sheila.' Jake replied, and then turned into a key and opened both of the steel armour.

Alana got up saw her mother for the first time in years. She couldn't believe her eyes! She ran towards her and gave her a big hug.

'We don't have much time, the soldiers will be here any second now.' Sheila finally said, and she was right. The soldiers marched in and stopped at the door.

'Let us go, otherwise you will pay for it!' Sheila yelled, but the soldiers didn't go.

She gently blew and a huge tornado appeared and wiped all the soldiers out.

'So that was wind bending!' thought Alana and ran to give her long-gone mother a hug.

When they got out, Lucy was waiting at the door, and as soon as she saw her mother and sister, she ran as fast as she could to hug them. Sheila gave a Jake a smile, thanking for all he did, and Jake was on his way.

Sheila turned to her kids and asked 'Are you two ready to start your training?'

The girls smiled and then nodded, they couldn't be any happier than they were at that moment.

GARNISH

ABBY PUGH
Dover, Huon Valley

2020 WINNER
YEARS 5-6 CATEGORY
 FEMALE DETECTIVES

I dug my fingernails into the leather steering wheel. I had never imagined myself coming back home, yet here I was, driving down the main road of Daineville, my hair sticking to my lips and the radio softly playing rubbish. I didn't know what brought me here, not exactly. Perhaps I was homesick, perhaps it just felt right. But I think I was looking for a new mystery, a new mystery that I would find here.

The world had evolved so much at this point, yet Daineville was stuck in the 80's, full of little motels, trashy old school buildings and a common enemy: Luke's Diner. Every time I had eaten there as a child, I had to stay home sick the next day, food poisoning every time. But no matter how many times I had fallen ill, we always ended up eating there one way or another. 'It was probably something you ate last night possum, perhaps Mum will stop cooking that for you.' My father used to say. It had always, and still did, drive me mad. Yet I pulled into the bumpy, half empty carpark anyway.

I pushed open the door and let the little bell ring. A few eyes looked curiously over their milkshakes at me as I walked up to the counter.

'Well, well, well, if it isn't Kara Brookestone, Daineville's own little Nancy Drew. How's the detective work going?'

Luke pulled his sinister, sarcastic smile as the words slipped through his teeth and started getting on my nerves. I tried to shake him off and tossed my coins onto the metal counter, clink, clink clink.

'I'll take a beer, Luke.'

He scoffed and dragged the coins towards his chest. Then, something on the menu caught my eye, an intriguing new item. I slid a $5 note towards him, 'Oh, and add the new spaghetti to that, would you?'

He snatched the five dollars out from under my fingertips, stuffed it in his pocket and proceeded to say,

'Sorry Love, that's only available after six. But thanks for the tip!'

I glanced up at the clock: 5:56. Wow. I slammed my fist on the table, a few hundreds in my hand.

'Pardon?'

He looked up at me and placed the five dollars back on the counter, clearing his throat.

'I- I said I'll add that for you,' he stuttered.

I smiled, picking up the five and placing a hundred down. He looked at the hundred, then back at my hand.

'What happened to the other three?'

I placed them back in my pocket and swallowed a lump in my throat. Whether I chose to admit it or not, Luke still intimidated me; I felt like I was a little girl.

'You lost them for being ignorant. Watch your sticky fingers next time buddy. I'll be at Table Five.'

Flabbergasted, he let me walk off, as he should. I pulled out my chair and flicked open my notepad as I sat down, wondering if I'd ever actually stood up to Luke, or if I ever would. I stabbed my pen into the pages repeatedly, trying to find a way to occupy my mind. The sour smell of hot spaghetti and boiling blood tickled my nose, it smelt like a mystery. The plate of food was dropped in front of me, along with my drink being placed so close to the edge it almost spilt onto my lap. The scrawny waiter gave a 'humph' under his breath as I caught the tipping glass and pushed it back towards the centre of the table. I noticed $100 hanging out of his oversized pocket, so I snatched it back as I dipped my finger into the golden liquid and flicked it up into his eye.

'Have fun telling Luke you failed your little mission, darling. Buh bye!'

He turned his back and walked off as I slipped a plastic bag from my back pocket. I sneer back at him,

'Let us see what is really going on here.'

I watched Luke's eyes dart back and forwards from me to his customer. I smiled and picked up my fork, trying to make him believe

I was actually going to eat my meal. He mouthed 'eat it' and I nodded, swirling my fork in the pasta. I couldn't believe I was going to do this. I stuck the fork into my mouth and pulled the pasta off. The instant, underlying taste of blood was disgusting, and something to be suspicious about. I looked up at Luke with a mouthful, smiling weakly. He nodded in confidence that this would be my last meal. Ugh, pathetic. He turned his back and rounded the corner, the customer's order scribbled onto a yellow sticky note. I dropped my fork onto the table and leant over the nearby bin, spitting out my food. I had never tasted anything more fake and disgusting in my life! I stared down at the indent I had made in the swirling dish, sauce, well what I assumed was supposed to be sauce, dripping down. I pulled the plastic bag from my lap and wrapped it over my hand, staring at the little green garnish on top. Its purple-tinted edges were something I hadn't seen before. I had to nab it before anybody saw! I picked up the little plant and flipped the bag inside out, trapping the peculiar green. I sealed it and shoved it back into my pocket, being cautious that I didn't damage the plant too much. I swigged my beer and walked out the door, drink in hand and the extra $100 I stole back from the waiter. I felt the little garnish rubbing against me, making my curiosity and craving for mystery a lot more real.

'KARA!' Luke called from inside the store as I sat in my car, holding the steering wheel with a satisfied grip.

I backed out and began driving towards the motel as he burst through the door, shaking his fist. I glanced over at the car's clock: 6:14. People were out on the sides of the road, drooping down the walkways with a pale, dead look on their faces. They had all come from the direction of the diner, making me speed up, eager to get to my room. I pulled into the motel's pothole-filled carpark and grabbed a black case from the boot. I sped past the reception desk,

'Room 24 checking in!'

I heard Darla, the reception lady's pencil tick me off as I raced up the stairs. I fumbled for my key card as I approached my room. I had only been home for two days and I had already lost my key card.

'Great,' I said sarcastically. 'Oh, wait-'

It fell out of my pocket and I ducked for it, shoving it against the sensor. Beep! I flew through the door and tossed the case onto my bed, pulling the plastic bag out of my pocket and slamming the door shut

'Keep it down, Love!' Darla's voice echoed up the stairs.

'Sorry!'

I opened my laptop and researched before anything. What does it mean if the edges of your plant are purple? The search results were scarce, but I found an article with everything I needed and more. I stared at the screen, analysing every little detail as my stomach swirled.

Mistopocatia-The Purple Death

The Purple Death, scientifically known as Mistopocatia, is a deadly plant that has been proven to have a zombie-like effect on anybody who may come in contact with it. The name 'Purple Death' came from the plant's strange lilac edges and stem, containing the toxins. If the plants stem is broken, crushed, or opened in any way, the poison will secrete. If bare skin or the digestive system comes into contact with the poison, people have been known to go into an undead state at 6:15pm, a state they cannot escape until they die 24 hours later. Mistopocatia has a strange taste, nearly identical to thyme, making it almost impossible to distinguish between a dinner garnish and an untimely death.

Click here to read more

My heart sank. That's why everybody was slumping down the pathways! They had eaten the purple death! I dashed to my bed and flicked open the case, a mini laboratory emerging. I open a little drawer, grabbing the gloves and slipping them on. Carefully, I opened the plastic bag and took out what I assumed was Mistopocatia, sliding it under the mini D3CRYPTER. I waited for a good fifteen minutes for the results.

'The D3CRYPTER at the lab works better,' I say, annoyed.

Finally, I got my results.

'You're in trouble now, Lukey!'

D3CRYPTER

Mistopocatia: Status-deadly

I dived for my phone and dialled the police, all the evidence I needed right in my grasp.

'Hello? Yes, this is Detective Brookestone. I've found evidence of Mistopocatia used as a garnish to the spaghetti at Luke's Diner. Yes, I can prove that. Alright, I'll head to the station now.'

I hung up, clipped my case and shut my laptop. Within seconds, I was down the stairs and out the door, Darla barely catching the tail end of my checkout. I sped to the station and burst through the door.

'I've got the proof; your turn to get the guy!'

I held up my evidence and they nodded in approval. They sped down to the diner behind me. I had finally done it! We parked in the now empty carpark and stormed through the door, disregarding the 'closed' sign.

'We'll take the spaghetti, Luke,' the chief said with his gruff, professional voice.

Luke's face was priceless! He looked up at the officers, then to me, swinging a pair of handcuffs around my finger.

'It was Kara. She told you, didn't she?'

I smirked. All those years…

'Luke Letsport, you are under arrest for the endangerment of others and serving poison to customers.'

He started whining pathetically, making my ears sore.

'Please, I did it for the money! If my brother hadn't offered me the big bucks, this would have never happened! Please!'

But it was too late.

At 9:24pm, Saturday 5th July, Luke Letsport was arrested, likely to be a life sentence for first degree murder. I slid my hand into my back pocket and watched them drive away with him. Something felt… wrong. My pocket…it felt…wet? I pulled out my hand and stared at the purple liquid seeping into my skin. I remembered the small snap in the stem, the small hole in the bag, and my heart stopped. I had just infected myself with the Purple Death, and there was no going back.

My throat swelled up, my veins went deep purple. I felt exposed. I felt unsafe. I felt dead.

TABITHA'S EARRINGS

TESSA GORDON
Lindisfarne, Tasmania

2022
YEARS 5-6 CATEGORY
 AGATHA CHRISTIE IN TASMANIA

The aeroplane landed with an ear- splitting screech of its wheels. Tabitha Cherry walked out the side door of the plane, the gravel from her old farm crunching and falling out of the little holes in the soles of her shoes. She wanted to be back in Edinburgh. But now she was stuck in the tiny, hidden island of Tasmania. Her mother rushed through the crowd to get to her daughter. Tabitha's mother got divorced with her father a year before then. Two days ago her father had a heart attack and died.

Tabitha had been very, very sad in her life ever since it happened. It was like one moment her life was full of colours, and then the next moment all the colours had been drained away. Her life was like a black and white picture now.

'Oh, darling! I wish I never moved here. What was I thinking, leaving you and going to live here?' yelled Rose, Tabitha's mum.

'Okay, Ma,' said Tabitha, embarrassed. They walked, hand in hand, to Rose's car. Rose stopped the car at a playground.

'Go on, hop out! I'm friends with a lady whose daughter goes to the same school you will go to in two days. Her name is Kristin Perkins, but she likes to be called Kristy, okay? Go play with her!' said Rose.

"Kay,' Tabitha said as she got out of the car. Rose rushed home. She called the news office.

'Hello? Clyde Clive from the news office speaking,' said Clyde through the phone.

'Hi, Clyde. I just wanted to tell you something to put in the news show tonight,' said Rose.

'Okay, Rosie.' said Clyde.

'I want the people on the news tonight to say to everyone not to mention that Tabitha's great, great grandmother is Agatha Christie. All of Agatha's books scare her. Thank you,' said Rose, and she hung up.

Two hours later, at 6:00, Rose took Tabitha home for dinner. They lived on a farm in Sandford.

Tabitha ate her Pasta a la Puttanesca, and she went to the kitchen to get dessert. There was one choc chip cookie in the cookie jar. There was a label on the jar that said DON'T EAT ME. It looked like Tabitha's mum bought a jar of cookies that said, 'EAT ME', and then she wrote 'DON'T'. Tabitha was SO tempted to eat the cookie, so she did. In one big CRUNCH.

'Tabitha! Tabitha Cherry! Did you eat the cookie we were meant to share?' Said Rose.

Tabitha mumbled a reply. 'I … guess? But I didn't know it was meant to be shared! Didn't you eat the rest? I mean-'

'Do as I say, Tabbi! You're gonna brush your teeth, get dressed into your jarmies and go to bed with no reading, young lady! NOW!'

Tabbi walked up to her new room, groaning and moaning the whole way. She turned on her new nightlight, and she saw a little box that said something in a typewriter sort of font, actually, it might've actually been from a typewriter. Here's what it said: To Tabitha Myra May Cherry, the girl who is destined for greatness or peril. Signed, 1 7 1 20 8 1 3 8 18 9 19 20 9 5.

Tabbi thought it was some sort of code.

She remembered she had $100 in her bank account, so she had a plan. In the morning, she'd buy a spy coding book from QBD bookshop, because they were going to Eastlands the next day. For now, she thought, I'll just open the box. So, she did. It was a pair of jade, emerald, amethyst and silver hoop earrings. The next part of my plan is to ask Mum if I can get my ears pierced tomorrow.

At 7:30 pm, she fell asleep. At 10:00 am, she woke up to a sunny day. She knew that because glistening sunlight seeped through her curtains, waking her up in what she thought was one of the most delightful ways to be woken up.

She got out of bed as soon as she woke up. She sprinted out to her mother. 'Mum! Mum! Can we go to QBD at Eastlands today please? Please?' begged Tabbi.

'Tabbi, no, darling. We can order it online though! It will take about two to eight weeks to arrive.' said Rose, feeling guilty about what happened the night before.

The truth is, Rose deliberately ate all the rest of the cookies except for one to lure Tabbi into her trap. Rose was planning on sending Tabbi to bed early so she couldn't watch the news, like she usually does. 'What book is it? I'll look it up,' said Rose, ignoring her guilty thoughts.

'Codenames and Codes: How to Decode Spy Codes for Little Brainiac Spies,' replied Tabbi, out of breath at the end of the sentence.

'Hmm... Aww, sorry Sweet Pea. It says pre order only, Hon. That means 8 weeks.' CLICK! 'There you go. Mum saves the day! I ordered it! It's coming in 8 weeks, baby!'

Mum is so weird! OMG I totally forgot Mum was so awkward! Oh, where'd I go wrong! I-

'Honey! Get dressed and brush your teeth and hair, then get your coat and come with me to the car! C'mon! We're meant to meet the Perkinses at Liv Eat in an hour! Chop chop!' said Rose.

'Oh! Mum? Can I get my ears pierced at Price Cutters today? If yes make an appointment now!' snapped Tabbi.

'Okay, okay. Yes, okay and you're fine. Now get ready!' Said Rose. Tabbi got ready in 20 minutes, and they were on the road at 10:25. They got to Eastlands at 10:55, and they were at Liv Eat right on time.

'Tabbi!' yelled Kristy.

'Kristy!' yelled Tabbi.

'We thought you weren't coming!' said Kristy. 'Guess what! I'm getting my ears pierced at 12:00 at price cutters!'

'No way! I'm getting mine done at 12:10! What are the chances. Hang on a minute. Mum?' Said Tabbi suspiciously.

'He he. Oh alright. I did set it up so you were ten minutes after Kristy's appointment at Price Cutters. Sorry, kiddo.' Rose said.

Tabbi said 'That's okay, Mum. Okey dokey! I want a-'

'Wait, wait, wait. Here, take my card. Order yourself!' Rose said, handing Tabbi her credit card.

Mum never gives me her card! Thought Tabbi. Boy, am I lucky!

Tabbi and Kristy walked up to the counter, and Tabbi said her order, then Kristy said hers. 5 minutes later, Kristy had eaten her Quinoa bowl and drank her orange juice, and Tabbi had eaten her cheese toastie and drank her The Good Apple, and they were off to Price Cutters.

Kristy went in first, and 10 minutes later, she came out with a bottle of ear spray and Amethyst studs in her ears.

Tabbi rushed into the shop. 10 minutes after that, she came out with a bottle of ear spray and Aquamarine studs in her ears. Mrs Perkins left at 12:30, and Kristy had a big bag in her hands.

'What's going on?' asked Tabbi. 'I'm having a sleepover at your house tonight!' said Kristy.

'Yay!' cried Tabbi.

Eight weeks later, Tabbi was well into the school term. She had been counting down the days 'til she could change her earrings, and, on her birthday, which was that day, she finally could take them out and replace them with the silver, jade, emerald and amethyst hoops. She changed them 1 hour before she got her book. When she got her book, she immediately started to decode the signature. A. Ag. Aga. Agat. Agath. Agatha. Agatha C. Agatha Ch. Agatha Chr. Agatha Chri. Agatha Chris. Agatha Christ. Agatha Christi. Agatha Christie. Agatha Christie.

Tabbi realised straight away what she had done terribly wrong. She went straight to the bathroom to take the earrings out, but the next four words will change the cheery melody of the story. They. Wouldn't. Come. out. No matter how hard Tabbi tried, the earrings wouldn't come out.

Tabbi stayed awake reading most of that night. But when she finally dozed off, a few seconds later she woke up on a train. A scary looking man started walking towards her. She squeezed her eyes shut, and she woke up in her bed again. Tabbi got up straight away and got ready for school. When she got to school, the teacher said 'Okay class. What the?'

The classroom walls started cracking. All the kids huddled together like penguins on one side of the room. Train tracks started forming on the ground. Suddenly, the same train that was in Tabbi's 'dream' burst through the walls.

The creepy man stared at her from the window as the train passed. The toilet on the other side of the room flushed. Timmy Carter came out, and said 'What'd I miss? Whoah! Wicked!'.

School ended early that day. Tabbi told her mum everything, and Rose said 'Tabbi, there's something I need to tell you. You know those earrings you're wearing? Your great-great grandma gave them to you. Agatha Christie. Your great-great grandma's Agatha Christie.'

'Oooooh! That explains it! Hahaha. Can I call Kristy when we get home?' said Tabbi.

'Sure, but what? You're not scared, or confused? You realise you have great power? That train was from one of Agatha's books, Y'know!' said Rose.

'Cool.' said Tabbi. When Tabbi got home, she video called Kristy.

'Hey, guess what?' said Kristy.

'What?' said Tabbi.

'My great-great-great grandma or something was Mary Shelley! So apparently I have, like, Frankenstein superpowers!' said Kristy.

'Wow! My great-great grandma was Agatha Christie! I've got, like, superpowers from HER books! Maybe we could, like, make a little 2 person club!' said Tabbi.

'No to the club idea, but cool!' said Kristy.

Those two eleven year old girls have a lot to learn about the great powers within them. They have had an amazingly unique life together, so far. And that is the end of this story.

SCONES, STONES AND SUSPECTS

ARIELLA LAMBETH
Hobart, Tasmania

2022
YEARS 5-6 CATEGORY
  AGATHA CHRISTIE IN TASMANIA

7 September 2022

Droplets of water cascade down our raincoats and umbrellas, covering the ground below with puddles. Whenever someone accidentally steps in one (which is often) ripples gently float out from the unlucky shoe. After seeing a soaking disposable mask stuck to the ground, all of us remember to take our soft cloth masks out of our pockets and wrap them around our faces, warming them.

We work our way through the network of stalls until I spot the brightly painted tent of Scones & Stones around a corner. It's flapping in the wind, the shredded canvas edge barely distinguishable from the cluttered cobblestones laid into the path. Alyssa and Chris stop their play-fighting, and walk a little faster to get to the warm, comforting atmosphere of the familiar space.

We veer around one last stall as we chat about what little artefacts we think Jessie has collected since last Saturday, when we see the destruction. Scones are scattered all over the bumpy stones like mulch on a garden, and a dirty plastic table with a bright tablecloth has been tipped over. The artefacts have been shoved into one corner, out of the rain, with a few of them chipped and scratched. A figure stands in the middle of the wreckage, her face in her hands and her curling black hair hiding herself from everyone and everything. All of us quickly recognize her as Jessie, the stall owner. I run up to her immediately to put an arm around her shoulder, Alyssa and Chris following suit.

After a while she looks up and wipes her eyes with the back of her hand.

'Thanks. I don't know who did this. I saw someone...' She seems so dejected and sad.

'Do you want us to look for the person who did it? Or at least try?' I blurt out. Jessie jumps at my suggestion.

'Are you sure you can handle it?' she asks, slight worry lines creasing her soft face.

'I can definitely try. And I'm sure that Chris and Alyssa will help too!' Alyssa nods excitedly, her eyes already roaming around for clues. Chris, on the other hand, seems a bit less sure, but still gives us a small nod.

'Thank you. And remember, if you don't find anything, that's okay,' Jessie tells us as we start looking around the shop.

'Alright, everybody,' I command, gathering Alyssa and Chris into a corner. 'First, we look for any clues. Trails, things that shouldn't be here, footprints, anything. Even crumpled fabric could work as a clue.' Alyssa and Chris bow their heads in response and begin searching.

A few minutes have passed when Jessie calls out to us, her voice almost carried away by the wind.

'I forgot to tell you something!' We all lean in closer, interested. 'When I got back to the shop, the last thing that I saw of the person was the edge of a fraying, navy blue shirt disappearing around the corner.'

'Hey! We can look for any threads from the person's shirt!' Alyssa jumps up and starts looking. But before she's found anything, Chris notices something.

'Look! There!' Alyssa and I stop, and look down at the ground where Chris's pointing. There, leading away from the shop, is a small, winding trail of crumbs. At the start of the trail lies half of a crumbling scone. The crumbs are sparse, some big, some small, but we still decide to follow it.

'Good luck!' Jessie calls after us as we run down the trail.

We peer at the seemingly endless path of crumbs that twists and turns all over the place as we attempt to follow it. Inevitably, though, our task gets harder as the trail gets sparser and we start to lose track. We've mostly lost the path when we hear laboured breathing coming from behind a stall. Alyssa and I nod at each other, and each creep different ways. Chris, unsure of what to do, follows me to the left. I've been mentally counting down from ten since I left the front of the stall, and I'm meant to jump out on zero. Five... four... three... two... one... I pounce, as does Alyssa, both of us shouting at whomever we're pouncing on... or whatever, because it turns out to be a shaggy dog with a patchy coat, puppy eyes and a scone clutched in its jaws. I sigh.

'Seems like we're back to square one,' Chris sighs, hanging his head.

'We should go back to Jessie's stall and look for more leads there,' I reason with them until they get up and walk back to Jessie's stall, the dog following behind us with its tail wagging hopefully.

Jessie hears our feet thudding along and turns from her cleaning, a slight frown creasing her normally joyful brow.

'Did you find anything?' Her hands are covered in dirt, and she's soaked from the dripping rain. None of us wants to be the one to break the news to her, so we all avoid her eyes and scuff our shoes in the dirt. We can see her face fall as she realizes what happened.

'You didn't find anything, did you?' I'm the first one to nod, a slow, dejected nod, and the others follow suit. Jessie breathes in, long and sharp.

'That's fine. Are you going to keep looking?' She furrows her brow at us.

'Of course,' I say definitively. Chris and Alyssa nod, and we set off looking for clues again.

After a few more minutes of looking, a young man appears from around a corner. He has a grey t-shirt with a ninja star, blue jeans and a black backpack slung carelessly over one shoulder. He walks up to Jessie and plants a kiss on her cheek. Strange. But then I recognize him as Jessie's brother, Simon. I wave at him, and he turns and nods at me in response. His piercing blue eyes illuminate his face, and a light frown creases his brow, as if he's been worrying about something.

After a few minutes, Jessie's head pops up.

'I think I know what's missing! It's a little blue ninja star,' Jessie calls as she points at Simon's t-shirt.

'It's a shuriken,' he tells her. Jessie shrugs.

'Thanks, Jessie,' I call back, and keep looking.

After a long time of looking, examining and peering, Alyssa finds something. She calls us over to a spot that I had overlooked before, where all of us can see the small navy-blue threads caught on a screw. She then points to a spot a few meters up ahead, where another few strands are caught on a tree branch.

'Look. The threads make a sort of trail. If we follow them, we might find something,' Alyssa tells us. 'I think we should still follow it, even though the last trail led to a dead end.' I nod, and both Alyssa and I look to Chris for conformation. Instead of nodding as well, like we expected, he scuffs his foot in the dirt and kicks a scone gently.

'What if this is just a dead end as well? Then we're just wasting our time. Maybe we should just stay here and help Jessie clean up.' Chris stares down at the ground. I'm about to try to encourage him when Simon jumps in.

'Chris has a point. Maybe you should just wait and help Jessie clean up. It is quite a mess…' he says, gesturing out at the scattered objects. I give him a weird look, as does Alyssa.

'Anyway, I still think we should go,' I say. 'And if this doesn't work, then we can just come back and help Jessie.' Simon attempts to argue, but by that time Chris has already nodded his head and we're off, following the sparse trail.

The rain has slowed to a light drizzle, and the grass sparkles beneath our feet as we pad over it following the threads. Simon started off following us, but left a little while ago to help Jessie. He's a mysterious character.

Chris marches on ahead, finding the threads before anyone else gets to even attempt to find them. Alyssa and I hang behind, chatting to each other. Even though we seem happy, our words are filled with tension.

It's not long before we reach a gate leading out of the market and down to the water. A bored-looking official with a black umbrella stands at the exit holding a sheet for us to sign.

'Should we go through? I can't see any threads on the other side,' Chris remarks. As I'm about to nod my head in agreement, I see a boot-print in the mud right at the base of a tall tree. I glance up, and it seems like a pretty normal tree… except for the small hole in the trunk, where I can see a little glint. I can't quite reach up there, since it's quite high. But Alyssa can! I point out the glint to her, and she nods and stretches her arm up until her fingertips brush the object, and she manages to grab it out of the hole and bring it down to us. Sure enough, it's a little blue ninja star, rusted at the edges with age.

'Look! We found it-' As I'm saying those words, Simon marches up and snatches the blue star right out of Alyssa's hand.

'Found it, did you? Well, you lost it again now!' He yanks a fraying denim jacket out of his bag, pulls it roughly over his shoulders and takes off, leaping over the flags and down to the water. I gasp, and clumsily jump over the flags to chase after him. Chris slides under easily as Alyssa flies over the flags, both of them dashing after Simon. I ignore the shouts from the officer, my mind only focused on getting to Simon.

The chase is hard and tiring. My feet barely touch the ground as I race after him, my heart pounding in my chest. We go up and down, racing along beside the choppy cerulean waters, the people in Salamanca Market slowly gathering to watch the chase on our other side. A light wind flaps my hair in my face, and pushes me along from behind. Simon is a fast runner, though, and we're falling too far behind him. All of us start to lose stamina, our breath going in and out even faster then before. But just when we think we've lost him, we see a woman with black curling hair and a peachy raincoat flying over the gravel towards him from the other side. It's Jessie, running into the wind, her face set with determination. Simon tries to swerve, and all of us put on one last burst of energy.

'Gotcha.'

14 September 2022

I stroll happily into Jessie's stall, the warm sun beating down on me. Jessie stands happily behind one of the tables, all of the things neatly organized. One particular new thing catches my eye, though. The blue ninja star is sitting in a little box made of clear plastic, with a sticky note on the front. 'This is a shuriken, otherwise known as a ninja star. It was bought by my great-great grandfather in Japan, and was then passed down through many generations of our family. This star stands here today courtesy of Simon, who found it and helped to keep it preserved.' Underneath, a few small, scrawled letters read 'not for sale'.

Just then Simon walks in, wearing the same grey shirt with a ninja star, but this time with shorts. It's quite hot for early September. He glances at the sticky note on the box, winces and turns away, grabbing a couple of scones from a nearby table.

'Do you want to have a scone with me?' he asks me.

'Sure.'

A STRANGE FAMILY

LINH LE
Tighes Hill, NSW

2021
YEARS 5-6 CATEGORY
SCENE OF THE CRIME

Cheap glass shattered as it hit the bare concrete floor on the second storey of Brooksby Mansion. You'd expect cries of 'is everything alright?' to follow, but there were none. However, this silence did not last very long – it was the screams that caught everybody's attention. Melinda Brooksby's cries were heard from villages far away, yet it was her daughter's disappearance that made brains throb.

Nanny Alice Campleton

Melinda had a daughter named Tori who was only four years old when she vanished, but eight years later, she came back. How and why she came back remains a mystery, but not to me.

I was Tori's nanny and knew nothing more than what Melinda knew about her own daughter. In fact, I may have even known a bit more about Tori than anybody expected. We had a strong bond that connected the both of us. Tori could understand me and I could understand her like no other. Telepathy, maybe, but she always let me know what she wanted. From the simple things like telling me she was full or didn't want to go to bed, to the more mysterious things like secrets she knew about her mother.

The night she went missing, I heard her. She said, 'I'm coming back soon, but I need to find him.' I had to trust my senses and listen to her, however, I couldn't send messages back. That was the only problem.

'And where were you that night, ma'am?'

'At my house, feeding my own children.'

'How old are your children?'

'9 and 13.'

'Your husband looks after them, yes?'

'Yes.'

The woman I had once known as Melinda Brooksby was planted in a chair, swollen eyes taking up most of her face. She had answered when needed and kept silent when expected. Thick auburn locks fell from her head, and the proud, motherly figure she used to own had left her.

'My child, my only child, is gone. Why does everyone I love disappear?'

Her murmurs were barely audible, but I could hear them. I placed a hand on her knee and smiled warmly. 'The police will find her in no time'.

One night, I woke up gasping for air as the last scene of my dream danced in my head.

Tori was there, amidst a black and white room. Her mother stood just in front of her.

'I have to find him. I must find him.' Tori repeated. Melinda shook her head, fear printed across her features. This child was fragile like the glass that broke that day, mysterious as to why the window broke. She dropped her teddy onto the bare black floor. Her weight making the red chair creak as she sat on it. 'Mum, I need to find Dad.'

Andrew Brooksby was gone. How could Tori know he was missing, let alone know that he existed? She was only seven months old when her father left. Andrew had a dark side to him and rarely interacted with his only child. When he was sleeping one night, he disappeared without a trace. Forty one months ago.

DETECTIVE ELISA KENNEDY

Another family member had disappeared. We hushed it down, didn't want the public to be afraid. Why the same family? The Brooksbys were a wealthy family, known by many. But since the passing of Mr Hudson Brooksby (Melinda's grandfather), the family had lost their fortune. Melinda helped her father sell bread, and her younger sister cleaned the house. Together they worked towards a brighter future, and their poverty all changed when Melinda was hired to be a server at a restaurant – a real job.

The house was the first place to search for clues, given the entire place was a crime scene of sorts. Maybe even the smallest curio would help.

'Detective Kennedy, you there?'

'Yes, I'm here.'

'Have you found anything?'

'No, I jus' started.'

'Okay. Call me back if you find something interesting that could help us...'

''Kay.'

I clambered up the mighty granite steps. Hail descended relentlessly, clonking on to my head. No signs of anything strange happening within the walls of this house were visible. No telltale signs of the two disappearing family members. I opened the door with a grunt as the weight finally fell to the other side. Moths fluttered around my head, while woodworms worked away on a wooden windowsill. My heavy-duty sneakers make their way up to the second floor as quietly as possible. I have investigated many missing-person cases, but this one is especially gave me bad vibes.

Beside a smashed window lay a teddy bear. Its head was awkwardly positioned, and a paw was missing. I picked it up, but it felt too heavy to be a child's stuffed toy. Ripping it open, I discovered a minuscule camera... and it was recording me. My vision became dazed and stars danced around in my head. Smoke began to rise from my satchel. I ripped it open to find the teddy's eyes glowing vividly. Wispy puffs of air emanated from its eyes, choking my vision. Gag reflexes kicked in, and my head jerked away from the teddy. Its hand lurched towards my face. I brushed it off, only to find out my face wasn't the thing it was going for - it wanted my neck.

Lunging for the space beneath my chin, the paws yanked at a pendant on my chest. The metal did not resist, and the chain snapped. An amber stone fell from the prong setting, clattering to the floor.

'Elisa! Can you hear me?'

Distressed mumbles filled the room. I opened my eyes to the scene of people crowding me. Their faces were painted with concern. 'You were supposed to be tough, aye?' Ailsa mocked. She yanked me up and grasped my shoulders.

'What did you see?'

'Not much.'

'You found a teddy, right?'

'Yeah…'

'And?'

'What do you want me to say?'

'Just tell me what happened!'

'Well, the teddy, it had some sort of camera stuffed inside it-'

'And?'

'It was definitely recording, but when I picked it up, the camera stopped.'

'We know. There are no fingerprints on it, however.'

'Huh.'

NANNY ALICE CAMPLETON

Just as I heard my 13-year-old daughter flick her light switch off, a cry arose from the window. I stepped over and saw a teddy sitting on the windowsill. The sound of a camera clicked, and a screen popped up from its head. It displayed the face of Tori on the screen, and she whispered a couple of words to me.

'I found Dad.'

DETECTIVE ELISA KENNEDY

Someone by the name of Alice Campleton came to the police station today. She explained everything.

Tori had set a remote control teddy bear to find her dad. Tori herself went missing because the bear had a small malfunction. The window smashing was a distraction to get out of the house. And Tori was not Tori Brooksby, but an adult who had dwarfism and posed as Tori to find her dad. Because that adult was Gabriella Brooksby, Melinda's sister, who suffered from the guilt of forcing Andrew out of the house to live for himself when he played a life-threatening prank on her.

Nanny Alice Campleton

Andrew stood on the doorstep, a foolish grin plastered on his face. Melinda rushed out to greet him, and when he finally came inside to the warmth of the fireplace, he explained everything about the joke, and how he stayed at his mates' houses while he tried to figure out a way for everything to be fixed. Tori was safe with him, and they lived for years until Gabriella found him and convinced him to come back to the place his family lived.

I guess that's the end of the story. Their family was happy that they were all back together. I headed back to my house to be with my family and enjoy their company. However, as I left, I noticed a small note on the floor. It said: Thank you Alice. Love, Tori.

Maybe I was hallucinating. Maybe that wasn't real. But even if it wasn't real, Tori still loved me and I would always be a part of her life, even if I was just the nanny.

4D SLEUTHING

AARON LEE
Hornsby, NSW

2021
YEARS 5-6 CATEGORY
  SCENE OF THE CRIME

I looked at the ornate halls of the museum, a century-old building created on festooned pillars and the minds of curators of art. The calm zephyr brushed against the trees and grass, causing them to wave lissomly. I stepped in, almost losing myself in the world of wonder at the sight of marble sculptures.

Why did you need me, Officer Ronald?' I inquired.

'As you can see here, Detective Joe, the so-called Wisdom Artifact has been stolen. We have gathered a few suspects here,' he replied, much like a soldier reporting anything and everything that had happened.

I took my magnifying glass from my pocket, as if I was roleplaying as Sherlock Holmes in a movie, one where a millennium-old part of the book of history was at stake.

I frisked through the suspects as if I was a dog, trying to catch the slightest whiff of foul play. I checked the DNA. It had surprisingly been modified. This was planned well, wasn't it? My mind thought. I asked each suspect where they had been and what they had done. Nothing seemed off. I checked for fingerprints. I found one.

On it were three words.

Drop. Some. Sand.

That's why it's called the Wisdom Artifact.

'Ronald, I found something over here. It says drop some sand,' I report. He came over like a wolf that had caught the scent of prey, the scent of the prey of evidence.

'Well, let's try it,' he said, the words imbued on the fingerprints apples of his eyes. We went outside, picking up motes of dirt. From it came Morse code and a string of binary.

A few hours later, we arrived at a wall of wire saying 'NO ENTRY'. I took out my wire cutters. A scintillating light almost engulfed me. My heart skipped a beat. My legs shook. My brain was stuck in a maze of confusion while being in overdrive. I found myself waking up.

'Why are you here?' someone questioned.

'Coordinates… from a fingerprint I found somewhere,' I replied, my mind thinking 'am I going to die trying to solve this?'

'This is literally top secret, hidden behind a smokescreen that is area 51. How would you find this?' the same voice asked, this time much louder.

'Where even is this?' I demand.

'Lab D4. We are trying to get into 4 dimensional space,' the same voice said.

'Well, I got a Morse code message from some sort of anomaly. It says fold 6 cubes together to get a tesseract and touch it to enter 4D,' I say, thinking what I said was useless. The voice was stunned.

2 minutes later, a once-hypothetical 'supercube' was brought to me. I touched it, to find myself in a strange world. Time seemed to be a physical dimension. I saw the real culprit- Officer Ronald.

Did I just solve this with science? My brain wondered.

I left the 4D space by collapsing the tesseract, but not before sending Morse code and binary. I found myself putting a handcuff on Ronald's hands.

Case closed – with science, I write.

THE TALE OF THE MISSING CHERRIES

INDY LEONARD
Victoria

2020
YEARS 5-6 CATEGORY
  FEMALE DETECTIVES

Dashy is a beautiful black kitten, but nobody knows the things she gets up to at night. It was late and Dashy's owners were tucking her into bed. They each said good night and closed the door to the crate she slept in. Dashy closed her eyes and waited until the house was quiet, then she stood up and said to herself, 'Where should I go tonight? Hang on, first I must go and get Lucky, my bestie!'

Dashy put her paw through the metal wire crate, opened the latch and slipped out. 'Now where are they?' Dashy said to herself. 'Here they are' she said, as she jumped up onto the mantelpiece and grabbed the keys to the back door. She flung them up onto the couch, then she sprung up herself and picked up the keys in her mouth. She leaped up at the door handle and caught on with one paw, swung for a moment, then unlocked the back door with the key in her other paw. The door slowly creaked open as she dropped to the floor. Dashy stepped through the doorway and out into the cool night air, paused, then hopped down the stairs, leaped across the back yard and up over the fence to Lucky's house. Lucky was waiting out front, together they headed down the street.

Many cats were out going to different places, night was a busy time for cats. They came to the human ice cream parlour, but passed it and went around the back of the shop. People never see the cat ice cream parlour because it's well hidden. It was run by a tabby cat named Franko, each night he would move a brick to reveal the entrance to his ice cream parlour, and hang the sign 'Gatto Gelato - Open'. Franko belonged to the owner of the human ice cream parlour. He was a happy friendly cat who enjoyed a bit too much of his ice cream.

Dashy and Lucky walked inside and picked out their flavours, they both decided on cherry panna cotta. They walked over to the park and had their ice creams sitting in a tree watching the shimmering moon. Next they went shopping at Katmart. They were walking down an aisle when Dashy saw a beautiful red neck scarf she wanted to get. So they went to the catregisters and paid. As they walked out of the shop, in the distant sky they saw the moon beginning to set and decided they should start making their way home. Just as they were passing the ice cream parlour a cat stepped out and said 'We are looking for two cats called Dashy and Lucky, have you seen them?'

'That's us' said Lucky.

'Then could you please come inside.' They stepped inside and the doors slammed shut behind them. Dashy felt uncomfortable, Franko was nowhere to be seen. There were about seven other cats inside, looking worried. A big cat stepped out in front of the small crowd and said, 'Tonight there has been a thief in the shop, most of the cherries have been stolen. The cats assembled here are the only cats that have been to Gatto Gelato tonight, so you are all suspects.' Three cats sprang out from behind the big cat in charge, and inspected each of the cats as they passed.

'Over here' cried one of the cats 'This one here!' All the cats turned to stare at Dashy. 'You are guilty!' said one of the inspector cats.

'No, I'm not!' cried Dashy.

'What is this on your fur then little miss? Looks and smells like cherry!'

'I didn't take the cherries! I brought a cherry panna cotta ice cream earlier tonight, some must have dripped on my fur' Dashy tried to speak confidently, but it was hard because she was feeling worried.

'You are banned from this shop!' Said the big cat in charge, 'Be off all of you! Be off and don't come back! Except for you black cat.

'But I didn't do it' said Dashy' she was feeling cross now, 'and I'm going to prove it!' Dashy turned to lucky and winked, then they both leapt up on the counter and out through the high window into the dark night.

They sat high up in an oak tree overlooking Gatto Gelato. Dashy needed to come up with a plan. 'I have to solve this mystery and prove my innocence,' said Dashy to Lucky.

'I know you didn't do it Dashy, we will sort this out I know we will' said Lucky.

Dashy thought as she stared down at the ice cream parlour.

'What are cats best at?' Dashy said.

'Um sleeping?' replied Lucky.

'I guess we are pretty good at that, but I was thinking, hiding and night vision!' Said Dashy. 'Let's creep down closer to the window and we can see if the thief strikes again!'

The cats waited for what felt like forever, Dashy had nearly given up when they heard a rustle and a flap of wings. They watched as a little bird sat on the window sill of Gatto Gelato with something in her beak. The bird took off up into the oak tree, landing in a nest for a moment, then flew back down to the ice cream parlour. Dashy made their way up through the tree branches to the birds nest. Dashy felt something sticky on the branch she was walking on and stopped to lick her paw.

'Cherry Juice!' As the cats peeked up into the nest they knew they had solved the mystery, it was overflowing with cherries!

The cats rushed to Franco's house to tell him what they had found and asked him to come back to Gatto Gelato to explain the mystery to the big cat and his inspectors.

The big cat had to admit that their story checked out, he seemed pretty annoyed!

Dashy and Lucky were free to go! As they were leaving they heard Franko mutter to himself, 'first cherries, now the cream, I'm losing everything tonight!'

Dashy and Lucky walked out of the shop, in the distant sky they saw the first light of dawn. The cats looked at each other in horror! They had to get home fast. Then Dashy remembered her magic powers. The moon was just about to disappear, so the cats ran and ran till they caught the last moonbeam. As Dashy stepped into the moonlight, glowing stripes began to appear on her fur, then she said to herself 'Home.'

A wind blew by and picked the two cats up, it carried them through the air back to their houses. Dashy leaped inside, jumped into her kitten crate and closed the door just in time. She lay there with her eyes shut pretending to be asleep. Her owners said good morning and opened the crate, but Dashy didn't come out. She was fast asleep. Just then one of Dashy's owners asked 'Did someone feed Dashy cream? It's all over her face'

THE GHOST MURDER IN THE WILLIAM MANSION

LISSETTE SHU
Surrey Hills, Victoria

2021
YEARS 5-6 CATEGORY
  SCENE OF THE CRIME

During winter, detective Arthur was invited to The William mansion. The mansion was located on the top of an isolated hill and was heavily guarded in every direction. Driving into the parking lot of the mansion with his Ferrari, Mr William Taylor, the owner of the mansion, was standing on the luxurious Marble stairs, waving his hand in a friendly way. Being polite, Arthur waved back with a smile. He noticed something about Mr. William's smile. It was forced and not natural. He did not think much of it at the time and prepared to enter inside. The moment he stepped foot inside, he saw many people dressed in expensive suits and dresses, who gave him warm and welcoming smiles.

Before he could wave back, Mr William invited him nervously into the 'Honoured Guests' room, where they could talk in private. Arthur was surprised at the sweatiness of Mr William's palms on this cold winter's day. As soon as the door was shut, Mr William took out his handkerchief to wipe his sweat, and introduced him to the eight members of his family. Arthur couldn't help but notice that Mr William's mood was quite foul.

When dinner was about to finish, Mrs Amelia, daughter of Mr. William and Mrs. Olivia stood and used the restroom. As soon as Arthur was about to take a sip from his glass of water, a scream was heard coming from outside. He immediately placed down his glass of water and rushed to the restroom to see what was going on. He saw Mrs Amelia on the floor, horrified as she stared into the restroom. He came closer and saw that Mrs Olivia's body was on the floor and had a bullet in her back. Arthur felt a lump rise in his throat and heard his heart thumping loudly in his ears. He knew that he had to act quickly in this situation. He demanded Emergency Services right away. Arthur, who was a detective by nature and instinct, took Mrs Amelia, who was paralysed in shock, into a room to interrogate her. Mrs Amelia explained that as she was walking out of the restroom, she heard a gunshot coming from inside so she turned around, and Mrs Olivia was lying on the ground, with a bullet on the upper part of her back. It was like a ghost shot her.

As soon as it got late, Mrs Amelia begged Arthur to stay, since she wanted him to solve the death of Mrs Olivia. Arthur agreed, since he also had a desire to solve the case. Mr William invited Arthur to the guest room and bid him goodnight. After a good rest, Arthur woke up only to see that Mr William's brother, James was now also dead. This time, there was a knife in his chest. The odd thing was that the knife didn't have a handle, only the blade was there. Arthur crouched down to take a closer look and found a small badge with the logo of a cat on it. Arthur put on a poker face and refrained from shaking or showing any signs of fear. He gave it to Mr William, who was now failing to resist crying, and asked him if he knew anything about it. He was silent for a while before telling Arthur that it was the family's company Logo. Arthur requested that Mr William tell him more, like who could be wearing the badge. He said that the badge was for everyone, and everyone in the house had one.

The police arrived once more and got to work immediately. According to the police, the bullet in Mrs Olivia's back was from a Ruger pistol. The bullet was found to be half rusted, as if it was loaded inside for quite a while without being fired. Suddenly, a thought came into Arthur's mind. If the bullet was shot into the back of Mrs Olivia, that meant that the shot came from the direction of the wall. Arthur rushed back into the restroom and began investigating the wall. He noticed a very thin black line running around a small portion of the wall and he pushed against one side of it. The sound of concrete scraping on luxurious marble was heard as the wall flipped open. Arthur knew he was onto something. Instead of going in all alone, he called some police officers to tag along in case something unexpected happened. The room was surprisingly neat and tidy. There was an old vintage table located on the right side of the room with a lamp in the corner. The table has very neatly drawn blueprints of death traps that Arthur thought could possibly be used soon by the 'Ghost'.

Before he could get to investigating more, he heard Mr William let out a loud screech. Along with the officers, Arthur rushed downstairs where the scream was coming from and saw Mr William looking at the body of a man in his 30's. Mr William sobbed as he held his lifeless youngest son, John, in his arms. Arthur saw that this time, the blood was coming from the John's torso, so he put on his gloves and turned over the body. After trying to see if he could match any information together, something clicked. He asked Mr William about his wife, and her position in the company. He told Arthur that she was the co-owner of the company. Next, Arthur asked about Mr William's brother's position in the company, and he said that James, his brother, was the manager for finance, another important position. Arthur figured out the Ghost's plan now.

Taking Mr William into a room where no one could eavesdrop, he asked who else in the family had an important position. He told Arthur that it was his daughter, the second youngest born before John. She worked at the leading manager, since her special skill was managing many tasks at once. Immediately, he asked Mr William where she was but he didn't know. Another scream could be heard before Arthur could think any further. Arthur rushed upstairs into the room where the scream came from and opened the door as fast as he could. He saw that both her hands were chopped and there was a bloody knife blade on the carpet floor. Out of the corner of his eye, Arthur spotted a door leading up, so he asked Mr William to take care of his daughter and climbed up into the ceiling. He could hear the faint sounds of the Ghost crawling and rushed as fast as he could to follow the direction of the sounds. Finally, he was one turn from reaching the Ghost, he heard a sigh, but couldn't tell if it was a man or woman. Extremely keen to know the person, he carefully took a peek. However, without paying attention behind him, the Ghost knocked him out and carried him to another room.

It was now dark. Arthur woke up in his room, with Mr William sitting on a wooden stool beside him. Arthur asked in a soft voice what happened, and Mr William explained that he found Arthur on the floor of the other guest room. Arthur immediately stood up and said that there was no time to waste, and they had to catch the Ghost as soon as possible. He quickly left the room as Mr William followed him nervously.

Arthur asked Mr William to list out all the important positions of the family members and he did. Instead of listing the positions of the five people alive in the mansion, he listed six. Arthur asked who the sixth was. Mr William was nervous, but decided to explain anyway. It was his oldest son. He was always loved by people and as he grew up, he was loved by the co-workers in the company. It all went well for him until his siblings joined. He loved attention, so when he lost it, he went mad. He left the mansion and went out to live on his own. He bought a medium sized house and found a partner. He would still come to work occasionally, but never talked to his siblings or anyone in his family. Arthur requested that Mr William give him the location of his oldest son's house and to take over the situation at the mansion. Without wasting any time, Arthur rushed to the location given to him.

After 30 minutes of driving, he reached the location. He rang the doorbell 3 times, but there was no answer. He looked around the place, and there was no car either. He noticed that the plants were dry and withered, and the grass was around 50cm tall. Arthur was now convinced that no one was home. Since it was night and there weren't many cars, he drove a little faster back to the mansion and quickly made his way inside. Mr William rushed to him, saying that another person died. This time, it was the middle son. Arthur investigated the body, and found that they had been choked to death, since their face was red, and they showed signs of struggling before death.

Arthur informed Mr William of the prime suspect, his oldest son. He was shocked to hear that a member of his own family would murder others like that. He fell to the ground crying. Arthur, with the list of important positions in his hand, found that now there were only four people left, excluding the oldest son. He quickly searched the house and found their daughter.

He took her into her room and asked her to stay there while he got things prepared. He asked her to pretend that she was sleeping, since it was night anyways and she agreed. Arthur, with his pistol and a taser was now waiting at the door outside of the room. The moment he heard a clicking noise from the ceiling and saw the door open, he barged in. The daughter screamed as the killer was on the bed with a gun, staring at Arthur. He turned on the light as the Ghost's identity was revealed. It was indeed the oldest son. He dropped his gun and put his hands in the air, as he knew that he had been defeated. The police were immediately called as he was tied up by Arthur. The Ghost's identity had now been discovered. Mr Williams was tearing up, knowing that his son was the murderer. The police thanked Arthur and drove away with the oldest son. Mr William said that he couldn't thank Arthur enough as he was preparing to leave. As he was about to leave, Mr William ran to him and handed him a scarf and said that it was a gift for helping him. Arthur took it and made his leave. As he drove out, he praised himself on his performance on the case and happily drove off. Almost arriving at his house, he was blocked by a car accident.

As he observed the accident closely, he saw a man holding a gun run away from his car and into the night. Arthur rushed outside only to see that the tires of one car were shot. Arthur thought to himself 'After one case is solved, another pops up right away.' as he began his next investigation.

THE GOLD NECKLACE

ENZO SZTEJMAN
Caulfield South, Victoria

2021 WINNER
YEARS 5-6 CATEGORY
 SCENE OF THE CRIME

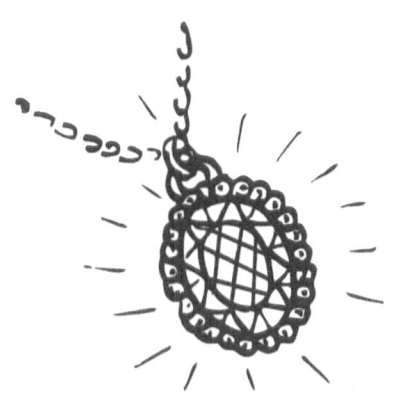

A crash came from upstairs. I throw my messy lunch plate in the sink and instantly speed in that direction. Something must be wrong. I look around slowly, staying alert at all times. I turn the lights on. While I'm searching in my parents' room for, well, something that can help me figure out what had just happened, I notice trace evidence of glass on the floor and when I look up I see a smashed window. I run to my mum's drawer. Her priceless necklace is missing!

Oh no! but also Oh yes! Oh no because my mother's priceless necklace is gone but oh yes because I am a huge fan of mystery and crime movies, especially the CSI series, and here I have a real crime in my hands. It's like fate chose this moment. This would be a dream come true for Jerry and the boys in my chemistry class. Anyway, there is no time to lose.

I quickly start searching for clues that the robber might've left behind. I suddenly remember that my parents are coming home from their work trip tomorrow and mum would be furious and devastated if she saw that her necklace was gone. So it is now up to me to solve this case.

It just so happens that I have a 'detective set', which my grandma got me ten years ago for my eighth birthday. At least it's something. Unfortunately there is only one piece left in the set, the fingerprint powder. I go to my room and search the perimeter. Sorry just trying to sound like a real detective. There it is, on my bedside table, the fingerprint powder. I grab it, then walk back to the contaminated site (A.K.A. my mum's drawer) and start dusting for prints. A minute passes, nothing. Two minutes passes, still nothing. Finally, I see something, a few lines, so I keep dusting and a bit more of the fingerprint reveals. Within a few minutes, all of the print is visible. Now I've got what you call a latent print. I can't believe that this old powder actually works. I'm going to hold onto it for the time being. Part one of my investigation, done and dusted! There are still many more clues I need to decode.

Subsequently I see a piece of paper on the floor right next to mum's bed. It reads '20, 15, 16 19, 5, 3, 18, 5, 20 1, 7, 5, 14, 20'. I don't have a clue about what it means but I'll keep it. I keep searching for more evidence of the crime scene.

I notice that some weird type of gadget is lying in my mother's room on the carpet and go check it out. It looks a bit like a watch, except that it has hundreds of buttons. I think that the robber dropped this, probably, while he was stealing the necklace. Then I see blood on the shards of glass from the window. I take a few pieces and put it in my stash of clues - the fingerprint, the note, the gadget and now the bloody glass. This all reminds me of Season Two, Episode Nine of CSI Miami so I go downstairs and turn on the TV. I fast forward to the part where the detective is close to solving the case.

That's it! I'll copy the detective. I'll look in more places. In different parts of the house. I'm just so happy that I'm solving a real crime. I'm going to search for even more clues. This time, downstairs. Could he have escaped from the front door? A window? That's for me to find out.

I shoot up and begin to dust the tiled floor with the powder I have left. The dusting is going longer than I expect and I'm starting to lose hope. Then I see a footprint! I grab the black tape from dad's tool bag, hoping this will work as well as gel lifter which forensic detectives use. Fantastic, it works. I am actually holding another latent print. I can't wait to tell Jerry. How weird, the toes are pointing away from the door so that means the thief entered the house from downstairs. How? I was eating lunch. I would've seen it. Could the suspect have been upstairs already before I started eating? If he entered downstairs that means he exited through the window upstairs. Then how did he survive? It's a long way down.

You know what, I need to get some fresh air and maybe I'll head over to the two dollar shop across the road to do something about my mother's necklace. I put on my jacket, in the middle of summer. Melbourne is crazy. I arrive at the two dollar store and I see, right in front of me a gold necklace that, to be honest, doesn't actually look like mum's necklace but she won't know the difference because she would never suspect it would be replaced.

I place the plastic necklace on the counter.

The bored looking man said, 'That will be $3.50 mate.'

I reach into my pockets trying to find some money and to my surprise I find exactly $3.50.

'Cheers bro,' I gush.

I rush back to my house, open the door, dash up the stairs and put the fake necklace in exactly the same spot it was in before it got stolen.

I just want to know who stole my mother's necklace! It's dinner time. All this detective work is making me hungry. But maybe I should go downstairs and call the police first. I head down.

Then, all of a sudden, the front door opens. I scream so loud the neighbours eardrums could pop. It can't be Mum or Dad.

He then appeared right in front of me. 'Hello, you must be Scott?'

I'm thinking to myself, *How does he know my name I have never seen him in my life?*

'I am a secret agent. My name is Adam and I was the one who stole your mother's necklace.'

'But why?'

In a deep voice he continued, 'Because this necklace is extremely dangerous and cannot be in the hands of an ordinary human. This necklace has a tracking device in it that is monitored by some very dangerous people. Probably the person who sold this necklace to your mother had no idea how dangerous it is. That's why I need to take it. It will be safe in the hands of my crew. I hope you understand.'

'Yes, I understand but one question. Could you just take the tracking device out so I can have the necklace?'

'Sure you can but I am going to need a decoy necklace to give to my boss.'

'I've got just the thing!' I fly up the stairs to get the cheap necklace and hand it to Adam.

He is pleased. 'Perfect! Now buddy, you must promise that you won't tell anyone about me or about what is happening right now. Got it?'

'Yes sir. I'll get rid of the evidence at once. Oh, here's your weird gadget thingy and a note I found on the floor. Could you tell me what it means.'

'Well, if you decode it, it says - Top Secret Agent.'

'Oh cool.'

'Thank you because for a while I thought I had lost those two things. By the way, you'd make an amazing detective.'

'Thanks. Bye!' I said.

'Till we meet again kid.' He then left.

Now I have the necklace in my hands. I went to my mum's room and stared at the returned necklace and then closed the drawer. Did all that really happen?

I think I need a feast from Maccas. A great meal to top off a great day.

I go to bed full and exhausted.

The next morning I wake up feeling relieved that the crime is solved and I don't have anything to worry about for the little time I have left of the holiday. I walk downstairs, fully dressed, ready for my parents to come home in just a few minutes. I set up my cereal and while I am about to have my first spoonful, my parents arrive home.

'Hi Scott!' They both exclaimed.

'Hi Mum and Dad,' I mumbled with a mouthful of Coco Pops. I'm trying to contain myself. It is so hard not to tell them.

After I finish breakfast, dad asks 'Hey, Scott, what have you been doing while we were gone?'

I simply replied, 'Not much, just watched TV and read some books.'

FOUL PLAY AT SUMMERVILLE SCHOOL FOR GIRLS

LUCA SZANDALA
Uki, NSW

2020
YEARS 5-6 CATEGORY
FEMALE DETECTIVES

Why do people always stare at me? I'm no different to the rest of humanity, just a little bit inquisitive. My name is Hilda Grey and I'm 13. I am a huge bookworm and can start dancing randomly. Along with my strange self, I have another strange human that I am best friends with, Gwen Bate. See here, Gwen is a lot like me but again, she isn't. She can be psycho sometimes, correction, all the time except for one second out of all the years from Kindergarten to year seven she stopped and thought about her decision.

Gwen is 13 as well, but sometimes I wonder if she is a goat (she has a strange laugh). Now you can understand slightly why people stare at me? Answer – because I hang out with a goat. Now that you know me and Gwen, let me get started on a strange period of time when we were on our way to Summerville School for Girls. Gwen and I were standing waiting at the bus stop with our bags when a man approached us.

'Hey girlies, have you met a girl called Rachael Davis?' Gwen and I were professional detectives in-the-making, so we knew to be suspicious right away. We did know a girl from our primary school called Rachael Davis, she was the only one who respected us, so we decided to play it cool.

'Nope.' We said in unison, looking very satisfied. Without noticing a girl called Rachael Davis walked up to us and exclaimed, 'Hi Hilda, Hi Gwen!' My brain automatically turned off like a bullet had hit my head.

The man started up again. 'Hi Rachael, remember we need to talk,

about some medical stuff.' Rachael blinked and replied, 'Right, yeah.'
They walked off and started talking about something (assuming I'm
right) secretive.

'That was weird, hey Hilda?' Gwen wondered. I shuffled slightly.

'Yeah, what a way to start school up again, I'll end up with that
question stuck in my head at midnight' I replied. Before we could talk
more about what we thought was going on, Rachael walked back with
a frown.

'You, okay?' I asked with uncertainty. Rachael nodded and pulled her
bags on her back. The bus pulled up and we embarked on our journey
to college. The ride to college felt longer than eternity and many men
in suits, who looked exactly the same, kept appearing. We departed
and strode into our old home, though it certainly didn't feel like home.
As us, the trio, walked into school something felt eerie and unsafe. It
certainly looked like fog was covering the rough concrete. Once we
made it further into the school we saw a TV crew for some news channel
and police tape around the entrance of the gym. Gwen and I exchanged
looks and bolted to the crime scene. Alerted, we asked many questions.

'What happened?' Gwen interrogated. The police officer glanced at
us with disrespect.

'Do you go to this school?' The police officer demanded.

'Yes, duh. Can you answer my question, official?' Gwen craved
sarcastically. The police officer frowned.

'Well, do you know Mrs Miracle?'

'Yeah.' I answered, just wanting his answer.

'She's my step-mother and we... we found her dead, in the gym. It
looks like she got stabbed from behind.'

The police officer was nearly in tears. I gasped.

'When did it happen?'

'It seems as though it was late at night. She told me she would be
working late because of a special class project the next day.'

Gwen clasped her notebook out of her pocket and scribbled away.
Gwen attentively looked up.

'Where about in the back was she stabbed, have you measured the
length? You should check across the road or in this area for knives
dropped around, measure them and if the wound is the correct length

as the wound, get the fingerprints and arrest!' Gwen stated, slightly boasting. Don't tell her I said that.

'Huh huh, seems like we have a smart one, I hope you guys aren't scared of gruesome stuff, because I believe we may need your help.' The police officer urged, gobsmacked. We simply indicated that we were keen and, within minutes, we were in a police car, on our way to the police station, ready to start an interview – an interview to see if we were ready to become junior detectives or forensic police officers. The police officer kept going on and on about how smart we were and how good it would be for the police team to have junior detectives. They can fit in small spaces, run fast, etc.

When we arrived at the police station, there were several scary looking people being questioned by the police. One I recognised, he was the man that talked to Rachael earlier, which made me even more suspicious about that dude. All the rest looked like bikies, with their leather jackets and spikes.

While we strolled inside, I had a very important inquiry to ask the police officer.

'After all this time, what is your name?' The young man stopped.

'Long name. Oliver Bee Birch Bay Byrn Miracle. But you can just call me Olly.' Gwen wrote something down in her notepad. Olly led us into the police station and immediately took us to a room. A scary looking Grandpa guy started asking us questions.

'Age?'

'13.'

'Name?'

'Hilda Grey and Gwen Bate.'

'Abilities?'

'Great detective skills. We have solved multiple murder cases.'

'What would you like to do here?'

'Become junior detectives, sir.'

'You've got the job. You may leave the room and start investigating this peculiar case.' Gwen and I reluctantly left the room and then Gwen sped-walked straight to Olly, to ask more questions.

'What is your father's name?'

'Dr Miracle'

'How old is he?'

'50'

'Where were you in the time of the crime scene?'

'At work, and then I got a call'

'What time do you work?' I questioned.

'Day shifts' said Olly. Gwen smiled.

'That is all I need right now.' Together we walked off. Gwen held her head up high.

'Will we discuss this-'

'Not till we speak to Dr Miracle.'

Gwen progressed up to Dr Miracle, who gave a polite grin.

'How can I help you girls?'

'I just have a few questions for you' I gritted my teeth.

'We' Gwen went on, ignoring me.

'Where was Olly when the crime scene happened?'

'He went out for dinner.'

'Where were you?'

'At home, watching the footy.'

'Okay and–' Multiple police officers marched up to Dr Miracle.

'You are under arrest for murder, Dr Miracle.' Dr Miracle gasped.

'I didn't-' A crowd started to form around the scene. The police handcuffed Dr Miracle.

'STOP! I believe that I am a qualified junior detective and I command you to stop what you are doing right now! I have evidence of who it was and it was not Dr Miracle. If you please take the handcuffs off the man, I will explain.' Gwen shouted.

I leaned over and whispered,

'I thought we were meant to solve the case together?' Gwen frowned.

'We did.' By this point I was very confused, but then it all made sense.

'Yesterday Oliver Miracle murdered Mrs Miracle.' Oliver started to protest but the police officer held her hand up.

'Go on.'

'How did we find out? When we saw the crime scene at our school, we asked Olly when did it happen? He said it seemed to be overnight. I had come to gather that Olly was suspicious. I asked him some more questions. I said 'where were you at the time of the crime? and he said he was at work'.

Then my lovely partner here, Hilda, asked the key question, what time do you work and he said 'day shift'. Little did Hilda know that she was the one who solved the case on the spot. 'I had already got enough evidence for him to be arrested but I decided to talk to his father for further evidence. I asked his father where Olly was at the time of the crime and Dr Miracle said Oliver had told him that he was going out for dinner. It is clear that Oliver killed her. Dr Miracle had a wonderful and friendly relationship with Mrs Miracle. To me it seems that Oliver killed her, possibly because he was jealous of how well she was getting along with her Dad. Perhaps he missed his mum and thought that his step-mum didn't deserve his Dad.' Gwen took a deep breath and I patted her on the back. The senior policeman blinked.

'Well, what do you have to say for yourself, recently fired police officer?'

'I didn't do it.' Police started to surround him as they handcuffed the correct assassin.

'You will be seen in court and I believe you will be found guilty.' The crowd started to disperse as the TV crew started to film the local news.

'Breaking news! I am here at Summerville Police Station as two young girls have just arrested an assassin who murdered his step-mother. I will hand it over to the two girls who solved this mysterious case.' The cameraman steered over to Hilda and Gwen who were laughing and embracing each other.

'Hello clever girls, what are your names?'

'I am Hilda and this is my partner in crime, haha, Gwen.' I smiled at the camera.

'How does it feel to solve a case?'

'Wonderful, except that we've solved heaps before already.' Gwen bragged.

'WOW! Have you got a job at the police station?'

'Yes we do, we are junior female detectives.'

'I believe you have inspired many young and older girls to be a strong person in life.' Said the reporter.

Gwen smiled and yelled into the camera, 'Go for your life girls, you are strong and if anyone wants to join the junior female detectives, have an interview and join the club.' The reporter grinned and said into the camera.

'Well, there you have it, a once in a lifetime live interview, on Summerville News.' The cameraman strolled off with the reporter looking delighted.

The girls turned to see Dr Miracle standing before them. 'Hey kiddos, thanks for sticking up for me back there.'

'It's what we do, you do not deserve to go to jail when you didn't do a thing wrong.'

The head police officer barged into the conversation. 'Well done girls, after showing amazing leadership I am raising you both to Head Junior Female Detectives.'

The girls started jumping up and down on the spot.

'That's a big title.' Gwen replied. The girls had many more interviews and conversations that day before they headed back to school. I guess it was half happy ever after?

THE MIDNIGHT MURDER

SHAKAYA TRIFFITT
Mowbray, Tasmania

2022
YEARS 5-6 CATEGORY
AGATHA CHRISTIE IN TASMANIA

So, my name is Shakaya, and this short story is about a murder at what was my favourite place to enjoy a coffee, 'Blue Café' in Invermay in Tasmania. Blue Café has outside and inside dining areas at Inveresk beside the Tasmanian Museum and the University of Tasmania. In addition, a tram line runs right past on which my brother is a conductor. My life at Blue Café and in general is pretty good with the ups and downs of being a young woman. Sometimes things are 'rough' and other times or sometimes at the same time things are pretty good.

I have lots of people in my life some of them are good and others are not so good. These people are in my story too such as Allianah, Zabia, Bridget, Connor, Oliver, Tate and Amelia. I could tell you who is good and who isn't but that will become clearer during this story. But I can tell you that one of these people is the murderer and that person is someone I really do not like!

So on with this story. Often, I get coffee cravings. This night I had one at 11.30pm on a Friday night. Crazy I know as coffee doesn't help sleep but well it's just what I wanted. I live nearby so walked to Blue Café hoping they were still serving late dinners. And they were, thank God! As I walk into Blue, I get that feeling that brings goose bumps to your skin and creepy and suspicious feeling seeped through my mind. I looked around and everything seemed normal, but I still felt all wrong from the surroundings. I had never had this feeling so strongly before. It is weird. It made me think that something bad was going to happen! But I decided to ignore these feelings and thoughts and I focused on getting my coffee.

I ordered a large latte and of course made eyes at the cakes and then decided to also have a cake. The cake I chose was a delicious looking carrot cake. I haven't the words to describe how good the cake looked other than to say, *It was so good!* After ordering I noticed a voice that was familiar coming from the kitchen area. Who was that? I knew that voice, a male voice with a noticeable high soft tone. I looked but couldn't see anyone. The voice stopped and I thought perhaps I had imagined it.

So, after ordering the latte and cake at the counter, I took my table number and found a spot to sit. This was outside on the deck below the night sky. I had a clear view of the beautiful midnight sky that was covered in stars. While looking up and admiring the view I relaxed into my seat. I began daydreaming, or should that be sky dreaming, about nice things. I was thinking about wanting a sweet cuddly kitten like my mum has. I had enjoyed playing with mums' kitten today and now I allowed myself to consider what it would be like to have a kitten all of my own to love and hold and feed and clean up after. (Cross that last bit out as that wouldn't be so much fun). A kitten would be a buddy at home.

While I was dreaming about kittens, under the night sky, the waiter came out with the cake and latte. She said 'lovely evening' having looked at me with eyes to the sky.

I jump in surprise at her voice. 'Yes yes, it is. Thank you very much for the latte and carrot cake to make my night the very best.'

'You're welcome,' says the waiter with a glance at the sky and a smile.

As she walks away I turn my eyes to what she has brought me and sat on my table. The cake looks perfect and the latte looks like it had to be sipped straight away. I pick the latte up with fingertips of both hands as the glass is hot and carefully take a sniff, I note it smells warm and strong and then I take a sip. The taste is amazing, and I quickly follow with a slurp! I place the cup down and look at the cake already anticipating the sweet, moist smooth taste. As I reach for the cake fork I notice a burning deep in my throat. I start to feel dizzy and lightheaded. I felt worse and worse, this was a feeling of death! I felt really scared before collapsing onto the deck where I quickly died!

Although I was dead, I could see what was happening around me! What had happened? I decided to have a look around to find out what had killed me. I started by looking at the latte. I realised there was something off about the latte. At the bottom of the clear glass latte cup was a powdery substance that was not coffee! This was poison. I had been poisoned by latte!

An investigator, D.I. Connor, came to view the scene 3 hours later. He examined my body due to my surprising death, 'This girl has been poisoned by the latte!' he declared. D.I. Connor knew it was the latte because the carrot cake had not been eaten and the latte had a few sips out of it.

The next day D.I. Connor came by to interview the people that were present when the crime happened. The first person he interviewed was the person who made the latte.

'So, I hear you were the one who made the latte?' D.I. Connor asked. 'Yes, sir I am the Barista and I made the latte. I did leave it sitting in the kitchen for a minute or two to do something but when I came back it all looked fine.'

'Ok thank you for that. But I do need to ask some questions. Is that ok with you?' he says.

'Yes that's ok with me.' The barista says.

'Ok where do I start, what did you put in the latte madam?' he asks, 'Sir I put coffee, water and milk in a latte!' she says.

'Ok madam thank you for your time, I don't have much time but what is your name may I ask?' he asks.

'Oh, my name is Bridget and the person who has sadly passed in the café was my daughter and I love her with all my heart!' the mum says.

'Really!! Ok have a good day!' said D.I. Connor.

D.I. Connor then moves on to speak with the kitchen hand, Tate.

'Hello there, is your name is Tate, am I right?' he asks.

'Yes, my name is Tate!' Tate says looking away from D.I. Connor's face.

'Ok so you do know there was a crime here yesterday?' he asks. 'Yes, umm yeah I know why... erm?' Tate says suspiciously.

D.I. Connor gazed at Tate, and says 'Did you go near the latte yesterday?' Tate mumbles 'Eeermm, no I didn't...why?' again suspiciously.

'Are you sure about that?' D.I. Connor asks.

'Umm yeah why do you have to ask anyway?' Tate says once again.

'Ok, I don't think you are telling the truth I'm going to have to take you down to the station to find out more.'

Tate yells, 'You can't do that!' he yells.

'I think you killed Shakaya, and you are going to the station,' said D.I. Connor.

D.I. Connor takes Tate to the unmarked police car and drives him to the station to question him more about the murder at Blue Café.

As Tate climbs out of the car at the station he tries to get away from but the investigator held him so tight so he couldn't get away. Tate is taken inside the interrogation room.

At the same time another detective arrives to interview the only other employee of Blue who had been working that night. The chef.

'Hello, my name is Meg and I'm investigating the murder of Shakaya,' says the detective.

'Hello Meg, my name is Zabia. I miss Shakaya so much; she was like a sister to me! I can't get over her death. Do you know who murdered Shakaya!? If so, please tell me! I need to know! I love her a lot and now she's dead.' Zabia says starting to tear up.

'Ok I see your really upset about the death of Shakaya. And we have took Tate up to the station to look him up a bit more. Due because he was acting weird a bit.' Says the investigator.

'Ok thank you for telling me. Tate was funny about Shakaya. Sometimes he thought he was in love with her and then he would get jealous of her and my friendship. I'm not sure because he didn't want to share me or Shakaya. We were meeting up here and I didn't know she sat outside, and I thought we were sitting inside. I must of not asked her where to sit. I must have forgotten to ask! This is all my fault that's she's dead!' says Zabia crying his eyes out.

'No it wasn't your fault. Someone bad hurt her and I don't think that was you,' said detective Meg.

So, there it is. Days after my death someone was arrested after confessing to the murder. Can you guess who it was? It won't be a surprise really. Tate killed me because he hated me for taking Zabia away from him! He was jealous and wanted me out of the way.

I watch over my friends and family now and love it when they talk together. I wish I could take their pain away, like when Zabia said to my mum, 'I'm very sorry. I feel like Shakaya's death is all on me. Can I do anything to make it up to you?' he says started crying a bit.

'Well, no Zabia, you didn't do anything it is Tate's twisted mind. I know you think it's your fault, but it isn't,' says Bridget.

Although I'm dead I have been very lucky to have such good friends and family. Plus, hey if you must die, dying by coffee isn't so bad.

425 AVENUE STREET

RUBY WELSTEAD
Dover, Huon Valley

2020
YEARS 5-6 CATEGORY
FEMALE DETECTIVES

The worn leather on my jacket settled on my shoulder blade perfectly without any help. I lock the bedroom door before weighing myself down on the cotton fibres of my soft bed. I stare effortlessly up at the chipping ceiling, and stare at several important newspapers I have hung along with it.

Isla Lockwood killed, Lucy Greenfield killed, Emily Tiger killed, Yama Owe killed, Uki Signs killed.

I know somehow the killer is leaving clues for me, but their identity remains unknown. It's driving me crazy! The descriptions of how they were killed mean nothing, a small paragraph each of how the weapon was used, and no clues. The names are what I'm focusing on. I met all of them the day before they were killed, so I know I have a stalker, a very secret stalker. I renounce having to see anyone right now, they might be killed as well.

I've been staring at these as long as I can remember. Every time I bought one, the puzzle was harder to put together. The pieces don't fit. It takes time, but in a situation like this, I don't know if I have any time before the alarm goes off.

I shut my eyes, slowly after I feel a shock of cold metal dig into my head.

'HEY!' I yell, grasping my head in immense pain. It's only a matter of time before I acknowledge the headache that the gash has given me and fall backwards. The killer has escaped. Painfully, I step up, and watch the car screech along the dirt road. My vision goes blurry, so I take this chance to stare at my crumpling newspapers. The capitals on the headlines from all their names glow in the pale moonlight. Did they do something to my newspapers?

'Snap out of it!' I tell myself. Nothing is happening. It's just my mind. But just to be safe... I rip the newspapers off the ceiling and tear away the first letters on their first and last names. Is it a pattern? How should I arrange it? Alphabetically? Seems not. The order I hung them? No.

'The order they were killed,' I say out loud. For a second I try to control my eye focus. It's painful but working. I rest the pieces on the floor as it reads out:

ILL GET YOUS

I pivot around until eventually I land on my bed. I'll get yous. The puzzle has been put together. Who are they looking for, is it me? Seems so, they have just stabbed me after all. But why is it a plural? Are they looking for more than me? Why? And who? This make no sense. Who will die? Do I know them? Is that why their after more than me?

The questions hurt even more that my headache. Is it my family? Because nobody touches my family.

I push my weak body off the bed and force its only strength down the loopy staircase. I clumsily grab my fedora off the wooden hat rack. It takes a minute to get down through the archway and out the heavy door. The rubble trips me more than once in the first five steps. I feel severely ill, but I need to find them.

My family.

No clues, just relying on that detective instinct of mine. I pull my black fedora over my bloody wound and continue down the street. I don't need any attention right now. I check my wristwatch for a precise time. Five-thirty A.M. I don't feel restless. Probably because I have better things to worry about.

Ding dong!

That's the sound I hear before the pounding rushed footsteps. The pounding becomes adjusting of locks, and the door swings open to produce my mother and my stepsister, Linda.

'LIA!' screeches my mother.

'Yes?' I reply, forcing to hide my fear and pain.

'It is FIVE FOURTY IN THE MORNING!!' she says in a terrible scream that is only pleasant for things without ears.

'I realise that. Where is he?' I ask.

Mother looks back into the house and screams his name. The house repels the echoes of her voice and it sends a chill down my spine.

'MAX! MAX!' But yet she is unintended with his reliving reply. My head sears in pain and I remember what I came here for. I know what has happened.

'Out of my way!'

'LIA!'

My stepbrother, Max. He's in trouble. I need to find him before it's too late.

I bolt up the rickety stairs and try remembering which room he was in. Think, think, think! The room at the end of the hall! I push through the door and a bloody body, dying in his bed. His bloody body, dying in his bed.

'Max...?' I whimper.

His chest is bruised and in there is a deep gash in the middle, oozing deep red blood.

'Hey Lia.'

'Don't leave me!' For life, he has been the only one to support me, the only person who I would obey the rule; respect your elders.

'I'm sorry,' he said. 'You have to find who is doing this.'

He hands me a bloody piece of paper the killer must have left behind. I push some of his thick, brown hair out of his crystal eyes.

'NO! DON'T LEAVE ME!'

'Goodbye Lia.'

I whimper until the colour drains out of his face, till the last tear rolls down his blood-stained cheek.

I push his eyelids over his eyes, being careful of his long eyelashes. Before I leave, I plant a wet kiss on his lips and sit on his rug and watch him in his peaceful rest.

Mother and Linda walk into the room and jump at his appearance. I take off my fedora to pay my respects, and forget I was trying to cover up something.

'W-w-hat is going on?' Mother is almost inconsolable. His face rolls to the side and she sees his and my wound.

'LIA! YOUR HEAD!' Linda screams.

I stumble over, realising what a terrible mistake I made, and swiftly force the fedora on my head. They stare at me, thinking if they saw that or not. Mother comes over and rips the hat off my head.

'Lia?' she looks worried.

'Yeah?' I say, covering it as if that's going to do anything.

'OUT!' she screams.

'What?'

'I don't need some witchcraft happening! That was MY SON!!'

'But mother it wasn't-'

'OUT!' she says, signalling me to the door.

I swiftly take the fedora out of her hand, and head on my way. Before I leave, I sneer at Linda so close to her face that she stumbles over and lands on the carpet.

I take the note and read: 425 Avenue Street.

Is this some sort of code? Or just an easy access to their house? Either way, I'm going to find this house. I take the ten-minute walk back to my house and hop into my caravan. I have no clue where this house is, but it has to be somewhere around here. I place the desired key into the keyhole and start the engine. I tear away the curtains on the windows, letting the soothing moonlight flow into the driver's seat.

I take time to think about Max and how I couldn't be there to save him. But was this just to aggravate me? Or was he a part of this? This war between detective and murderer? No, he couldn't have. Too kind, too gentle. Never in his life would he have seen the world in the way of my eyes. He's not that kind of guy, he never would have been.

I feel the little shock of the cold-water flow from my cheek onto the leather steering wheel and drop to my blood-stained pants.

I look at the note and turn on my google maps. 'Siri, locate 425 Avenue Street.' I hear the beeps of approval and watch as the screen lights up with the road around me. It seems about fifteen minutes away. Why? This isn't a proper chase? Fifteen minutes? This seems like a trick. But even though the brewing thoughts remain in my tiny head, I continue.

I look outside the window and watch for any suspicious activity. Nothing yet. This can't be the killers address. Maybe it was their next destination, the next destination for a murder.

I halt at the next stop after seeing a man, close to the road, desperately looking for something.

'May I help you, sir?' I ask.

He stares up at me and smiles, 'Yes, yes, I'm looking for a small piece of paper. You see, um, yes, it has a very important address on it.'

My eyes agog in shock. Could this be him? A middle-aged man who looks like he has no business stabbing knives into people's heads. I try not to look stunned; it will only give away my character. Wait, why doesn't he know my character? Was I rolled to one side? Was I too quick bolting up that he didn't see my face? Does he think I'm dead? Because if he was attempting that, the heart is the best way to go.

Is it because I have the fedora on...?

'Sorry sir, I will be back. I just need to make an important call.'

Before he can reply, I run back to the van and call the police. I tell them where we are, and that I'll distract him till they get there.

I hop out of the van and return to him. 'Ugh, sorry, had to call mother. She was worried where I was.' I try to look realistically emotional, and not play that fake sarcasm I always seem to give off.

'That's fine dear,' he says.

The wind howls vigorously and makes a snap in one of the trees next to him. He turns around to investigate the sound. As he does, my fedora blows away over the gate next to me. I let out a howl and turn around when he comes to look back at me. He sighs and then comes and wraps his arm around my shoulder. I squeeze into a ball to release his grip.

'What the matter?' he cries.

Just before he says that I hear the loud monstrous sirens as the police cars screech down the road. He jitters and then turns back to me.

'I really have to go,' he says, stumbling over one foot and then the other.

'Sorry, but you're not going anywhere!'

I grab his arms and hook them around mine. He stares up at me, and then screams, finally realising who I am.

'Remember me?' I say drunkenly.

The cops pull up in front of my van, and take him away, forcing him into the somewhat small vehicle.

He curses at me as the car becomes smaller and smaller. I start walking home, feeling my head delicately. It's fine now, thank the gods.

I stop and say one thing before I carry on:

'You've done good Lia, you've done good.'

THE CASE OF THE MISSING DOG

LAUREN WHITE
ACT

2020
YEARS 5-6 CATEGORY
  FEMALE DETECTIVES

'How do you plead Mr Rumplesturgess?'

'Guilty, your Honour'. Archibald Rumplesturgess shook his head and looked down, defeated by the system he tried to cheat.

I looked over the old, crowded room to see I had won the case! I turned to see my two greatest allies smiling at me.

'Good job El! We did it!'

'Mike, I can't believe it! We did do it!' I grabbed my friend's hand in excitement. Suddenly, I remembered – school. I quickly got my friends and ran back home. I had to feed my dog Luna and get her into the backyard. She needed her breakfast and a chance to play. Mike and I rushed to school and arrived just in the nick of time. RING RING! The red bell screamed.

'Well, well, just in time Miss Magnolia,' I looked up to see the towering giant who was Mrs Anderson, my Year 10 Head of School. She had always frightened me, perhaps it was her height or the tone of her voice. She sounded like thunder most of the time and she had the personality to match.

'I uhhh was ummmm...' I was lost for words; I was just like a statue. Mike grabbed my hand and hurried me off to class. He knew I wasn't going to say or do anything useful standing there with Mrs Anderson. Why was I such a dummy around her?

The school day passed without incident. I was preoccupied with thinking about Mr Rumplesturgess and how he tried to steal his father's car. Mike and I stopped him when we realised that he had pretended to be his father's valet when he picked it up from the mechanic. He had a lot of gambling debt and wanted to sell it to pay it all off.

'Sigh, they never learn do they?' I thought. All these people doing bad things in the world. I smiled a little, still, plenty of work for amateur detectives then!

'See you Monday Magnolia.' Mrs Anderson woke me from my daydream. Where had she come from? How could someone so large move so quietly? I groaned.

Mike caught up with me in the corridor as we walked out of school at the end of the day. I wanted to go to the Cruft's Dog Show in the morning. We both loved dogs and l wanted to enter our dogs into the show.

'Hey meet me at Cruft's tomorrow and bring Lilly 'kay?' I asked in an excited tone. Lilly was a Doberman and she was beautiful.

'Sure, see you then,' Mike replied with an ounce of distaste in his voice. Mike really loved dogs but was not excited about entering Lilly into the show. Mike's mother was very private and wasn't keen on having the family's dog made famous because of the show.

The next day the already busy streets of London were crowded with more tiny heads because of Crufts dog show. I met up with Mike and his Doberman, Lilly. Luna was jumping with delight to see Lilly. They were good friends and had known each other since they were puppies. We entered the arena to see thousands of different dogs and people. So many people! It was a little overwhelming I had to admit. Still, I was determined to enter Luna in the competition.

As we wandered around, I noticed an enormously overweight man in a nice white suit. He was wearing a monocle and had the most ridiculous handlebar moustache.

'Ah yes hello! I'm Mr Abercrombie and this is Princey!' he said, showing us his Shiba Inu. Princey was a beautiful tan coloured dog with a black and white diamond collar that sparkled in the arena lights. I couldn't take my eyes of it.

'I will get first place! You look like a twentieth place with your mutt! Oh, ho ho!' Mr Abercombie said in a snooty tone.

'My dog is actually a Labrador crossed with a Kelpie which only lives in Australia! That's pretty interesting actually so you can stop being so boastful!' My eyes were flaming with anger because of this aristocratic knuckle head! I could not get over how rude he was.

Before Mr Abercrombie could reply and before I had a chance to glare at him further we were interrupted by another man. He was extraordinary looking with a top hat, a black suit and a gold monocle. He was also very tall and very slim.

'Hello Miss, I'm Charles Hamilton!' The man said.' You look new to Crufts and as runner up last year, I am definitely the person to help you if you need it.' He was holding the lead of a King Charles Spaniel that reminded me of Lady from Lady and the Tramp. She was beautiful and I could see why he was runner up last year. The winner must have been stunning.

'Runner up,' Abercrombie said with disgust. 'There's only one winner around here and that's me.' I watched him poke himself in his chest with his thumb. It was clear that the two men did not like each other.

'Miss, you had better go and get set up for the show before this unpleasant man ruins the day for everyone,' Charles Hamilton said, glaring at Mr Abercrombie. Mike and I walked away as quickly as we could. They were two very strange and angry men. I was hoping they wouldn't interfere with the show and we could enjoy our day.

A short time later Mike and I heard a shriek. We turned and looked to see Mr Abercrombie crying and wailing.

'HELP!! PRINCEY IS MISSING!!! HELP!!!' He was screaming and yelling like a toddler having a meltdown. Mike and I rushed over to see what was going on.

'Mr Abercrombie, what's happened? Where's Princey?' I asked. I disliked him but I didn't like to see anyone in so much distress.

'Someone stole my Princey,' he sobbed. 'There's blood on the floor so whoever stole him must have been bitten by Princey when they took him.'

I could see there were drops of blood on the ground. Princey's lead was on the table nearby but there was no sign of Princey or his diamond collar. I wondered whether he was stolen to get the collar or if it was because he was the prize winner.

'Mike, what do you think, can we do this?'

'El, of course. I'm already thinking of who we need to talk to. First on my list is Hamilton. The two of them clearly don't get along and I think there's some jealousy there. That's a good motive!'

'Don't be so rude, Mike. He seems like a nice man. Perhaps we shouldn't jump to conclusions so early. Let's start with Mr Abercrombie's staff. They may know something.'

We grabbed my blue ruled notebook and a cherry red ink pen. Mike and I spent the rest of the morning racing around the arena talking to people we thought could be suspects. It didn't take long to rule out the head of the Crufts because he was allergic to Shiba Inus. Mr Abercrombie's staff were all out the back at the time of the theft and hadn't heard or seen anything. We were getting desperate when we noticed Mr Charles Hamilton near the First Aid office.

Mike and I stood back, watching. We saw him through the window, clutching at his arm. The nurse pointed to the spot on his arm where he held a handkerchief which, from a distance, looked like it was soaked in blood. I gasped. Surely he wasn't our thief?

Mike and I ran over to the First Aid Office and burst through the door. We saw Princey and Charles Hamilton's dog sitting next to each other in the corner.

Charles Hamilton looked shocked. 'I can explain everything,' he said. 'All the years I have been in this dog show Ronald Abercrombie has been rude and nasty to me and my dog Ruby. Princey has always loved seeing me and Ruby and the two dogs are good friends. I decided I would take Princey as payback for Ronald's rudeness over the last few years.'

I was torn. Mr Abercrombie was a rude, horrible man but he deserved to get his dog back. Mr Hamilton was a good man but did the wrong thing. The Crufts owner came through the door and said that he heard the conversation and decided that he would ban Mr Abercrombie from the show from now on for being a bully and for being so horrible to other competitors.

Mr Abercrombie got his dog back and Mr Hamilton left Crufts with a dog bite and nothing else to show for his efforts. Mike and I felt sorry for him so we invited him and Ruby to join us for ice cream after the show. He was grateful for the company so we left, having not even managed to enter our dogs in the show. What a day!

We walked out of the arena as the London sky faded into darkness littered with glittering stars.

SNUFFED IN SNUG

NEVE WINDSOR
Huonville, Huon Valley

2022
YEARS 5-6 CATEGORY
AGATHA CHRISTIE IN TASMANIA

It was a sunny morning and Miss Marple was preparing herself to go out to catch up with a friend from Western Australia. Her name was Mrs Clarise Gordon. Miss Marple was her usual self, so she couldn't wait to dig up some gossip from this particular friend who shared the exact same interests as herself.

Miss Marple got in her car and started the engine. The roar of the engine was enough to drown the sound of a dragon's roar. Miss Marple was going to Longley's Hotel with such an energetic smile you thought she would've crashed her car. As Miss Marple hopped out of her car she heard her friend calling her name in the distance.

Miss Marple and Mrs Gordon sat at the bar where they could see almost everyone in the room.

'How have you been going my old friend, it's been long time no see!' exclaimed Mrs Gordon.

'I hear you've moved apartments to a cosy flat down in Snug.'

'Well it's been wonderful. How's it been going in Western Australia.'

'Hang WA! I read some jolly good gossip in the paper about Dr Randle marring a woman half his age. Her name was something like Elenore Leone, she probably only married him for the money, I mean if it was me, that's why I would marry him.'

Mrs Gordon turned around and said with a quiet voice, 'Why, would you look at that, there's Mrs Randle over there!'

'Clarise I hate to cut in, but the man she's sitting with is not Dr Randle', whispered Miss Marple.

Miss Marple and her friend watched Mrs Randle and the man holding hands and having a rather romantic lunch. How odd was that? Miss Marple thought.

She said her goodbyes to Clarisse and said 'I hope to see you again soon dear friend.' And off Miss Marple went.

Later that day Elenore Randle was out outside of the start of the Snug Falls track. Dr Randle and she were side by side waiting for the host of their hiking club to arrive. Johnathon Nero was next to arrive all loaded with his walking sticks and hiking boots. He was followed by Nigel Lovelace the head of the walking group. 'Ok everybody we are right to start walking.' Exclaimed Nigel.

The walk would've been quick but since they were advanced walkers they made their own track and walked up to the top of the waterfall. Everyone else went for a look around whilst Dr Randle and Elenore stood and admired the view of the waterfall. Elenore could hear a clicking noise as if one that would come from some sort of mints container.

The next day there was a case in the newspaper saying Dr Randle slipped whilst bush walking at Snug Falls and fell to a deep dark death. Now Miss Marple being the town busy body decided to walk up Snug Falls to see where Dr Randle had supposably fallen to his death.

She hired some one named Sam Brooklyn to walk her up to the top of the waterfall. When she saw the way the rocks were and how the waterfall was formed she knew almost instantly this was no accident. Only a fool could've fallen off there and Dr Randle was no fool. This had to have been murder that was the only conclusion Miss Marple had.

Soon she saw a detective come out to the top of the waterfall to check it out himself. Miss Marple had no time to waste. Later that day she saw Mrs Randle and asked her a few questions. She said 'it was just such a terrible accident he slipped and then he fell.' Miss Marple knew this was obviously a lie. From the corner of her vision Miss Marple remembered seeing a purple mints container on top of the waterfall and wondered what this could mean. She went to talk next to Nigel Love lace. Seeing him she remembered him from the pub he was the man out at lunch with Mrs Randle.

Nigel said, 'Me and Johnathon left Dr Randle and Elenore at the top of the waterfall together and then later on Johnathon needed to do a bush-wee, so he went off to do his business somewhere.'

'Thank you very much Nigel.' Expressed Miss Marple.

Next, she was off to talk to Johnathon Nero. Johnathon was playing with a purple mint container and he was clicking the lid up and down impatiently.

'I just needed to do a wee, so I left that is all. Well and then Elenore came running back and told us about the you know.'

Miss Marple started to put all her facts together and called everyone down. Nigel, Johnathon and Elenore faces as white as sheets were all sitting ready to listen, so Miss Marple began. 'Elenore and Randel were left on top of the water fall whilst Johnathon and Nigel were exploring till you Johnathon needed to wee. Though we all know that wasn't really your intent. You hid in a bush with your lolly container clicking. You were spying on Elenore and Randle. Nigel and Elenore had secretly been having a love affair as I discovered whilst having lunch at Longley's pub. Johnathon stood there and watched Elenore push Randle off the cliff. You Elenore like any other had a motive you wanted money. Johnathon watched you and then came out and threatened to share your secret if you didn't kiss him. He was blackmailing you. To then pull the facts off your self you placed a mints container you knew he always had on him at the top of the waterfall leading all suspicions onto him.

'Well I just needed money.' Yelled Elenore. 'None the less I am afraid you're going to jail. I've already notified the inspector and the police. I'm afraid you're going away for many, many years.'

SOPHIE AND THE LOST KEY

JOANNA WU
Hobart, Tasmania

2022
YEARS 5-6 CATEGORY
  AGATHA CHRISTIE IN TASMANIA

Sophie always longed for an adventure.

As a six-year-old girl, she might surprise people with her insatiable curiosity about life. Even her parents sometimes needed to find good reasons if they wanted her to obey, not to mention her elder sister Meg, whom Sophie often called a 'goodie-goodie'.

On a Friday, Sophie and her family went to the State Library of Tasmania after school. Sophie was keen on the visit, though Meg didn't seem so. As they entered the main room, Sophie grabbed her favourite book, The Holidays. She loved the adventurous dramas and heart-warming moments in the story. Meanwhile, Meg took her favourite book, Camille and Madeline. This novel was a bit similar to The Holidays. But it also distinguished itself by those fancy French words in it.

The family had gone back downstairs when Sophie spotted an entrance featuring an old-fashioned door framed with luxuriously carved wood and adorned by erstwhile black-and-white photos. Even more photos and paintings decorated the walls leading to the entrance door.

As I mentioned earlier in the story, an adventurous child like Sophie wouldn't just shrug their arms and walk past such a peculiar place. They would either keep pestering their guardians until they allowed them or sneak there before anyone noticed. Sophie decided to try the former first, for she knew that if she begged her dad with that spoiled but convincing tone, he would let her. Anyway, let's proceed to the interesting part of the story – hopefully, I didn't bore you readers with too much voice-over.

'Look,' said Sophie promptly, pointing to the vintage door, 'Can we go there?' Most of the time, Sophie's parents were not averse to a harmless, novel experience. So Dad said with an interested tone, 'We certainly can.'

Above the door frame was a sign: The Alport Family Exhibition. Next to the door, there was a desk with a computer on it. On the computer screen, you could see live surveillance footage. A man was working at the desk. He looked somewhat nervous. Too kind to ignore him, Meg said, 'Are you alright, sir?' The man didn't seem very keen to answer a thirteen-year-old girl's question. However, the sparkles in her soft blue eyes made it impossible for him to say, 'Mind your own business.'

'I'm looking for a key. An antique key,' the man said.

Meg looked puzzled.

'For heaven's sake, Meg,' said Sophie, 'You don't even know what he is talking about!'

Apparently, the little girl was impatient at her sister's goodie-goodness.

Meg ignored Sophie and wished the man luck in the search.

'Sophie, don't talk to your sister in that manner,' said Mum, 'It is not very nice.'

'This place looks fun,' said Dad, 'Let's go and explore.'

Sophie went ahead of her parents, desperate to see the exhibition.

The first room, where the man was sitting at the desk, had a marble floor with a frosty sheen. A table with a glass top was also in the room. Peeking through the glass top, Sophie saw books that looked very old, and one of them lay open. It was a manuscript full of words made up of strange alphabets.

Meg explained to Sophie that this was how people wrote in the past. Then, near the table, Sophie saw a shelf containing even more old books and an exquisite fan appealing to her the most.

In the next room, Sophie saw paintings of men and women elegantly dressed, Chippendale chairs, and cupboards full of delicate porcelain cups with patterns of flowers, birds, and some unique shapes.

Then, they moved to the adjacent bedroom furnished with a Chippendale bed draped with fine linen fabric, beside which a classic wooden dressing table was positioned.

In the dining room that adjoined the bedroom, Sophie saw a huge portrait of a graceful woman in a turquoise silk gown. Neat ringlets defined her ruddy face, while a large bun secured them at the back of her crown. Suddenly, something caught Sophie's eyes – with an odd symbol on it, a rusty lock hung to the left of the painting. But just before she could reach the lock, Sophie heard Meg's voice—'Sophie, time to go'.

'I'm coming,' Sophie answered, gazing at the mysterious lock on the wall.

As Meg was dragging her to the exit, Sophie asked, more or less with a tone of disappointment, 'Can we come back tomorrow?'

'Of course,' Dad said without hesitation.

'I'd like to check the reading room upstairs, too,' Mum added.

The next day passed quickly. By the time Sophie finished the reading class, Meg had already been standing outside her classroom waiting for her.

'Sophie, your sister is here to pick you up', said Miss Murphy, Sophie's form teacher, with a cheerful smile. Sophie leapt out of her chair and said goodbye to Miss Murphy. Meg also said goodbye to the teacher, and the two girls headed straight to the library.

'Mummy and Daddy can't come with us today', said Meg.

'We'll be fine on our own,' answered Sophie.

When the girls arrived at the library, they went upstairs into the reading room. Meg quickly walked off to the shelves and started searching for books. Sophie was roaming about until she spotted a thick book entitled The Alport Family Album lying on the bottom of the shelf. She picked it up immediately. The book was full of photos and paintings of the things she had seen in the exhibition the day before. After swiftly turning the pages, Sophie put the book back.

As soon as she left the aisle, Sophie caught sight of a stranger figure out of the corner of her eye. It was an elderly woman – actually, the oldest one she had ever seen. From her pocket, the woman withdrew an old, rusty key; it bore the same symbol as the lock. She then hid the key in the book Sophie had just finished reading.

'Meg,' cried Sophie as she hurried towards her big sister.

'Shh!' Meg whispered angrily to Sophie, feeling embarrassed when several people turned and looked at them. 'This is a library; we're supposed to be quiet!'

Sophie paused and waited until everybody returned their attention to their reading. Then, she dashed to the bookshelf, took the key out of the book, and hurried back to Meg.

'Let's go to the Alport Family Exhibition,' Sophie suggested, in a hushed voice this time.

Meg was still feeling so embarrassed that she wanted to leave, too. So the two girls exited the room and headed downstairs. Upon reaching the ground floor, Sophie rushed into the exhibition despite Meg's lecture on proper behaviour in the library. She stopped by the painting of the beautiful woman and climbed onto the dining table once the coast was clear. With the guilt of doing something inappropriate, Sophie inserted the key into the lock beside the painting and turned it. All of a sudden, the painting opened like a door. Inside, Sophie saw nothing but a blazing light. She removed the key and promptly climbed in without giving it much thought. Immediately, she found herself in a daze.

'Why is it cold and wet?' This was her first thought when she regained her senses. It only took her seconds to find the answer to her confusion: she was in the middle of a creek, and the cold water was rushing past her feet.

'Are you alright?' Sophie heard a voice out of nowhere.

'I'm fine,' Sophie replied instinctively. She looked around and saw a young woman standing on the bank. Sophie made her way out of the water and approached the woman, closing the distance between them. To her surprise, the woman before her looked exactly like the one in the painting. In her hand, she held a fan that also looked familiar to Sophie.

'Who are you?' asked the little adventurer.

'I am Lily Alport,' answered the woman, 'And I know you are Sophie.'

'How do you know...' Sophie was so stunned that she couldn't even finish her question but stood there in disbelief, mouth agape.

'The key has already told me everything,' Lily smiled, 'It has chosen you over my great-great-granddaughter.'

'Do you mean the old lady I saw in the reading room?' asked Sophie.

'Yes,' answered Lily, 'You are a clever girl.'

'She failed to open the portal, though she knows how to read our family manuscript about the magic key.'

The images of those books filled with bizarre words floated into Sophie's mind again.

'Why did the key choose me?' Sophie asked. She has never been so curious before.

'I don't know yet,' Lily shook her head, 'But there must be a reason. We will probably find out in the future. Now that you are here, let me show you around.'

Lily led the way as her little guest followed her into a mansion near the creek. During the tour of the mansion rooms, Sophie saw all kinds of Chippendale furniture and exquisite porcelain. Elegantly dressed men and women ambled about, beaming warm smiles and nodding welcomes to Sophie as if they had already known her.

'This is amazing,' Sophie exclaimed, 'It's just like the exhibition.'

'C'est du déjà vu, n'est-ce pas?' Lily smiled, 'It is good to know that everything is well-maintained.'

Suddenly, it occurred to Sophie that Meg must be looking for her in the exhibition room.

'Lilly, I'm sorry, but I really have to go now,' said Sophie. Meanwhile, something sprang to her mind.

'Shall I give the key back to you?' She asked Lily, extending her hand that held the key.

'No,' the kind hostess replied, gently waving her hand. 'The key itself knows where to go. Don't worry.'

Lily led Sophie back to the creek.

'Step in, and you will return to your time,' Lily told Sophie, 'You might want to close your eyes.'

Sophie followed Lily's instructions after they bid each other farewell.

The next thing Sophie knew was finding herself in the Alport Family exhibition again. She scanned the room and then dashed off to search for Meg and found her at the 'Silver collection'.

'Don't run. There is no need,' Meg frowned at Sophie.

Sophie stopped, feeling a little puzzled.

'How long have we been here?' she asked seconds later.

'About fifteen minutes,' Meg answered calmly.

'I've got some good news for you,' Meg continued, 'The librarian found the key he had been looking for in that reading room'.

Astonished, Sophie opened her hand that had held the key tightly – yes, it had gone!

'It does know where to go,' Sophie murmured to herself.

'Somebody hid it in the book called The Murder of Roger Ackroyd,' Meg added, ignoring Sophie's self-talk, 'Anyway, I don't think it's something appropriate for young kids like you. Hey, what are you doing?'

Unexpectedly, Sophie hugged Meg fiercely, who then nervously looked around to see if anyone had noticed the scene.

'We are in a library, Sophie. How many times must I tell you—'

'Yeah, I know we're in a library,' the little sister chirped, 'So I want to find out more about the Alport family.'

Resignedly sighing, Meg said, 'That's okay. But no matter what you are imagining, you need to be quiet here.'

Together, the two girls carefully observed and read everything as they continued their visit in the exhibition. At the same time, it is about time that we turned our heads away and read another story about mysteries in Tasmania.

LADY JESS

GRACE WINSPEAR
Hobart, Tasmania

2019 WINNER
YEARS 5-6 CATEGORY
FEMALE BUSHRANGERS

I flew through the bush. I could feel the hot pulsing of my horse under my fingers. My breath came hard and fast. I allowed myself a fleeting glance to check behind me, all was quiet. I slowed, looking all around, alert and listening.

Suddenly, I heard the drumming of hooves and shouting voices. I cursed under my breath and urged my horse into motion, faster, faster. Soon we were cantering, then galloping. The voices were not very distinct. One moment, they were right on my tail, the next, fading off into the distance. Still, I pushed my horse blindly faster. Suddenly, there was a gunshot, then another, then another. The first two went wide, but the third really drove home.

I cursed again, out loud this time, as I felt searing pain in my left leg. I fought to stay focused, ignoring the burning and searching for a way to lose my pursuers.

Aha! Salvation. An enormous clump of Bottlebrush coming up on the right. I steered my horse towards it and urged him into a flying leap, right smack bang in the centre.

It was prickly and uncomfortable, but we waited there for much longer than absolutely necessary. Only when it began to grow dark did we begin our journey back to base.

We arrived late, and I was met with a great flurry of anger, which immediately turned into concern once my limp was noticed. I hobbled over to the infirmary and proceeded to extract the bullet and bound the wound tightly. Many offered to help, but I refused. You don't grow up in a circus without knowing how to treat a bullet in the leg.

We gathered round the fire and everyone grinned.

'What'cha bring for us tonight Jess?' Asked one of the new boys.

I flashed him a glare and he shrank back. Suddenly, I grinned and threw a sack at his feet. He chuckled and rifled through the contents. Pulling out three loaves of bread, a bottle of brandy, some slices of meat and, laughing, a packet of tea leaves.

We feasted on the bread and meat, toasting it over the fire. We laughed and joked, while taking slugs of brandy.

As was custom, Jerry brewed me a cup of tea while the lads shared impressive stories of past felonies. I found myself scoffing at the same new kid's daring tales of villainy. Robbing three stagecoaches in a day singlehandedly? Not likely. Still, I admired him. After finishing one of his tall stories he leaned back and asked me mockingly:

'Want a scone with your tea, Lady Jess?'

With a swift flick of my hand I swiped my gun from my holster, cocked it and levelled it at his head. All without taking my eyes off my tea. The whole bush seemed to hush. All eyes trained on the weapon I held in my dainty hand.

'No thank you.' I said. 'Who's on watch tonight?'

A tentative hand crept into the air.

'I will relieve you.' I rose and drained my mug. 'Goodnight all. Unless there's anything else you want to add?' I gestured to the kid with my gun.

'N-no Jess.' He stuttered, never taking his gaze off the dormant gun.

'When speaking to me, you will address me by my proper title.' I demanded haughtily.

'Lady Jess. Sorry.' He then bowed deeply.

In the tense silence that followed, time seemed to stop. Everything watching and waiting to see what I would do next.

I chuckled, and then laughed so uproariously that it startled a few of the boys out of their drink-induced slumber.

'Good one kid.' I laughed. 'It takes a lot to make me laugh.'

I wiped the tears from my eyes then finally holstered my gun. There was a collective sigh of relief. Tipping my head to the boys I then proceeded to take up my post by the edge of the camp.

It was getting late and my leg had begun to pound again. I was lost in my thoughts.

I had only been a bushranger for a few years but I already had a pretty fearsome reputation. At first, people wouldn't believe that a woman could be a bushranger, and now look; a band of followers and my face on wanted posters within every ten miles.

Perhaps if I had not been shot, or if I had let someone else be on watch, or if the boys hadn't have had so much brandy, it wouldn't have happened. But happen it did, so there's nothing I can do but recount the events.

It was probably 3 in the morning when I heard shouting coming from the base. I rushed back, expecting that we were under attack. I arrived to a blaze of flames and burning heat.

'What the hell happened here?' I shouted over the crackling of flames.

'Some idiot forgot to put out the fire.' Yelled Old Tim. 'Now you stay back Jess. You're injured, we'll sort this out.'

I reluctantly consented, limping back over to my post. It was probably a few seconds before I noticed the rustling and thumping of hooves far off in the distance. I pricked up my ears and listened closer. Shouting now joined these sounds and I realised that the fire had alerted the Snitches on duty. (Snitches is our fun little name for the local policemen) I grabbed my gun and prepared myself for the oncoming battle.

I wasn't much a good shot with the pain muddying my brain. I remember lots of cussing and gunshots. Pain in my right leg, but wasn't I shot in my left? A crack as a baton connected with someone's face. I suddenly found myself bundled up by Old Tim and locked in one of the caravans to stop myself from getting shot a third time. I was left to kick uselessly at the door and scream myself into a fevered, dreamless sleep.

When I finally woke, I saw two people hovering over me with bandages and worried expressions. I struggled to sit up.

'Wha–?' I slurred.

'Don't worry Jess.' Said one of the men. 'You got shot again, in the other leg this time. You've been asleep for three days. We have already moved base and none of our numbers were killed in the battle, though some injured. Does that answer all of your questions?' I nodded dumbly and relaxed back into the makeshift cot bed.

I smiled broadly.

'What's she smiling about?' Whispered the man who had been silent until now. I wanted him to be quiet again.

'I love the bush life.' I said.

'But you got shot twice!' He exclaimed. 'And you're a woman. Shouldn't you prefer sitting at home cooking cakes?'

I stared him down, not an easy feat lying down I can tell you.

'If I made a cake, would you eat it?'

'No,' he said, averting his gaze. 'It would probably be poisoned.'

'And burnt to a crisp.' I added.

'With salt instead of sugar,' chimed in the other man.

We all laughed. I slumped back into the bed and closed my eyes, surrendering to sleep's warm, gentle pull. I only had one thought on my mind: Get better so I can go back to being the most feared bushranger in Australia.

DETECTIVE APPLE-HAT AND THE CHERRY TREE MANOR MYSTERY

ARTHUR DENDLE CRERAR
Gardeners Bay, Huon Valley

2022 WINNER
YEARS 3-4 CATEGORY
 AGATHA CHRISTIE IN TASMANIA

Just after midnight, in a private study at Cherry Tree Manor on Bruny Island, Lord Cherrington was reading over his speeches for the next day's anti-logging event. Suddenly the door creaked. He looked around and saw a tall, looming black silhouette approaching. He screamed.

The following day was gloomily wet. Detective Apple-Hat was driving along in his Rolls-Royce when a man jumped out in front of him. The detective pulled over, checked his secret knife was well hidden, and stepped from his car.

'I am a messenger from the Cherrington family,' the man said. 'Lord Cherrington is dead.'

Later, at Cherry Tree Manor, Detective Apple-Hat gathered a group to investigate Cherrington's murder. Seated around the table was a man named George, a tall young girl, a woman with blazingly red hair, and two wrinklies, who clearly wanted to be elsewhere.

'I am the brother of the late Lord,' said George. 'I consider it my duty to discover his murderer. I believe the suspect is seated at this table. You were the only ones in the Manor last night.'

The first suspect was a tall, ten year old named Josephine, daughter of a local logger. She had black hair, glasses, and a friendly smile.

The next was Rose, a blind young woman with wild red hair, who had been looking after Lord Cherrington for many years.

Then 95-year-olds Sal and Pip, twins with deeply wrinkled skin – and matching scowls. They were the cooks, though they should have been kept out the kitchen.

The detective watched them carefully. All wore poker faces.

That evening over dinner, Detective Apple-Hat and George were discussing the suspects.

'Who do you think did it?' asked George.

'Not sure, but my guess is Rose,' replied the detective.

'Why? She's blind!' exclaimed George.

'Or so she says,' replied the detective. 'Trust no one.'

'I think it's Josephine,' said George, tucking into his fish.

'She's just so young,' said the detective, but at that moment George fell to the ground.

'The fish,' he said, clutching his throat 'the fish...'

Next morning, the detective woke up early at Cherry Tree Manor.

Walking downstairs for breakfast, he heard footsteps behind him. He jumped behind a suit of armour as a pole came down hard. He bolted away as the suit of armour smashed.

Suddenly the attacker dropped the pole and pulled out a sword and revolver, one in each hand.

The detective ran for his life.

Four things happened in quick succession.

The sword slammed into a column.

The detective darted out the way.

The revolver fired, a stray bullet hit the hilt of the sword.

The column fell, crushing the sword and revolver with a deafening crack.

The figure stood unarmed. The detective pulled out his secret knife.

As the figure ran away, her glasses fell to the ground.

The detective cried, 'We won't catch her now!'

'No need,' said George, stepping from the shadows with Josephine's fallen glasses in his hand.

THE MISSING 'CHINA CHINA' (IN THE MONA)

NADRAH ABDULLAH
Lakemba, NSW

2021
YEARS 3-4 CATEGORY
SCENE OF THE CRIME

Rrrrrriiiiiiinnnnnnnggggg! The fire alarm suddenly went off scaring the living day lights out of me and causing people to scatter all around like cockroaches. Staffs were pacing around, trying to get everyone to evacuate. I followed my sister out the door. 'Get your butt over here, Amelia' she yelled angrily beckoning me over near the parking lot. I looked anxiously inside expecting flames of furious fire taking over the museum but instead I saw... two men suspiciously lurking around instead of following everyone out, I slowly watched one of them step on my pen I dropped on the way. Suddenly, my sister pulled my hand and we drove home.

One the way home, near the Tasmanian sea I spotted two men in black, they had a large bag. My curiosity increased as I saw those two guys back at the MONA.

Tonight, on the news they announced that the famous 'China China' was missing or in other words – stolen. The police offered $2,500 to anyone who had information about the crime. And a big grin spread across my face, 'what are you smiling about?' asked Charlotte, my stepsister at dinner.

'Nothing' I replied still smiling

'Come on...'

'I said nothing, are you deaf?'

'Hmph' she crossly said, crossing her arms.

The next day, I grabbed my bike and rode my way to the station.

'Good morning, I've come here report something I witnessed earlier, yesterday' I said as I walked in.

'Hurry up dear, don't have all day' one of them replied quite impatiently.

'Yesterday at the MONA when the fake fire alarm went off, I saw two men in black hanging around inside instead of following the others outside, then on the way home I saw the same guys near the sea with a large bag'

'I'm sorry love, but we don't except anything from children under the age of 16 or unless they have proof'

'Oh, sorry for wasting your time then' I said walking out.

On the way, a light bulb moment hit me – I DID have proof. I turned my smartwatch on to see and as I had imagined, it was all there. I decided to come the next day just in case they got suspicious. And my pen that they stepped on... they're shoes must have had the neon yellow ink under it.

The next afternoon, I asked my sister to drive me over to the police station, she got curious, but she said yes anyways. We walked inside and showed them everything, they decided to take in the evidence.

We drove to the crime scene next, and showed them too, they were surprised since the voice recognition showed that it was two of their important staff.

Tonight, on the news, they found the criminals because of the broken neon pen and the traces they caused and of course my recordings. Gladly, we got the $2,500 they promised. Charlotte and my mum got all emotional and hugged me a little too much for my liking.

HANNAH SHRILLCOCK

IZABELLE BORZAK-BELL
Gardeners Bay, Huon Valley

2019
YEARS 3-4 CATEGORY
 FEMALE BUSHRANGER

Hannah Shrillcock was born on January 15 1889 in Western Australia, but was heartlessly abandoned by her parents at the age of three. She was taken in by an orphanage at the age of five. She fled from the orphanage at the age of 12 because she despised the way they treated her and desperately wanted to leave the continent.

Whilst in the orphanage she heard many stories of distant lands and opportunities to make herself a better future. So, dreaming of a new life, she made for the docks, in search of an opportunity to stowaway. An official and mean looking man spotted her and demanded she identity herself. Not knowing what to say she ran and hid quickly in a crate. Too terrified to move she stayed hidden for so long that she fell asleep in the cold night air In the morning she awoke to find the crate she had chosen as her hiding place had been loaded upon a ship. She would soon discover was bound for Africa.

For the many weeks that followed she bid aboard the ship, sneaking out under the cover of dark and poor weather in an effort to steal food and other items whilst not being found. When the ship finally reached its destination, Hannah crept from her hiding place, half-starved and exhausted from the lengthy sea journey. She stood and stared at her new surroundings, realising with shock and a gasp of excitement, that she had arrived, in Africa After leaving the ship and spending time in the dangerous world of the docks of this part of Africa, Hannah realised that from now on she would have to be tough and often fight to survive in this new country.

Her criminal career began as it did for so many in her situation, through necessity. She started off stealing food and clothing. At the age of 17 she formed a gang with other thieves, and began stealing cattle together. She and her gang were often pursued by the police for stealing valuable clothing too.

Once or twice Hannah and her gang would go to jail for short periods of time. Once they were sent to jail for 4 years for stealing a whole herd of cattle, however as soon as they were in jail they managed to escape. Hannah's gang rode off on cattle, stolen from a nearby farm. But Hannah, unable to find any more cattle, had to escape riding to her freedom on a domesticated elephant!

The story goes that she fled to the famous Victoria Falls where she leapt over the edge of the colossal canyon, disappearing into the misty spray of the giant falls. About a year later Hannah's gang, upon hearing reports of her being alive, discovered her living, hidden by a river at the bottom of the canyon. No one knows how she survived the treacherous descent but she became famous for that mighty jump.

Hannah Shrillcock died as a result of a meningococcal infection on July 20th 1952 aged 63.

This account of Hannah's life was told by Franklin Lastscar (one of Hannah's many partners in crime).

THE COOKIE THIEF

CHARLOTTE BROWN
Mornington, Victoria

2021
YEARS 3-4 CATEGORY
SCENE OF THE CRIME

'Woosh!' went the wind on the stormy beach.

Waves bashed against the bumpy rocks.

Clouds turned pitch black.

It was getting late.

At a hotel a young girl named Mal was getting tucked in bed while she listened to the waves crashing.

'We had a big day at the beach today, so get some rest,' Mal's mother said softly.

'We go to the Louvre tomorrow.'

Her father gave her a kiss and both parents walked out. They worked at the Melbourne State Library but were staying in France to bring Mona Lisa back to Melbourne. The two museums were having a swap. The Louvre was swapping the Mona Lisa for Ned Kelly's Armour.

Crash! Boom! Bang!

Mal's parents woke suddenly.

'They're gone!' exclaimed Mal's father.

It was exactly 3:00am. Ned Kelly's Armour and the cookie jar had been stolen.

In all the commotion Mal woke up too.

'What going on?' she asked half asleep.

'Ned Kelly's Armour and the cookie jar have been stolen. Back to bed.' Mal's mother sounded worried. Mal decided not to argue. She went to bed, but couldn't sleep. What is going to happen?

Who stole the armour and the cookie jar?

Her mind was full of questions.

Five hours later they went to the Louvre. Police cars were everywhere. The Louvre staff were all standing where the Mona Lisa was usually hung.

'The Mona Lisa has been stolen!' cried a worker.

'We heard a crash, boom, bang and then it was gone.'

'That's exactly what had happened with Ned Kelly's Armour!' said Mal's mother surprised.

'Ned Kelly's Amour has been stolen too?' yelled the Boss of the Louvre. 'Munch!'

'Alex! I know you love cookies, but this is no time to eat!' The boss was very mad, so she put some lip-gloss on.

'Why do you put lip-gloss on?' Mal asked quietly.

'The pink fruity smell helps me calm my nerves' replied the boss.

'May I have a look of where the painting was?'

Mal didn't wait for an answer. She went over to the Mona Lisa's place and looked for clues. All she found was cookie crumbs. She picked them up and sniffed them.

'We need to go back to the hotel' Mal said seriously.

Everyone got in their cars and drove as fast as they could. Once they were there Mal sprinted up to their room. She asked her parents where the Amour had been. They showed her and Mal immediately saw more cookie crumbs.

'Can I see your lip-gloss?'

Mal sniffed the lip-gloss.

'It was you!' Mal said pointing at the boss.

'You stole the cookie jar to make it look like Alex had stolen it.' Everyone was shocked.

'Except your lip-gloss scent was on the crumbs.'

'Fine it was me, but—'

'Police – get her!'

The boss went to jail and was never seen again.

GREAT GRANDPA'S SECRET

LILY CLARK
Geeveston, Huon Valley

2020 WINNER
YEARS 3-4 CATEGORY
FEMALE DETECTIVES

Katie and Sophia were upstairs in their attic reading on their great grandfather's old bed. Sophia had fallen asleep and was snoring loudly, as she rolled over she knocked Katie out of bed. As she was getting up off the floor she could see something carved into the wood of the bed. Written below an old metal key:

National Archives Hobart Library 1782 Page 3 Pearl Necklace

What does that mean? asked Sophia. 'I remember Grandma telling me that her Mum had a valuable pearl necklace stolen' said Katie. As the library was open they hopped into their silvery blue car, Katie was driving and her 14-year-old sister Sophia was the passenger.

The drive took 2 hours to Hobart from Southport. When they arrived Katie asked Sophia if she had written down the words carved under the bed. 'Of course, did you think I would leave that knowledge at home?' said Sophia.

Both girls decided to look in the old newspaper section hoping to come across something.

After about half an hour searching they found the microfilm newspaper reel for 1782, 'Let's put it on' said Sophia. Page 3 showed an article of a suspected jewellery thief with a picture of an ugly man with what appeared to be a pearl necklace tucked into his swag bag. The article said that he may have hid his treasures in a cave around Hastings, but none were ever found.

'I wonder if we could find the cave and Great Grandmas pearl necklace?' asked Sophia.

'I'm pretty sure there is a cave at Hastings that collapsed years ago and isn't open to the public because it's dangerous,' said Katie.

'Do you think we can go? asked Sophia.

'Yes, so long as we got some gear to keep us safe'.

The girls needed to go through Dad's shed.

'Wait in the car while I grab some stuff,' said Katie.

'Fine but be quick' warned Sophia knowing her Dad wouldn't be happy.

When Sophia was sitting in the car all the things that could go wrong were racing through her mind.

'What about getting lost? yelled Sophia.

'I'm bringing white chalk' said Katie

The girls looked around the bush for 2 hours before they found the overgrown, long-forgotten cave. They cautiously entered the cold, dark cave.

'I hope there are no bats,' whispered Katie. Wide eyed she could make out something ahead. As they got closer they realised it was an arrow carved into the stone. Pushing where the arrow pointed made an entrance to a room carved out of rock open. Inside was an old rusty locked trunk.

'Wait, Sophia cried, this is what the key is for!' The lock squeaked but opened with the key.

Inside was a beautifully preserved letter. It read:

Congratulations, you have followed the clues and shall be rewarded. This letter gives the finder all the treasure I have taking from this cave, and stored at the Old Bank Geeveston.
Signed
Stanley Alfred Petersen.

'Our Great Grandfather!' the girls said.

BUSHRANGERS

TESS BURGESS
Geeveston, Huon Valley

2019
YEARS 3-4 CATEGORY
FEMALE BUSHRANGERS

Around about 1840 I was born, I lived in a fancy house, but no one appreciated me as much as my rich and handsome husband it made me sick. So I decided to change the way I lived to make myself happy. I would be a bushranger and then my husband wouldn't be the only one with money!

My name was Emily Johnson but that had to change if I was going to be a bushranger. No one shall know who I am or what real name is. My aliases are the Lady Knight and the Evil Crimson. My life got exciting and I had more money than my horrid husband!

It is night time and I am approaching my next victim, a lady riding in a coach with a necklace covered in jewels and purse spilling out with money.

I pulled out my gun and told her to give me her money or I would open fire. After getting that cash I still don't think have enough for my liking I need to wait until my husband has another of his 'tea party's' and rob his guests as they leave.

Tonight my husband is having a another tea party so I better get ready, I will have time because I am not invited to his party's he doesn't think I am good enough to join him, but that's good because I would have no pleasure accompanying him and his guests. It has been 3 hours of them laughing and eating little cupcakes, and finally they are getting ready to leave.

So I better get ready to rob them and take their money. They are in their carriage leaving and I am approaching, I raise my gun and tell them to give me their money or I will shoot. They didn't have much money on them at that moment, but I still got quite a bit. I think when I have robbed most of the people in this town I will move across the country and find new victims. I have now robbed 50 people! so far but if I move across the country I might get twice as many. I about am packing my bag, I won't bother saying by to my husband because he probably won't notice I am gone he doesn't really care.

I pack some food for the first couple of nights before I get to the town, I mount my horse and ride across the desert. Three days later I reach a tavern and order a meal, I eat then I leave. I still have long way to travel and I need to feed my horse, I get some bread out of my satchel and give it to my horse, she thinks then eats it with no more hesitation. I find shelter and tie up my horse, I get a potato sack for a pillow then I sleep. A couple months later I was caught for stealing 200 pounds and I am about to be sent to Australia as a convict for 4 years. And when I return I will continue my story as a bushranger.

CHARLOTTE SMITHTON

NEVE GILL
Petcheys Bay

2019
YEARS 3-4 CATEGORY
  FEMALE BUSHRANGERS

Fierce winds tore through my hair as Bonney ground to a halt, grunting in despair. I closed my eyes as I was anxious that it was those dreaded men.

I finally opened them and saw their unwelcoming figures striding towards Bonney and I, and it occurred to me our chance of escaping was narrow, being a crumbling clifftop.

Panicking, I mistakenly cried out for Bonney to dive off the overhang and was soon leaping after him, plunging into the depths of the churning water below.

Breathlessly, I hauled myself onto the withered land, shaking from the icy waters. I glanced around but there was no sign of Bonney anywhere.

After losing Bonney to the treacherous river, weeks became months and months became years. To survive, I had mastered horse rustling, and acquired a new horse named Dale, although Bonney was still alive in my heart. He was significant to me – my only company for years, as after the droughts Mother and Father went for supplies to mend our farm, a journey that should take two weeks – but never returned. I awaited them for a month, but after such a time I was doubting their return and grew worried, so left to search for them. I had no idea where to look, and never found them. Bonney was all I had as company for endless months.

Although not proud of robbing an ill looking man on a busy route in south west NSW I had gained a great few shillings and was prepared to ransack any other people unfortunate enough to come across this way. Though I didn't know how long we could survive on the supplies we already had.

Most people may think of us bushrangers simply as criminals and thieves, but our reasons for doing so may all be entirely unique. Dependent on theft and deceit I had barely anything call my own.

Days later, ravenous, we had to do something to stay alive but I had lost my snare and slingshot and felt so weak. Our only option was to thieve. There was a chance would be captured but I had no choice.

Bursting into the store, snatching piles of items off the shelves, we soon took off, leaving the owner behind, threatening and yelling at me. We had enough supplies to last us days, so our journey continued.

Years afterward, I had grown weaker and could barely move on my own. Without Dale I would be long gone. Passing through an isolated town, the familiar men in large, blue trench coats draping down their sides were beside the inn, muttering to each other. Before they could recognise us, I leaped off the nearby cliff face and hurtled into the dark murky waters beneath, only this time, I didn't come back up either.

ELISABETH AND THE MISSING WALLET

LAVINIA PEARCE
Hobart, Tasmania

2022
YEARS 3-4 CATEGORY
  AGATHA CHRISTIE IN TASMANIA

One afternoon at the Richmond gaol, Elisabeth was cleaning Edward's quarters. This is her story.

Elisabeth was sent to Richmond gaol when she was 18. She stole a loaf of bread and she was deported from England and travelled for 4 months before reaching Van Diemen's land. Now she must clean the top guard, Edward's quarters every day.

Elisabeth shares a cell with Fanny and Mary. They used to cook together but Edward liked Elisabeth and now she cleans his quarters. Edward is very kind to Elisabeth so Fanny and Mary are jealous of Elisabeth.

One day after cleaning Edward's quarters she saw Fanny and Mary walking together complaining. Elisabeth thought it was normal because they usually come to the cell looking disappointed. They all sat down in the cell waiting for dinner when Elisabeth heard Fanny say 'the same?' but it was hard to hear because Fanny and Mary always sit away from Elisabeth and whisper.

When they finished dinner, they went to sleep as they all had a very busy day so they were very sleepy. 4 minutes later the guard John woke the three up and said 'don't worry girls you're not in trouble Elisabeth here is'.

Elisabeth just stayed quiet as she didn't want to get in any more trouble. As John was leading her to Edward's quarters she thought to herself whatever John thought I did Edward thought I did it too. But he couldn't have as he was so kind to me. Then she realised she was at Edward's door. She was one step closer to finding out what she had done and if Edward thought she did it.

She stepped into the room and saw Edward sitting in a chair.

John said 'sit down'. She sat down. John sat down and said 'You know why you are here'?

'No', she replied.

'Well, let me explain. You cleaned the room and Edward's wallet is missing. You did it'

'No, no, I would never'.

'Don't play dirty on us, we will find out. You're in solitary confinement for 2 days and you will get whipped starting tomorrow. Remember clean the quarters then solitary confinement. Have a good night'.

She walked back to her cell. The girls were asleep. She lay down. She couldn't stop thinking about it. It kept her up all night. In the morning, she woke up, cleaned Edward's quarters and was coming out when John took her arm and brought her to solitary confinement. He gave her some food and then said 'don't waste it because you are getting less dinner'.

John was walking to Edward's quarters and at the door he saw a strand of blonde hair. He picked it up and ran to the women's cells. The hair was long so he thought it was a girl's.

He asked every girl with blonde hair if it was theirs. None of them looked guilty. As he was about to walk out of the room he saw Fanny and asked Fanny. Fanny gulped and then said 'No, of course not'. John thought it might be her hair. Maybe it just got caught on Elisabeth's dress and fell of when she got to the door.

The next morning he went to give Elisabeth breakfast and on his way back he thought that he might talk to Edward and see what he thought about the wallet mystery. They talked but Edward said he didn't know who it was so John left the room went to the kitchen. When John gave Elisabeth her dinner he said 'you are getting whipped tomorrow' then he left the room. Elisabeth heard him chuckling to himself as he left the room.

The next day he was ready to solve this mystery. All he had to do was make Elisabeth tell the truth and then she would get whipped as a punishment. He had 20 minutes until Elisabeth was going to get whipped. He thought that maybe Edward would have left his wallet in his drawer but when John looked in the drawer, he saw finger prints made with flour from someone's hands. He went into the kitchen and saw a photo fall out of Fanny's pocket of Edward's sister. He took Fanny by the hand and explained it all the Edward. Then he put Fanny in solitary confinement and took Elisabeth out. He said to Elisabeth she would not get whipped and Fanny would get whipped every day for 20 days. They found the wallet in one of the air holes in the cell and they all lived horribly ever after except for one, named Elisabeth.

THE CASE OF THE TWO MYSTERIES

STEPHANIE MCGRATH
Caboolture, Queensland

2021 WINNER
YEARS 3-4 CATEGORY
SCENE OF THE CRIME

I skip through Old Ron's peeling yellow gate. The smell of cake swims up my nose.

Then dirt. Dainty is digging intently in the yard. That dog never stops.

An hour later: 'Morning tea was wonderful, Ron.' I say that every week.

I'm cautious going back through the gate – don't want to be sprayed with dirt again.

Wait. There's no dirt. There's not even a Dainty.

Dainty's disappeared!

'Ron, Dainty's gone!'

'What do you mean Dainty's gone?' There's shuffling in the house and Ron appears at the door.

'She was digging here before and now there's just pawprints leading out the open gate...' My sentence trails off because now I know what's happened. I slap my forehead.

'Oh, man, I'm so sorry, Ron. I must've left the gate open.' Oops.

Ron isn't mad. 'Well, what are you doing just standing there, kid? Go find my dog.'

I know nothing about being a detective, and now Ron wants me to find his dog. That's not going to happen.

'Ron, you see–'

'Go find my dog!' I have no choice.

I start with the pawprints. They head out the gate, along the footpath, and into Dr Dan Daniels' place.

We ring the door bell. Dr Dan appears almost immediately.

'I'm so glad you're here, Ron. I have something urgent to ask you.'

Guess who is on the couch, tail wagging? You probably already know if you've been following the story. And I just gave it away because I said 'tail'. Oops again.

'Dainty!' Dr Dan lives on our street, so of course he knows Dainty – she steals sausages. 'I told you not to chew on that bone.'

He takes it away from her and shows us.

I can't imagine that Dr Dan would know the first thing about bones. He's a psychologist.

'This is a human femur.' He raises an eyebrow at Ron. 'Why have you got human bones buried in your yard?'

Ron laughs nervously. He has a good way of pretending to be innocent. I raise my eyebrow too.

'Oh, all right,' He takes a deep breath. 'I had a friend once – must have been in our twenties or so – such silly boys we were. We were drinking. My friend sat on the balcony railing.' Here he paused, not making eye contact with any of us, 'and he fell and broke his neck. I buried him in my yard.'

My first thought is: Shouldn't he have moved house by now? My second thought is: Oh. Wow.

'So you didn't tell the authorities?' Dr Dan wonders.

Ron sighed. 'No, I didn't tell the authorities.'

'You do know that if you bury someone on private property, you get a big fine, and if you bury someone and don't tell anyone, you can go to gaol?' Dr Dan is speaking slower now. This does not look good for Ron.

'You're not going to let them take me away, are you?' But Ron was too late. Dr Dan was dialing 000.

THE HUNT

BONNIE PULLINGER
Fern Tree, Tasmania

2022
YEARS 3-4 CATEGORY
  AGATHA CHRISTIE IN TASMANIA

'Mum, all I want is to not go to Auntie Sophie's house tonight. Can we not go?' I asked hopefully. But I knew the answer would be no.

'No.' She answered. I sighed. It's not that I don't like Auntie Sophie, it's just she's just a bit of a scatter brain. She's hard to take seriously. She's always going on about the book club she goes to, for people in their forties even though she's in her fifties. We walked out of Lipscombe Larder. (We had just been shopping.) We walked back to our house. I ran to my room. Threw down my school bag.

'SARAH, I DON'T SEE WHY WE HAVE TO!'

'FINE!' Mum and Dad shouting at each other, again. I listened closely; Mum was crying. Again.

I got changed into a blue top and denim shorts. We got into our Volvo and made our way to Auntie Sophie's house. We arrived; her car wasn't there. I didn't want to wait in the car. 'I know where the spare key is.' Mum said. Mum went to the welcome mat. She pulled out a key from underneath it. She unlocked Auntie Sophie's door. We all rushed inside. I went to the calendar. Auntie Sophie would've marked our dinner on it. It said nothing about a dinner. It said,

Going to Hugh's. His boy is such The Whaler.

I thought Auntie Sophie was good at English. Then it hit me, so rapidly that I stumbled backwards. I knew where Auntie Sophie was. The Waler. Me and Mum had walked past it on Saturday.

'Drive me to the Whaler.' I said to Mum. It wasn't a command more a plead.

'Yes.' she answered determinedly. We drove through Hobarts's streets. 'Mum, this isn't Salamanca.' I cried. Mum had got lost! Mum never got lost. Dad did occasionally but Mum, never!

'Darling be patient.' She said. It was a whisper. Her cheeks were wet. She was crying. I suddenly realised that the car wasn't moving. It had happened. They had finally broken up. I knew it would happen except I didn't think it would be so soon.

'Mum,' I said shakily. 'We have to go.' The car revved. We parked out the front of the Waler. We got out and made our way to where we saw Auntie Sophie sitting. With a man. She glanced up at us.

'You have got alot of explaining to do,' Mum said crossly.

'Me and Hugh are dating, I didn't want to tell you because I would be embarrassed if we broke up, so I acted like a scatter brain so you would think I would forget about our dinner,' she said.

'Oh, that makes sense.' I said, not really paying attention. And that's how we found Auntie Sophie.

A couple of months later Auntie Sophie showed us her hand. There was a diamond ring on her ring finger. Then I found some divorce papers. Dad said he had to move for 'work'. Not the real reason.

MURDER ON THE WISP

JOSIE RICHARDSON
Snug, Tasmania

2021
YEARS 3-4 CATEGORY
SCENE OF THE CRIME

I looked at the open sea around us. If I had known when I left, I would never have agreed to go.

On our boat 'Wisp', there is Captain Alfie, the Fielding brothers, Sam (first mate) and Jackson (second mate), Lookout Billy, Admiral Jo (me), India (able seaman) and the Cabin Boy Byron.

It was a normal day for us. Alfie shouting out orders, India scowling, Billy in the crows nest, Sam at the helm, Byron at the jib and me at the main sheet. We all though Jackson was frying eggs in the galley, but when nine o'clock came, neither Jackson, nor breakfast appeared.

'Hey Jo' Sam called. I handed the sheet to India and hurried over. 'Do you like some people better than others?'

'I think you're really nice, but her on the other hand' I nodded toward India and shrugged.

The afternoon passed and by bedtime there was still no sign of Jackson.

I woke up several times that night and felt something was wrong but couldn't imagine what. Until morning, when we heard the scream.

Alfie came bursting into our cabin breathless and terrified. 'Murder... Sam...' he gasped before he passed out.

'Quick India, cold water. NOW!' Images kept flashing through my mind – like... too gruesome. I can't tell you. I ran up to the deck and what I saw nearly made my heart stop. Sam was lying on the deck with a knife through his chest.

There was a footprint on the deck near the body. At that moment I wished that water didn't dry. I pulled a pencil out of my pocket and quickly traced the footprint and the body. 'Jo' I heard India calling. She ran over and knelt down by the sail. 'You're my only hope. Everyone th-thinks I'm a-a murderer' the girl sobbed.

'I know you're not,' I said 'and I've got proof'. I spoke to her kindly as we went down and as I spoke, I started to believe what I was saying.

'The murderer! The murderer and her accomplice!' was the first sound that reached my ears. 'Don't be silly' I said. 'Why would you think India's a murderer?'

'I have proof' Jackson yelled. 'She was up last night,' he said triumphantly.

'So were you! I saw you committing the murder Jackson Fielding' India yelled.

The cabin was silent for a long time.

'Jackson' I said, 'what is your favourite food?'

'Crumbed scallops. Why do you need to know anyway?'

'Because I saw half a crumbed scallop near the body. See here, and not only that, you're the only one onboard who wears size 10 Blundstones'.

Jackson knew he had lost. He'd never fulfil his ambition to become first mate now.

Looking back on the whole gruesome episode, I sometimes wonder if I shouldn't have lied about the scallop.

ANNABETH AND THE CASE OF THE MISSING CREST

ELOISE VANIER
Hobart, Tasmania

2022
YEARS 3-4 CATEGORY
 AGATHA CHRISTIE IN TASMANIA

It was seven o'clock in the morning and Annabeth Hill was eating her breakfast. She was looking at her phone and she was so bored that she could have dunked her head in her soaking wet cereal. Suddenly, she found something that got her interest. It was a message from her school principal, Miss Fry. It said the library was closed because the school crest tapestry was stolen! The school crest tapestry was very important to the school heritage as it had a Tasmanian Tiger on the top left-hand corner.

'Wow!' Annabeth exclaimed, this was serious. She got dressed and ran down stairs and as she ran out the door she yelled 'bye mum! bye dad!' and shut the door behind her. Then she rushed to school and dashed through the creaky gates and raced to class just in time. The bell suddenly rang the second she sat in her seat.

'Where is Miss Olive?' the class whispered. Miss Olive is Annabeth's favourite grade 2 teacher. Then Miss Fry, the principal, entered the room 'All students must enter the hall as soon as possible' she said, sounding very agitated. Annabeth and her class scurried down the long hallway, they passed the library, reached the hall and gathered next to the other classes. The whole school had come to hear what the frustrated principal had to say.

Everyone was talking, then once Miss Fry put up her hand they all fell silent. 'I have called you all here to talk to you about something. As some of you may know, someone in this school stole our school crest tapestry and the library is closed for investigation.' 'No' Annabeth muttered under her breath. She loved the library, she also loved to read, she was so upset she buried her head in her hands.

'Hey' said the boy next to her 'are you okay?' It was Liam.

'Oh, um yes, I think so.'

'Why are you crying?'

'Oh, I'm just upset because... the library's closed.'

And yes, everyone in the hall was listening, it was so embarrassing then Miss Fry cleared her throat 'Are you done talking, Miss Hill?' she said in a stiff voice.

'Well, um, yes.'

Miss Fry kept speaking, and just at that moment Annabeth thought that if she stayed long enough to hear about the robbery she could quickly sneak in to the library and see the scene of the crime and maybe, just maybe, crack the case! This would also mean breaking every school rule but it was going to be worth it. When Miss Fry finished speaking, Annabeth quietly crept out of the hall and dashed to the library, but just then a big guard stepped out and said 'Hey little miss, what are you doing out of class?'

'Oh, I'm Miss Fry's assistant.' Annabeth said quickly.

'Oh, come right in missy.'

Wow, they're pretty dumb, she thought, very dumb indeed. She tiptoed into the quiet room and looked around until she spotted a big hole in the wall. She gasped! Wow! It was as big as the crest.

'Hey! how did you get here so fast?' Annabeth asked Liam as she realized her friend was standing next to her.

'I sprinted.'

'Oh,' said Annabeth 'Well I'm glad that you're here, let's start looking for clues.'

Liam exclaimed 'Look over there, a pen. Who would leave a pen lying around here? Let's follow it and find out.'

'Hang on!' Said Annabeth. 'Let's think. Who has a pen that we know?' They gasped! 'Millie!' They raced to the science lab which was where she always was. They burst through the door. 'Millie!' they cried.

'What? I'm science-ing,' said Millie.

'Did you lose a pen?'

'Duh, no. I keep my pens in the lab.' Then Annabeth asked another question 'Where were you yesterday?'

'In the library. Duh,' said Millie.

So hmmm, Annabeth thought, could Millie be the criminal? 'What were you doing there?' Annabeth asked.

'Um, reading...duh.'

Wow Millie loves saying 'duh' doesn't she? Annabeth thought.

'Hey Annabeth can I speak?' Liam whispered. He cleared his throat, 'Millie, what were you reading?

'Um, well, err, I...I was reading on, well, you know, science.'

Liam and Annabeth had a quick conversation and agreed it was not her and then said, 'Thank you Millie for your time.'

'Um, no problem.' Millie said as they left the room with a sigh.

'Maybe we – hey what's that?' said Annabeth as someone ran past them and dropped something. 'It's one of those things that you use for PE.'

'You mean a whistle?' Liam corrected her.

'Same thing, anyway, we should get back to the case. Let's go.' said Annabeth.

'Go?' Asked Liam. 'Go where?'

'Mr. Oaks office,' said Annabeth. Mr Oaks was the PE teacher.

'Oh I suppose that makes more sense.'

'Of course it does,' she said impatiently. 'Now can we go?'

'Oh right, we probably should.' They ran to the corner and nearly passed it, as most people do, as it is squished in between the computer lab and the teachers' staff room. They had to be quiet because in the staff room there was a meeting and if they were seen, they would get in so much trouble and would probably get banned from all the camp activities! Without thinking, they pushed open the PE office door and walked in to find it was completely empty except for a big desk in the middle of the room. They searched the desk when suddenly the door slammed shut. Annabeth pulled at the handle and it did not move. 'We're locked in! Oh no! What do we do?'

'There's nothing to do.' Came a voice from behind them. 'Mr. Oaks?' Annabeth thought, what? No way he was here the whole time.

'You aren't where ya supposed ta be. Unless y'all lookin for somethin 'ere?'

'We're looking for...' Annabeth started to say when Liam cut her off and shook his head.

'I know what ya lookin for. It's the crest! Well I can give y'all a clue.... well y'all know that the crest's a tapestry right?'

'Umm, yes.'

'Well, Mrs Clive loves 'em but her best friend loves 'em more. So ask her for information, instead of breaking in ta some guys office. 'Kay.'

They left the office and sped see Mrs Clive, the old science teacher. She has brown hair and always wore high heels and a red dress. They walked over to the almost-empty staff room and in the biggest chair sat Mrs Clive.

'Oh hello, Annabeth. What do you want?'

'Who is your best friend?' Annabeth asked.

'Oh, why do you want to know?'

'Umm, err, to give her a gift.'

'Oh right. I'll tell you. My best friend is ... Mrs Fry.'

Mrs Fry? But how? Where? Why?

'Thanks Mrs Clive, you were so much help! Liam, let's go!' They hurried as quick as a leopard towards Mrs Fry's office and knocked on the door and ran in. 'Aha! You're the thief!'

'Yes, I am. You see, I stole the tapestry because it has the most powerful thread in the world in it – the thread made from Tasmanian Tiger fur! And with the magic powers of Tasmanian Tiger fur, I won't need to do this horrible job. I closed the library for research on the Tasmanian Tiger until I learned all the secrets of its magical fur! And now I can make the whole of Tasmania know my name for all of history – I am Sophia! Sophia!'

'Your name's Sophia?'

'Shut up fool. Let me take over Tasmania.'

'No! Said Annabeth. 'No!' And she pulled the old and tattered tapestry in two and the Tasmanian Tiger fur thread broke into dust.

'Noooooo! You idiot! I'll get you for that, I'll get you!'

But just at the moment the police burst in with their sirens wailing as loud as the bell. The chief of police said 'Sophia Fry, you are under arrest! As for you two, come with me you have broken all your school rules.'

Liam and Annabeth said 'Yes, sir.'

The chief of police went on 'but you will receive special awards for catching your principal' 'Thanks, sir. But it wasn't just us, we couldn't have done it without Millie or Mr Oaks.' Said Annabeth. 'Thank you, but we don't want awards. Can we all have a party instead?' Said Liam. 'Of course!' said the chief of police, 'we'll have a party!'

So that night they had a big party.

MURDER IN LILYBROOK STREET

MAKAN WANG
Turramurra, NSW

2021
YEARS 3-4 CATEGORY
  SCENE OF THE CRIME

It was a snowy evening; hot steam was building up on the windows of Lilybrook Street, and a sophisticated detective lay thinking that he could get rest in his house, Number 67.

Hilton Berlin got up, but immediately someone thrashed at the door. He opened slowly, half expecting a criminal. But it was a messenger boy. There must have been trouble in the city, the culprit escaping in the white.

'Crime! Crime!' he shouted.

'Is it theft?' Berlin cried.

'Worse! Murder!'

Now Berlin's ears flipped on, 'Where?'

'Number 5 Lilybrook Street!'

Meanwhile, in an alley, a dark shadow of a middle-aged man loomed over a dumpster; blood was dripping from a shiny steel object. The shadow ran behind a building.

Berlin took a short but chilly walk with the police to the scene of the crime. He walked into the room but was stunned at how the body was there, left untouched to be examined.

'Here you are,' Sergeant Gregory said, taking a bow, 'the fresh body.'

It was horrible what Berlin saw. A poor fellow lay dead on the floor, stained full to the brim with blood all over. No poison could bring blood stains; it must have been a weapon of some sort that ended him. To the look on his face, Berlin could tell he was shocked at his death, but it looked disgusted, as if there had been something sinister about the death.

Gregory said, 'Age 24. Male. His name's James.'

'Who reported the body?' Berlin asked.

Gregory replied, 'Brawley, friend of the dead man, middle-aged man, new to the town, loves gambling, spotted him dead on his casual run; says here.'

Berlin noted this in his head. Brawley couldn't have seen him dead if the murder was made in the house. He was very suspicious of him. 'Then I shall go to his house to interview him, for any information' Berlin said. Gregory said, 'then I will accompany you'.

Together, they headed towards Brawley's house, trampling the snow and making footprints. Berlin noticed there was no blood soaked in the snow; the murder was made in the house, that was clear.

'Stop interviewing me! Ugh, I'll tell the story, I was running along the streets, when I heard a scream then I turned and thought it was coming from the house behind me. There was steam on the window so I scraped it off–'

'Excuse me, was this from outside the house?'

'Yes, so then I saw the body, long story short. Happy?!'

At this, Berlin said, 'arrest him, Gregory.'

'Wait, what?' Brawley said. 'I'm his friend! You can't accuse me for something–' '-you did do. Arrest him first, and I'll tell the story.' There was a click of handcuffs and Berlin spilled the beans out. He showed Gregory out. 'Can you rub the steam off the window?' He tried, but it didn't work. 'Ohh, the steam's inside, so he lied dreadfully!' 'Exactly!' They both left to get good nightmares for their lovely efforts.

HELEN THE HATED

ZARA STRONG
Geeveston, Huon Valley

2019 WINNER
YEARS 3-4 CATEGORY
FEMALE BUSHRANGERS

This story was found by Harry Viper after the death of Helen Viper.

Hello my name is Helen Viper and I was a woman convict.

I was sent to Van Diemen's Land on the 15th of November 1839 for stealing a loaf of bread.

I was so terribly hungry, it was only a small loaf of bread and the baker I stole it from had loads of them anyway so I don't know what the big deal was?

I married a man called Harold Viper who owns a bakery downtown so I'm hardly ever hungry anymore.

I usually do all the work in the house.

In the mornings I cook Harold and my adopted son Harry a big plate of eggs, bacon and two slices of toast before mopping the floors, dusting the window sills in the bedroom and taking the big rug in the dining room and beating it with a stick over the balcony until all the dirt has been shaken out.

It was a gloomy afternoon when I went down town to visit my husband's bakery when I saw a gorgeous brown horse with the most majestic black mane I ever saw on sale so I immediately decided to buy her for 500 pounds but I bet my mansion it was worth it!

I was very poor after that and there was no way Harold was lending me money because after all the bushrangers going around and stealing bread he was keeping every penny he could lay his hands on.

Then I thought...

Bushrangers make millions by stealing money and bread and other stuff so maybe I should become one, so I did!

My first crime was a quite successful bank robbery.

After that deed people were trying to join my gang all over the place but of course I only chose the best!

I ended up with a gang of 5. Mike the Man Killer. Ben the Betrayed, Daniel the Demanding, Andrew the Annoying, and me Helen the Hated!

We robbed banks, stole horses and as I predicted we made millions! Richer than Harold who still didn't know where I was!

After years of camping out with my gang and getting richer and richer I was finally caught and I was hanged in the prison, my neck broke straight in two then doctors in training took turns at cutting me to bits and running tests on because you see the churches didn't want my body and didn't want to put it in a coffin and care for it because I was a bad person so if you don't want to end like I did, don't turn bad!

After I was hanged my gang still lived on.

Mike the Man Killer took over my role as gang leader and they were actually a quite successful team!

Then Mary Ann the Misled joined the gang and things went to chaos from there on.

All my gang mates were hanged immediately but since Mary Ann was shot in the foot everyone had to wait until she healed before she was hung.

As for Harry...

MONKEY MYSTERY

OLIVIA KRISTENSEN
Hobart, Tasmania

2022 WINNER
UP TO YEAR 2 CATEGORY
AGATHA CHRISTIE IN TASMANIA

Once upon a time there lived a girl and a monkey. They lived in a beautiful cottage just outside Hobart city. They both liked solving mysteries.

One day the girl woke up and Monkey was gone. She looked around the room and she thought he might be having breakfast. He was not there so she looked outside instead and he was not there either.

It was her birthday and she wanted to celebrate it with Monkey. Which made her sad. So she went back inside.

Then she thought we like solving mysteries maybe he has left me a clue. She looked around and saw a note in the pantry when she went she to have breakfast.

The note said... you have to figure out the letters to find were I am. The first letter comes after O and just before Q. The next letter is always at the beginning. The next letter is at the beginning of rabbit and the end of car. The final letter is at the beginning of Kate and the end of crock.

The girl looked up and thought P-A-R-K park! and she rushed to the park. There was a giant party just for her and she got to celebrate her birthday with Monkey after all. They had so much fun at the party.

THE END!

LUCKY BOOTS

JACK KELLY
Beaufort, Victoria

2021
UP TO YEAR 2 CATEGORY
SCENE OF THE CRIME

CHAPTER 1 – WHERE WAS JOSH DAICOS?
It was a dark and stormy night and I was playing junior footy at the MCG at half time. I saw Josh Daicos wasn't on the field for Collingwood. Where was Josh Daicos? We need Josh!

CHAPTER 2 – LOOKING FOR JOSH
My heart was pounding and I decided it was time to go looking for Josh. I told my coach I needed to go to the toilet. 'Hurry up,' he said. I went into Collingwood's change room and there was a big, muddy footprint. I looked in Josh Daicos' locker and I found a size 10. It was the exact size.

CHAPTER 3 – THERE YOU ARE!
I looked in the Cat's change room and I saw there was another footprint the exact same shape. I saw another one in front of Joel Selwood's locker. It creaked. I opened it slowly, and there was Josh Daicos.

CHAPTER 4 – THE FINAL GOAL
'What are you doing in here?' I said.

'Stinkin' Selwood threw me in here!' Said Josh.

'Aren't those his lucky boots?' BEEEEEEEP. The siren went.

'Get the boots and come on the field. The Pies need you,' Josh said.

I grabbed the boots and ran onto the MCG. It felt great when the crowd went wild. They were 5 points in front and Selwood bumped me.

'Free kick to Collingwood!' Said the umpire. 20 metres out I kicked the ball. BEEEEEEP. Goal! Collingwood win!

And that is the story of Jack and Josh.

THE THIEF

ETHAN LI
Castle Hill, NSW

2021
UP TO YEAR 2 CATEGORY
  SCENE OF THE CRIME

One day Mark woke up. No! He was late for work!

He quickly ran to the car. But when he opened the wooden front door. He stood there confused. Where was the car?

'Someone must have stolen it!' Mark thought. He parked it yesterday but overnight, it disappeared.

He quickly called the police on his phone. Beep beep beep.

'Hello, this is the police station. What has happened?'

'Well...I woke up this morning and was going to go to work, but my car has disappeared!'

'My...we'll be right there.'

They arrived in 20 seconds! After they examined the grounds, they realised a little something... footprints. They followed them, leading to a house.

They reached for the doorknob. They policemen peered into the door. They saw a dirty man.

He saw them and started to run. The criminal crashed through his wooden wall. The policemen followed knowing that it was the right criminal.

'I've found it!' a policeman exclaimed. It was Mark's car.

The policeman jumped over the criminal, smiling.

'Hands up!'

They put handcuffs on him and sent him to prison. From that day on, Mark never saw the criminal ever again. He even put some very strong walls around his house and car to protect. But...he was late to work...again!

AUDREY
THE BUSHRANGER

ELEANOR MONK
Franklin, Huon Valley

2019 WINNER
UP TO YEAR 2 CATEGORY
 FEMALE BUSHRANGERS

In a tiny, little, home in the middle of the woods on a very windy and freezing cold day there was a 20 year old girl called Audrey. She had fiery red hair, freckles, and always had a smile on her face. She was a bushranger. She always had at least 5 loaded guns on her. She was 6 feet tall.

Audrey had a pet dog called Misty who was a greyhound, scruffy, dirty and grumpy. Misty barked a lot every full moon.

Audrey had a sister who was a convict in Australia at the time. Her sister's name was Edith. Edith had a transportation sentence for 3 years.

A few months later, after Edith had gone to Australia, Audrey hatched a plan to help Edith escape her convict prison. Audrey hired a galleon ship to take her to Australia as she was very rich from bushranging. The captain had a long beard, brown hair, and dark brown eyes. He was a little grumpy so she knew it would take a while for him to warm up to her.

Audrey was extremely confident to get her sister Edith out. Audrey pretended to be a beautiful lady so no one knew she was a bushranger. On the long trip from England to Australia Captain Lewis and Audrey became good friends and trusted each other. Captain Lewis also enjoy the company of Misty, who also came along.

Once they had arrived in Australia they discussed putting their plan into motion. Captain Lewis was staying at the ship while Audrey would travel to the convict prison to free her sister Edith.

Audrey had a basket full of food, but the food had a special chemical that puts people to sleep. She said to the guards, 'I have food to give to the poor hungry soldiers that work so hard all day.'

All the guards thought it was lovely so they all took some food. They all drifted off into a deep sleep so Audrey took the keys off one of the guards and went into the prison. She found Edith's prison cell and put the key in the lock and set her free. They embraced so hard! They both cried with joy. They hadn't seen each other for a year.

Audrey handed Edith a ladies outfit and they fled back to the ship where Captain Lewis was ready to set sail.

Captain Lewis brought them back to England where Edith's and Audrey's mum was waiting for them. They all reunited.

Captain Lewis took them to America where they bought a lovely house. Audrey married Captain Lewis and they had many adventures on his ship together.

ACTIVITY IN THE BUSH

CONNOR MCGUIRE
Kingston, Tasmania

2020
UP TO YEAR 2 CATEGORY
FEMALE DETECTIVES

Roger is sitting in the shade of the Neika bush when he sees something peculiar – a young boy being dragged along by two rough men. Roger stays in the shadows and watches the two men.

Roger sees the two rough men take the young boy on a small rowing boat, so he grabs his phone and calls Tasmania Police. He gives the information to the police operator and they tell him to sit down and wait for the police to arrive.

50 minutes later, the police arrive, and they all hear a loud 'BOOM' and a big boat comes round the bend in the river. The police then realise there is a small rowing boat smashed upon the bow of the big boat.

A group of men are on the big boat. Roger is feeling terrified and is worried there is going to be a gang war. Then Roger hears the sound of sirens and a 'whoomph whoomph' noise which he looks up to see are helicopters. In an instant 19 police abseil out of the helicopters.

The men stand on the deck of the big boat in a defensive line. The police fire their stun guns and the men drop to the ground. The young boy is released.

The police run to rescue the young boy. The police ask the boy 'what was all that about?' and the boy replies 'I am the first person to extract DNA from a Tasmanian Tiger bone and those men wanted it.'

THE LOST BABY

WREN MILLER
Peregrine School

2020
UP TO YEAR 2 CATEGORY
FEMALE DETECTIVES

It was a dark night and a little girl looked out her window. Her little sister was not usually this quiet, she thought. She went down the stairs to check on her, but when she looked into her little sister's cot, she wasn't there.

The little girl, whose name was Emma, screamed! 'Mummy!'

Her mum came rushing down the stairs.

'Come quickly now' said Emma. '

Where did our baby go?' said Mum.

'That's the point' said Emma 'she's gone.'

Her mother said, 'Let's look everywhere.'

They looked under the cot and everywhere around the house. There was no sign of her.

Emma's mother called the police, and they came immediately.

'Go to bed sweetie' said her mother. Emma went to bed and heard the police searching for clues. The girl detective was coming in the morning. Emma drifted off to sleep.

In the morning Emma came into the kitchen for breakfast and the detective was there. She had long brown hair and a black dress, blue tights and shiny black shoes. She was looking for clues to find the person who had stolen the baby.

Emma was desperate to find her little sister. The detective asked Emma a question. 'What does your sister look like?' 'Well,' said Emma 'she has short black hair and blue eyes.' 'OK' said Detective Wren. 'We'll have a look.'

First Detective Wren looked under the cot. There in the dust was a licence card. The name on the card was Lily, their next door neighbour. Lily's baby had just died. It would make sense if she had done the crime. So, Detective Wren and Emma went to Lily's house. No one was home.

They started to look for signs of the baby. 'Let's look in the cellar' said Emma. She said that because there were noises coming from the cellar. It sounded like a baby crying.

They looked in the cellar, and there was Emma's baby sister Philia. Emma rushed over to hug the baby. 'Let's go home to Mummy' said Emma.

When they got home, Emma's mum was delighted.

THE CASE OF THE MISSING GOLD

ASHA OLIVER
Heathmont, Victoria

2021 WINNER
UP TO YEAR 2 CATEGORY
SCENE OF THE CRIME

One day Alex the cat was playing with a bouncy ball when someone called for help through Alex's cat tag. It was Katy, her gold had been stolen after her cat guard Callie fell asleep.

Alex went to the scene of the crime, a jeweller's shop. She saw that someone had painted a skull and bones on the wall. She sniffed the wall and realised the paint was still wet, it had been painted one minute ago. She knew that it was a pirate that painted the skull and bones, and there was a trail of gold and tyre tracks.

She followed the trail that led to the sea. Alex got on her surfboard and followed. Soon enough she found the pirate ship. She put on her swimming gear. She used her net to stop the engine and get the gold.

The only thing the pirate could do was turn back to shore. Alex called the police by pressing a button on her cat tag. The pirate went to jail. Alex was a superhero!

THE MYSTERY
OF THE MISSING WAND

DAISY WALTER
Huonville, Huon Valley

2022
UP TO YEAR 2 CATEGORY
  AGATHA CHRISTIE IN TASMANIA

Once there was a fairy ball in Hobart and all the fairies came. Suddenly Twinkle realised she'd lost her wand. The fairies looked, but couldn't find it. Twinkle's friend Elfie spotted a map under a mushroom, with little dirty fingerprints all over it. She showed Twinkle the map. It had a wiggly path to a building with a funny face drawn on it. They decided to follow the path.

The forest was pretty, with ferns, bandicoots and lots of little fairy homes. They saw a big building up ahead and felt excited. They realised the face on the map was on top of the building, so they flew up, but couldn't find anything. Then Elfie said, 'it might be inside the roof!' So she magicked them inside, and there was Twinkle's wand!

Just then, the robber appeared, and the fairies magicked a net over him. His goblin fingers matched the prints on the map!

'Are you a good or bad goblin?' asked Twinkle.

'Good,' said the goblin.

'Why did you steal my wand then?' said Twinkle.

'I needed magic to stop the bad robbers trying to steal all the fairies wands. I forgot which house I borrowed the wand from so I hid it. I came to get it to figure out whose it was.'

So Twinkle and Elfie let him go and thanked him for stopping the robbers. Then Twinkle and Elfie went back to the fairy ball and let their new goblin friend come with them.

THE MYSTERY OF THE DINO MODEL

AUGUST WALTER
Huonville, Huon Valley

2022
UP TO YEAR 2 CATEGORY
AGATHA CHRISTIE IN TASMANIA

Once, in Huonville, three kids were playing cops and robbers after hearing that a dinosaur model had been stolen from the Hobart museum.

Dan said, 'I wonder how it is for real life?'

'I think it'd be the same as our game!' said Jenny. 'But harder.'

The next day Dan's mum said, 'Why not go for a picnic?'

While spreading the rug, Jenny spotted something on the ground.

'It's an old map,' said John.

'Yes, but...' said Dan excitedly. 'It's a map of our house! How strange, it seems to say there's a secret trapdoor!'

The kids searched all over Dan's house for the trapdoor, when suddenly Dan disappeared! They spotted a hole.

'Quick get a ladder!' said Jenny. They climbed down into an underground room. Suddenly, John spotted something. 'The dino model!' he yelled, then the others saw a footprint and a glove. They copied the print, and took the glove.

Dan hid the model, and they went to Jackman & McRoss for cake. There, right outside, they saw a man with only one glove and it matched the one they'd found!

'Quick! Call the police!' said Dan. The kids shadowed the robber and heard that his name was also John.

'Good John bad John little John big John!' giggled John. The police arrived, handcuffed the man, and thanked the children.

'Well, it wasn't quite like our game!' said Jenny.

'No,' said John. 'But I think we need to change the rules a bit!'

THE MYSTERY OF THE SILVER LLAMA

STEPHANIE SHANNON
Taroona, Tasmania

2020 WINNER
UP TO YEAR 2 CATEGORY
FEMALE DETECTIVES

Gloria was awakened by her sister rolling on top of her. It was a lovely morning in the Llama pen. Gloria the llama overheard two humans talking about a stolen Incan Silver Llama. Gloria loved to solve mysteries and was quite the detective around the farm.

The next day she snuck out of the llama pen and started on a journey to find the thieves. She travelled through the Andes Mountains and finally reached Quito in Ecuador. She went into the city and started looking around.

A sparkle from an open window caught her eye, a cat sat next to a pouch. Gloria was sure it had the missing Incan Llama in it!

The cat started to run and Gloria tried to catch the cat but she was too quick.

Night came and Gloria fell asleep, tired from her long journey.

The next day she woke with the sun shining through the open window. She remembered she needed to find that cat. She went back to see if the cat was still there. She was!

Gloria caught her, she hissed and scratched. The bag she was carrying fell and the missing Llama rolled out. Gloria let her go and picked up the silver Llama.

The cat came and introduced herself, her name was Sabina and she was trying to return the silver Llama to the museum where it had been stolen from.

The next day they returned the silver Llama.

They became very good friends and told each other all their stories.

Sabina told Gloria how she had seen the bad guys who had stolen the silver Llama and knew she had to get it back.

When they arrived back at the Llama pen all the other Llama's welcomed Gloria and her new friend. The next morning was different. Gloria woke to a fussy fur ball on her back, all curled up in her warm fur. They were ready to start a new adventure together.

www.ingramcontent.com/pod-product-compliance
Lightning Source LLC
Chambersburg PA
CBHW030649020726
47493CB00006B/1940